PASSION'S PAWN

"Take off your clothes, Alexa, and get into bed," Adam ordered brusquely, unbuttoning his shirt as he spoke.

"I think not," retorted Alexa, deliberately turning her back. "You will not use me as an instrument of revenge."

"You think not?" Adam smiled thinly. "I'm perfectly capable of undressing you should you refuse. In fact, I might even enjoy it. Which will it be?"

Alexa glared at him murderously, refusing to budge. Perhaps if she displayed courage he would go away and leave her alone. But she was mistaken. Adam would not be put off.

It took but two strides to reach Alexa's side and too late she turned to run. His body rigid with desire, Adam easily captured Alexa's struggling form in his arms, turning her until she was crushed against his chest. . . .

Other Leisure Books by Connie Mason

TENDER FURY

CARESS AND CONQUER

FOR HONOR'S SAKE

CONNIE MASON

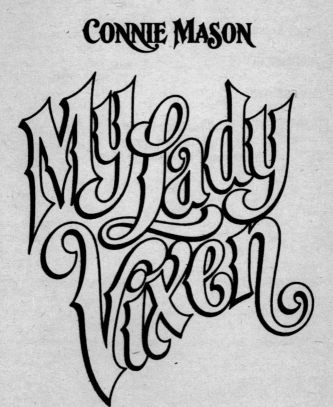

MY LADY VIXEN

LEISURE BOOKS NEW YORK CITY

To all my faithful readers,
especially those in Clermont,
Florida and Buchanan, Michigan

A LEISURE BOOK

Published by

Dorchester Publishing Co., Inc.
6 East 39th Street
New York, NY   10016

Copyright ©1987 by Connie Mason

Printed in the United States of America

My Lady Vixen

PROLOGUE

London 1763

Thin wisps of mist settled above the damp ground, shooting ghostly tendrils heavenwards as leaden-gray skies released weak rays of dawn. From his vantage point some distance away behind a line of trees a lad just beginning to fulfill the promise of youth watched, his distinctive silvery eyes hardened into slits of granite that were to become harder and colder as the years matured him.

Unbeknownst to the boy he was not the only interloper that chill fall morning. Some distance to his left a closed carriage waited on the path. A woman's pale face, hauntingly beautiful yet strangely sad, stared fixedly through the curtained window into the gloom, her magnificent violet eyes wide and horrorstruck as she silently watched two men enact a drama in the clearing ahead.

She sighed audibly as a case containing a magnificent

pair of duelling pistols was offered to each man. As if aware of the woman's indrawn breath the boy echoed her response, adding a grimace, distorting the features that held but a hint of the rugged good looks that would one day be his.

Formalities dispensed with, the two duelists stood back to back, weapons held aloft. At a signal the counting began, and to the watching boy each step was magnified and intensified until he imagined he heard the exaggerated pounding of each footfall against the spongy earth. But they were only his own heartbeats thundering in his ears.

The lad had been instructed to remain at home, as was the woman. Both had deliberately disobeyed, choosing instead to watch from a distance the one-sided match. Each viewer had their own reason for being present, but the common bond that compelled them was love.

Suddenly the opponents in the clearing halted, slowly turned and took aim. Simultaneously two shots rang out but only one man spiraled from the impact and crumpled to the damp ground; the other remained standing. A cry of despair left the boy's bloodless lips to mingle in the still air with the woman's heartwrenching wail. Such was their concentration that neither heard the other's outcry.

A tall, cadaverous man, presumably a doctor, knelt over the prone form. Shaking his head negatively, he swiveled to face the victor, spreading his hands helplessly, suggesting the wounded man to be beyond mortal help. Shrugging negligently, the victor impatiently turned away to a waiting carriage just as the doctor bent to cover the fallen man's face with a square of linen he had withdrawn from his pocket.

His gray eyes consumed with hate, the boy watched as the wheels of the carriage disappeared from sight, lost in the shrouding mists. "One day you'll pay for this!" he shouted to the silent heavens, shaking his fist to emphasize his words. "Someday, somehow, I'll take from you something or someone you hold dear, just as you took from me! By all that's holy, I swear it!"

Silent tears slipped unbidden from his eyes as his rage focused on one man and his unfaithful wife. A rage that was to consume him body and soul for many years to come as he grew to manhood, waiting for the right time to exact his revenge. With faltering steps he stumbled from his concealment to kneel numbly beside the body sprawled in the dirt. Suddenly his shoulders straightened, and in those few short moments he seemed to pass into adulthood.

Inside the carriage, the woman, her face a pale reflection of death, slumped boneless against the cushions. The man's death foretold the ending of her own useless life. Living no longer held any meaning. Not even her love for the precious three-year-old daughter waiting for her at home possessed the power to alter the course of events.

BOOK ONE:

The Lady

1

London 1778

Lady Alexa Ashley pirouetted on dainty feet, setting her voluminous white skirts awhirl about her shapely ankles. Her engagement ball was all that she had hoped and her violet eyes sparkled with excitement. Her father, Sir John Ashley, confidant and advisor to King George III, had only moments before announced her betrothal and impending marriage to Lieutenant Charles Whitlaw of the Royal Navy, only son and heir of Sir Brandon Whitlaw. It was a marriage Alexa's father extolled until Alexa herself became convinced that Charles, though staid and somewhat dull, was the handsome Prince Charming she had always yearned for.

It was true Charles was handsome and young, as well as completely besotted by her. Rich, too. What more could a girl of eighteen hope for? Alexa often asked herself. Surely marriage to Charles would settle once and for all the nagging doubts that plagued her. Charles would be a wonderful husband, kind, thoughtful, loving.

What did it matter if her heart never sang out with joy when he kissed her? Or that her body ached for something she could only guess at? She supposed, given time, Charles would teach her body to respond to his. Smiling beguilingly, Alexa knew she was the envy of all her friends as she bent her thick mass of ebony curls toward her dashing betrothed, allowing his arm to curl possessively about her slim waist.

"Are you happy, my dear?" beamed Charles, his smile slightly askew.

Alexa hesitated but a moment. "Of course, Charles, extremely so. Are you?"

"Ecstatically," Charles assured her, giving her waist an intimate squeeze. "Even more so when I'll have the right to lead you off to our bedroom and close the door."

"Charles!" Alexa scolded, somewhat shocked. It was unlike Charles to speak so boldly, but she had watched him consume a large quantity of hard liquor and supposed the drink lent him courage. She stifled a giggle at the thought of Charles exhibiting the passion she had thus far only read about in books, and concentrated on the dance steps.

From across the crowded room the cold gray eyes of Adam Foxworth never left the slim shapely figure swathed in virginal white who appeared to melt into the uniform-clad arms of her young fiance. He surreptitiously studied her face. It was a lovely face, delicate and fragile, a face of strange contrasts, deep violet eyes black-fringed and smoldering against pale creamy skin, translucent as alabaster. And her mouth, unexpectedly full-lipped and sensuous. A cloud of raven hair, shiny as glass, was arranged in an artful mass atop her proud head with wayward tendrils framing her perfect features.

Against his will Adam was thoroughly beguiled by the face and form of Lady Alexa Ashley. Slim of waist, her full breasts rose enticingly above a low, square neckline. When she turned he saw a provocative expanse of smooth back and sloping shoulders. He imagined her legs beneath her full skirt were long and shapely. Deliberately he forced his mind and eyes from the innocent beauty to concentrate on her father, Sir John Ashley, a man truly deserving of his hate. A small twinge of regret at what he was about to do twisted his handsome features but he hardened his heart as he remembered his pledge of long ago. Fifteen years had done nothing to ease his rage or lessen his thirst for revenge. If anything, the long, lonely years only added to his resolve. Finally fate had intervened and his moment of vengeance had arrived, just as he always knew it would.

"Are you having second thoughts, Adam?"

Adam reluctantly turned his gaze from the dancing figure in white to eye his companion malevolently. "Never!" he denied vehemently. "Did John Ashley have second thoughts? By now you know me well enough, Mac, to realize I don't easily back down from a vow once given. Though young when it was made, I have not wavered once in the intervening years."

"Don't do this, Adam, please," begged Mac, his blue eyes intent upon the silvery orbs of his friend. "In the end you'll hurt no one but that innocent girl, and yourself."

Adam smiled ruefully, smoothing back hair the color of thick, tawny gold with long, splayed fingers. "She's the spawn of the devil and his mate, how innocent can she be?" he replied tersely.

"Be reasonable, Adam. That girl knows nothing of this vendetta of yours."

"She'll soon learn," answered Adam coldly, his icy gaze finding and locking on Lady Alexa once again.

"Adam," Mac whispered urgently, "let it go. We have

more important business at hand. You know Captain Jones . . ."

"Quiet, you fool!" hissed Adam angrily. "Do you want all of London to know why we are here? I know my duty as well as the next person and nothing will interfere with it. And if you're worrying about the girl, don't. No harm will come to her. Unlike her father, I am not entirely heartless. I intend to use her, not kill her."

Alexa could not help but notice the tall, handsome man dressed entirely in muted gray. For some time now his eyes had followed her every move and when she turned to meet his gaze she was shocked by the animosity that flew out to meet her from those slitted orbs the color and texture of cold cement. A chill of foreboding shook her slight frame as he bowed mockingly and smiled at her with a smile that failed to reach his eyes.

Raw masculinity exuded from his every pore, enhanced by the cut and color of his clothing. Though drab in comparison to the other males present, his garb accentuated the strength of well-muscled limbs and shoulders that put every man Alexa had ever seen, Charles included, to shame. His profile spoke of power and ageless strength. His teeth, even and white, contrasted pleasingly with suntanned skin pulled taut over the elegant ridge of his cheekbones. It was a stubborn and arrogant face, Alexa decided.

Nervously Alexa's gaze shifted to the imposing man's companion. Though nearly as tall, his flaming red hair and beard gave him a comic appearance. His bulging biceps left little doubt as to his strength should it be put to the test, but unlike his silver-eyed companion, there were touches of humor around the mouth and near the clear blue eyes. Both men looked to be in their late twenties or early thirties.

"Who is that man, Charles?" Alexa could not help but

ask. "The one dressed in gray satin. I've never seen him before. Is he a friend of yours?"

Charles swiveled his neck and met head-on the icy eyes of Adam Foxworth. "Good God, he's no friend of mine, Alexa!" he shuddered. "I thought your father invited him."

Alexa sighed, exasperation clearly etched on her mobile features. "But do you know who he is?"

"Of course," admitted the young man, shrugging. "He's a Colonial come to collect his inheritance. Seems that his uncle, some earl or other, died, leaving some obscure holdings in Cornwall. Thank God he's not one of those rabble-rousers from the Colonies who are fighting for Lord only knows what. Penwell, that's it, the Earl of Penwell. He's here at your father's invitation, no doubt."

"No doubt," echoed Alexa, wondering at the man's thinly veiled animosity. She didn't even know the man, so why should he hate her? she wondered nervously.

"It's damn hot in here, let's go outside," suggested Charles suddenly, running a finger under his tight collar. "Besides, I haven't had a minute alone with you in days."

Nodding distractedly, Alexa allowed Charles to lead her from the crowded room through the tall French doors and out into the soft June night. She smiled wryly as he staggered tipsily before righting himself.

Alexa followed meekly as Charles led her to a deserted corner of the vast gardens of her father's country estate outside London, unaware that a tall, somberly-clad man followed at a discreet distance. When they came upon the deserted summerhouse Charles hesitated but a moment, then drew her inside The revelry of the party seemed far away as Alexa settled herself beside Charles on one of the cushion-strewn couches placed strategically about the cozy room.

The silence between them grew as Charles gathered his courage, prompting Alexa to fill the void by remarking idly, "Did you hear the talk tonight about the Fox and all the trouble his ship, *The Gray Ghost*, is giving our navy?"

"That's all I did hear," snorted Charles, moving closer to Alexa. "That damn Colonial is causing all sorts of mayhem. He's credited with sinking six vessels in the last two months. He's as wily and cunning as the animal he's named after. He comes out of nowhere and strikes swiftly, disappearing to Lord knows where. Some even believe him to be a ghost because he seems to evaporate into thin air."

"Have you ever seen his ship?" asked Alexa, warming to the subject.

"Once. From a distance. Our ship, *The Gallant*, gave chase, but it was as if the sea swallowed him. I'd give anything to be the one to blow him and his pirates out of the water."

"Is he? A pirate, I mean."

"He's a privateer, same thing. Those damn rebels don't know when to quit. They sail under legal sanction of their government and are becoming more bothersome as the war progresses. It's said that more than two thousand armed privateers ply the seas carrying more than 18,000 guns and 70,000 men. How those ignorant Colonials could organize to such an extent remains a mystery."

"Do they have a chance of winning?" asked Alexa, feeling a surprising empathy for the people who fought so bravely and tenaciously for their freedom.

"None whatsoever," assured Charles confidently. "Our navy is the strongest in the world and our soldiers the best trained. No one is capable of defeating us."

Alexa slowly digested the facts Charles had just imparted. For some obscure reason she felt almost sorry for the fledgling country across the ocean struggling for independence. She had always prized her own independence, exercising her mind freely, and she could well understand America's valiant struggle. Since her mother's sudden death fifteen years ago her father had allowed her free reign, leaving her to make her own decisions. Should her freedom be curtailed, she too would rebel against those unfair restrictions.

So engrossed was Alexa in her own thoughts that she failed to notice when Charles lightly fingered the fastenings marching down the back of her gown until the cool night air fanned her bare skin.

"Charles, what are you doing?" she asked, shocked by the actions of a man she had always considered mild-mannered and rather shy. But of course she had never seen him drunk before.

"We are engaged, Alexa," pouted Charles childishly. "You know I must leave tomorrow for sea duty, thanks to the Fox, and I won't be back until a few days before our wedding. What will it hurt if we consummate our marriage early? Others do it. I want you, Alexa. I need you."

Not waiting for her reply, Charles literally pounced on her, his clumsy kisses and thick, fumbling fingers revolting her. Many times of late she had fantasized about sharing intimacies with Charles once they were married but it was never anything like this.

"Charles, behave," she scolded, becoming alarmed when her pleas did little to cool his increasing ardor. "You know we can't . . . we can't . . . do what you suggest. It isn't right. Besides, you're drunk. Now take your hands off me!"

Thoroughly incensed by the sight of milk-white breasts partially bared when he attempted to pull down her bodice, Charles became a madman with but one purpose—to possess Alexa. Nothing she could say or do had the slightest impact upon his alcohol-soaked brain.

Alexa heard her fragile ballgown rip as she resisted Charles's advances, determined to fight him tooth and nail. Her long fingernails found his face and he cursed roundly as she dug bloody grooves down his cheeks.

"Whatsa matter, honey?" Charles asked petutantly, slurring his words. "I won't hurt you. If you loved me you'd let me. Just lay back and relax."

Drunk as he was Alexa was no match for his superior strength and against her will she found herself flat on her back with Charles sprawled atop her. His slobbering kisses fell on her bared breasts as he eased her skirts above her thighs. His own heavy limbs prevented her from kicking out, struggling against the indignity he was forcing upon her. How could she have ever thought she loved him? Alexa wondered, astonished by her response, or rather lack of response, to her husband-to-be.

Her screams were trapped in her throat as his mouth plundered hers, whispering obscenities against her lips. "I've dreamed about this, Alexa," he moaned. "It will be so good, you'll love it just like I will. Your breasts feel so silky, so do your thighs. I'm so hot for you. Open up, honey, before I explode."

At that moment Alexa felt as if she had never really known Charles although they had been friends for years. Can it be he had a completely different personality he kept hidden from her? She gagged when he forced his tongue between her lips and managed a hoarse scream when his fingers invaded her secret place that until now had been sacrosanct. Charles mistook her scream and writhing for rising passion.

"That's it, honey, move," he grunted as he prepared to mount her. "I knew you'd like it. Soon we'll be man and wife and can do this as often as we like."

The thought sobered Alexa as she prepared herself

for his violation. Surely this isn't the way it's meant to be, she silently lamented. So much for romance! Cringing inwardly she felt something moist and hard probing between her thighs. Then suddenly the weight was gone from her body and she drew in a long, shuddering breath.

"Are you all right, Lady Alexa?" a deep voice asked.

Abruptly Alexa sat up, squinting in the moonlight as she tried to identify the figure framed in the doorway. There was no mistaking those broad shoulders and muscular thighs encased in dull silver. Although they hadn't been properly introduced she spoke his name easily.

"Lord Penwell! What . . . what are you doing here?"

"Saving a damsel in distress," he quipped arrogantly. "Or did I make a mistake?"

"No . . . no mistake. I'm . . . I'm afraid Charles has had too much to drink and . . . and . . . well . . . how embarrassing," she stammered, blushing in the darkness.

"No need to explain, milady. I have two good eyes, as well as two good ears. I knew what your fiance was doing and I can't say I blame him."

Eyes like two shards of ice reflected in the moonglow, fixed on Alexa's full breasts almost completely exposed, and then fell to her slim legs and shapely thighs. Immediately Alexa's hands flew to set her clothing right and she turned her back on Adam as she covered her breasts as best she could with the torn edges of her bodice and smoothed her skirts down over her hips and thighs.

Suddenly a loud groan drew both their attention as Charles picked himself rather painfully off the floor where Adam had unceremoniously tossed him.

"Wha . . . what happened?" he asked, dazed. For the first time he saw Adam and grew indignant when he realized what had happened. "How dare you interfere!" he snapped peevishly. "My fiancée and I were having a private conversation. You owe us an apology, Lord Penwell."

"From where I stood it looked as if you were attempting more than mere conversation," said Adam suggestively. "When the lady protested I felt obliged to step in."

"You Colonials presume too much," Charles protested violently. "You don't belong in polite society, you're no better than savages!"

A taut smile twisted Adam's mouth as Alexa watched the two men warily. She felt certain something dreadful would happen if she did not intervene. But what could she do?

"Charles, please," Alexa pleaded, "I don't want any trouble. Lord Penwell did what he thought best under the circumstances. I'm certain you'll feel differently in the morning."

With the mention of morning Charles grew livid with rage. "Perhaps you've forgotten that I'll be gone in the morning, Alexa, and this was our last chance to . . . er . . . talk privately before I sailed. I am your fiance, after all. What business has this Colonial to butt in where he's not wanted. I have a good notion to teach him a lesson."

Heedless of his drunken state, or perhaps due to it, Charles launched himself full tilt at the unsuspecting Adam, only to be neatly sidestepped by the quick-thinking new lord. Not to be thwarted, Charles roused himself for another attack, but this time he met the solid front of a doubled fist as Adam's natural reflexes required that he defend himself. Charles hit the floor like a sack of potatoes as Adam rubbed his knuckles thoughtfully.

Alexa was stunned. From the moment she walked out the French doors with Charles things had happened so swiftly that she could do little more than stand and gape at the inert form of her fiance.

"You've killed him!" she gasped, finally finding her voice.

"No such luck," sneered Adam scathingly. "Your young popinjay will recover to take to the sea tomorrow."

"You didn't have to hit him so hard," she accused.

"I could have just gone away and let him assault you," Adam challenged cynically.

"I'd better go back to the house and get some help," Alexa said, ignoring Adam's gibe.

"Looking like that?" Adam asked, cocking one well-shaped brow suggestively. "That ought to cause quite a stir."

Glancing down at her tattered and rumpled gown, Alexa realized that Adam spoke the truth. Somehow she'd have to sneak up to her room and send word down to her father that she'd developed a sudden headache.

"I can sneak up to my room through the back entrance, but what about Charles?" Alexa asked. "We just can't leave him lying there."

Had Alexa looked into Adam's eyes at that exact moment she would have run for her life. An unnatural light glowed from those silver orbs and he smiled as if destiny was about to be fulfilled. "I'll have my friend see him safely to his ship. By tomorrow he'll be so busy looking for the Fox that he'll forget everything that happened tonight. I've a good notion he's too drunk to remember anyway."

"I . . . I don't know," hedged Alexa, sitting on the horns of dilemma. "Shouldn't we tell someone?"

"Do you want it bandied about by the scandalmongers that your fiance got drunk and assaulted you? That he was knocked cold by an earl of little account? It's entirely up to you, milady."

"No . . . no," protested Alexa, picturing in her mind the embarrassment she would endure by returning to the ballroom practically naked. "Your way is much more discreet. I'll . . . I'll make it up to Charles when he returns. He would have never acted so rashly had he not been in his cups."

"You show good sense, milady," mocked Adam. "Wait here while I summon my friend. Then I'll see you to the back entrance." He slipped out the door so silently Alexa had to look twice to make sure he was gone.

Sighly heavily, Alexa sat down, trying to puzzle out just where the evening went awry. One moment she was laughing and dancing with her dashing fiance and the next she was fighting off a drunken rapist she barely knew. And how did it happen that Lord Penwell should show up at so crucial a moment? It wasn't as if the summerhouse was in a likely place for a stranger to be casually strolling by. That's why Charles chose it. Something here didn't quite mesh but for the life of her Alexa couldn't figure it out.

In a surprisingly short time Adam returned with the redheaded man she had seen him conversing with in the ballroom. "Lady Alexa, may I present my friend, Logan MacHugh? Everyone calls him Mac. He graciously agreed to take your . . . uh . . . fiance safely back to his ship."

Alexa thought Mac looked slightly dubious but put it down to the unusual circumstances. Embarrassed by her dishevelled appearance, Alexa said, "I'm pleased to meet you, Mac, and I'm grateful for your help."

Mac shot Adam a scathing glance before replying. "Anything to help a damsel in distress, milady. I only hope you won't come to hate me for this."

Misunderstanding his meaning, Alexa smiled gratefully. "How could I? You've but come to the aid of

24

a friend and in so doing helped solve my dilemma. My fiance has imbibed too freely and it is best for all concerned that he is returned to his ship before his actions cause a scandal."

"I'll look after him well, milady," promised Mac. "He'll soon be safely in his bunk sleeping it off."

With surprising ease Mac hefted Charles's limp body over his shoulder and left the summerhouse, soon disappearing into the dark shadows. Now all Alexa had to think about was getting up to her room without being seen and sending a maid to inform her father of her indisposition. She looked to Adam expectantly.

"I think we'd better leave," she suggested, peering anxiously into the darkness. "Someone might take a notion to come out here."

For the first time since he had unexpectedly shown up inside the summerhouse, Adam slowly approached Alexa until he stood within inches of her slim form, his warm breath caressing her cheek. Against his better judgment he drew her close until their bodies touched, her ripe breasts pressed intimately against his gray jacket, their lips inches apart. Mesmerized, Alexa felt certain he would kiss her and for some unexplained reason her heart beat faster in anticipation.

But when she dared to look up at him his silver eyes regarded her with barely concealed contempt and she instinctively drew back, breaking the spell. Her own violet eyes regarded him with confusion. For a brief moment his gaze softened to a caress but just as swiftly disappeared to be replaced by an expression of cool amusement tinged with something she could not decipher.

"Come along, Lady Alexa," Adam said, grasping her firmly by the elbow. "You're right, of course, we'd best leave."

Silently they left the summerhouse with Adam guiding

her in a circular path to the back of the mansion where darkness enveloped them like a shroud. So engrossed was Alexa on entering the house without being seen that she did not notice the closed carriage standing close by the back door.

The noise from the party was muted back here and the revelry only remotely apparent. Evidently the servants were occupied at the front of the house seeing to the many guests. Alexa heaved a sigh of relief as she made unerringly toward the door. For some unexplained reason she felt tense and ill at ease. Though attracted to the handsome Lord Penwell, Alexa did not trust him. Those compelling gray eyes did strange things to her, things she could not explain, but feared.

"Thank you, my lord," Alexa said, turning to Adam. "I'll be fine now. Don't let me detain you."

The grip on her elbow tightened and Alexa knew a moment of panic. It grew and magnified when Adam's hand fell to her waist, dragging her backwards, away from the door and safety.

"What's the meaning of this, sir?" she cried out in dismay. "Let me go this minute!"

"I'm sorry, milady, but you're coming with me. Your family owes me a debt and I've come to collect."

"Then see my father," Alexa retorted. "I'm sure he'll be glad to pay you."

"Oh, he'll pay, all right. With something dearer than money," insisted Adam cryptically. "Come along quietly and you won't be hurt."

Alexa's first thought was that she was being kidnapped for ransom. But she quickly discarded the idea when Lord Penwell said he wanted more than money. What could he want? Alexa wondered fearfully. Some favor? He said he wouldn't hurt her, could she believe him? For want of a better idea she decided to scream, but Adam anticipated her and clapped a restraining hand over her mouth.

"I told you to come along quietly," he reprimanded, annoyed. "I'm afraid you're forcing me to become rough."

Without warning a cloth was jammed into her mouth and she was slung over one of Adam's broad shoulders, her head dangling helplessly down his back. Her arms and legs beat ceaselessly against his well-muscled body but he paid it little heed. When he reached the carriage Alexa had failed to notice, he flung her inside and flopped down beside her. Almost immediately the carriage jerked forward and Alexa cast one frantic look back at her home slowly disappearing as the carriage gathered speed.

Alexa had no way of knowing, but from that moment on her life would never be the same.

2

Finding her hands free Alexa pulled the cloth from her mouth, gasping and sputtering in an effort to catch her breath. Fear and anger knotted inside her and she began to shake as fearful images built in her fertile mind.

That Lord Penwell was a dangerous man she never doubted. He exuded strength and authority from every pore. His very presence commanded respect and attention. Alexa held little doubt that the man could be brutal when crossed. But what did he want with her? she asked herself, puzzled. From the few words he spoke she gathered her abduction had something to do with her father. And her mother, even though that poor woman had been dead and buried these fifteen years.

Beside her, Adam was tense, his eyes and body alert for any sign of pursuit. He doubted if Alexa had even been missed yet, especially since she was last seen with her fiancé. And if Mac had done his job, Charles should be safely in his bunk sleeping off his hangover. If luck was with him *The Gallant* would sail off in search of the elusive Fox without Charles ever knowing Alexa had mysteriously disappeared.

When they reached the deserted docks Adam heaved a sigh of relief and turned to face an enraged Alexa. "We're nearly there, milady," he coldly informed her.

"Nearly where?" shot back Alexa, peering into the darkness. Though the tangy odor of the sea assaulted her senses she would not give him the satisfaction of admitting she knew where they were.

"You'll know soon enough," replied Adam as the carriage skidded to a halt.

Grasping Alexa by the wrist Adam hauled her from the conveyance and pulled her toward a long wharf at the end of which a shadowy ship rode quietly at anchor. The moment she realized their destination Alexa balked, digging her heels into the rotted wood of the quay.

"No!" she gasped, panting in terror. "I won't go! Why are you doing this to me, Lord Penwell?"

"You may as well become accustomed to using my name," Adam replied, ignoring her outburst. "It's Adam, Adam Foxworth. Lord Penwell is too new and sits uncomfortably upon my shoulders. In America a title means nothing."

"Please, Lord Penwell . . . Adam," anything to placate him, she thought, "if you release me now I won't tell anyone what happened. I'll return quietly to my room and you can go about your business."

"You are my business, milady." Adam smiled tightly. "I've waited too many years for my revenge." So saying he scooped up her resisting body in his brawny arms and hastened to the end of the dock, closing his ears against Alexa's loud protests and cries of distress, telling himself that one insignificant woman mattered little in his scheme of things. Using the daughter was his one chance to avenge himself on a man he had despised for almost half his life.

Nearly to the end of the dock, Alexa saw that the

gangplank of the ghostly ship had been let down and that Adam, impervious to her pleas, was heading directly for it. Panic like she'd never known before welled up in her throat. It seemed impossible that this could be happening to her. Wasn't she the daughter of Sir John Ashley, a powerful man at court? Just what was Adam Foxworth going to do with her? That quick and disturbing thought tore at her insides.

Up the gangplank of the seemingly deserted ship, across the deck and down the ladder to a dark passageway. Then a door opened and Alexa found herself inside a small, damp cabin with little to commend it. A langern hung from a hook on the ceiling swinging slowly too and fro as gentle swells lapped against the dark hull of the mystery ship that was to be her prison. Once inside Adam set her on her feet. Gazing at him, Alexa could read nothing in his expression for it had become a mask constructed of stone.

"Your castle, milady," he mocked, affecting an exaggerated bow.

Forgetting everything she had ever learned about how ladies should act, Alexa flew into a rage. "Damn you!" she cursed. "You'll pay for this! My father won't rest until you're caught and punished for this cowardly act!"

"He'll have to catch me first." Adam smiled grimly, his dark face set in a vicious expression. With trepidation Alexa noted his tightly clamped mouth and glazed eyes and her heart sank. Instinctively she realized none of her wiles, or even her anger, would have the slightest effect on a man of Adam Foxworth's calibre.

"Why do you hate my father?" she asked in a burst a resentment. "I'm sure he doesn't even know you exist."

"He'll know, all right, after tonight. And he'll remember, more than you know," Adam assured her confidently. "Now I'll bid you goodnight, milady. I hope you'll be comfortable." His tone suggested he cared little for her comfort.

"You're leaving?" asked Alexa, dismayed. "Where are you going? You're not going to leave me alone, are you?" As if to emphasize her words she clutched convulsively at his satin-clad arm.

"I thought you'd be pleased to see me go," Adam quipped. "Don't worry, you'll be well taken care of in my absence. No one will harm you."

When she continued to cling to him, her wide violet eyes dark with fear, Adam nearly lost his resolve as her nearness began to affect him in a strange way. She seemed so helpless, so lost that he felt an urge to protect her, to keep her safe, even from himself, which was impossible. For some unknown reason he wanted no other man to touch her, not even the estimable Charles, particularly not Charles, he thought grimly. He wanted to be the one to initiate her to love, to awaken her desires, to hear her cry out his name in passion.

Frozen in the grip of his storm-gray eyes, Alexa could neither move nor breathe. Her mouth was dry, her breath a hard knot in her throat. His face wore the smile of a wolf just before it closed hungry jaws on the rabbit. There was a hard arrogant strength in his expression, a repressed violence about him that called forth feelings she had never experienced before.

Then suddenly, in heated, vibrant and explosive need, his mouth caught hers in a kiss so deep that she was filled with wonder. Never had she been kissed in such a manner. Not even by Charles. When his tongue plundered the moist cavern of her mouth, she felt shock . . . and something else. A yearning in the secret recesses of her young body. Almost like an awakening.

When Adam slid his lips against the soft skin of her neck, slowly stroking it with his tongue, Alexa gasped aloud, tossed on the waves of her near-surrender. The sound served to clear her head. It also alerted Adam to the passage of time and he reluctantly pushed Alexa's limp form away from his own hardening body. Now was not the time to dally with his enemy's daughter, he thought ruefully. Plenty of time for that when they were safely away from London.

Finding herself without visible means of support, Alexa sat down heavily on the narrow bunk, eyeing Adam warily as he straightened his clothing. "As pleasant as this has been, milady, you'll have to wait until later for my . . . uh . . . attentions. I must hie myself back to your party so I won't be connected with your disappearance. There is also the matter of a note to be delivered to your father. Until later, Lady Alexa." Then he was gone, the harsh grating of the key turning in the lock assaulting her ears.

"Wait!" cried Alexa. "Don't go! Don't leave me here alone!" Her words echoed hollowly through the empty cabin.

Dejected, Alexa bit her lip until it throbbed, her misery so acute it was like a physical pain. But she refused to be defeated. Until she found out Adam's purpose she had to endure. And if the chance for escape presented itself she must be prepared. Tears would solve nothing. Furthermore, she must fight the strange attraction she felt for her handsome abductor. It was an indisputable fact that Adam Foxworth was a man who would have his way.

Forcing herself to be calm, Alexa lay back on the bunk and gave in to her exhaustion as sleep claimed her. She had no idea that hours later a black-clad, masked stranger quietly opened the door and stared at her through hooded eyes.

The first rays of errant sunlight filtered through the dirty pane of the small, round porthole, stabbing Alexa in the eyes until she was forced to rouse herself. She groaned and stretched, wondering how her soft down mattress had become so lumpy all of a sudden. She turned, thinking to ring for her maid, and nearly fell off the narrow bunk. Her eyes opened wide and she stifled a scream, abruptly recalling everything that had happened the night before.

Rising on unsteady legs she straightened out her torn and rumpled ballgown, pinned up her hair the best she could and walked to the door, gingerly turning the knob. Of course it was still locked, she thought, chagrined. Thoroughly enraged, she began beating on the panel, regardless of the pain it caused her, and crying out loudly for attention. Her efforts were met with silence. Rubbing her bruised fists she gave up in disgust, returning to the bunk to wait impatiently for someone to come to her.

From the sounds of activity filtering through the bulkheads she knew she wasn't alone on the ship. Somewhere above men were working. Did anyone besides the despicable Adam Foxworth know she was being held captive aboard this ship? she wondered bleakly as she got up and began pacing.

Suddenly a noise outside her door alerted her and she whirled, prepared to face her abductor. But when the panel opened a tall, red-haired man entered, smiling disarmingly. "I trust you slept well, milady," Mac said, a hint of humor lurking at the corners of his wide mouth.

"Where is Lord Penwell?" Alexa asked, ignoring Mac's greeting. "Have you come to release me?"

"I wish I could, milady," Mac said, sobering. "But it's not up to me. I owe Adam a favor and promised not to interfere."

"But what he's doing is wrong!" cried Alexa. "I've done him no harm. Please, let me go! He doesn't have to know it was you who released me." His soulful expression gave her a surge of hope. But it was short-lived.

"I'm sorry," murmured Mac. "Adam assured me you wouldn't be harmed. I'm to look after you until he can join us."

"Where is he?"

"He went back to the party last night. When he is certain no one links him to your disappearance he will return to the ship. No longer than a day or two."

"So I am your prisoner."

"A guest, if you will."

"Like hell!" shot back Alexa, thoroughly incensed. "I'm here against my will, carried away from my own home by force!"

"Is there some problem with our guest, Mac?" a raspy voice interjected.

Both Mac and Alexa swiveled to face the speaker. "No, Captain," Mac replied, darting a swift glance at Alexa's startled features.

Alexa could only stare open-mouthed at the tall, imposing man who filled the doorway with his brawny frame. It wasn't just his dark garb and commanding air that startled her but the fact that his features were completely hidden from view by a mask that concealed his entire face but for his lips and chin. His hair was covered by a scarf worn pirate style and knotted at the nape. But even more shocking was the mask itself. Upon its dark surface was superimposed the features of a fox. Though she had never seen him his identity was obvious.

"You!" she breathed, trembling. "It's not possible! You're the Fox! How could you be in London harbor? The entire British navy is looking for you. How did you escape them?"

"Easy, milady," rasped the Fox, his voice a thick whisper. "We fly the Union Jack atop our mast. A devious trick, I'll admit, but one that works."

"But . . . why am I aboard your ship? Where is Lord Penwell?" Warily Alexa looked from Mac to the Fox for an explanation.

It was Mac who answered. "Adam and I have been friends for many years. We traveled on the same ship to America. When war was declared with England I was recruited by Fox to serve aboard his privateer, *The Gray Ghost*. In time I became his first mate.

"While in London a few days ago on a secret mission I happened to meet Adam, who asked my help in enlisting Fox's aid in a scheme that included you, milady."

"Lord Penwell paid well," continued Fox, taking up where Mac left off. "And his plans fit in with my own, so I agreed. When he returns we will sail under the noses of the British navy to a secret destination."

Alexa was astounded. The man's daring was legend but never did she expect to find the privateer berthed in London harbor. Evidently neither did the navy. "If it's money you want," Alexa offered bravely, "my father will pay well for my return. Far better than Lord Penwell."

"I gave my word," whispered the Fox. "Besides, I don't deal with the enemy. My ship will carry you and Lord Penwell to your destination. Now, if you will excuse me, milady, I'll leave Mac to see to your needs." Such was his presence that when he vacated the small cabin he left a definite void.

"Your captain is a strange man," Alexa mused, once he had disappeared from sight. "Why does he wear a mask? Is he so ugly he doesn't want to be seen? Or horribly scarred?"

"The Fox deems it wise to keep his identity a secret. By so doing he can operate more effectively."

"Bah!" scoffed Alexa. "Not only is he a pirate, but a spy!"

"Perhaps." Mac shrugged, unconcerned.

"Does no one see his face?"

"I do. So do most of the crew. But we are all loyal and would never reveal his identity."

After Mac left Alexa mulled over the first mate's words. Evidently Fox was able to move about freely in society while remaining unidentified as the Fox, a renowned privateer, the scourge of the British navy. The man had no scruples. It was obvious she could expect no help from him. She must rely on her own resourcefulness if she wished to escape from Adam and the fate he had planned for her.

During the long day an array of palatable food was provided by Mac as well as water with which to bathe. Of Adam there was no sign. Nor had the Fox returned. When Mac picked up her supper tray that evening he bid her goodnight and locked the door behind him for the last time that day. Stripping to her brief shift Alexa climbed between the sheets and was soon sound asleep, her dreams wild and unsettled.

The grating of the key in the lock did not awaken her. Nor the nearly noiseless rasp of the well-oiled hinges as the door slid open. Rather it was an awareness of another presence other than her own in the airless room. Alexa's eyes flew open to a darkness deeper than the depths of Hades. The moonless, starless night allowed not one glimmer of light through the porthole.

Icy fear twisted around her heart as the whisper of soft footsteps commanded her attention. Rising on one elbow she swallowed the lump in her throat and called out, "Mac, is that you?" Absolute silence. "Answer me, damn you, who is it? What do you want?" And then, "Adam?"

A raspy chuckle gave Alexa her first clue as to the identity of her nighttime visitor. "Fox! What do you want? I know you're there."

A hand caressed her face and Alexa gasped, jerking reflexively. "Captain, what are you doing in my room? Get out!" she ordered, despite her rising terror.

"This ship is mine, I go where I will," rasped Fox in his distinctive, hoarse whisper.

"I'll scream," Alexa threatened.

"Go ahead. No one will come."

"Mac . . ."

"Has orders to remain in his cabin."

"Adam, then. I'll tell Adam!"

"Do you prefer Adam Foxworth to me?"

"I prefer neither of you," insisted Alexa hotly. "I wish only to return home to my father."

"One of us will have you, milady," the Fox whispered. "Count on it. The choice is yours. Give over to me now or Lord Penwell later. Which will it be?"

"I told you, neither," Alexa retorted, knowing full well that given his superior strength he could easily take what he wanted.

The mattress sank beneath his weight and Alexa knew a moment of panic as he reached for her and pulled her roughly, almost violently to him, holding her snugly. The touch of his lips on hers sent a shock wave through her entire body and her senses reeled as if short-circuited.

Gently he eased her down on the bunk as his lips slid from her mouth to caress and tantalize a breast one large hand had bared while the other explored her thighs and hips beneath her thin chemise. His touch was light and painfully teasing. Never had she been touched in such a manner before.

With a swiftness that left her breathless her shift was lifted over her head and off, leaving her nude and vulnerable to his exploration. The moment his lips touched her sensitive nipple she realized the Fox was not wearing his mask. Immediately her hands flew to his face, finding it surprisingly smooth and free of even the slightest blemish. His amusement at her action was evident in the low chuckle that rumbled through his breast.

"Are you so eager to know me, Alexa?" he rasped huskily.

"Yes . . . no!" she contradicted, confused. "I care nothing about you."

"I burn to know you." The stroking of his fingers sent pleasurable jolts through her as she fought his gentle seduction.

"Please, don't do this to me," Alexa begged, writhing beneath his lust-arousing exploration of her soft flesh. "I'm to be married in a few weeks."

His hands stilled and he whispered throatily, "Are you a virgin? Has neither your fiancé nor Lord Penwell sampled your treasures?" His low voice sounded dubious.

"Of course I'm a virgin!" retorted Alexa indignantly. "I've been taught a girl's virtue is her most prized possession."

Mocking laughter met her ears. "So be it. Now that your fiancé is out of the running for the time being it remains between Lord Penwell and myself to experience the pleasure of claiming your virtue. I will give him a sporting chance, my lovely Alexa, choose between us."

"Choose?" she scorned. "Choose between a pirate and an abductor? You're mad!"

"Then I will choose for you," he declared authoritatively as his hands moved gently down the length of her back and his body bent to partially cover hers.

Uttering a cry of dismay Alexa quickly slid from beneath him. This couldn't be happening to her! she screamed in silent supplication. She had to stop him before it was too late. A delaying action was preferable to lying there and mutely submitting to Fox's lovemaking.

"Wait! Stop!" she cried as she felt him part her thighs. "I prefer Adam! Yes, yes, I prefer Adam Foxworth to you!"

Abruptly the pressure lifted from her slim form as the Fox shifted to sit beside her. She had felt his excitement in their struggle and Alexa wondered if he was capable of exerting the control necessary to walk out the door and leave her untouched. Evidently he was for he arose from the bunk. Alexa could feel his eyes piercing her through the darkness.

"We are far from finished, milady," came his husky whisper. "One day we will meet again and finish what we began. Until then, I bid you goodnight."

Holding her breath, Alexa listened to his light footfall as he made his way to the door, and then paused. If only she could see his face, she thought. "You have no idea how I envy Adam Foxworth," Fox rasped softly in parting.

Alexa collapsed against the mattress, fighting the overwhelming feeling of deprivation. What was wrong with her? First she was inexplicably drawn to Adam by a strange magnetism, and now to the pirate, Fox. In their own way both were powerful men, sensual, passionate. Both instilled in her an inner excitement that took all her strength to combat. Yet Charles's kisses left her cold and the thought of his lovemaking filled her with dread. Was there some flaw in her character that caused her to welcome the caresses of rogues while resisting good men like Charles? she wondered dully.

No answer was forthcoming and Alexa finally fell asleep, the mysterious face of Fox and the magnetic gray eyes of Adam warring within her brain.

3

The ship was underway! From somewhere below came the creakings of chains and from above Alexa heard the distinct sound of sails flapping in the breeze. Not only that but the gentle swaying motion reaffirmed her belief that *The Gray Ghost* had slipped its moorings and left London harbor. Glancing out the grimy porthole Alexa recognized the banks of the Thames gliding by at a respectable pace.

Quickly pulling on her ruined ballgown Alexa raced to the door and was shocked to find it unlocked. She pulled it open and stepped into the dim passageway, heading unerringly toward the ladder leading to the deck above.

Alexa stepped onto the deck and was lost amid a whirlwind of activity. If she had once thought the ship was deserted she now knew her assumption to be incorrect. Men of all sizes and descriptions were doing all the things it took to sail a ship the size of *The Gray Ghost*. Glancing upwards she grimaced ruefully at the Union Jack flying boldly from her mast. Evidently the crew had their orders for not one of them glanced her way.

"Have you had breakfast, milady?"

Alexa whirled about to face a smiling Mac, brilliant sunlight setting his red hair and beard ablaze. "N-no," she stammered, startled.

"Come, I'll escort you to the galley so cook can prepare something for you." He gallantly offered her his arm.

"You mean I am no longer confined to my cabin?"

"It is no longer necessary, Lady Alexa." Mac smiled. "As you can see we left London on the morning's tide."

"Then Adam must be aboard," Alexa mused aloud.

Mac eyed her strangely but only nodded.

"When did he return?"

"At dawn."

"Where is he now?"

"Still sleeping. I'm certain you'll see him later."

Alexa sniffed disdainfully. "Who cares," she declared hotly. "Both Adam and your captain are men of questionable morals."

"Fox? What do you know of him except that he's a privateer?"

"Believe me I know all I want to know," replied Alexa cryptically.

Before Mac could question her further they had reached the galley and he seated her at a table where the officers took their meals. Then he left her to her excellent breakfast prepared by a beaming elderly cook named Hayes.

Afterwards Alexa roamed the deck, enjoying the fresh salt air after a long day and night confined to her tiny cabin. Standing at the rail, her dress plastered against her long legs and high breasts, ebony locks blowing freely in the breeze, Alexa breathed deeply. She had always longed for a sea voyage but certainly not under these circumstances.

As she turned to continue her promenade she caught sight of Fox standing on the bridge, legs spread in typical seaman stance, looking more imposing than she remembered. His face was concealed by the inevitable mask but his powerful form, balanced on the balls of his feet had the appearance of a sleek tiger, coiled and ready to spring. His massive muscles rippling under his black silk shirt open at the neck quickened her pulse and she recalled vividly the feel of his strong hands on her body.

Sensing her silent appraisal Fox jauntily cocked his head to one side then nodded mockingly. Flushing angrily, Alexa stiffened, haughtily tossing her mass of windblown black curls. A low mirthful rumble reached her ears and she abruptly turned and marched back to her cabin.

Later that afternoon Adam visited her cabin. Not bothering to knock he barged in, his profile strong and rigid, his icy eyes hooded. "I see you've fared well in my absence." His voice was courteous but patronizing. "Have my friends seen to your needs, milady?"

"Well enough," snapped Alexa. For some unknown reason his commanding presence irked her as much as that of the pirate captain. "You choose strange friends, Adam," she accused. "A rogue privateer and his first mate who take your money without a qualm. But then, you are not much better despite your title."

Adam laughed raucously, evidently pleased by her show of spirit. "The lady has spunk. Be careful, milady, you may bare your claws once too often with me. You are bound to pay the consequences."

"What are the consequences, Adam?" Alexa asked quietly. "Why have you taken me from my home and what do you plan for me? You owe me an explanation."

After a poignant pause, Adam answered, a look of inflexible purpose on his face. "It's no more than right that you should know. Your father and mother caused a man's death fifteen years ago. A senseless death that could have been avoided, the problem settled less harshly. One man was an excellent shot, the other had never held a pistol in his hand much less fired one. The outcome was inevitable."

Alexa sucked in her breath and involuntarily stepped backwards, the hatred in Adam's cold eyes frightening.

"As you might have guessed, the expert shot was your father; the man he killed was mine. And your mother, whore that she is, was the cause of it all."

"No!" screamed Alexa, striking out at him blindly. "How dare you call my mother a whore! How can you speak so of the dead?"

"Your mother is dead?" asked Adam, startled by her disclosure. "I . . . I didn't know. But that still doesn't excuse her. She led my father on, made him fall in love with her, knowing there was no hope for him, for your father would never let her go. How . . . how did she die? An accident?"

"I . . . I'm not sure. All my father would tell me was that she died suddenly fifteen years ago. I don't even have a picture of her. I thought it was because he loved her so much that he burned everything that reminded him of her."

"It matters little." Adam shrugged carelessly. "However she died my father is gone because of her and your father. I made a vow to avenge his death one day by depriving your father of something or someone he values highly." He stared at her pointedly.

"Me!" breathed Alexa. "You're punishing me because of something my parents did fifteen years ago! It's so unfair! How am I to be punished for the sins of my father?"

"You won't be hurt, Alexa," Adam assured her stonily. "I don't abuse women physically."

"Then how. . . ? Oh, no," she gasped, her violet eyes dark with horror. "Fox was right, you do plan on . . . on ravishing me. But if that's what you intend why didn't you just do it and let me go?"

"There's more to it than that, milady. I intend to keep you with me and make you my mistress until I tire of you. Your father has already been given a message outlining my intentions. He knows that you are being held by the son of Martin Foxworth, the man who stole the heart of his wife. How do you think he'll react to the information that his innocent daughter is being corrupted time and again by the son of the man whom his wife loved?"

Alexa could only stare at Adam, amazed at the amount of hatred stored within his tall frame. Fifteen years of hate. All directed at her father, and indirectly at her. Adam expected to hurt her father but it was the daughter who would ultimately suffer.

"My father won't let you get away with this," Alexa declared, lifting her small chin belligerently. "No doubt he has already informed the king and you are being hunted down this very minute."

Adam smiled complacently. "Looking for whom? No one knows that the newly created Lord Penwell is Adam Foxworth. In my note I identified myself only as the son of Martin Foxworth. It will be like looking for a needle in a haystack. Besides, we'll soon be far from London and I've been careful to leave no clues as to our destination."

"If you think I'll give in to you without a fight, you're sadly mistaken," Alexa informed him, eyeing him warily from beneath lowered lids.

Adam chuckled, vastly amused. "Your reluctance does not overly worry me," he told her with typical male conceit. "The fact remains that in my own good time I will bed you and make you my mistress. In due time you will be returned to your father no worse for the wear. Every time he looks at you he will be reminded that I have had my revenge for my father's death. Two women he loved were taken from him and used by the Foxworths, both father and son."

"You're mad!"

"Of course. You would be too if you were forced to wait fifteen years for vengeance, your hate festering with the passage of time."

By the set expression on his hard features Alexa could tell he was implacable. Nothing she could say or do would change his mind. Would he ravish her now? she wondered desperately, slowly backing away from his salacious intent.

But Adam's only reaction was a thin-lipped smile, bleak and derisive. "Have no fear, milady," he informed her with cool hauteur. "I'll have you in my own good time, when and where I choose."

"Monster! Cad!" she shot back hotly. "I'd rather bed . . . Fox!" The moment she said it she was sorry, clapping a hand to her mouth. Adam's face wore a stunned expression as his mouth dipped into a deep frown and his eyebrows shot up in amazement.

"Is that so, milady?" he mocked.

Alexa found a perverse pleasure in the challenge as she nodded vigorously, eyeing him with cold contempt. She would not be cowed by this brute! she vowed silently.

Their eyes met and a vaguely sensuous light passed between them. His power and self-confidence were awesome and Alexa fought against his charisma. Her wild emotions were quickly eroding her courage and she looked away. Adam chuckled, enjoying her struggle to capture her composure.

"We reach our destination tomorrow, Alexa," Adam informed her, using her name for the first time. "We will leave the ship together."

Before Alexa could find her voice and question him further concerning their destination, he was gone.

That evening Mac brought Alexa a tempting tray and bid her good-bye, telling her he would be busy the next day and wouldn't see her before she left the ship. "Where am I being taken, Mac?" Alexa asked anxiously.

"Adam will tell you, I'm sure."

"Adam!" Alexa scoffed derisively. "How could you condone what he is doing when you know what he intends?"

Mac had the grace to look embarrassed, his face nearly as red as his hair. "I won't interfere, milady. I couldn't even if I wanted to. No one meddles with Adam when his mind is made up. He has promised me you won't be mistreated and I believe him."

"What do you call rape? It is the worst kind of mistreatment."

Shifting uncomfortably from foot to foot Mac refused to meet her gaze. "I'm . . . sorry, Lady Alexa, truly I am. But my hands are tied. In parting I'd advise you to allow Adam his way in this. He's not as bad as you seem to think. Many women would envy your position."

"Then let them have him! I just want to go home and marry Charles."

"You still can marry your Charles after . . . after . . ."

"After Adam tires of me, is that what you're trying to say?"

"Good-bye, Lady Alexa," Mac said, flushing darkly. "Perhaps we'll meet again." Then he was gone.

Once again Alexa was alone with her thoughts. If they were to reach their destination the next day surely they weren't too far from London. They could be going to France or some remote section of England where no one would think to look for her. Raging at the unfairness of it all, Alexa readied herself for bed, stripping to her brief chemise and climbing between the sheets.

Glancing toward the porthole she noticed that it was another moonless, starless night and she shuddered when she thought of what had nearly happened the night before. As long as she was aboard *The Gray Ghost* she was physically threatened not just by one man, but by two. Breathing deeply and trying to forget her predicament, Alexa finally fell asleep.

The door slid open noiselessly but the sound of the key turning in the lock startled Alexa into wakefulness. "Who's there?" she called out, her voice trembling. "Go away, Adam!" For some unexplained reason she was certain her intruder was Adam. A raspy chuckle soon disabused her of that notion.

"Fox, my God, what are you doing here?"

"You fooled me, milady," he whispered hoarsely. "You told me it was Lord Penwell you preferred when all the time it was me you wanted."

"No! No! I didn't mean it! I want neither of you!" Her eyes narrowed suspiciously. "How do you know what I said? Were you listening at the door?"

"I know everything that takes place on this ship." The huskiness of his voice mesmerized her. "I have my ways of finding out. I'm here to grant you your wish."

Before she could protest the mattress sagged beneath his weight. Immediately her hands flew to his face and she wasn't a bit surprised to find that the inevitable mask was missing. Her fingertips found his mouth which was spread in a wide grin. When they slid down his torso she was shocked to discover he was bare to the waist.

She opened her mouth to protest but his lips robbed her of reason and thought. His tongue surged between her lips, exploring the velvet recesses of her mouth in a way that sent her pulses racing and filled her with a strange excitement in the pit of her belly. Her skin registered the slight roughness of his fingertips as they traced the delicate knobs of her spine through her shift. Her breasts surged against his chest begging to be freed to the feel of his hands. Eagery he obliged her as he lifted her shift and drew it over her head.

"Alexa," Fox groaned huskily. "You set me afire."

His words seemed to bring her out of her trance and she realized she was about to lose her virginity to a pirate, a rogue and an enemy of England. She began to struggle, pushing against the solid wall of his chest, lightly furred with thick curly hair.

Searing the soft skin of her neck with his lips, he slowly stroked it with his tongue. Roving downward he found a rosy nipple and sucked it into his mouth, nipping it gently with his teeth. Alexa knew the only reason she did not cry out was because she was holding her breath, helpless to halt the yearnings that washed over her. When he slipped his fingers between her thighs, a shiver of protest gripped her, but his rhythmic stroking soon quieted her as she spiraled higher and higher, searching for something . . . something . . .

Suddenly his weight left her as he struggled to cast off his trousers. Then he was back and she felt something hard and hot probe at the softness between her thighs. It managed to wedge itself a little ways inside, and she squirmed uncomfortably, trying to escape it. It prodded at her again, harder this time, and she arched to escape it, thereby aiding Fox as he broke through her maidenhead. Pressing his advantage he slid into her so far she was certain she would die of the sweet pain.

A cry rose in her throat but was lost in the depths of Fox's mouth as his tongue darted inside like a rapier to pierce her resistance. He stilled his hips, savoring her while she grew accustomed to his size before moving in the age-old rhythm of love.

"Alexa, Alexa," Fox murmured throatily against her breast. "you are so sweet. Come with me, my love."

Alexa moaned, tossed on the waves of her own surrender. This couldn't be happening to her. Only her lawful husband had the right to possess her, not a man who hadn't the courage to show his face. And then his forceful thrusts were carrying her away on a spinning cloud and she was too weak to fight him. A trembling began in her thighs as something fluid and mysterious began to build in her.

Smiling to himself Fox was aware of Alexa's excitement and the pleasure he was giving her despite her initial reluctance. As he surged into her moist, silken sheath, he felt waves of ecstasy encompass her, and she cried out rapturously as he branded her flushed face with his kisses. Only when she was still did he allow his own passion free rein as his huge frame shuddered convulsively and he joined her in paradise.

Alexa came to her senses first, pushing at Fox until he raised himself and shifted his weight to rest beside her. "You're incredible," he sighed breathlessly, running his hand possessively along the rise of one slim hip. "Virgin or not, you have more passion in your petite body than a woman with years of experience. You've given me something precious to carry in my memory for years to come."

Alexa was stunned by her response to Fox and his lovemaking. Never in her wildest dreams had she imagined making love could be so pleasurable. Of course she had her romantic musings, what girl didn't? All she really knew of sex was what she read in romance novels she bought without her father's knowledge. And they stopped far short of full disclosure. Quite often she had tried to envision what it would be like to make love with Charles but the thought usually left her cold and depressed. From all she had overheard or been told she assumed it was a duty she must perform perfunctorily, giving her little pleasure. But Fox had just proved otherwise.

"Why so quiet, love?" Fox purred in a low, raspy voice. "Have I disappointed you?"

"Oh, no, I mean, oh, I don't know," Alexa answered, confused. "I should hate you but I'm not certain how I feel."

"Did I give you pleasure?"

"You know you did," Alexa admitted, blushing. She was glad the cabin was too dark to make out her features.

"Then don't feel remorse at what we did. What you felt was natural and right."

"Will I feel the same with anyone?" Alexa asked curiously.

"I hope not," Fox teased, bending his head to press a kiss on her trembling mouth. "But any man worth his salt has the power to bring a woman to climax and give her pleasure."

Alexa said nothing but seriously doubted another man could give her the same pleasure as the mysterious Fox. At that precise moment thoughts of Adam Foxworth were so far removed from her mind as to be nonexistent, for Fox's hands and lips were once again carrying her into a world where no one existed but the two of them.

Before she fell asleep she heard him whisper huskily, "We are far from finished, my lovely Alexa. We will meet again."

A persistent knocking roused her from a dreamless sleep and Alexa immediately looked to the pillow beside her, knowing instinctively that she was alone. No doubt Fox had risen long before dawn to return unseen to his own cabin. "Who is it?" she called out sleepily.

"It's Adam. We've arrived. As soon as you've dressed and had breakfast meet me on deck."

Alexa was out of bed like a flash, gazing out the porthole. She gasped in delight at the awesome panorama spread out before her. The ship appeared to be anchored a short distance from shore in a small sheltered cover. Above her on three sides rose steep gray cliffs stark against a cloudless blue sky. Atop one majestic outcropping hung the outline of a castle, magnificent yet bleak and forbidding with tall turrets pointing skyward in splendid artistry.

Catching her breath in wonder Alexa hurried into her clothes and rushed topside to the small wardroom where Hayes, grinning toothlessly, served her breakfast. She reached the deck just as a longboat was being prepared to be lowered into the sparkling blue water. Adam was waiting for her.

His eyebrows arched mysteriously as he asked coolly, "Did you sleep well."

Alexa froze in terror as he searched her face. Did he suspect something? she wondered bleakly. What would he do if he knew Fox had come to her bed last night and made love to her? Aware that Adam was waiting for her answer, she stammered, "I . . . yes, of course I did."

"Good," he answered, his mouth twisting wryly. "When I noticed those dark shadows beneath your eyes I thought perhaps you had trouble sleeping."

Automatically her hands flew to her flushed face, her dark sooty lashes lowering to hide her embarrassment. But she was saved from responding when the longboat hit the water with a splash and Adam gripped her elbow. "Shall we go over the side, milady?" he asked smoothly.

"O-over the side? You mean climb down to that boat in the water?"

"Exactly. Shall we go?"

"No! I can't!" refused Alexa stubbornly. "This ballgown I'm wearing is hardly suitable for such activity."

Adam eyed her narrowly, silently agreeing with her. Suddenly he turned and marched her back to her cabin. "Wait here," he ordered brusquely, "I'll be back directly."

Curious as to what exactly he had in mind, Alexa patiently waited for Adam's return. Fifteen minutes were to pass before he re-entered the cabin carrying an array of sailor's garb over his arm. "Put these on," he ordered. "It's the best I could do on short notice. At least they are clean."

Alexa grimaced at the white pants and shirt as she held them gingerly between her fingers, but realized they were far better suited to climbing ropes than a ruined ballgown. She began to remove her dress until she suddenly remembered that Adam was still in the room. She looked at him pointedly.

"Soon your body will hold no secrets, milady," he bowed mockingly. "But if it will make you feel better I will wait for you topside."

Changing swiftly, Alexa returned topside, glancing around for Mac so she might bid him good-bye. But he was nowhere to be seen. Instead her eyes came to rest on the Fox standing loose-limbed on the bridge, his mask firmly in place. His hand raised in a gesture of farewell and she managed a tremulous smile before Adam came forward to help her over the side. If he noticed her wistful expression he said nothing. And then she was far too busy concentrating on descending the side of the ship without mishap to worry about anything else.

The longboat set them off on the narrow strip of sand

below the cliffs and returned immediately to the ship. Alexa gazed about her forlornly, feeling as if she were stranded in another world.

"Come along, milady, Adam urged, pushing her forward.

Alexa eyed the cliffs warily, fully aware that she could not scale those lofty heights. Not even comfortably clad in her sailor's garb, which surprisingly was a fair fit. The pants were too big in the waist but hugged her hips enticingly while the shirt was a snug but adequate fit if she rolled up the sleeves. The look on Adam's face when he first saw her dressed assured her that she was not unattractive in her new clothes.

"Adam," she finally said, exasperated. "There is no way I'll be able to climb those cliffs."

"I know," he smirked confidently. "But there is no need for such tactics. Follow me."

Keeping close to Adam, Alexa was astounded when he led her toward a small cave whose yawning mouth was completely hidden behind a huge boulder. When he crouched to enter, Alexa obediently followed. Taking a flint from his pocket Adam struck a light to a torch conveniently placed in a sconce on the stone wall and Alexa was surprised to see that the cave was large and roomy, allowing them space to stand erect. Holding the torch with one hand and Alexa with the other, Adam led her toward a small passage to the right of the cavern.

With the torch lighting their path the passage led steadily upward and Alexa panted from her exertions. Suddenly they came to a flight of stone steps which they slowly negotiated. Then another, twisting to the left. Then another. And finally a door set into the stone wall. Adam extracted a key from his pocket, fit it in the lock and the door creaked open, protesting loudly from disuse.

Adam stepped into the room first, bowing low as

Alexa crossed over the threshold. "Welcome to Penwell Castle, milady," he said, his brooding face breaking into a half-smile that did little to allay her fears. "I hope your stay will prove enjoyable."

4

Cornwall 1778

Alexa stared moodily out the tall window of the lovely room assigned to her. A high, canopied bed accessible only by climbing three steps onto its surface dominated the room decorated in varying shades of blue. A wardrobe, chest of drawers, delicate French desk and several satin-covered chairs complimented the attractive decor. It was obviously a woman's room. A fire was blazing in the fireplace to ward off the chill that permeated the stone walls despite the fact that it was summer and they were adorned with thick tapestries. Alexa had been at Penwell Castle for two days and it seemed to her that in all that time the wind blew constantly.

It was obvious to Alexa that the castle was ancient, built by one of Adam's ancestors. He had finally confided to her that they were in a remote section of Cornwall and the castle and lands were part of his inheritance. Alexa knew there must be a village nearby for the servants who served the castle had to come from somewhere in the vicinity.

But, Hilda, the elderly woman assigned to see to her needs, might well have been deaf and dumb for all she communicated. It was evident that the servants were intensely loyal to the master of Penwell and though they treated her with respect they obeyed only Adam. Alexa had the run of the house but was not allowed outdoors to walk the wild moors as she longed to do. With the well-stocked library she realized there was no chance of her becoming bored, but she missed her father and all her friends.

Still, she was eternally grateful that Adam had not yet carried out his threat to make her his mistress. During the day she was left much on her own and at night his only demand was her presence at supper.

Most times he remained cool and courteous, but at other times the hate and contempt he felt for her father was transmitted to her, his icy blue eyes conveying his feelings adequately.

What proved most distressing to Alexa was the fact that she had no suitable clothing. The sailor garb was taken from her when she first arrived and she found nothing in the wardrobe or dresser but filmy night-clothes, most unfit to be seen in. When she complained bitterly to Adam he only smiled blandly and said, "You have nothing to hide from me, milady."

Alexa could read nothing in his stony expression so chose not to pursue the meaning behind his cryptic words. The less they spoke about his reason for bringing her to this windswept land the better she liked it. So in the end she had worn the gowns and robes, grateful at least for something with which to cover her nakedness.

From her vantage point high above the cliffs and the sea, Alexa could not see the small cove where *The Gray Ghost* had put her and Adam ashore, for her room was situated in a corner where the cove was not visible. She had since learned from Adam that the cave and passageway into the castle were used at one pont in time by an ancestor involved in smuggling, which made her think of Fox. She supposed that by now he was back harassing the British navy. She sighed wistfully as she thought of that last night aboard his ship when he had made love to her.

So deep was her reminiscence that she did not hear Adam enter the room or see him pause in the doorway to study her enchanting face and slim figure. Her great, black-fringed eyes were set aslant like a pair of sparkling amethysts against the porcelain texture of her skin. Her small straight nose and rosy lips were made expressly for kissing, and framing it all, coal-black hair shiny and sleek, nearly touching the curve of her hips and held back by a thin ribbon.

Beneath the satin robe every luscious curve was clearly outlined and defined. The high upthrust breasts with impudently protruding nipples, slim waist that had no need of a corset, hips and thighs gently curving and shapely. For two days Adam had refrained from taking her, preferring to wait until she became accustomed to her surroundings. But he could wait no longer. His eyes turned smoky, thinking that revenge would be more pleasurable than he had imagined. Lady Alexa Ashley was a tempting morsel and he had much to teach her. There was nothing she wouldn't know about the art of love by the time he returned her to her father.

"Dare I hope you're thinking of me, milady?" Adam asked softly.

Alexa whirled, surprised to find Adam in her room. "Hardly," she answered haughtily.

"Surely Charles isn't the recipient of those wistful sighs. He hardly strikes me as the type to evoke romantic fantasies," he taunted.

"You've only seen Charles once when he was drunk.

He isn't like that all the time," Alexa defended. Adam walked further into the room, shutting the door firmly behind him. "I didn't hear you knock!"

"No, you didn't."

Alexa deliberately turned her back to him to stare out the window, noticing as she did that the sun was slowly disappearing below the horizon. It was a magnificent sight.

"What do you want?" she asked, studiously avoiding his eyes as she concentrated on the cliffs and the sea below.

"Turn around, Alexa, look at me," Adam commanded sternly.

Alexa turned slowly, waiting until the last possible moment before lifting her eyes to meet his gaze. She gasped audibly. His eyes, smoldering gray, pierced her very soul. He was so handsome he took her breath away. If only they had met under different circumstances, she mused. Even his eyebrows were beautiful and thick with a sardonic arch, and very expressive in conveying moods without words. There was something about the man that ignited her interest. Something mysterious about his aloof, superior manner. Only he wasn't aloof now. His probing gaze conveyed his desire more adequately than words.

"No!" whispered Alexa, backing away in an effort to combat the devastating magnetism that threatened to destroy her willpower.

"My revenge, Alexa. I must have my revenge. I will not rest until I have thoroughly demoralized your father."

"And me, Adam. It's me you will be hurting."

"I'm sorry it has to be this way." For a fraction of a second his face softened, but just as quickly resumed his facade of cool indifference. "Don't fight me, milady, and you won't be hurt."

It was true, Adam had no desire to hurt Alexa

physically, but neither did he mean for their coupling to be construed as anything other than what he intended. He was determined to take her with cold detachment. He would leave her romantic yearnings for Charles to assuage when he returned her to be married to her young fiancé. It never occurred to Adam that he might be the one to form attachments, for love had no place in his heart.

One day he would marry, to be sure, but for political and financial advancement only. He even had a wife picked out at home in Savannah who would serve his purposes admirably. There was no room in his life for a violet-eyed girl who had the power to turn his life upside-down given half a chance. Without remorse or recrimination he would take her, enjoy her fully, and return her to her father only slightly used. Or so he thought. Such was the extent of his hate that not only did it include Sir John Ashley but his innocent daughter, Lady Alexa.

Alexa watched the play of emotion upon Adam's face, hardly daring to breathe. His expression told her he was determined to have her and she was just as determined to resist.

"Take off your clothes, Alexa, and get into bed," Adam ordered brusquely, unbuttoning his shirt as he spoke.

"I think not," retorted Alexa, deliberately turning her back. "You will not use me as an instrument of revenge."

"You think not?" Adam smiled thinly. "I'm perfectly capable of undressing you should you refuse. In fact, I might even enjoy it. Which will it be?"

Alexa glared murderously, refusing to budge. Perhaps if she displayed courage he would go away and leave her alone, she thought futilely. But she was mistaken. Adam would not be put off.

It took but two strides to reach Alexa's side and too late she turned to run. Not that it would have mattered, for she had no place to run to. His body rigid with desire, Adam easily captured Alexa's struggling form in his arms, turning her until she was crushed against his chest. Bending her over his arm he took her lips savagely, his tongue stabbing with hot insistence into the moist recesses of her mouth.

Her protests died as he kissed her and were replaced by a shuddering sigh. Adam paused, momentarily dismayed by her sweet response. But his next act dispelled any softening of his resolve he may have felt. Grasping the neckline of her fragile nightgown and robe, he tore viciously, ripping it from her trembling body.

Adam stared . . . and stared. Clad in nothing but a luxurious cloak of long black hair, Alexa was breath-taking. She could feel the intensity of his smoky gray eyes upon her and she shivered beneath his bold regard as he measured and assessed her. Sweet magnolia-blossom flesh the color of rich cream except for coral-tipped nipples filled his gaze. He marveled at the perfect symmetry of her.

"You are beautiful." The words sprang spontaneously from his lips despite his reluctance to say them.

He reached out to caress her and a shiver of arousal gripped her as he played with the ripe swells of her breasts. "No!" Alexa cried out, struggling to retain her dignity as well as her willpower. To be taken against her will was reprehensible.

"Aye, milady," Adam countered, dragging her closer. His lips were insistent as he ravaged her with his hands and tongue.

With every ounce of will left to her she resisted being used, battled against being conquered like an enemy, fought the ravisher of her flesh, but it was useless . . . useless. A drugging sweetness enfolded them as they swayed in passion.

Scooping her up in his arms, he swung her onto the surface of the bed and flung himself down beside her. Immediately Alexa rolled to the opposite edge but Adam had only to reach out one long arm to sweep her back into his embrace.

"Adam, don't do this," she pleaded softly. Her large violet eyes bright with unshed tears left him unmoved as he lowered his head to her breasts and tongued her swelling nipples until Alexa wanted to scream.

Suddenly Adam grimaced as he realized what he was doing. He was making love to Alexa, tender love, when his original purpose was to take her without consideration for her feelings. He had meant to ravish her quickly, to satisfy his lust furiously, painfully, aware of the way she was affecting him and hating it. But somewhere along the way another urge had overtaken him—the inexplicable urge to fill those violet eyes with passion, to open those luscious red lips with cries of shuddering pleasure, even though his better judgment told him she was the spawn of a devil and a whore. Didn't she deserve to be taken coldly and remorselessly? As long as he did her no harm wasn't it right and just to seek vengeance in any way he saw fit? Aye, he decided, answering his own question, what Alexa felt or thought was unimportant. Vengeance must be served.

Stiffening his resolve, Adam methodically removed his clothes, all the while holding Alexa firmly in place beneath him. Rising up he parted her thighs with his knees and touched his swollen manhood where his fingers had been only moments before, fully intending to thrust viciously and finish swiftly.

At the first touch of his manhood, Alexa stiffened, raising her sooty lashes to gaze appealingly into Adam's face. His mouth was chiseled, hard granite; his narrowed eyes were sculpted marble. A tear slid down each cheek as Alexa recalled the night she had lost her virginity to Fox. He was so tender, so gentle, nothing at all like what Adam intended now.

"Go ahead," her voice quivered dangerously. "I'm no match for you physically. Do your worst, I won't beg or cry for mercy. You're a cold-blooded bastard, Adam Foxworth!"

Hearing her words and watching the play of emotion upon her face, Adam's resolve collapsed like a house of cards. "Alexa, my sweet Alexa," he groaned, his breath warm against her ear. "I can't hurt you. I want to make love to you. I want to give you pleasure, not pain."

He kissed her eyes, her nose, the rapidly beating pulse at the base of her throat, and then her lips, tenderly, thoroughly, until she lay gasping for breath. At his first touch the satiny flesh of her breasts shivered away from his lips, then rose treacherously against his mouth as her body reached to his soft words.

His touch was deliberate yet honey-smooth as his hands slid between her legs, and a moan left Alexa's lips. His scent titillated her, a mixture of soap and the faint aroma of tobacco and a male musk that was uniquely his. When his lips nestled momentarily against the ebony fleece that shielded the treasure between her thighs her control was nearly shattered.

He entered her slowly, savoring her, pausing only a moment when he encountered no obstruction. His lips worked their own magic while he thrust deep inside her, moving upon her sensuously, stroking vigorously. Fire grew in her loins, her blood was a pulsing river of lava that ran hottest at the joining of her thighs. Amid those all-consuming sensations, Alexa's last prickling of conscience lay buried.

A cry of joy burst forth unbidden from her parted lips. "Yes, yes . . ." Adam chanted in a husky voice, urging her on, coaxing her to revel in the glory of her response.

And then his own cries of completion lent her courage as they soared together upon the wings of ecstasy.

It was nearly dark when Alexa awoke, still cradled in Adam's arms. She felt his gaze upon her and was startled to find his eyes kindled with a strange glow, searing her soul, plumbing the depths of her being.

"You think you have defeated me, milady, but you have not," he commented coolly. "Don't think that because I find you desirable I have changed my mind, or that you have made a conquest of me. I am only a man, with a man's desires. And you are a beautiful, passionate woman."

In the terrible moment of silence that followed, Alexa sought her voice but could not find it. Despite the fact that Adam had just made tender love to her his thirst for revenge remained unquenched. "I would expect no less from you," she finally said.

"Had I known you weren't a virgin I might have reacted differently. I thought I was claiming virgin territory but found the ground already plowed."

"How dare you talk to me in such a disgusting manner!" Alexa ground out from between clenched teeth. "I'm glad! I'm glad you're not the first!"

"Who was it? Charles? When I interrupted your tryst in the summerhouse I thought I arrived in time, but evidently he managed to deflower you. Or had you given yourself to him before?"

Like a match to a powder keg his words ignited her anger. "It's none of your business!" Best to let him think what he will, Alexa decided, than to tell him it was Fox who had stolen her virginity.

"What does it matter," Adam shrugged carelessly, "as long as the proud John Ashley believes his daughter was dishonored by a Foxworth." His eyes darkened with an emotion Alexa could not define.

Soon afterwards Adam arose, donned his clothes and

left, only to return a short time later followed by a servant carrying a heavily laden tray. While their supper was being laid out Adam stoked up the fire and lit a lamp, for while they had been pleasantly engaged in the canopied bed, full darkness had descended.

"From now on we will take supper in your room," Adam explained, glancing meaningfully toward the bed. "That way I won't have so far to go to take my pleasure. A mistress should never be allowed out of bed. Especially when she is as exciting as you." Chuckling at his own cleverness, Adam began to eat heartily, ignoring Alexa's murderous looks in his direction.

Alexa ate in silence, fuming with impotent rage at the indignity of her position. Once she was allowed to return home all of London would know she had been the mistress of Adam Foxworth, the Earl of Penwell. What would Charles think? Would he still want her? If he loved her as much as he said, it would make no difference to him, Alexa decided guardedly.

After their supper was cleared away, Adam had thoughtfully arranged for a bath to be prepared for her. She balked when he settled himself in a chair, intending to watch her bathe, but in the end he had his way, his hooded gaze resting on her while she washed. He said nothing, barely moving a muscle until she reached for the towel and arose from the tub all rosy and glowing from the hot water. Then suddenly his muscles flexed as he lifted himself from the chair with the silent grace of a stalking tiger.

Taking the towel from her, he began to dry her dripping body, paying meticulous attention to those certain parts of her body that intrigued him the most. When he dropped the towel Alexa tried to grab her robe but Adam stayed her hand, lifting her in his arms instead and carrying her to the bed still rumpled from their earlier encounter.

"I've not had my fill of you, milady," he said, smiling sardonically. "I've not always been so fortunate to be serviced by so desirable a mistress. During the next weeks I intend to use you well and often. Charles will probably thank me when I return you to him."

"He'll kill you!" spat Alexa, determined to fight against the spell he wove around her senses. "If he doesn't, my father will!"

"They'll have to find me first," laughed Adam, vastly amused. "By then I'll be far from English shores."

"When, Adam?" Alexa asked, her eyes luminous with unshed tears. "When will you release me?"

"When I'm ready, milady, when I'm good and ready," came his terse reply as he moved with exaggerated slowness, pulling her lissome body against the length of his.

"You don't really want me, Adam," Alexa contended bleakly. "Revenge is a powerful emotion. Is there room in your heart for no other emotion?"

"Leave my heart out of it, Alexa," Adam snapped. "I give it freely to no woman. But that doesn't mean I can't enjoy you for as long as we're together. My thirst for revenge has no adverse affect upon my ability to perform in bed, nor does consummation require the use of my heart, only my . . ."

"Oh, you're despicable," Alexa cut him off angrily, blushing furiously.

"Aye," he concurred amiably. "But as long as you understand you are here for one purpose only we shall get along admirably. Now, milady, if you'd be so good as to be quiet I will show you just how capable I am without the use of my heart."

And in the end Alexa did just that as he proved to her once again that he was a consummate lover, inventive, irresistible. As he made love to her, confused images animated the corners of her mind. He became

Fox, gentle, tender, burning away all her resistance with the subtle seduction of hands and lips. But when she opened her eyes she saw only Adam, tawny-maned, silver-eyed, his face hard and inflexible. When finally his hands parted her thighs she lay quiescent, her eyes closed, every nerve and fiber concentrating on the waves of feeling sweeping over her, wild and wonderful, waiting for him to fill her. She couldn't think, she could only respond.

When she was certain she would die of sweet wanting, he took her fiercely, ardently, driving between her thighs with ever deeper strokes until he freed them both in a burst of ecstasy that left them exhausted.

When Alexa awoke the next morning Adam was gone. And not just from her bed. The dour Hilda informed her that the master had left at daybreak without a word as to his destination or purpose. He was gone for ten days and when he returned gave not the slightest clue to where he had been. During his absence Alexa was guarded by a huge man named Curtis who told her he came from the village not far away. He seemed a simple man, albeit one blindly loyal to his master. It appeared Adam had effectively cut off all avenues of escape and until he released her she was his to do with what he liked.

Following Adam's return to Penwell Castle he took up where he left off with Alexa, making passionate love to her nightly, most times tenderly. But there were other times he took her roughly, as if to remind her that she was nothing to him but the daughter of the man he hated above all others.

At the end of the first month in Penwell Castle, Alexa asked for her release.

''Not yet, Alexa,'' he informed her coldly. ''The pleasure your body affords me is still too great for me to let you go. You'll be sent back, milady, when I tire of you, and not before." Then he proceeded to make love to her with a tenderness that left Alexa's mind whirling with confusion.

Afterwards, she dared to ask, "If you hate me so much why do you make love to me with such . . . caring?" Her face flushed becomingly at her temerity but for some strange reason it was important that she know.

"Don't mistake my motives, Alexa," Adam replied sternly. "It's your father I want to hurt, not you. You're just the instrument of my revenge. It's not in my nature to mistreat a woman.

"I tried, Lord knows how I tried to take you callously, without a thought for your feelings. But it went against everything I've ever been taught. Not even a whore deserves such treatment. If I prefer to make love to you instead of raping you, you should be grateful and not question my motives."

"So, I'm no better than a whore!" Alexa said angrily.

"You said that, not me. What I said was . . ."

"I know what you said and you're right. I am your whore."

"Mistress is a better word."

"It will make little difference to my father."

"Exactly." Adam smiled cruelly.

After that encounter Alexa struggled desperately to curb her response to the devastatingly handsome Lord Penwell. But he was an expert in the art of arousal and she could not resist his tender ministrations. In the end Alexa was the one clutching at his broad shoulders, crying out for release. Oh, yes, he was adept and experienced and Alexa considered his lovemaking more devastating than if he had physically abused her.

Sometime during the second month Adam mysteriously disppeared again, staying away nearly two weeks this time. But at least Alexa had gained a concession from him before he left. He had agreed to allow her outside as long as the bumbling Curtis accompanied her. She readily agreed and was given the sailor garb she had worn previously, for it was obvious she couldn't walk the wild moors clad in the fragile nightclothes Adam insisted she wear.

Alexa spent hours outside, roaming, exploring, enjoying the waning summer days out in the open. One day she came upon the secluded cove where *The Gray Ghost* had set her ashore. Inexplicably her thoughts flew to the Fox and the one night they had shared. And then a strange thing happened. In her mind the Fox and Adam became one and each tender moment she spent with Fox dimmed and faded into a single image. It was Adam's face behind the mask but Fox's hands and lips upon her body.

Ridiculous! she scolded herself, shaking her dark head to clear it of such confusing thoughts. It was only natural that she should confuse the only two men who had ever made love to her. No one could be as gentle and tender as Fox had been with her despite the fact that he was a pirate and enemy of England. Her romantic soul yielded to him, forgave him all, for he was a man around which dreams were spun.

Adam returned but refused to reveal to Alexa where he had been. It was now two months since she had been taken forcibly from her home and still she had no idea when her captivity would end. She couldn't exactly say she was unhappy. She wasn't mistreated, she was well-fed, and most of the time had Adam's stimulating company to keep boredom at bay. During his unexplained absences the well-stocked library sufficed.

The servants were polite, if remote, and Alexa's long walks along the moors and cliffs helped immeasurably to work off her pent-up anger and anxiety. And of course there was Adam's lovemaking. She grew so accustomed to it that she actually missed him when he was gone; his strong arms, warm body, and lips and hands that drove her wild. Alexa often wondered if Adam hadn't planned it that way. Though she tried, she couldn't really hate him. What she despised was her growing addiction for the man, Adam Foxworth.

Adam was absent twice during Alexa's third month at Penwell Castle deep in the wilds of Cornwall. This time when he returned his lovemaking took on a frantic quality and when she sought to question him she encountered a nearly imperceptible clouding of his features. For over two weeks his unleashed passion rose in devouring fury to consume her, as if he were driven by an urgency to prove his mastery over her. Though his eyes often told her he cared for her his lips were still.

Then abruptly one night, without warning or provocation, Adam took her without apparent emotion or any attempt to arouse her, as though she were truly nothing but a means of exacting vengeance as he had so often insisted; a vessel into which he poured out his need. The hands and lips that had always intoxicated her with their tender caresses now denied her any satisfaction. She endured it in silence, never more aware of Adam's power over her.

Alexa awoke with a vague feeling of dread hanging over her, but blamed it on Adam's strange behavior the night before. It was almost as if he were trying to tell her something. She pulled on a robe just as Hilda brought in her breakfast tray, but she could only push the food around the plate in a distracted manner. A hard lump formed in her throat, preventing her from swallowing.

The hard, cold facts were that Alexa was faced with a dilemma. She knew little about the workings of the human body but what little she did know all pointed to the fact that she was pregnant. For over a week she had become queasy upon arising and she had not had her woman's time since arriving at Penwell Castle.

Moreover, her breasts were tender to the touch and appeared to be fuller, the nipples darker. She was torn between telling Adam and remaining silent, certain that it would make little difference to him. In fact, her pregnancy probably would fit into his plans admirably. How fitting that he should be returned to her father not only dishonored but pregnant. How Adam would laugh when he found out! In the end she kept her own counsel.

Fighting off twinges of nausea rumbling through her stomach, Alexa wandered downstairs, wondering if Adam was about or off on another of his mysterious jaunts. On a whim she entered the study, for she rarely sought him out there, and spied him instantly, standing in an outpouring of sunshine as he stared somewhat pensively out the window. Only it wasn't Adam. Almost immediately Alexa realized her mistake. Their muscular forms were nearly alike but there the similarity ended. The unruly mop of red hair could belong to no one but Mac.

Something must have alerted Mac to Alexa's presence for he whirled to face her, his bright blue eyes twinkling merrily at the sight of her lovely face. He opened his arms wide and Alexa had no compunction about flying into them.

"Oh, Mac," she sighed, "it's so good to see you again! When did you arrive! Does Adam know you're here? Where is he? Not off on one of his mysterious trips, I hope."

Mac laughed, happy and relieved to see Alexa looking so well. Adam had not lied to him. He had done Alexa no harm. "One question at a time, milady. I arrived last night and I've already seen and spoken to Adam early this morning."

"Is . . . is Fox here also?" Alexa couldn't help but ask.

Mac eyed her curiously. "No, I'm here alone."

Alexa bit her tongue to keep from inquiring further into Fox's whereabouts. Instead, she asked, "What are you doing here? Where is Adam?"

"I'm here at Adam's request, Lady Alexa." Alexa's heart rose like a stone in her breast.

"He's gone, isn't he?" To her dismay, her voice broke slightly and a shadow of alarm touched her face. Every fiber in her body warned her what was coming next and she steeled herself against the impact by sitting in a chair, her thin fingers tensed in her lap.

A look of tired sadness passed over Mac's features. "Aye, Alexa, he's gone. I'm to take you back to your father."

A flash of wild grief ripped through her, and when she lifted her eyes, the pain still lingered. Beneath his breath Mac cursed Adam a hundred times over for hurting this young, innocent girl.

"It's what you want, isn't it?"

Biting her lip she looked away and stirred uneasily in her chair. Her composure was a fragile shell around her and she measured her words carefully. "Of course I want to return home. It's what I've always wanted."

"Good." Mac smiled uncertainly, though her brave words did not fool him one bit. He could read in Alexa's eyes the truth of her feelings for Adam. That damn fool had somehow made Alexa fall in love with him. Mac wondered if Alexa knew the extent of her own feelings for Adam. "How soon can you be ready?"

"I'm ready now." She shrugged carelessly. What did it matter when she left? "But if Fox isn't here, how will we leave? By coach?"

"I have a ship, milady. A captured British frigate. Fox has been so active in these waters the past three months that *The Gray Ghost* is too easily recognized and he dares not venture into London Harbor as he did previously. It was agreed that I should escort you home. I . . . I renamed my ship. I call it the *Lady A*," he said shyly. "I hope you don't mind."

Alexa smiled warmly. "Of course I don't mind, Mac. It was thoughtful of you. I'll be proud to sail aboard my namesake."

"Er . . . I hope you have something more suitable to wear, milady. I'm afraid my men would forget their duties if you were to come aboard dressed like that."

Only then did Alexa give a thought to the inadequacy of her attire. She blushed hotly at the warm look kindling in Mac's eyes as he swept her thinly clad form from head to toe, liking what he saw. "I . . . I still have the sailor's garb Adam gave me. I'll change immediately."

Alexa was out of the chair and nearly to the door when she turned to face Mac, asking, "About Adam. He's with Fox, isn't he?"

Mac nodded solemnly. "Fox was ordered back to American waters by Captain Jones and Adam went with him. The search for Fox was becoming too heated for the Captain's liking. As for Adam, it was past time for him to return to his home."

"What about his inheritance?"

"He never intended to remain long in England. He signed the lands over to a distant cousin, the money and title he kept for various reasons."

"So this is how it is to end," Alexa stated with finality. "I'll never see him again. Did . . . did he leave a message for me."

"No, milady, I'm sorry."

"No need to be sorry, Mac." Alexa smiled a parody of a smile. "I believe he left his message loud and clear last night."

Alexa thought of the cold, perfunctory way Adam had made love to her last night, and what he was trying to convey to her. His callous actions revealed to her that she was little more to him than a warm body, that his only interest in her was her close relationship to John Ashley, her father. Through her Adam was finally able to avenge his own father's death. Now he was free to go on with his life, forgetting Alexa as if she never existed. Little did he know that he was leaving a part of him behind. Already she felt possessed by the child she carried beneath her heart.

Dragging in a deep breath, Alexa controlled her trembling and left the room. Behind her Mac cursed the day he met Adam Foxworth and agreed to his harebrained scheme.

Halfway up the stairs, Alexa froze, every nerve-ending tingling with a new discovery. There was one chance, albeit a remote one, that Fox had fathered her child, not Adam!

5

London 1778

Because of her unorthodox garb Alexa was grateful to
Mac for hiring a closed conveyance to take her to her
father's house. Aware of the fact that the London season
had just begun, Alexa knew her father would be at their
townhouse located on a fashionable square surrounded
by a green park. She prayed desperately that her arrival
would pass unnoticed for soon enough her name would
be on the tongue of every scandalmonger in London.

When they arrived at the gates of the huge two-story
mansion, Mac insisted he accompany Alexa to the door,
but she quickly disabused him of that notion. "No,
Mac," Alexa shook her dark head. "It's best for all
concerned that you not be seen. I have no idea how my
father will react or what he might do."

"He won't harm you, will he?" Mac asked anxiously.
According to Adam, John Ashley was the devil's own
disciple."

"I'm his only child, Mac," Alexa assured him confidently. "He won't punish me for something over which I had no control."

Mac was not at all certain about that, but had no recourse but to allow Alexa her own way. "All right, Alexa, you know your father best. But if you should need me for any reason I'll be staying at the Stag and Horn for two weeks before I leave London."

"Will . . . will you be seeing Adam any time soon?" Alexa could not help but ask. She could have bit her tongue once the words were out of her mouth and she turned her face aside before she noticed Mac's pitying look.

"I don't think so, Alexa. But if I should do you wish me to convey a message to him?"

"No," Alexa lied unconvincingly. "The sooner I forget him and get on with my life the better. I'm certain Charles and I will be married once he learns I have returned."

Her words were spoken so bravely, with such conviction, that Mac felt compelled to place a tender kiss on her forehead. "Be happy, milady."

There was great sadness in his eyes as he watched Alexa's small form leave the carriage, and Mac knew he could remain no longer. From the first moment he laid eyes on Alexa he had lost his heart to her. Had he been on the same social level with her he would have offered marriage rather than return her as Adam ordered. But he knew his dreams were impossible. He was but one son among ten offspring of poor Irish immigrants. He could offer Alexa nothing but his love. Better she should marry her Charles and take her rightful place among her peers. Had he known from the beginning how deep his feelings ran for the beautiful Alexa he would never had allowed Adam to carry out his devious plan to avenge his father's death through the innocent body of Lady

Alexa. Friend or not, Mac would have fought Adam to the death rather than allow him to defile Alexa.

Alexa felt her small frame shake violently as she grasped the large brass knocker in trembling fingers. Why should she feel such fear? she asked herself dully. This was her home and her father would no doubt be happy to find her safe and sound. Banging the knocker three times, she stood back to wait.

Within minutes the door was opened to reveal a pleasant-faced older woman dressed in a black dress covered by a voluminous white apron so spotless it dazzled the eyes. Her gray hair was drawn into a neat bun and her dark eyes viewed the bedraggled figure standing on the doorstep with compassion.

"Beggars are fed at the back door," she said not unkindly as she started to close the door.

"Maddy, wait, it's me!" Alexa cried, dismay clouding her perfect features. "I've come home!"

The housekeeper recognized her mistress the moment she heard Alexa's voice. "Oh, my lady Alexa!" she cried, throwing her apron over her head, "you've come home!"

Alexa stepped inside and shut the door behind her, then moved to take the sobbing Maddy in her arms. Maddy had been their housekeeper for as long as Alexa could remember and the closest thing she had to a mother. Maddy had bestowed love and understanding freely on the motherless child when Alexa's father was too busy to care.

"I'm home, Maddy," Alexa crooned consolingly. "Don't carry on so. I've not been harmed."

"But the note, milady! The note your father received said you were . . . were . . ."

"We'll talk about it later, Maddy," Alexa said, fully

cognizant of Adam's cruelty. His note to her father must have been explicit in revealing his intentions toward Alexa. "I need to talk to my father first. Is he home?"

John Ashley stood at the top of the stairs, thoroughly annoyed at having his work disturbed by loud voices. Still handsome and trim at forty-five, he frequently displayed a raging temper and mean streak that kept the servants terrified. To Alexa, he rarely showed this side of his nature, but with his cohorts he earned the reputation of being a man easily aroused to vindictive acts when crossed. He was invaluable to King George for he could be counted upon to deal swiftly and ruthlessly with enemies of his country and his king. No compassion existed in his stalwart body.

With the possible exception of his daughter, John Ashley exhibited strong feelings for nothing or no one. At least that had been so for the past eighteen years. And had Alexa not been such a loving and dutiful daughter, his disposition would have been entirely different. After he had killed his wife's lover he watched carefully throughout the years for some manifestation of his wife's unfaithful nature in her small daughter. But thankfully the child had grown up in her father's shadow exhibiting no sign that she would develop into the wanton her mother had become. Until now, that is.

"Oh, Sir John!" Maddy cried joyfully. "Lady Alexa has returned!"

Sir John stared incredulously at the slim figure ill-clad in a dirty white shirt and trousers, her long dark tresses covered by a wrinkled kerchief. "Alexa, is it truly you? What are you doing here?"

Alexa had been in the process of throwing herself into her father's arms when his words stopped her cold. Her violet eyes gew wide with confusion as she watched him slowly descend the stairs until he stood before her.

Alexa gasped as he skimmed her slim figure with barely concealed contempt.

"Father, what's wrong? Aren't you glad to see me?"

"I would think you'd have the decency not to return."

"I . . . I don't understand."

"Well, I understand only too well where you've been and what you've become. Your lover's note explained all too clearly. To think that a daughter of mine should become whore to the spawn of Martin Foxworth, the man responsible for your mother's death!"

"My mother! You said my mother died in an accident."

"So she did. One of her own making. When I killed her lover she took her own life. They wanted to go away together. Did Foxworth tell you why I killed his father?"

Stunned, Alexa nodded miserably. "He told me."

"Your mother claimed she loved him. She wanted to take you and go away with him. I threatened to kill them both before I'd allow that to happen. I did kill Foxworth, quite handily, I might add. Who knows, I might have killed your mother had she not been too cowardly to face me and taken her own life. You were abandoned by her, Alexa. Abandoned because her life held no meaning without her lover. And now you, my own daughter, have been corrupted by another Foxworth. Bah! You disgust me!"

"Father, you must know I didn't go along with Adam willingly! I was taken against my will, forced to submit in order to satisfy one man's thirst for revenge. I was nothing but an instrument through which Adam Foxworth gained his end. Surely you can't hold me responsible when I am innocent of any wrongdoing."

"All these years I've done my best to raise you into a decent young woman," Sir John contended coolly, "despite the fact that your mother was a slut. But to what end? You've proved that you're both cut from the same cloth. You allowed yourself to be corrupted by a man whose name I have reason to hate above all others. Did you swoon in his arms and cry out with ecstasy when he touched you?"

Alexa flushed. Did her father know how close he came to the truth? "It wasn't like that! What was I to do? Kill myself?"

"Aye!" Sir John shouted despite Maddy's loud gasp. During the entire exchange Maddy had stood helplessly by while her employer heaped abuse upon his daughter. "That's exactly what any decent woman would have done. She would have killed herself rather than submit. Just how did Adam Foxworth manage to carry you off from your own party beneath our noses? How did he get into the grounds?"

"You don't know, then?"

"Know what?"

"That Adam Foxworth is Lord Penwell. It was you who invited the man into your home."

A string of vile oaths assaulted Alexa's ears. "I invited that viper into my home? How was I to know that bloody Colonial was Adam Foxworth? Now that I know I'll see him hunted down and hung. The king will uphold me in this."

"It's too late, Father. Adam has already left England. He's accomplished what he set out to do. No doubt neither of us will ever see him again."

"Damn!" cursed Sir John. "You've become the scandal of London. And I'm the laughingstock. Fifteen years is not long enough for people to forget how my wife cockolded me with Martin Foxworth, or what followed afterwards. That the same thing should happen again with my daughter is too much. He could not have done me more harm had he driven a knife through my heart."

"I am not my mother," Alexa declared stubbornly. "It

is unfair of you to accuse me unjustly or make comparisons."

"Get out of my sight, Alexa, you disgust me! I'll summon you when I decide what's to be done with you."

"I'll save you the trouble, Father. I'll send for Charles and we'll be married immediately. You needn't worry over my future."

Raucous laughter met her words. "Charles! Oh my dear deluded daughter," he mocked. "Charles broke off the engagement the moment he returned from his tour at sea and learned what had happened to you."

"Who told him?"

"Why, I did. Don't you think he deserved to know that his future bride had become whore to another man? He broke the engagement immediately."

"No!" Alexa denied vehemently. "Charles loved me! He wouldn't do such a thing!"

"He would and did."

"I'll go to him. Explain. I'm certain he'll understand."

"It's too late, Alexa. Only last week Charles announced his engagement to Lady Diana Paine." His cruel words smote her like stones.

"Diana! Why she's several years older than Charles and quite . . . er . . . matronly," Alexa protested, devastated by Charles's lack of faith in her. Yet, somehow it didn't surprise her.

"Money has a way of disguising a multitude of flaws," said Sir John. "Lady Diana's dowry is larger even than yours would have been. Now, do as I say. Leave me. I've a lot of thinking to do."

Stunned by her father's rejection and Charles's desertion, Alexa had no choice but to obey. Squaring her slim shoulders she slowly ascended the stairs, followed by a thoroughly confused Maddy. Never had she expected to see her darling Alexa treated so shabbily, and by her own father!

"And take off that disreputable costume." Sir John called out as Alexa disappeared into her room.

Immediately Maddy became solicitous and began fussing about her woebegone charge. "Oh my dear Alexa, how you must have suffered at the hands of that . . . blackguard! My heart goes out to you. I don't know how your father can treat you so shabbily?"

"Nor do I, Maddy." Alexa shook her head sadly. "And . . . and it wasn't as bad as it sounds. Adam wasn't cruel, or abusive. It's not in his nature. I wasn't hurt . . . physically." But I was hurt in other ways, she thought to herself. Ways that don't show but are much more cruel than any bruises he could have left on my flesh.

Soon Alexa was soaking in a hot tub with Maddy clucking around her like a mother hen. The bewildered woman couldn't seem to do enough for her poor abused chick no matter what Alexa had told her to the contrary. She just knew Alexa wasn't telling the whole truth. After all, the young virginal girl had been cruelly abducted and made to submit to a man whose hatred extended to an innocent child still in her teens.

"Maddy, does . . . does everyone know about me? All my friends?"

"Everyone, Alexa, I'm so sorry."

"Who told them?"

"Your fiancé, of course. The moment he heard about your disappearance and who had taken you he became livid with rage. I was nearby when your father told him and heard everything. For some unexplained reason he appeared angrier with you than with that Foxworth fellow. He even went so far as to suggest you went along willingly. He flew out of here muttering something about you giving freely to a rogue what you denied him," Maddy revealed confidentially.

Alexa was stunned. Surely Charles couldn't be so

petty! What happened to the undying love and commitment he spoke of? Evidently he was angrier than she would have guessed over her resistance to his advances. And to think she had once considered Charles the perfect mate.

"But why would Charles deliberately set out to ruin my reputation?" Alexa mused aloud. "Perhaps no one would have known what had happened to me had Charles not bandied it about so freely."

"Oh, they would have found out anyway, my lady," Maddy said scornfully. "Some lord or other, I forget his name, but he attended your party that night, well, he brazenly announced to the whole assemblage that he had seen you go off with another man in his carriage after Charles left to go back to his ship."

"Oh, no!" gasped Alexa, dismayed. Adam had certainly been thorough.

"When he returned, Charles acted the properly jilted bridegroom, moaning to all who would listen how you had run off with another man nearly on the eve of your wedding. It wasn't long before he was being consoled by all your friends of marriagable age."

That night Alexa took supper in her room. Her father had made it perfectly clear that her company would be neither welcomed nor tolerated. Would all her friends feel the same as her father? she wondered bleakly.

The next day she put them to the test. Dressed in her most becoming outfit, Alexa arose early and left the house shortly after her father's departure for the palace and his daily interview with the king. Before noon she had called on two of her closest friends and had been refused admittance after she left her calling card.

The afternoon went much the same. Two more of her acquaintances sent messages that they would not be home to her. She was even snubbed in the street by Betsy Cummins who had been her bosom friend during the years they attended Miss Marchand's Finishing School for Young Ladies. Not one of her so-called friends allowed her the opportunity or the courtesy to explain about Adam Foxworth.

No matter that she was the innocent victim of a man bent on vengeance. In the eyes of her friends and family she was held responsible, even blamed, for being forced to submit to a man who wished to destroy her father. And from all appearances he had succeeded only too well. Mother and daughter, each in their own way had both become the victims of a Foxworth.

But John Ashley could think of no one but himself. The framework of his entire life had been torn apart when his daughter became the mistress of Adam Foxworth. Everywhere he went he imagined his friends' laughter, pointing a finger at a man twice a fool.

Alexa was home a week before Sir John required her presence in his study. During that week she had neither seen nor spoken with him. Her meals were sent to her room and, since all her friends snubbed her, she had kept mostly to her room, pondering the sad predicament in which she found herself. She had been cruelly taken and then summarily abandoned by a cold, calculating man who left her carrying his seed without a thought to her future. What would happen to her when she told her father she was pregnant? she wondered fearfully. Would he, too, abandon her, casting her adrift to fend for herself and her child as best she could?

In the days since Adam had abandoned her Alexa refrained from thinking about him. When she did, the pain became unbearable. She expressly forbade herself to analyze her feelings for the vengeful Lord Penwell, for strange as it may seem she could not hate him as she should. She could only remember those days and nights in his arms when she was fulfilled beyond her wildest yearnings. But neither could she give him her unqualified love. For the pain and embarrassment he brought to her was beyond bearing. He had shown her tenderness, gentleness, all the while reminding her that she was in his bed for one purpose only. What hurt the most was that Adam had left without so much as a good-bye, his heart totally intact though her own lay in tatters.

Alexa entered her father's study and waited silently for him to acknowledge her. When he finally looked up he thought he had never seen her so beautiful. Though she wore a simple gown of buttercup yellow her face glowed with an inner, almost mysterious quality that took his breath away. He had finally come to the realization that Alexa might have repeated the sin of her mother but she was still flesh of his flesh, blood of his blood, and he owed her a future. Charles was no longer her fiancé but Sir John hadn't been idle in the week since Alexa had returned home in shame.

Clearing his throat, Sir John motioned Alexa to a chair. "No matter what you might think, Alexa, I am not entirely heartless," he informed her grandly. "This past week I've gained my senses and calmed down long enough to consider your future. I owe you that much. You carry a proud name and I won't abandon you."

"Oh, Father!" cried Alexa, her heart leaping with joy, only to plummet when she heard his next words.

"I've found a husband for you. It wasn't easy what with all of London aware that you were sharing the bed of an upstart earl no one had ever heard of. But Sir Henry is so anxious for an heir he is willing to overlook your indiscretion. His wife and grown children were all taken by the plague and if he doesn't produce an heir his line will die out. It's a good match, Alexa. When he dies you'll be rich beyond your wildest dreams," he added when he saw dismay cloud Alexa's features.

"But . . . Sir Henry is an old man! Old enough to be my grandfather! I remember him well. He always looked at me as if he could gobble me up."

Sir John chuckled crudely. "I doubt Sir Henry has the stamina to devour you, much less bed you. You are right in naming him aged, though. Under the . . . er . . . circumstances I find much favor with the match. And should Sir Henry prove us both wrong and you give him an heir, all the better."

Alexa's face grew still and white, utterly devoid of all color as her mind worked furiously. Would it not be to her advantage to marry an old man like Sir Henry? she asked herself, thinking of the child she carried. How easy it would be to foist Adam's child off on Sir Henry who desired a child so desperately he would not question one born far too early. But to do so would require she bed the man, lie beneath him uncringing while his aging and sagging flesh touched hers intimately. After Adam's thrilling caresses how could she endure it? Perhaps, for the sake of her child, she answered silently.

"Alexa, do you hear me? I asked you a question."

Alexa shifted her attention back to her father who had been speaking to her. "What did you say, Father? I didn't hear you."

"I asked if your lover left you with child. It's not an impossibility, you know. You shared that bastard's bed for three months." Sir John's question stunned Alexa. Never had her father spoken so bluntly to her.

"Well, are you? Don't lie. I could have Maddy summon a midwife to examine you if you'd prefer."

"That won't be necessary, Father, I have no intention of lying to you," Alexa declared, aware that her disclosure would put an end to any marriage plans her father had for her once and for all. It was almost a relief to speak the truth.

"Aye, I am with child," she admitted with forced

equanimity. "I learned of it before I had the opportunity to tell Adam."

"Excellent!" exclaimed Sir John, shocking Alexa into silence. "Sir Henry will be thrilled to produce an heir so soon after his marriage. It is up to you to do what is necessary in order for him to believe the child is his. You must have learned something those three months in Foxworth's bed and should have little difficulty in doing your part."

"Father," Alexa whispered raggedly, "I can't marry Sir Henry, no matter what you say. He . . . he's repulsive to me."

"What of your child, Alexa? Surely you don't expect me to welcome a Foxworth bastard into my home, let alone support it! Why do you insist on heaping dishonor upon my head when I am doing my best to restore your good name? I insist you see Sir Henry and give him a chance."

Sir John's reasoning defeated Alexa. Perhaps his way was best after all. "All right, Father," she agreed wearily. "I'll see Sir Henry but I won't promise anything."

"He's coming tonight, be ready to receive him," Sir John said, dismissing her with a curt nod. "In years to come you'll thank me for thinking of your future when I should be reviling you."

After supper one of the servants summoned Alexa to the drawing room where Sir Henry waited with her father. Short, squat, with wispy gray hair combed sideways to cover a bald spot, Sir Henry appeared every bit his age. Heavily wrinkled, he gazed through myopic blue eyes at Alexa when she entered the room. As Alexa had dryly remarked to her father earlier, he looked as if he could devour her.

Alexa greeted her father's crony warily, but Sir Henry

grasped her hand and planted a wet kiss on it before she realized his intent and could snatch it away. It nearly sickened her.

"I'll leave you and Sir Henry alone to become acquainted, Alexa," her father informed her as he hastily left the room, careful to close the door behind him. "I'll see that you're not disturbed." It's a good thing that Alexa missed the conspiratorial look that passed between her father and Sir Henry or she would have left immediately.

"Come, my dear," Sir Henry grinned salaciously, "and sit beside me. If we are to be married we should get to know one another. I don't believe in long engagements and your father led me to believe you would be receptive to any suggestion I might make."

"I promised my father nothing," Alexa insisted, already regretting her decision to see Sir Henry alone. "I . . . I'm not at all sure I wish to marry you."

Sir Henry smiled condescendingly. "Your choices are necessarily limited, my dear. I am willing to take damaged goods. What other respectable man would make such a statement? I know I am an old man desperately in need of an heir. My own choices are not the greatest, for under normal circumstances I would be forced to consider older widows beyond childbearing years.

"That's why I am prepared to overlook your . . . er . . . transgressions. I am not too old to father a child, or bed a young woman, if that be your worry. So shall we seal our bargain with a kiss?"

Alexa was completely unprepared when Sir Henry reached out with talon-like claws to grasp her in a strangling hug. "No!" she cried, alarmed and shocked by the strength in his aged body.

"Don't be shy." Sir Henry chortled crudely. "I'm not asking for more than you've already given away. I just want to show you I'm still capable of passion."

Fleshy dry lips converged on hers and Alexa felt nausea rise in her throat when his hard tongue stabbed repeatedly into her mouth. Then suddenly his hands were everywhere, on her buttocks, breasts, under her skirts, prodding and probing relentlessly into her private places.

"Sir Henry, stop!" Alexa cried out, struggling with all her strength against certain violation. Where a man of his advanced years found such vigor remained a mystery to her. "I'll tell my father!"

Sir Henry chuckled. "Do you think he cares? He'll be relieved to have you off his hands. Now be a good girl and lie back, it won't take me long."

Sickened by Sir Henry's slobbering kisses, weakened by his hurtful hands, Alexa despaired of escaping the old man's lecherous attentions. She felt cool air touch her bare thighs and with renewed strength born of desperation exerted one mighty shove against Sir Henry's barrel-like chest that sent him flying. Alexa took instant advantage of Sir Henry's confusion at finding himself flat on his back. Running out of the room and up the stairs she reached the safety of her room, immediately latching the door against unwanted intruders.

Seeking the relief only tears could bring, Alexa collapsed on the bed sobbing. She remained there for a long time, cursing Sir Henry, cursing her father, but mostly cursing Adam for casting her into such a predicament in the first place. And with her tears came the first real stirrings of hate for Adam Foxworth. Before the tears dried on her face, sleep claimed her.

Maddy's frantic knocking was the first sound Alexa heard since she had fled in panic to her room the night before. Disoriented and sluggish, Alexa was surprised to find sunlight streaming through her window and that she was fully dressed lying on top of her bed. The knocking continued. "Lady Alexa, please let me in," the housekeeper begged. "I have a tray for you."

"Go away, Maddy, I'm not hungry."

"You have to eat, my lady. Please let me in."

Unwilling to cause the tenderhearted Maddy undue distress, Alexa opened the door. "Is my father home?" she asked.

"No, my lady," replied Maddy, carefully placing the tray on a table. When she turned to face her young mistress she was distressed to see the beautiful face ravaged by tears, and Maddy immediately went to the girl, hugging her to her ample bosom. "What is it, Alexa? You can tell Maddy about it."

"Oh, Maddy, what has happened to my life?" Alexa wailed miserably. "One minute I was the pampered daughter of Sir John Ashley, fiancee of Charles Whitlaw, and the next I am a pariah, disowned by my father and reviled by all my friends. Even Charles has forsaken me. And now my father intends to give me to Sir Henry."

"That old lecher!" snorted Maddy, scandalized. "Why, he's old enough to be your grandfather. You've done nothing to deserve such treatment. You're but an innocent babe thrust into a situation that began when you were but three years old."

"You know the whole sordid story, don't you, Maddy? About my mother, I mean."

"Aye," Maddy admitted grimly. "You must remember I've been here for many years."

"Tell me what you know, Maddy. Please," begged Alexa. "I've heard Adam's version, and my father's. Both biased. I want to know the truth."

"The truth is, my lady, that your mother and Martin Foxworth, an attractive young widower, met and fell desperately in love. At first they fought against the attraction but soon their love became an obsession that demanded consummation. It wasn't long before they began meeting secretly in different places, and it did my heart good to see your mother glow with happiness after so many years.''

"Didn't my mother love my father?"

"It was an arranged marriage, advantageous but not necessarily happy."

"What happened then?"

"Your father found out, of course, and challenged Martin to a duel. Martin was an honorable man, soft-spoken, more of a poet than a fighter. He abhorred violence of any kind. The outcome was inevitable.''

"Father said my mother killed herself," Alexa said hesitantly.

Maddy nodded sadly. "She confided to me that she carried Martin's child and feared that Sir John would kill her once he found out. Or make her life so miserable she would wish for death. But I never suspected she would take her own life.

"She came back from the duel and called me to her room. She told me about Martin's death and placed you in my care. Your mother never was a particularly brave woman and life without Martin held no appeal. Before your father returned from the duelling field she slit her wrists and bled to death.''

"Father was right," Alexa whispered forlornly, "mother cared nothing for me."

"Oh, no, Alexa, never think that," Maddy countered. "Your mother loved you dearly. You were the only thing good in her life besides Martin. And she knew your father would never harm his own flesh and blood. But knowing she carried another man's child she chose to take her own life rather than risk death at the hands of Sir John. You see, she truly believed her husband would kill her.''

"Would he, Maddy? Is father capable of such cruelty?"

"She believed he was and your mother knew him better than anyone."

Alexa brooded silently, assimilating every word Maddy said. When she spoke it was with a desperation that hardened her beautiful features into stubborn resolve. Maddy recognized the expression immediately and prepared herself for the worst.

"I have to leave here, Maddy, and you must help me. I . . . I'm expecting Adam Foxworth's child. And since I will never agree to marry Sir Henry, it's imperative I leave. Father as much as told me he would not accept my child in his house. And after what you've just told me I can no longer remain here."

Maddy's blackberry eyes grew round as saucers. "A baby you say? On, my poor Alexa. What has that monster done to you?" Then she began crying and carrying on so that Alexa was forced to shake her to gain her attention.

"Maddy, please don't fall apart on me. It's not the end of the world. And I need you."

"I'll do what I can, my lady." Maddy sniffed despairingly. "But what will you do? How can you survive on your own with a child to care for?"

"I have my jewels and some money I've saved. That should suffice until I can find work. But we must hurry, Maddy. Once Father learns from Sir Henry how I reacted to that old lecher he will surely punish me or force me into that despicable marriage."

"What can I do, Alexa?"

"Help me pack, quickly. Only the necessities, nothing fancy. Include all my jewelry, my warmest cloak and sturdiest shoes. And please hurry, Maddy."

Together they managed to stuff a large portion of Alexa's vast wardrobe into two large carpetbags. While Alexa took care of last-minute details, Maddy disap-

peared for a few minutes. When she returned she
pressed a heavy purse into Alexa's hand. When Alexa
demurred, Maddy insisted.

"It's of no use to me, Alexa. I have a good home here,
no relatives to support. You're the closest I've ever had
to a daughter. Please take it."

In the end Alexa took the money, promising to pay it
back one day. Then she sent the housekeeper out to hire
a public conveyance. Before Sir John returned home late
that afternoon expecting to force Alexa into marriage
with Sir Henry after hearing all about Alexa's deplorable
behavior the night before from the old man, Alexa was
gone, taking with her all her valuables and Adam
Foxworth's child.

6

Alexa had no doubt as to her destination. A new life beckoned to her. A life far from England and the people she once considered her friends, and the father upon whom she once doted. Alexa realized that the waterfront was no place for an unaccompanied lady, but she had no choice. She prayed that it wasn't too late, that Mac was still at the Stag and Horn, that he hadn't finished his business early and sailed away.

Alexa bade the coachman wait while she made her inquiries at the inn. To her chagrin she learned that Mac had indeed concluded his business and checked out that very morning. Her face crumbled with dismay and she looked so woebegone that the innkeeper was emboldened to add, "He mentioned he would not sail until this evening's tide so perhaps you can find him aboard his ship, milady."

"Oh, thank you, thank you," cried Alexa with such obvious relief that the inn keeper had the distinct feeling his disclosure spelled the difference between life and death for the beautiful young lady.

It was but a short ride to the docks and Alexa was filled with anxiety while she waited for the coachman to return. Once they reached the harbor she had pressed a coin on the man and sent him to find out if the *Lady A* was one of the ships anchored in the Thames and where she was berthed.

Just as Alexa was certain she could no longer stand the suspense, the coachman returned from his visit to a nearby tavern where he learned the *Lady A* did indeed ride at anchor in the harbor. She was slated to sail with the evening's tide. Not only had the obliging coachman ferreted out the information but he brought a crewman back with him.

After questioning the man Alexa learned that the sailor, Andy Beggs, had been engaged in rounding up any straggling crew members who still lingered ashore. His duty completed, he was about to row himself the short distance across the water where the *Lady A* was moored.

After wasting precious time convincing the skeptical Beggs that it was imperative she be taken aboard the ship to speak with her captain, the doubting sailor reluctantly agreed to row her to the *Lady A*. The coachman loaded her bags into the longboat and with Beggs manning the oars they were soon bumping the hull of Mac's ship. In answer to Begg's bellow a dozen hands appeared to lower chains to the boat and winch her aboard. A short time later Alexa stood before an astounded Mac.

"My God, Lady Alexa, what are you doing here?"

Alexa found herself enclosed in two strong arms and she felt as if she had come home. "Oh, Mac," she pleaded, her courage suddenly deserting her. What if he sent her away? "I need your help. I'm so miserable and afraid."

Alexa's impassioned plea stabbed directly into Mac's

tender heart. "Alexa, you know I'll help you. Calm yourself. Sit down and tell me what's troubling you."

While Alexa struggled for composure Mac went to the desk and poured a generous splash of brandy into a glass, handing it to Alexa. She took a sip, coughed, then drank again, this time more deeply. "I want to go with you, Mac," she blurted out.

"I don't know when or even if I'll return to England again, Alexa," he said hesitantly. He wasn't sure what she was asking.

"I don't care if I never see England again," she was quick to respond. "I intend to make a new life for myself. You can put me ashore anywhere, France, America, even one of the islands." She sounded desperate and Mac wondered what had happened to cause her such anguish.

"What happened to Charles? Wasn't your father happy to see you? My God, Alexa, what took place during the past week?"

The pain visible in Alexa's huge violet eyes was nearly more than Mac could bear. "Charles no longer wanted me. Adam ruined me for marriage and his peculiar method of revenge made a scandal of the Ashley name, just exactly like he planned."

"What of your father? Surely he loved you enough to . . ."

Alexa's harsh laugh cut off his words in the middle of a sentence. "I learned a cruel lesson. I never really knew my father. He could no longer stand the sight of me. In his eyes I had been corrupted by a Foxworth and no longer deserved his love and protection. He . . . he was forcing me into marriage to a man old enough to be my grandfather. When Sir Henry tried to force me in my own home I decided to leave."

"That bastard!" gritted out Mac. "Where was your father when all this took place?"

"Sir Henry obviously had my father's blessing. My father decided that under the circumstances I could do no better than Sir Henry. So I left. Please don't turn me away, Mac. I've no one else to turn to, no place to go."

"I'll always be here for you, milady," Mac assured her. "If you're serious about leaving England I'll take you with me. I'm going to Virginia and . . . and I'll take care of you if you'll let me." It wasn't exactly a marriage proposal but Mac felt it was too soon to declare his feelings. Perhaps by the time the voyage ended . . .

All that Alexa heard was that Mac would take her away and she would have a chance at a new life. The rest was quickly forgotten in a rush of gratitude so profound that Alexa immediately threw herself into Mac's arms, completely unaware of his tender feelings for her. "Thank you, Mac, you're the best friend anyone could have. And I'll try not to be a burden to you."

"You could never be that, milady," Mac assured her, his blue eyes twinkling merrily. "I'll show you to your cabin. Did you bring any luggage?"

Alexa nodded, her eyes swimming with tears of gratitude. She started to protest when he showed her to the captain's cabin, but he would hear none of it. "I insist, Alexa. I'll bunk in with the first mate." He grinned jauntily. "I'll see that your bags are brought to you so you can get settled." He would gladly give all he possessed to share the cabin with her.

At high tide the *Lady* A slipped her moorings and quietly sailed from London Harbor, her journey down the Thames uneventful. In the darkness she easily slid past several warships in the English Channel unchallenged and finally into the endless Atlantic. Once they were well out of sight of English shores the Union Jack was hauled down from the mast amid much cheering and clapping by the crew members whose hatred for English oppression was well-known.

Alexa felt nothing but immense relief when the last sliver of English soil slipped beneath the horizon. No matter what the future held it was better than what she left behind.

Though the weather was cold and brisk, often laced with driving snow or sleet, Alexa spent a good part of each day on deck. Often, fearing for her health, Mac was forced to send her to her cabin. But despite of, or perhaps because of, the harsh weather, Alexa's health prospered. Each day Mac became more and more enchanted by her sparkling eyes, rosy cheeks and glowing complexion.

They chose not to speak of Adam. Alexa knew that once she spoke his name painful memories would rise up and haunt her. In her estimation it was best not to dredge up feelings better left untouched, or to analyze those same feelings too closely, for surely hate existed somewhere in the compartments of her heart. But what of those times he made love to her with such tenderness that she lay swooning and unresisting in his arms? It was all part of his grand plan for revenge, she told herself bitterly.

How could a man make love to a woman with such feeling and yet care nothing for her? Obviously Alexa had never known a man like Adam, for that's exactly what he had accomplished. And yet . . . yet . . . a small kernel of indefinable feeling lurked in her heart. An emotion ready to burst into bloom given the slightest provocation. Some might call it love. Alexa put no name to it.

Mac was just as determined to keep thoughts of Adam from invading Alexa's mind and body. In his heart he knew she had fallen in love with Adam and truly believed those feelings would never be returned by his friend. Adam had plans that didn't include the daughter ot John Ashley. Mac's own course was much less complicated. He would care for Alexa until she came to realize the extent of his love. When that happened they would marry and live happily ever after. But then, Mac had always been a dreamer.

One fine day Alexa stood at the rail of the Lady A, staring westward. As it happened so often of late, her mind dwelled on the babe growing inside her. Already she had to let out her dresses and wondered if she could complete the voyage without Mac finding out.

Inexplicably her thoughts turned to Fox, a man Alexa knew would never treat her cruelly despite the fact that he was a pirate and a rogue. Their all too brief encounter had initiated her to a thrilling new experience that Adam had finely honed in their months together. Would she ever see Fox again? she agonized. Probably not, she decided. If only her baby belonged to Fox . . . Unikely . . . but . . .

Almost as an afterthought, Alexa's hand fell to her stomach where she lightly outlined the slight bulge she was careful to keep hidden beneath her cloak and numerous petticoats. And then, in a motion so common to pregnant women she pressed her other hand to the small of her back, forcing her stomach and pelvis forward. In the several seconds she held that position her pregnancy was all too apparent.

Merry eyes akindle, Mac watched from the quarter-deck as Alexa leaned into the wind, staring westward. Her beautiful face reflected her inner turmoil and Mac wished there was something he could do to ease her fears. Then suddenly her movement caught his attention and his breath caught painfully in his throat. Alexa's unusual stance emphasized the unnatural bulge of her stomach, with one slim hand outlining the slight swelling while the other eased her back, as if to take the pressure off her burgeoning middle.

Mac knew a moment of intense hatred for Adam Foxworth. Pregnant! The bastard had left Alexa pregnant without a thought for her future! Hadn't he realized such a thing could happen? Mac thought with impotent fury. It was obvious Adam's vengeful mind failed to take into consideration the consequences to an innocent young girl. Never had Mac felt the urge to kill so strongly.

Mac spent the rest of the day coming to terms with the certain knowledge that the woman he loved was expecting another man's child. Holed up in his cabin with a bottle of brandy, he pondered long and hard and finally came to a painful decision. Armed with the knowledge that what he was about to do was right for Alexa, Mac spoke briefly to his navigator, then went to bed, his mind much eased. From the beginning he knew his dream had been an impossible one.

Alexa hardly noticed the slight change in course. What she did note was that the closer they came to their destination the warmer it became. As the nights passed into days, and days into weeks, Alexa's pregnancy advanced apace. The day finally came when she could no longer hide it from Mac. He came upon her one day when she was forced by the hot sun to remove her concealing cloak, and she caught him staring at her stomach. She did not flinch but faced him squarely.

"It's true, Mac," she admitted before he could ask. "I am expecting Adam's child."

"I know, Alexa," Mac acknowledged softly. "I've known for some time."

"You must hate me."

How could she think such a thing? "Not you, milady, never you," came Mac's impassioned reply. "Only Adam for taking advantage of you and then abandoning you without a thought for what might occur."

"He didn't know."

105

"Don't make excuses for that blackguard. He should have anticipated that possibility and made provisions."

"I was going to tell him but he left without so much as a good-bye. Besides," Alexa said bitterly, "it would have made little difference to Adam. Knowledge that he had sired a child upon me would only serve to sweeten his revenge."

"Perhaps you do him an injustice," suggested Mac.

"We both know I meant nothing more to Adam than a means of getting to my father. This baby is mine and mine alone. I'll raise it to the best of my ability."

Mac marveled at Alexa's courage in the face of such adversity and he was determined that she would not suffer because she was unfortunate enough to be born the daughter of Sir John Ashley. Nor would her child. But for the time being Mac thought it best to keep his plans to himself for he knew Alexa would never agree to them.

"Alexa, you must know I'd never abandon you," Mac said tenderly. "I will do whatever is necessary to help you." And hope you don't hate me for it later, he silently added.

Somehow Alexa was comforted by the knowledge that Mac shared her secret. Whatever Mac was, pirate or no, he was her friend and could be depended upon for help.

They were nearly within sight of land when the *Lady* A crossed the path of an English merchantman. The first sign Alexa had of any trouble was the loud cheer arising from the men on deck who had been itching for a chance to engage the enemy in battle. She watched from the safety of the passage as Mac readied his ship for battle. It was obvious to Alexa that Mac had learned much during his years of tutelage under the Fox aboard his *Gray Ghost*.

The crew immediately sprang into action, loading and

priming the twenty-four eighteen-pounders on the upper deck and eight nine-pounders on the quarterdeck. A brace of pistols and cutlass were strapped about each man's waist in anticipation of hand-to-hand combat.

Before allowing the British ship the advantage, Mac turned the Lady A leeward and ordered a warning shot fired across the bow. "Strike the colors!" he yelled to his crew. Immediately the Stars and Stripes were hoisted up the flagpole, caught the breeze and waved proudly above the Lady A. The British ship returned a warning shot of her own.

"Look lively, men, we're coming about!" shouted Mac as he brought the sails into the wind, coming up almost on the prow of the enemy ship. "Fire your guns on the swivel deck!" came the crisp order.

The volley that followed rendered the merchantman nearly helpless. Mac ordered the sails lowered as he came up against the hull of the English ship which was unable to fire her guns, for by that time the Lady A was far too near. Much to the chagrin of the American sailors the fight was finished before it really began.

In quick order a boarding party led by Mac leaped nimbly across the short distance separating the two ships and swiftly subdued the last pocket of resistance. After impressed American seamen were ferreted out, the remaining English crewmen were set adrift in their longboats to be picked up by another of their ships in the vicinity while Mac made an inspection of the merchantman's cargo. He was well pleased with the variety of goods he found aboard which would bring a good price in the West Indies.

A skeleton crew was put aboard the merchantman to sail her to Barbados and dispose of her cargo. Because the ship was old and slow, Mac thought it best to sell her also. It was a good day's work and each crew member would be richer for their efforts, Mac mused happily as he watched the merchantman sail away manned by his most trusted men.

Nearly six weeks to the day that the *Lady* A left London, the first green crescent of land came into view. But to Alexa's surprise the ship did not make for port but maintained a course parallel to the coast. When questioned, Mac explained his tactics.

"Just before I arrived at Penwell Castle to take you back to London, I saw Captain John Paul Jones of the Continental navy, who with a small squadron based on French soil carries on a series of raids against British coastal shipping. Fox and I are part of his operation—harassing British ships close to their own shores. Just this year France allied herself with the colonies so that the British not only had to contend with the colonies but with the French fleet.

"Captain Jones had recently received a dispatch outlining plans of a British expeditionary corps to march into Savannah in late fall. It's already December and I have no idea what I'll find if we sail directly into Savannah Harbor."

Alexa slowly digested all this, then suddenly something clicked in her brain. "Savannah! That's not in Virginia!"

Mac smiled slyly. "It's in Georgia, milady."

"But . . . I don't understand," said Alexa warily. "I thought we were going to Virginia."

"A slight change in plans, Alexa. One that will work well in your favor. Trust me, I would do nothing that would harm you," he assured her most emphatically.

Alexa shrugged. What did it matter where she went? One place would serve her purposes as well as another. She would pose as a young widow expecting a child and hope to find work eventually.

The *Lady* A appeared to hover just out of sight of land until nightfall. Only then did she cautiously nose toward shore. Under cover of darkness the ship unerringly made her way into a small cove with an opening barely discernible to the eye. Alexa held her breath as the ship gracefully traversed the coral reef and finally bumped against a dock in the deep but small body of water that Mac told her had been dredged out to accommodate a sailing vessel the size of the *Lady* A. It was on private property and not many people knew of its existence.

"On whose land is it?" Alexa asked curiously.

"It belongs to a friend of mine," Mac murmured noncommittally. "Are your bags packed, Alexa? We will be going ashore soon."

"Aren't we going to Savannah?"

Mac gave her a oblique look. "No, I'll leave you off here. You'll be safe enough."

"But . . . are you staying here too?" A shiver of foreboding shook Alexa's small frame and she pulled her cloak tighter about her slender shoulders. Some innate sense warned her that everything was not as it should be. Surely Mac wouldn't lie to her, would he?

"Alexa, I have to see to the docking right now. But the moment we are ashore, I promise to tell you everything."

Not entirely satisfied but unable to persuade Mac otherwise, Alexa returned to her cabin to finish her packing. By now she had let out every one of her dresses and her pregnancy could no longer be concealed beneath her skirts nor covered by her cloak. Well into her fifth month, her waistline had virtually disappeared. Somehow, during the weeks of the voyage the baby growing beneath her heart had become very precious to her. A tiny entity with a character all its own, living, breathing, taking nourishment from her own body. Against her will Alexa began to love the tiny being, to wonder what he or she would look like. Which invariably led her to thoughts of Adam. From there everything became muddled as images of Fox warred within her brain for prominence. Most times her child looked like Adam. But at other times she pictured her baby's face as being completely featureless, for she had no idea what Fox looked like.

A short while later Alexa's baggage was set ashore on the dock and then Mac came for her. Glancing at her warily he grasped her hand and guided her down the gangplank. Once on land he hesitated for a moment then led her along a well-defined path that crunched beneath her feet.

"Seashells," Mac smiled, sensing her question.

"Where are we going, Mac? It's so dark I can barely see the path."

"Just hang on and follow me, milady. I know this path well. You'll see the house as we come out of the woods."

Suddenly Alexa balked, her mouth set in stubborn lines. "I will go no farther, Mac, until you tell me where we are going. I think I've been patient long enough. What is all the mystery about?"

Mac sighed regretfully. What he was about to tell Alexa was sure to shock and anger her. "Alexa, I hope you won't hate me for what I've done but it's what I judged best for you and your child. One day you'll thank me."

Not only did Mac's words confound Alexa, but she felt as if a hand had closed around her throat. Frantically she searched for a meaning behind his words. "What . . . what are you talking about? Why should I be angry with you?"

While they talked Mac urged her along the path, and unconsciously she followed. Suddenly they came out of the woods and onto the well-kept grounds surrounding an imposing two-story house whose every room blazed with the light from thousands of candles. Dozens of coaches lined the curving driveway and it was apparent a party was in progress.

"Jesus!" breathed Mac irreverently. "I hope it's not too late."

"Too late for what?" Exasperation furrowed Alexa's fine brow. "Whose house is this?"

"Alexa, these lands belong to Adam and this is his house." Mac held his breath, waiting for the inevitable outburst. He was not disappointed.

"What? You've brought me to Adam? Damn you, Mac, I trusted you! What do you expect to gain from this? Or will you enjoy watching my humiliation when Adam turns me out?"

"Alexa, give me credit for something. I think I know Adam better than you do. He won't turn you out. I . . . I believe he'll do the right thing if it's not too late."

"To late for what?" she repeated. "You're talking in riddles again."

"Alexa, I'm asking you to trust my judgment. I'd never leave you stranded should Adam prove me wrong. What have you got to lose?"

"My pride!" bristled Alexa angrily. "Adam Foxworth has taken everything else and I'll be damned if I'll give him that, too!"

"You're coming with me even if I have to carry you the rest of the way!" Mac insisted, determination hardening his features. "Which will it be, Alexa? Will you go under your own power or must I prove my strength to you?"

Tossing her head to show her defiance, Alexa reluctantly moved forward. Mac smiled indulgently as he followed. He loved her most when her eyes spit violet flames and her cheeks burned with anger. A spirit such as hers could never be quelled. Beneath his breath he prayed he was doing the right thing, that it wasn't too late, for he was privy to Adam's plans for his future. But most of all he prayed that he wasn't thrusting Alexa into a situation more volatile than the one in which she now existed.

7

Savannah 1778

By all accounts this should be one of the happiest
moments in Adam Foxworth's life. To be sure the stately
blond on his arm was the most beautiful woman in the
room. The perfection of her face and figure was certainly not lost on Adam. Nor was the fact that she was
passionate in bed, for he had tested her charms often
enough in the past weeks.

The lady was Gwendolyn Wright, niece of the royal
governor who even now waited to announce the
engagement of Lady Gwen to Adam Foxworth, Earl of
Penwell and staunch Tory. It was an advantageous
match which would bring Adam a large dowry in addi-
tion to entrance to all the prominent Tory homes in
Savannah.

Until Adam had inherited a title he was just another
Colonial, but since returning from England he had been
besieged by royalists to join their inner ranks. He was
acquainted with Lady Gwen before he left for England

but it was not until he returned that he was in a position to offer marriage. All his scheming had worked out beautifully, Adam congratulated himself as he smiled blandly at his beaming fiancée.

But if the truth be known, Adam was far from pleased with himself. Inexplicably his thoughts flew back over the water to a raven-haired, violet-eyed girl whom he had callously used and discarded. The experience left a slightly bitter taste in his mouth. The knowledge that he was capable of employing such dirty tactics to gain his own ends had wrought subtle changes in Adam. For one, there was a certain ruthlessness in him now that was more refined. For another, he completely disregarded the feelings of others.

And at the root of it all was a woman. There had been many women in his life and he could not remember what most looked like, including the woman beside him who faded from his memory the moment they parted. But at any given time he could conjure up Alexa's beauty in perfect detail. She haunted his dreams until he grew to hate the vivid memory of her soft, warm body entwined intimately with his.

Their final night together Adam had attempted to demonstrate by his actions that she had no place in his life, and looking at her face when he took her callously, without apparent regard for her feelings, he was certain he had succeeded. No doubt by now Alexa was married to her Charles and could be carrying his seed. Somehow the thought was not comforting. Not once did the thought enter Adam's mind that Alexa could have conceived as a result of their own numerous couplings.

He was distracted from his bleak ruminations when the slim blond at his side nudged him with her elbow. "Adam, darling," Gwen pouted prettily, "where are your thoughts? Two of Uncle James's friends just spoke to you and you completely ignored them."

"I've been thinking of us, my sweet," Adam lied smoothly. "Soon it will be time for Sir James to announce our engagement."

"It can't be too soon for me," riposted Gwen, her clear blue eyes promising delights yet to come. "I want to be with you every night, not just on those occasions when we can slip away for a few hours."

"So do I, my sweet," Adam allowed cryptically, "More than you'll ever know."

Lady Gwendolyn Wright, the beautiful, pampered niece of Governor James Wright, had accompanied her uncle to the colonies to act as his official hostess since the governor's wife had died leaving no children. She became the immediate toast of Savannah, wined and dined by prominent Whigs and Tories alike. But her bright blue gaze fell upon Adam Foxworth and there it remained, though it wasn't until Adam had suddenly inherited a title and lands in England that Gwen's uncle had pronounced Adam a suitable husband for his beloved Gwen.

Adam's inheritance had changed his position in life overnight. Until Adam hinted he could offer much more after his return from England, Gwen had seriously considered accepting the proposal of Captain Lance Barrington who sprang from illustrious parentage. Although pushing twenty-six, Gwen waited and had not been sorry. Upon Adam's return they became lovers; shortly afterwards he proposed, and Gwen promptly accepted. Of course, Lance had been livid with rage at Gwen's reversal, but with Adam an earl there was nothing he could do about it.

Aware that many of his guests were looking at him expectantly, Adam decided that the moment had arrived to signal Governor Wright to make his announcement. His hand already extended to alert the governor, Adam's motion was halted before it could be completed by Jem, his butler, who approached his master with a puzzled look on his broad, black face.

"You have guests, Mastah Adam," Jem announced hesitantly.

"Show them in, Jem," Adam whispered, annoyed by Jem's sudden lack of protocol.

"They insist on seeing you alone," informed Jem. "I showed them to the study. I hope that's all right, Mastah Adam."

Adam nodded curtly, spoke a few words to a thoroughly disgruntled Gwen and followed Jem from the crowded ballroom. "Who are my mysterious visitors, Jem? Do you know them?"

"It's Mastah Mac, suh, and a lady I never saw before."

"Mac is here?" enthused Adam, hastening his steps. "Why didn't you say so? And you say he has a lady with him? That devil!" Adam grinned roguishly.

"Mac!" greeted Adam exuberantly as he burst into the study. "You sly dog! What are you doing here? I thought you were for Virginia."

If Mac's greeting was less than enthusiastic Adam seemed not to notice. Thus far he had not seen Alexa who had removed her cloak in the warm room and stood slightly behind Adam clutching the back of a chair.

No man has a right to be so outrageously handsome, Alexa thought distractedly. His thick tawny hair barely brushed his collar and was unpowdered. His nose was classic, straight as a blade, and arrogant, while the harsh lines of his broad cheekbones and wide brows could have been sculpted by a master. Elegantly clad for the occasion, his garments were neither gaudy nor elaborate, yet molded and enhanced his muscular form perfectly. Her heart jolted and her pulse pounded. Suddenly Alexa was anxious to leave his disturbing presence.

"You and your lady are just in time to join the party." Adam smiled.

"I'd hardly feel comfortable with all your Tory friends," answered Mac jerkily. "We travel in different worlds now, Adam."

Adam fixed Mac with a baleful glare, then shrugged. "Where is the lady Jem told me about? Introduce us," he said, whirling to search the room for Mac's elusive lady. Finally he spotted her and his steady gaze bore into her with silent astonishment. Slowly his eyes dropped from her face to her breasts, and finally to her protruding stomach. Tearing his gaze from Alexa's obviously pregnant form, Adam turned and glared defiantly at Mac.

"What in the hell is she doing here, Mac?" he gritted out angrily. "Why didn't you leave her where she belongs? I should have known from the beginning that your interest in the lady was more than passing."

"You bastard!" retaliated Mac. "Can't you see Alexa is pregnant? She's carrying your child, Adam. Doesn't that mean anything to you?"

Adam had the decency to flush guiltily. "You know my plans, Mac."

"Change them, damn it! You owe Alexa. Her father turned her out, she has no place to go."

"So she came crying to your for sympathy! You always were a fool over a pretty face and tears. What in the hell do you expect me to do?"

"The right thing, Adam," Mac insisted quietly.

Suddenly Alexa gained her wits and stepped forward, red dots of rage exploding behind her eyes. "Both of you, stop it! How dare you talk in front of me as if I didn't exist! I never intended to come here, Adam. Mac took it upon himself to bring me here against my will. I had no say in the matter. Besides, I knew I was expecting your child before you left Penwell Castle but I chose not to tell you. You owe me nothing because that's exactly what I want from you."

Though Alexa's unexpected arrival threatened to rip apart his months of planning and scheming, Adam could not help but admire her courage and spirit. His eyes settled once again on her stomach, and an unexpected surge of joy threw him into sudden panic. What was he thinking of? he asked himself crossly. It was impossible for him to marry Alexa and he must make Mac understand. Too much depended on his marriage to Gwen.

"Contrary to what you may think, I am not completely heartless, Alexa," Adam said tightly. "I'll see that you and the baby are taken care of. Neither of you will want for a thing. But . . . tonight is my engagement party. As soon as the announcement is made my betrothal to Lady Gwendolyn Wright will become official."

"Then we're not too late!" sighed Mac thankfully. "I was afraid . . ."

"Mac," Adam admonished sternly, "have you forgotten so soon the reasons behind my marriage to Gwen?"

"I've not forgotten, Adam. It's just that I believe this is more important. Your child deserves a name."

"Then marry Alexa yourself!" shouted Adam, his eyes widening when he realized what he suggested.

Mac's eyes narrowed dangerously. He thought he knew Adam but he had been mistaken. Moving to Alexa's side he gathered up her cloak and settled it about her slumped shoulders.

"Damn you, Adam, that's exactly what I'll do. It's what I wanted all along but I thought I owed you the opportunity to claim your own child. I'll have no guilt now over making Alexa mine. Go back to your Tory friends."

Adam made a strangling sound low in his throat but before he could form them into words the door to the study burst open. "Adam, what is so important to keep you from your guests?" demanded a petulant voice. "Uncle James grows impatient to make the announcement of our engagement."

Alexa stared at the lovely blond woman, thinking she had never seen anyone so beautiful. Soft blond hair the color of ripe wheat was done up artfully atop the regal head resting on a long, slender neck. Everything about her was golden, from her hair to smooth alabaster skin that glowed with pale gold undertones. Her lips were full and rounded over even white teeth, her nose exquisitely dainty. Her totally feminine figure swayed gently in a cocoon of gold tissue silk and gauze and she carried herself confidently. In Alexa's eyes her own dark beauty paled in comparison to this golden flower—Adam's bride-to-be.

For a long, tense moment Adam said nothing as he regarded Lady Gwen through slitted lids, his gray eyes murky as he balance on the horns of dilemma. "For God's sake, Adam, say something!" demanded Gwen icily. "Who are these people?"

Suddenly Adam came to life. "Excuse my rudeness, Gwen," he apologized, smiling blandly. "Surely you remember Mac? You met him in my home once before I left for England. The lady," he gestured carelessly, "is Lady Alexa Ashley. Both have just arrived from abroad."

Gwen nodded curtly at the pair who managed to disrupt the most important night of her life. "Can't your friends wait until tomorrow to speak with you? I'm sure they must both be exhausted. Besides, Uncle James is waiting."

Flinging an inscrutable look in Alexa's direction, Adam drew in a deep steadying breath before replying, well aware of Gwen's temper when things failed to go her way. "Gwen, I'm afraid there can be no announcement, not tonight, or ever. I have just learned something that changes everything."

Red blotches of anger mottled Gwen's lovely features and her lips twisted into a snarl of outrage, turning her face almost ugly. "No announcement! Do you mean there will be no engagement? What have these people to do with our marriage plans?"

Mac shot Alexa a triumphant grin, as if to say, "I knew I hadn't misjudged Adam!" Alexa could only gasp, too astounded to protest. At that point she was determined that she would marry neither Mac nor Adam. Both men were arrogant rogues but she'd show them. She would raise her baby by herself and to hell with both of them!

"Circumstances beyond my control force me to honor a prior commitment to Lady Alexa, whom I met during my stay in England," Adam said, startling Alexa.

"Honor be damned!" shouted Gwen angrily, fixing Alexa with a contemptuous blue stare. "What did you do, Adam, bed the little slut and get her with child?" Seeing Alexa's flushed face, Gwen knew she had guessed correctly.

"It matters little what happened between Alexa and me," Adam replied calmly. "I will do what I must. I intend to marry her as soon as possible."

"You little bitch!" grated out Gwen in a fit of rage. "It's all your fault. Why couldn't you stay in England where you belong? I'm sure Adam would support you and your brat without need for marriage."

"That's enough, Gwen!" countered Adam curtly. "I'm marrying Alexa through my own choice. You ought to know by now I can be coerced into nothing. Will you tell your uncle or shall I?"

Gwen stiffened, momentarily abashed. Never had she been treated so shabbily. It was a humiliated, deflated feeling. Her pride had been seriously bruised by Adam, but she was far from through with him. Not by a long shot! Whirling in a mist of gold tissue, she stomped angrily from the study. When she reached the ballroom, she immediately sought out her uncle, spoke a few sharp words into his ear, leaving him stunned, and together they left the crowded room amidst a buzz of speculation.

Sensing something was amiss, Captain Lance Barrington, ever one to seize an opportunity, followed. He still was angry at Adam for taking the woman he wanted, a woman he needed in order to further his career, and if something had unexpectedly parted the couple he wanted to be on hand to console Lady Gwen. After all, he had been her second choice and still had hopes of walking off with the prize. Unaware of the drama taking place behind closed doors, the orchestra played on and the party continued.

By the time the door slammed shut behind Gwen, Alexa was trembling with pent-up emotion. To be thrust into such an embarrassing situation was a horrifying experience, and at that moment she felt nothing but hatred toward both Mac and Adam for creating it. Suddenly, everything that happened tonight, combined with total exhaustion, began closing in on her. But it was the following exchange between Mac and Adam that finally pushed her over the brink.

"You finally got your way, Mac," Adam commented dryly. "I hope you're satisfied." His sarcasm was not lost on Alexa.

"Adam," Mac replied grimly. "I did not create this situation. It is one of your own making. I only did what I thought was best for Alexa and your child. But if you had insisted upon being bullheaded, I would gladly have married her myself."

"You can go straight to hell!" Alexa flung out. "If either of you had asked, which neither of you did, I would have refused you both. From now on I'm on my own. I don't need you, Mac, and I wouldn't have you, Adam!"

Astonished, Mac and Adam appeared rooted to the spot as Alexa made for the door, fully intending to leave and see neither man again. But she had sorely misjudged her own flagging strength. With one hand poised on the doorknob, Alexa's knees suddenly buckled and she began an inexorable slide to the floor before the astounded eyes of both men.

Willing his superb muscles into motion, Adam reached her first, scooping her limp form into his arms only inches from the floor. Dumbfounded, he looked at Mac, his expression suggesting he had no idea what to do next.

"What did you expect?" Mac shrugged helplessly. "The girl is five months gone with child and at the end of her endurance. No thanks to you."

"I'd best get her to bed." Adam said, frightened by the waxy paleness of Alexa's face. "Look out in the hall, Mac, and see if there is anyone about before I carry her upstairs."

Moving with alacrity, Mac peered out the door, then motioned Adam forward. Between them they managed to reach Adam's room without being noticed. When Alexa lay stretched out on the bed both men stared down at the still form, each to his own thoughts. Her bulging middle suddenly reminded Mac of why he had brought her here in the begining.

"You do mean what you said, don't you, Adam? About marrying Alexa, I mean. I care about her. Very much. I only want what is best for her and her child . . . your child," he quickly amended. "But I won't leave her if she'll be mistreated."

"For God's sake, Mac, what do you take me for! I didn't mistreat Alexa before and I certainly won't now that she's carrying my child."

"I'm not speaking of physical abuse, Adam, for I doubt you capable of that," Mac said softly. "But I've known you a long time and I trust you to do what's right." Suddenly he looked about the room knowingly. "This is your room, isn't it, Adam?"

Adam shrugged. "The guest rooms are all being utilized. The ball, you know." Mac nodded but said nothing.

His expression gone soft with tenderness, Mac gazed down at Alexa, as if trying to memorize her features. Stooping, he placed a gentle kiss on her smooth forehead, at the same time brushing a tendril of hair away from the curve of her cheek. "Be happy, milady," he whispered hoarsely. Before Adam could see the suspicious moisture gathering in his eyes, Mac headed for the door. "I'll have Alexa's bags brought up to the house. Make her happy, Adam." Then he was gone.

Perplexed, Adam did not move for several minutes. He was torn between making Alexa comfortable himself or sending for one of the maids. Deciding he'd best not delay, Adam worked at the fastenings on Alexa's gown. Soon she lay clad in her thin chemise and Adam let it remain, thinking it made an adequate nightgown. He was about to tuck her inside the covers when his eyes fell unbidden to her rounded stomach and thickened waist.

Like a kick to the belly, Adam came to the jolting realization that it was his child swelling her slender frame. Hesitantly he placed a trembling hand on the mound sheltering his child, smiling to himself as he felt an answering thump against his palm. Until that moment all that had happened tonight seemed unreal. But the moment he felt his child move the dream became a reality. With a tenderness he hadn't known he possessed, Adam pulled the covers over Alexa and gently tucked her in.

It was at that precise moment that Alexa's eyes fluttered open and she felt herself floating in a cottony void. Slowly she emerged from the suffocating mass to find Adam staring at her with an inscrutable look in his eyes. Was it concern? "Where . . . where am I?"

"In my bed," Adam replied thoughtlessly. "You fainted."

"Ridiculous!" declared Alexa, attempting to rise. "I've never fainted in my life."

Adam pushed her back down. "You never been pregnant before. Relax, I'm not about to climb in beside you and ravish you. Besides, I have a houseful of guests downstairs to see to."

"Where is Mac?" Alexa asked, aware that she and Adam were alone.

"Gone. I'll be taking care of you from now on."

"I'm perfectly capable of taking care of myself!" Alexa countered, rising once more only to be pushed down again. "I don't need your sympathy or protection."

"Alexa, be sensible. You're carrying my child and I won't have you going off and endangering him or yourself."

Alexa eyed him suspiciously. "A pretty speech, Adam, but why this change of heart? You had no such compunction when you went off and left me. Why now? I know I spoiled your wedding plans so why are you continuing with this farce when Mac is no longer here to see that you do the right thing?"

Why indeed? Adam wondered, his thoughts badly disjointed. From out of the blue Alexa turns up pregnant and disrupts his entire life. He had expected never to see her again. But if the truth be known, not one day went by when he did not think of the innocent girl he had ruined and left to her own devices without experiencing a twinge of regret. What is more amazing is that he overlooked completely the possibility that Alexa might become pregnant from their time together. And if the thought did lurk in the back of his mind it had been with the knowledge that it would only serve to sweeten his revenge.

But now, seeing her helpless and swollen with his child, he felt a great tenderness well up inside of him. A tenderness not just for a tiny part of his flesh growing inside her, but for the woman who nurtured his child. Seeing her again he realized he could not let her go; would not set her adrift without protection. Alexa would become his wife.

"Alexa," Adam began patiently, "believe it or not I want to marry you. I want our child. I'll see that you're taken care of. Neither you nor my child will want for anything."

"I had always thought I'd love the man I married," whispered Alexa brokenly. "And he would love me. Is that being so silly?" Alexa was well aware of the fact that Adam had not said one word about loving her. Nor did she expect it. She was an Ashley and in his eyes would never be anything other than the daughter of an enemy.

"Love is well and good, but how many couples do you know who marry for love? Do you think I loved Gwen?"

"Didn't you?"

"Hardly," laughed Adam harshly. "It would have been an advantageous match. Gwen has much to offer."

"And I do not. Forget it, Adam, go back to Gwen."

"You carry my child, Alexa. As difficult as it may sound, given our inauspicious beginning, we can still become friends. For the sake of our child. If you're willing to forgive me, I'm willing to forget you're the daughter of a man I've sworn to hate."

Alexa swallowed convulsively. Could she and Adam become friends? Somehow she doubted it. Lovers, perhaps, but never friends. Yet, if he was willing to try, could she do differently? At least for the sake of their child, she added hopefully.

Adam watched the play of emotion upon Alexa's expressive face, thinking how beautiful she looked lying in an ebony pool of her hair. Mac was right, he, Adam, had used Alexa foully and she deserved better than being relegated to the role of unwed mother.

"I don't know, Adam," Alexa finally said.

"Is there someone else in your life? Charles, perhaps? Or Mac?"

"Charles is a weakling. Not only did he turn to another woman the moment he learned what happened to me, but he created further scandal by talking too freely about it. As for Mac, he is my friend, nothing more."

"Then it's settled," Adam said in a firm voice that brooked no argument. "We'll be married within the week. Now I'll leave and let you rest while I attend to my guests. Many of them will be staying over. Goodnight, Alexa."

"Adam, what will your friends think? Weren't they expecting an engagement between you and Lady Gwen?"

"It doesn't matter what they think. When I go downstairs and inform them I am going to marry the daughter of Sir John Ashley there won't be a man down there who won't envy my luck in snaring the daughter of such a lustrous man." Try as he might Adam could not keep the mockery from his voice.

"Tell them? Now?"

"Aye," he nodded solemnly. "Goodnight, milady." Then he was gone, leaving Alexa trembling in his bed.

True to his word Adam marched boldly into the still

crowded ballroom, rapped for attention and announced his engagement to Alexa before one and all. A stunned silence met his words and each person present suddenly became aware that Gwen Wright, the lady who had commanded Adam's constant attention these past weeks, was suspiciously absent. And so was her uncle, the governor. No one knew what had happened, but the Ashley name was every bit as prestigious as that of Wright.

Almost timidly, some brave soul called out, "Where *is* the lady, Foxworth? Why are you hiding her?"

"Lady Alexa arrived just a short time ago. Her journey was long and arduous and she begged to be excused tonight." Loud groans met his announcement. "But to make up for the lack I cordially invite each and every one to witness our marriage vows one week from today."

Had Alexa heard his words she would have swooned for the second time in her life. For what woman five months gone with child would wish to have every prominent family in Savannah show up at her wedding?"

His face purposely blank, Adam stared down at the sleeping form of his wife-to-be. He had spent an uncomfortable night on a narrow cot in his dressing room, the only bed available to him last night, and arose at dawn to see his guests off and make some hurried arrangements. Now, nearly noon, the house was empty except for servants and Adam took it upon himself to arouse Alexa from her deep sleep.

How exhausted she must have been, Adam thought as he watched the steady rise and fall of her chest beneath the covers. How easy it would be to love her. But it was impossible. John Ashley stood like an insurmountable barrier between them.

If the truth be known, Adam had not originally planned to keep Alexa with him for three months. After he had taken her from her home his intentions were to keep her a week or two in his bed and then send her back in disgrace to the man who had killed his father and the woman who had brought it all about. Of course he had not known then that Alexa's mother no longer lived. It might have changed things but somehow Adam doubted it. At that point he had lived too long with the memory of his father's untimely death for it to matter.

Adam hated to admit it even to himself but the thought that Alexa might become pregnant did enter his mind but only in a vague sort of way. When he was faced with the actuality of Alexa growing large with his child, something snapped in his brain and he offered marriage, knowing full well it would never work. Yet, oddly enough, he wanted the child despite the fact that Ashley blood flowed in its veins.

Alexa was another matter altogether. How exactly did he fell about her? He enjoyed making love to her, that much he knew. More than any other woman he had ever bedded, despite her inexperience. He knew she hated him. What kind of future could they hope for?

Suddenly Alexa stirred, effectively halting Adam's disjointed musings. "It's nearly noon, Alexa," Adam said as violet eyes regarded him warily.

"You should have awakened me earlier." Alexa yawned.

"No need. Besides, you were exhausted. But the dressmaker will arrive soon and you need to get up now."

Alexa sat up abruptly. "Dressmaker! But I have clothes."

"Nothing appropriate for a wedding. I know for I've

already gone through your bags. Besides, every one of your dresses has been let out more than once. I don't want my bride embarrassed before my friends."

"Or for them to be embarrassed by your obviously pregnant bride!" shot back Alexa, flushing. Adam shrugged eloquently and left her to her ablutions.

8

Alexa hated to admit it but Adam had been right. The bright-eyed, twittering Madam Dubois, the dressmaker summoned from Savannah, was a marvel with needle and thread. She had taken one jaundiced look at Alexa's burgeoning figure and set out immediately to work a miracle. Or so it seemed to Alexa as she spun slowly before the pier glass in the stiff brocade gown so heavily embroidered with crystal beads that it nearly stood alone.

While the very low neckline emphasized Alexa's high, prominent breasts, the empire waistline fell from just below those enticing mounds in stiff, embroidered folds to the floor. And miracle of miracles, the telltale bulge in her middle was invisible. Taking into account her delicate coloring, Madam Dubois had fashioned the gown of soft pink to compliment the cloud of ebony hair and enhance her magnolia-blossom skin. All in all, Alexa was very pleased with the result of the dressmaker's handiwork.

Though Adam had yet to see the wedding gown, he

had commissioned Madam Dubois to fashion an entire wardrobe to accommodate Alexa's growing bulk. She was grateful to him but not deluded as to his reasoning. As the wife of an earl she had a certain position to uphold in the community. On that score Adam need have no worry for she was a lady born and bred.

Alexa had seen little of Adam this past week, what with fittings and all. In fact, he was rarely at home. One thing Alexa did learn in her time at Foxworth Manor was that for some unexplained reason Adam had firmly established himself with the royalists. At first Alexa found that difficult to believe in view of his friendship with Mac and Fox, both notorious patriots. But Alexa could not deny the obvious. All Adam's friends were Tories. And they in turn thought highly of him. In a sudden burst of insight Alexa felt certain she had more sympathy than Adam for the Colonists and their quest for freedom. How could she not after listening to Mac expound endlessly on the cause for which he fought?

In those all too swift moments before her marriage vows were to be spoken, Alexa allowed herself to dwell briefly on Fox, and wondered if he was still raising havoc with the British navy. Or was he even now resting at the bottom of the sea? Somehow she pictured him alive and well, his muscular legs balanced on the bridge of *The Gray Ghost*, a smile lurking at the corners of his lips visible beneath his mask. Fox, the man who had taken her virginity—Fox, who could well be the father of her child.

Suddenly, amidst the scattered thoughts of a man other than her intended hsuband, it was time. Hattie, the little black maid assigned to her, arrived to tell her everything was in readiness and that the groom was awaiting her appearance. Though Alexa had sworn many times during the past week she would not be

bullied into this marriage, she moved out of her room—
Adam's room, for she had not moved to another—and
began the slow descent down the curved staircase.

Instead of dwelling on her unlikely marriage, Alexa
surveyed her surroundings, still amazed at the beauty of
Adam's home despite her thorough exploration during
the last week. A two-story dwelling, it was set back half a
mile from the main road and reached by a long driveway
of crushed shells. On all sides of the mansion were
green areas interrupted by flower beds kept neat by
slaves. The house itself was simple with two double
chimneys rising above a slanting roof. Inside, a wide,
carpeted reception hall led the way into the house,
adorned with huge chandeliers and the grand staircase
which Alexa was now descending.

The drawing room where she was to be married was
huge, serving also as a ballroom. The mahogany floor
was covered with a large, round rug. Besides the
drawing room the first floor also contained a dining
room, library, and study that was solely Adam's domain.
An archway led to a covered arcade and the kitchens
beyond. Upstairs were six bedroom suites all lavishly
appointed. Alexa had certainly not been idle this past
week as she became acquainted with her new home.
She decided it was a fine place to raise a child.

Almost before she was ready, Alexa found herself at
Adam's side in the drawing room decorated with holly
and bayberry and crowded with strangers whose faces
reflected their appreciation of the beautiful bride. From
the corner of her eye Alexa saw Lady Gwen, her face
grim and unsmiling. Beside her sat a handsome, dark-
haired man wearing the uniform of an English officer.

Had Alexa looked at Adam she would have seen a
glimmer of admiration in his gunmetal eyes. Though she
had missed it, Gwen did not. Her automatic responses
to the marriage vows were given in a flat and unemo-

tional voice, barely registering upon her befuddled brain. Only when Adam's lips lightly brushed hers did she realize the ceremony was over.

The rest of the day was a blur as Alexa met and promptly forgot the names of most of Adam's prominent guests. The reception immediately following the ceremony must have been impressive, the food sumptuous, but Alexa did not remember. She felt relief that Adam had insisted upon an afternoon affair for had a dance been held Alexa knew she could not have danced a step in the heavy gown that disguised her pregnancy so well.

By evening Alexa teetered on the brink of collapse and she excused herself to retire to her room leaving Adam to bid good-bye to the last of their guests. With Hattie's help she removed her ornate gown and donned a beautiful sheer nightgown that had mysteriously been placed on her bed. Within minutes she was sound asleep.

Alexa had thought little about her wedding night. She had wrongly assumed that her protruding stomach repelled Adam and she had months before he would consider bedding her. Alexa viewed it as a kind of reprieve. She had no desire to bed Adam. At this point her emotions were too fragile to be bombarded by his masculinity. She hadn't had enough time in which to explore her feelings for the new husband who had previously been her tormentor. She hoped during the months she carried her baby to term she would get to know Adam and try to understand the intricate workings of his mind.

It was very late when Adam entered the bedroom he intended to share with Alexa. Though he was disappointed to find her asleep, he undressed swiftly and climbed in bed beside her. She was warm and smelled of violets, Adam noted, a scent he often associated with her long after he had left her. Alexa stirred as Adam tentatively explored the soft curve of a hip before moving on to full, soft breasts that seemed to fit his hands even better than he remembered. Parting the neckline of the pale mauve nightgown he had purchased for their wedding night, Adam's lips tenderly encircled a ripe, rosy nipple. He was rewarded by a deep, soft sigh.

Adam knew the exact moment Alexa was awake for he felt her violet eyes upon him despite the dark room lit only by moonlight. "Adam, what . . . what are you doing here?"

"I want you, Alexa." His words came to her on a gusty sigh and instinctively she knew he was asking—not demanding.

"Why?" Alexa was bewildered. "I'm certainly unlovely to look at right now. And I know you don't love me."

"Surely you remember how it was between us?" Alexa nodded, for she remembered far better than he how he had carried her to heights never before imagined. "Then how could you doubt that I would still want you? I went into this marriage fully expecting to share your bed. It's one of the unexpected compensations for marrying the daughter of John Ashley. Besides, strange as it may seem, I do not find you unlovely."

Alexa stirred uncomfortably, his words serving only to confirm her belief that Adam wanted his child enough to lie to her. "Adam," she hedged, immediately sensing his keen disappointment, "I'm tired."

"I won't hurt you, Alexa, if that is what you're worried about."

"Can't you understand that I don't want you, Adam?" she retorted, attempting to convey her feelings. "I married you to give our child a name. If it wasn't for you I wouldn't be in this embarrassing situation."

Suddenly the old Adam returned, one Alexa knew well from her stay with him in England, and she experienced a brief moment of stark fear. Bathed in moonlight, a scowl cut crevices in his stony face and his eyes matched the murky darkness of the room. A low chuckle filled the silence and Alexa felt the hackles rise at the back of her neck as he ripped apart her fragile nightgown, baring her body to his rough caresses.

"I tried to be gentle, Alexa. And I thought we might learn to enjoy what little we have together. I have no intention of harming you or the baby but I won't be denied my wedding night. Now relax and enjoy what I can do for you. Lord knows what we share is little enough on which to base a marriage, but it's better than nothing."

Thoroughly incensed by his arrogant words, Alexa decided Adam could go to the devil, and told him so. "The devil has already claimed me, my love," Adam mocked sardonically. The endearment sent a strange chord singing through her blood.

"Don't mock me, Adam," Alexa declared hotly, "by calling me your love when we both know why this marriage took place."

"Do you know, Alexa?" Adam asked softly, his voice suddenly gone hoarse. "Do either of us really know?"

A sigh of consternation fluttered past Alexa's lips as she sought an appropriate retort, but the words never left her mouth as the moon silhouetted a half view of his face, painting a silvery wash over his chiseled cheekbone and down to his determined jaw, and her heart gave a painful lurch in her breast.

Suddenly Alexa realized his naked skin was warm against the cool night air, and she felt herself drawn to him. Exultantly, Adam reveled in her moment of capitulation. The deep kiss he pressed to her parted lips was a demand and she responded without willing it, without wanting to as some hard kernel of denial dissolved within her.

His hand paused briefly on the bulge of her stomach, then moved between her thighs, and Alexa felt her flesh throb at his touch. Her fingers scored the tawny hair at the nape of his neck as her own hot nature triumphed treacherously and she surrendered to his need.

Sliding his lips to her breast, Alexa felt her heart catapult to her throat, then tumble down to pound against her ribs as his tongue teased its taut peak. Desire burned like liquid silver in Adam's eyes as he devoted special attention first to one engorged nipple and then the other, her body reacting violently to his masterful manipulation.

He tightened his hands about her waist to hold her close as he began to nuzzle the dark triangle of curls that beckoned to him with the promise of delights he could not resist. He felt the exquisite pleasure he gave her shudder through her body and he could wait no longer to share her joy. His body so taut and inflamed, he swiftly entered her. With each movement her body began to pulsate with sweet tormenting pleasure until she was engulfed in a maddening spell, gasping, moaning, calling out his name mindlessly. Then he freed her in a blaze of bursting stars and exploding lights, following close behind.

Afterwards, both were silent, thoroughly shaken by the flame that seemed to lick to life each time they came together. It left Adam shaken and confused, but Alexa, her perception keener in matters of the heart, knew exactly where to place the blame for her amazing and ardent response to Adam's lovemaking. Love! Against her will love had entered like a thief in the night and stolen her heart! Love possessed her, but its pain condemned her. Before she fell asleep she vowed never to allow Adam the satisfaction of knowing the depth of her feeling for him. His mockery could not be endured should he discover she loved him, she reflected bleakly as sleep finally claimed her.

His wedding night was all Adam had hoped. Alexa moaned softly as he awoke her with light, feathery kisses, and gently, considerate of her condition, he took her again, sweeping her with him on a magnificent upward journey to the very peaks of passion.

When Alexa awoke the following morning Adam was gone. Not only from her bed but from the house. To her chagrin she learned that he had placed his sprawling plantation into her care only when the overseer, Tom Forbes, called on her later that afternoon. Silently she cursed Adam for not warning her he planned on leaving so soon after their wedding. To Alexa it was the final insult, serving to reinforce her belief that Adam cared nothing for her. Thankfully, Forbes proved an able overseer, perfectly capable of running the plantation during Adam's frequent absences. Alexa liked him immediately and was delighted to hear that he had a wife and two children living with him in the overseer's cottage, promising herself to call on the Forbes woman soon. The reason for Forbes's visit was unclear but Alexa surmised his curiosity concerning Adam's hasty marriage played a big part in it. Whatever the reason she was glad that he came and looked forward to meeting his wife.

Alexa hoped her advanced state of pregnancy did not shock Forbes but he had the good grace to pretend not to notice as he concluded his interview and left. She did not fare so well with her next visitor to Foxworth

Plantation.

Two weeks had passed since Adam left so hastily and Alexa glanced up from her book to see a carriage make its way up the long driveway. Her first thought was that Adam had returned and she thoughtlessly rushed outside without first donning a cloak just as three women stepped down from the conveyance. Alexa stopped dead in her tracks, her face a pale oval as she faced Lady Gwen and her two companions.

"Lady Foxworth, we've come calling," Gwen called gaily.

Assuming a pleasant countenance, Alexa forced a semblance of cordiality into her voice. "Welcome, ladies. Come inside where we can chat over refreshments."

"Lady Foxworth," Gwen simpered, "these are my friends, Ellen Corby and Frances Lyme. Both are married to army officers quartered in town."

Alexa nodded pleasantly, then turned to lead the way into the house. "Please call me Alexa." As luck would have it, a sudden breeze caught at her full skirts, molding them against her protruding stomach. A collective gasp rent the air as Gwen and her friends stared fixedly at the unmistakable bulge beneath her dress. To make matters worse, Gwen laughed crudely while the other two ladies tittered behind gloved hands. Flushing with embarrassment, Alexa turned and entered the house, wishing her guests would disappear.

But luck was against her. Gwen waited until they were all seated before she began her malicious goading, egged on by her goggle-eyed companions. "At last we know the reason behind Adam's indecent haste to wed you. From the look of you he must have bedded you the moment he arrived on English soil. How did you meet?"

Connie Mason

"Lady Gwen, I'm certain our meeting and courtship hold little interest for you and your friends," Alexa hedged evasively.

"Oh, but you're wrong. I'm sure we'd find it vastly amusing, wouldn't we ladies?" snickered Gwen. Two carefully coiffed heads nodded in agreement. "After all," continued Gwen snidely, "if you hadn't arrived when you did Adam and I would be practically married by now."

"Why don't you ask Adam if you are so anxious to learn about us?" Alexa countered, refusing to be baited by the insulting trio.

"Rest assured I intend to," Gwen returned haughtily. "Where is the happy groom?"

Just then one of the maids entered the room with a tea tray and Alexa was saved from answering while she served refreshments. But Gwen was not about to let her escape so easily. "Well, where is Adam? No one has seen him since the wedding. Have you chained him to your bed?"

Alexa sighed, carefully setting her fragile cup back on the tray. "Adam has been called away on pressing business."

"I'll bet," snorted Gwen derisively, exchanging knowing looks with her two friends. "It's obvious the poor man was trapped into this marriage and now regrets the haste with which he complied with your wishes. Under the circumstances I'd leave, too, the sooner the better."

"Good afternoon, ladies." Four heads swiveled to where Adam lounged lazily in the doorway. Though giving the impression of total relaxation, Alexa knew him to be as tightly coiled as a sleek tiger ready to strike.

Gwen's two companions nodded nervously but Gwen

140

had the temerity to ask, "How long have you been here, Adam?"

"Long enough," he answered, cryptically as he uncoiled his lean length and moved on cat feet to Alexa's side, making a great show of greeting her by pressing a tender kiss on her startled lips. "How nice of you ladies to call," he continued smoothly. "It gets lonely out here for Alexa."

"Yes, well . . . er . . . just because you chose to wed Alexa doesn't mean we can't be friends," Gwen stammered helplessly. "Especially since we all know now why you married her, the poor child."

"Just why did I marry her, Gwen?" Adam asked in a soft voice that should have warned her.

"Come now, Adam, we're not blind. Any fool can see Alexa is pregnant. Five or six months, from the looks of her, you devil. What more can I say?"

"You can say that you came here to offer friendship, not criticism. From what I heard you and your friends were quick to condemn. What chance does Alexa have against your malicious gossip?"

"Adam, darling, we meant no insult. It's just that we were . . . shocked when Alexa showed up from out of nowhere to claim you. But of course we don't blame Alexa. Far from it, you rogue. How could she resist you? Even I was not immune."

Adam was not deceived by Gwen's sugary words but he smiled in order to ease the tension as the ladies finished their tea. Perversely, Adam chose to remain and the talk did not veer toward the snide innuendos that marked the first part of the visit. Indeed, Adam bestowed such lavish attention on Alexa that Gwen turned green with envy. As soon as was decently possible she ended the visit and, flanked by her twittery friends, departed in a flurry of rustling skirts.

The moment they cleared the door Adam searched Alexa's face reflectively. "Are you all right?" he finally asked. Miserably, she nodded. "It had to happen sometime, you know. It might be easy to lie about a month or two but a baby that is five months early cannot be so easily explained. Especially one as strong and vigorous as ours shall be."

Alexa smiled at that. "It doesn't matter, Adam. Of course, it hurts, but I'll get used to it." She was lying and Adam knew it.

In the two weeks since Adam had last seen her she seemed to have blossomed, literally. As sometimes happens to a woman between her fifth and sixth month, she appeared to have grown overnight. All in one direction—outward. He had hoped for a repeat of their wedding night but with a twinge of regret realized that until their child was born he had to put such notions out of his mind. The well-being of his child meant more to him than satisfying his lustful urgings. There were other ways to assuage those yearnings, he thought somewhat guiltily. Savannah was blessed with many good brothels.

"Where have you been, Adam?" Alexa asked in an effort to break the growing silence.

"On a business trip," Adam was quick to reply.

"Why didn't you tell me you were leaving?"

"There was no time. I received an urgent message early that morning and left almost immediately. Didn't Forbes call on you?"

"Aye," acknowledged Alexa with a halfhearted smile. "But I thought . . . a note . . . anything . . ."

"I'm sorry," apologized Adam. "It's hard to remember I am no longer a free agent to come and go at will. I'll try to do better next time."

"Next time! You mean there will be a next time? Will you be disappearing every few weeks just like you did in England?"

"Aye, Alexa, but I can tell you no more than that."

"Does it have anything to do with the war?"

"Aye. It's a well-known fact that the American cause is now aided by the French. Comte de Rochambeau arrived in Newport, Rhode Island, in July. In case you might not know, Newport is occupied by the British.

"Only recently an unsuccessful attempt was made to drive them out with the aid of French Admiral Hector d'Estaing and a French corps. Major battles and skirmishes still abound in that area."

"What does all this have to do with you?"

"It turns out the British are turning their attention to the weaker colonies in the south where much sentiment rests with the crown," informed Adam patiently. "From what I gather from Governor Wright the operations in the north are not to cease, but a poweful diversion undertaken with a view to complete conquest of this section of the country. Success here is believed to facilitate further movement to the north. They tried it once in 1776 with an isolated attack upon Charleston, in South Carolina, but were foiled by the unexpected fierce resistance of General William Moultrie."

"Whose side are you working on, Adam?" Alexa asked quietly. "And what does all this mean to you?"

Eyes narrowed thoughtfully, Adam searched Alexa's face for several minutes before answering. "I'm on the side of the English, naturally. England is the country of my birth, I lived there the first fifteen years of my life. I am the Earl of Penwell. I may have sold my properties but I am still a loyal subject of King George."

Alexa frowned. "I don't remember you as being excessively loyal to England when you were there. From our conversations I assumed your sentiments lay with the colonists."

"Did I ever say that?"

"No—not exactly. But what about Mac? And . . . and Fox?" Alexa wanted to know. "I've never known more zealous patriots than that pair and you claim them both as friends."

"Mac and I go back a long way. We would remain friends no matter what," Adam informed her. "As for Fox, I hardly know the man. I paid him well to do a job for me. And neither of them have ever discussed their loyalties or their plans with me."

"Somehow I find it hard to believe you'd forsake your adopted country because of a title. Have you no sympathy for these people fighting against political oppression and unfair taxes?"

"Do you? Where does your loyalty lie, Alexa?" Adam asked. "You sound like a proper patriot yourself."

Alexa flushed, confused. Was it possible for an arrival so new to the colonies to feel empathy for these struggling people? If so, then she surely was on the side of justice. With the sense of conviction that was part of her stalwart character, Alexa replied, "Perhaps I listened to Mac too long, but I sympathize with the colonists who have no rights of their own. I know what fear and oppression feel like. To me, freedom means everything."

"I take that to mean you are on the side of the rebels."

"Let's just say I'm not unsympathetic to their plight. It's you who are being evasive, Adam. Just what is it you do for the English?" Alexa insisted doggedly.

"If you must know, I offered my services as a courier to Governor Wright. He found he needed someone like me too much to hold a grudge against me for jilting his niece. I know these parts extremely well and am good at slipping around enemy lines."

Alexa stared at him, aghast. With a start she realized she never really knew Adam. Not only was he a confirmed royalist but a spy! Even Fox's pirating ways seemed far preferable to Adam's covert activities against his own adopted country. Clamping her mouth tightly shut she wisely kept her views to herself.

9

Adam remained home for two weeks, and in all that time he did not seek Alexa's bed. She assumed he was occupying one of the guest rooms and could hardly blame him. She was growing larger every day and looked hideous. Even the clever dresses designed by Madam Dubois failed to conceal her bloated body. Not many men cared to make love to an elephant, Alexa thought wryly.

Had Alexa been privy to Adam's thoughts she would have been startled to learn that despite her rounded girth he fancied her more beautiful now than when he first met her. There was a special glow about her that made her lovelier than ever, at least in his eyes. He longed to make love to her, needed her desperately, but effectively harnessed his desire by throwing himself into his work at the plantation and concentrating on keeping his secret life hidden from Alexa. Much of the time Adam spent in Savannah with his Tory friends, keeping up on the latest developments in the war.

Then, on December 19, Adam came riding home from

Savannah with the news that Colonel Archibald Campbell, with an expeditionary force of 3500 men from Clinton's army in New York, had captured Savannah, defeating the American force under General Robert Howe. Alexa's soft heart went out to the Americans as tears came unbidden to her eyes. It was a grievous setback but she felt certain the valiant colonists would not let it defeat them. Especially since they appeared to be made of the same cloth as Mac and Fox.

The following week Alexa learned about General Benjamin Lincoln, succeeding Howe, had undertaken to drive the British out of Georgia, but General Augustine Prevost, who had commanded in Florida, had moved up and compelled Lincoln to retire to Charleston. Prevost, making his headquarters in Savannah, now controlled Georgia. Adam informed Alexa that he had immediately offered his services to General Prevost, which were accepted with alacrity.

"The governor is hosting a ball in General Prevost's honor next week, Alexa, and we've been invited," Adam informed her grandly.

"Adam!" gasped Alexa, annoyed. "I can't be seen in public now! Whatever are you thinking?"

"It's imperative that I attend that ball, Alexa." Adam frowned.

"Then you'll have to go alone!" Alexa declared hotly. "I won't be made the laughing stock of Savannah for you or anyone else."

"No one will dare laugh at you, Alexa. I've already commissioned Madam Dubois to create a dazzling gown for you. You are Lady Foxworth and need fear no one. Besides, I want you with me," he confessed, stunned when he realized he spoke the truth.

In the end Alexa was persuaded to attend the General's gala. And when she dressed in the gown

Madam Dubois delivered to her the day of the ball she felt much better about her decision. The woman certainly knew her business.

The color, a true, vivid red, made her flawless skin appear as translucent as a fragile china plate. The dramatic contrast with her ebony hair drew immediate attention from her middle to her face. Fashioned with a empire waist hanging in full folds from just under her breasts, the gown cleverly disguised her pregnancy. Though not hiding it altogether, the gown nevertheless succeeded in minimizing the actual degree of her pregnancy. To further defy the imagination, Madam Dubois had designed a kind of transparent cloak made of the thinest silk to be worn over the dazzling concoction. The results were truly stunning and Alexa appeared to be floating on air as she walked with the cloak swirling about her ankles.

"You'll be the most beautiful woman at the ball and I'll be the most envied man," Adam said, admiration turning his eyes smoky.

Alexa flushed becomingly and turned slowly for his inspection. "You're sure I look all right, Adam?" she asked anxiously. "You're not just saying it to make me feel better, are you?"

In answer he drew her into his arms and kissed her as he'd wanted to do for weeks but was afraid to lest he hope control of his senses. Beneath his mouth her lips warmed and parted. Desire riding him mercilessly, his tongue surged between her lips, arrogant and demanding in its possession of her velvet recesses. Reluctantly leaving her clinging lips, his mouth traveled the curve of her cheek, then brushed against the velvet skin of her ear. He drew a shaky breath as his fingers explored the satiny mounds of flesh rising above her low-cut bodice.

Alexa gave herself up to the aura of his masculinity as the heat of his body and the scent of his skin spanned the distance between them to enfold her in a cocoon of sensual delight. It had been so long since he had touched her, since their wedding night, and she vividly recalled the hardness of him pressed against that part of her that ached for him.

Abruptly he pulled away, panting heavily; his face wore a look of amazement. He could not believe he could react so violently to one woman. A pregnant one at that! Was it because he could not have her now? he wondered wryly. Whatever the reason he had to remove himself before he ended up taking what he wanted and risked harming his child.

"My God, Alexa, I can't understand what it is you do to me!" Adam agonized as he placed her out of temptation's way. "I have but to touch you and I go crazy. Are you a witch?" Threads of confusion sent his mind reeling and his handsome face twisted in his own agony. With a willpower forged of steel he left the room to compose himself with a few stiff brandies while he waited for Alexa to finish her toilette in preparation for the ball.

Alexa was no less shaken by the encounter with Adam. Her whole body vibrated with a need for consummation. Surely six months wasn't too far into pregnancy to finish what they began, she rationalized. Then it struck her that she was most certainly correct in her original assumption that making love to a pregnant woman repulsed Adam. Unbidden, she wondered what woman was satisfying his needs, lusty creature that he was. A sudden burst of jealousy so intense that it nearly consumed her rose up to taunt her. Alexa knew a moment of hatred for the woman or women on the receiving end of Adam's special brand of love.

Adam was well into his third glass of brandy before

Alexa announced herself ready to leave for the ball. While attempting to drown his arousal, he came to the conclusion that until Alexa was able to share his bed, he would visit one of the better brothels in Savannah and engage the services of a whore—maybe two, the way he felt tonight. Perhaps he could manage to send Alexa home alone after the ball in order to indulge his lustful fantasies later. The only problem being that those fantasies usually included his own wife.

The reception for General Prevost proved to be the most elaborate affair Savannah had seen in years. Every prominent Tory, English officer and distinguished citizen for miles around attended the gala. Alexa was relieved to learn that there were far too many other things to interest the gossips for them to pay her much heed. One subject in particular seemed to be on everyone's tongue —Fox and his *Gray Ghost*. Because he had been active in the area of late, talk was rife concerning the method with which he managed to appear out of nowhere to engage English ships as they left they harbor, then disappearing into thin air—or so it seemed. The price on his head increased as his reputation grew. Alexa hung on every word during the evening until Adam began to look at her strangely.

Thankfully Adam did not leave her unattended during the long evening, until near the end when General Prevost, the governor and several prominent gentlemen congregated in the corner to discuss plans to take Charleston in the near future. While they talked Alexa waited as far out of the mainstream of dancers as possible. Nevertheless she was painstakingly located and cornered by Lady Gwen and her escort, Captain Lance Barrington.

"Your dress is lovely, Alexa." Gwen snickered

maliciously. "Concealing yet enticing, is it not, Lance, darling?"

"Very attractive, Lady Foxworth," Lance agreed, practically oozing charm. "And so is the lady inside. But then, I thought so the first time I met you."

"You mean at my wedding to Adam?" asked Alexa, a chill of foreboding prickling along her back.

"Why, no, milady, at your engagement party. Your engagement to Charles Whitlaw. You might not remember me in the crush of people that night but I remember you. It was Charles who invited me. We've known each other since our school days."

Alexa felt herself begin to black out and drew in deep breaths to keep from pitching forward and making a fool of herself. "That was a long time ago."

"At least six months ago," piped up Gwen viciously, staring fixedly at Alexa's middle.

"Am I interrupting?" At that moment Alexa was never happier to see anyone in her life as Adam appeared at her elbow.

"No . . . no," insisted Alexa with such obvious relief that Adam slanted a baleful glare at Gwen and Lance.

"Then come along, my love. General Prevost expressed a desire to meet you."

Moving with alacrity, Alexa wasted not even a backward glance as she took Adam's proffered arm. Her meeting with the general went well until the men began talking once again about the Fox, for the moment ignoring her as if she didn't exist. When General Prevost said, "Hanging is too good for a traitor and pirate. It won't be long before we have him and then we'll see how brave he is hanging in the town square."

Fuming inwardly, Alexa allowed her anger to cloud her judgment as she blurted out indiscreetly, "The Fox is fighting for what he believes in! For justice, for freedom for a country and people he loves!" All eyes turned in her direction as absolute silence reigned. Adam groaned as if in pain and General Prevost's face turned several shades of red. Governor Wright sputtered indignantly as did several of the other gentlemen.

"It seems, Lord Penwell, that we have a patriot in our midst," the general said when he finally found his voice. "Are you certain your wife is the daughter of Sir John Ashley?"

"I'm sorry, General," Adam apologized sincerely. "As you can see my wife is not herself tonight. Why, she is as loyal as I am. I'm certain her condition is causing her to say things she doesn't mean." All the while he made excuses for Alexa, Adam cursed inwardly, silently raging against Alexa for nearly ruining everything with her wayward tongue and traitorous leanings.

The general's eyes grew hard as nails until his gaze settled on Alexa's stomach, unnoticed by him before because of her ingeniously designed dress. Immediately his stony features softened and he allowed himself to relax. "Ah, I see, Lady Foxworth, your husband is correct. Indeed you are not responsible for your words. My own wife took to doing and saying strange things when she was in the . . . er . . . family way. I strongly advise you to take your lady home, milord, she seems to be exhausted."

"Of course, General," agreed Adam immediately, turning Alexa in the direction of the door.

"And Lord Penwell, I suggest you keep her there until she . . . feels better," implied the general sternly.

Adam hurried Alexa from the room as hundreds of people looked on in disapproval. "My God, Alexa, what are you trying to do, ruin me?"

"I don't care, Adam!" Alexa countered hotly. "He had

no business talking about Fox that way. Or about the brave people who want nothing but to be left in peace to run their own country!''

"Alexa, I find your strong support of Fox strange. Is there something between the two of you I should know?''

Alexa blushed guiltily, thinking about the night Fox had taken her virginity and could well have sired her child. "Don't be silly, Adam," she scoffed, dropping her eyes evasively. "It's just that I truly feel empathy with these Americans. They are tough, brave, and certainly not lacking in pride.''

"And you admire all those qualities?''

"What woman doesn't?''

"Obviously Fox is some kind of folk hero to you.''

"Aye, and Mac, too. They are both brave and daring.''

"And so are you, my little spitfire," Adam said softly.

They reached their carriage and Adam carefully handed Alexa inside. He was about to climb in beside her when he suddenly changed his mind. "You go on home without me, Alexa. I'm going back inside and try to placate General Prevost and the Governor.''

"But Adam, how will you get home?'' Alexa protested. For some reason she did not want to be alone tonight.

"I'll borrow a horse and follow later. Do as I say, Alexa.'' Adam frowned sternly. "I want to undo some of the damage you've created tonight.''

Irked by his cool, aloof manner, Alexa nodded jerkily and ordered the coachman forward.

Alexa was barely out of sight when Gwen, having followed the couple out of perverse curiosity, sidled up to Adam. "I knew she was trouble, darling," she drawled throatily, "the moment she turned up uninvited in your study and laid waste to all our plans.''

Adam slanted Gwen a bemused glance. "What do you

suggest I do, Gwen? Alexa is carrying my child.''

"Get rid of her once the child is born. Send her back to her father. Or . . . is it that she is better in bed than I am, Adam?''

"Surely you don't expect me to answer that!'' Adam replied, vastly amused.

"As big as she is she can't be doing you any good, darling. You know I'm crazy about you. No one has ever made me feel like you do. Why not let me provide what your wife is incapable of giving you?''

Her low seductive voice promised delights Adam had long denied himself while her lips, so soft and inviting, begged for his kisses. Without him willing it his mouth covered hers hungrily. Abandoning herself to his drugging kisses, Gwen melted into his crushing arms, not caring whether anyone might be watching. "Oh, Adam,'' Gwen sighed raggedly. "I know you still want me. Make love to me, my darling. I've been too long without you.''

Adam was stunned by his response to Gwen's blatant invitation. Desire throbbed through his veins as his body reacted instantly to the soft warmth in his arms. It had been ages since he had a woman; since his wedding night, to be exact. Gwen was a handy and obviously willing substitute for the woman he really longed to make love to, so why not accept what she offered? he asked himself, unwilling to moralize so long as need dulled his senses. Alexa need never know, and besides, Gwen was nothing to him but a willing receptacle for his lust.

"Where?'' Adam croaked hoarsely. "Where can we go?''

Triumph sparking her desire, Gwen whispered urgently, "The guest cottage, it will be deserted now while the reception is in progress. Come, darling, hurry. I want you so badly my body is afire for your touch.''

Needing no further urging, Adam swooped up Gwen's lithe form in his strong arms and turned in the direction of the cottage, a place he and Gwen had used often in the past for their trysts.

The carriage carrying Alexa had barely traveled to the end of the driveway before she realized she had lost her reticule in the excitement of her hasty departure. Flustered, she ordered the coachman to return to the Governor's mansion so she might ask Adam to look for it. Thinking she might have dropped it outside when she and Adam left the house, Alexa retraced her steps while she sent the coachman inside to look for her husband. And then she saw him, but he was not alone.

Gwen was pressed so close to Adam's hard frame that they appeared as one. After a kiss that Alexa was certain went on forever, she watched stunned while Adam took up his ladylove and started off for some unknown destination. Alexa's distress was such that she was unaware of the strangled sob that passed between her parted lips.

Startled, Adam heard the sound and whirled, fearing they had been discovered by one or more of the guests. He was completely unprepared to confront his wife's astounded face; one fist stuffed in her mouth, the other clenched in the folds of her red dress.

"Oh, God," he groaned as if in agony as he roughly set a smirking Gwen on her feet. "I thought you left." Dismay made his voice gruff.

"Obviously," Alexa choked out. "But you won't have to tell me twice." Turning in a froth of red, Alexa began running back along the path toward the carriage, desperate to escape the sight of Adam with another woman in his arms. The night was dark, the way strewn with loose stones, and Alexa's body awkward and ungainly. In her haste to flee from Gwen's smirking face and Adam's confusion, she tripped. Her ankle turned and she fell heavily to the ground, her stomach taking the brunt of the fall.

She was halfway up before Adam gained his wits and rushed to her side. "Alexa, my love, are you hurt? Oh my God, I wouldn't have this happen for the world!" He began a slow but frantic search of her limbs for any sign of injury, but thankfully found none.

"Don't touch me, Adam!"

"I'm sorry, Alexa," Adam rejoined lamely. "I never meant to hurt you."

"I want to go home, Adam," Alexa said shakily.

Still fearing she might be hurt in some way, Adam cradled her gently in his arms and carried her back to the carriage, settling her on the seat and sliding in beside her. "What made you come back?" he asked once she was made comfortable. The coachman, at Adam's signal, slowly started forward, doing his best not to add further to Alexa's distress. From a distance Gwen watched, frowning.

"I suddenly discovered I lost my reticule somewhere and came back to look for it."

"Are . . . are you certain you're not hurt? What about the baby?"

"There seem to be no bones broken," Alexa allowed grudgingly, fixing Adam with a contemptuous glare.

"Alexa, allow me to explain. I had too much to drink and . . . and . . . forgive me . . . Gwen means nothing to me. She offered . . ."

"It doesn't matter, Adam." Alexa cut him off in mid-sentence. "You owe me no explanations. I know why you married me and you never promised to be faithful."

Groaning inwardly Adam decided not to pursue the matter further, thereby adding to Alexa's distress. Plenty of time for explanations later when she had calmed down. For nearly an hour they traveled in silence.

Suddenly Alexa doubled over, clutching her middle convulsively. A groan of anguish escaped her throat and beads of perspiration dotted her furrowed brow. Adam turned deathly white, more frightened than he had ever been in his life.

"What is it, Alexa? Is it the baby? Oh, God, what have I done to you?"

"No . . . no!" cried Alexa, biting her lip against the pain, "it is too early! Help me, Adam! Help me!"

Her plea tearing him apart, Adam urged the coachman dangerously faster as he tenderly cradled Alexa's tormented body in his arms, all the while cursing Gwen, cursing fate, but mostly cursing himself. He had never felt so helpless or so useless in his life.

Adam was eternally grateful his plantation lay not too far from the city, situated on the south bank of the Savannah River. Traveling as fast as safety allowed, they reached Foxworth Manor shortly and Adam was galloping up the stairs two at a time with Alexa in his arms while the coachman was dispatched posthaste back to Savannah for the doctor.

With shaking hands Adam undressed Alexa, slipped a nightgown over her head and tucked her in bed. "Are the pains getting any better, my love?" he asked anxiously, hopefully.

Biting her lip to keep from crying out, Alexa shook her head negatively. In an attempt to ease her pain, Adam poured cool water into the basin and gently bathed the perspiration from her face and neck, though Alexa was in too much agony to appreciate his effort. Her one consuming thought as she drifted in and out of pain was that Adam would have made love to Gwen had she not interrupted at an inopportune moment. And she was about to lose her baby because of it.

Two hours later the doctor from Savannah arrived and Adam reluctantly left Alexa's side while he made a thorough examination of his patient. A half-hour later he confronted Adam in the hallway, shaking his head sadly. "I'm sorry, Lord Penwell, but I can detect no heartbeat. Your wife told me she fell. Evidently the child suffered the brunt of the fall. I'm afraid there is nothing more I can do except offer help in aborting the dead fetus."

Adam sagged against the wall, glad for its support. He was stunned at what his lust had wrought. "Does Alexa know, doctor?" he asked jerkily.

"No, I thought it best not to cause her any more anguish than necessary. She'll need all her strength for the birthing." He made to reenter the bedroom, then turned back to Adam. "If one of your people is experienced in midwifery, send for her. I'll be glad for the help."

Adam nodded and rang for Jem, asking him to summon Mammy Lou, the elderly woman who delivered all the babies born on the plantation. She was competent and intelligent and should prove capable of following the doctor's directions.

To Adam's tormented mind it seemed that he paced outside the door for hours, but in fact only two were to pass before Alexa emitted a piercing shriek that sent shivers up and down his spine. Then all was quiet. Fear for Alexa nearly caused him to go rushing into the bedroom despite the doctor's orders to remain outside. His hand was reaching for the doorknob when the panel opened and Mammy Lou stepped out carrying a tiny bundle swaddled in a white cloth.

At Adam's inquiring look, Mammy Lou said, "He didn't have a chance, Mastah Adam. His tiny skull was crushed."

"It was a boy?"

"Yas, suh. Perfect in every way, though he couldn't

have weighed more than three pounds. I'm sorry, suh."

"Tell Jem to have the carpenter build a small box, Mammy Lou," Adam said, his voice catching painfully in his throat. "We'll have the funeral in the morning." Mammy Lou started to walk away with her tiny bundle. "Wait!" said Adam suddenly. "I'd like to see him."

Mammy Lou looked dubious but finally uncovered the still form and offered him to Adam's view. Almost reverently Adam regarded the lifeless child, blood of his blood, flesh of his flesh, and then he turned away, unable to restrain the tears streaming down his cheeks. Mammy Lou continued down the stairs and Adam, steeling himself to face Alexa, entered the bedroom.

Alexa looked incredibly small and pale lying in the bed with her eyes closed. She did not stir when Adam entered, nor did she acknowledge his presence in any way. Immediately the doctor drew Adam aside.

"I did all I could, Lord Penwell," Doctor Lambert shrugged, his weary face etched with sadness. "It was as I expected. The child's skull was crushed in the fall. It's a terrible blow to your wife, I know, but Lady Foxworth is young and healthy, there will be plenty of time for other children."

"How is my wife, doctor?" Adam asked in a low voice.

"As well as can be expected. As births go this one wasn't particularly long or difficult. But I'm afraid your wife is taking the stillbirth badly. She'll need all your support and love to surmount this tragedy."

"By God she'll have it!" vowed Adam in a hoarse whisper. If she'll accept it, he thought but did not add.

His job done, Doctor Lambert prepared to leave, moving about the room gathering up his instruments and packing them in his medical bag. "Summon me immediately should a fever develop," the doctor said in parting.

"Is there much danger of that?" Adam asked sharply.

"There is always danger of fever. See that she takes plenty of liquids and stays in bed a week or two." Then he was gone.

Gingerly Adam approached the bed but refrained from speaking should Alexa be sleeping. When she slowly turned her head and opened her eyes, Adam was stunned as well as saddened by the hurt and bewildered look lurking in their violet depths.

"He's dead. My baby's dead, Adam," she said in a flat voice devoid of all emotion.

"I know, my love. It hurts me, too. I wanted him as badly as you did. But there will be other children. We've plenty of time."

Alexa blinked. Though she was weary beyond bearing, her voice, surprisingly strong, conveyed her contempt. "How can you say that, Adam? You married me for one reason only, to give your child a name. Now we have nothing! There is no child! Your obligation to me is ended."

"Alexa, my love," Adam reasoned, "you're tired and distraught, and this is no time to discuss our affairs. You blame me for our baby's death and God knows you are probably right. I blame myself. But don't judge me now, Alexa, wait until the hurt passes and we have time to talk."

"You're right, Adam, I am tired. I want to be alone. You can't possibly understand how I feel. My baby meant everything to me. At long last I would have someone to love me for myself. Now I have no one." She turned her face to the wall.

"You have me, Alexa," Adam whispered softly. But she was already asleep.

The next day the tiny baby was buried beneath a live oak tree in a small box lined with velvet. Alexa was in no condition to attend for she awoke burning with fever. The doctor was sent for and he immediately ordered cooling baths to bring down the fever. Adam insisted on performing that task for his wife and none could persuade him otherwise. For three days and nights Alexa waged a violent battle against the raging infection, and on the fourth day emerged victorious as the fever broke.

During those desperate days when Alexa hovered between life and death, Adam refused to leave her side, patiently forcing life-giving liquids down her parched throat, spoon by painful spoon. Only when Doctor Lambert assured him she would live was he persuaded to leave her side.

It was during his long vigil at Alexa's bedside that Adam learned of his wife's attraction to the Fox. Time and again she called out his name in her delirium, stunning Adam. They had met so briefly that he was astounded she could have formed such an attachment to the privateer. But obviously the Fox had impressed Alexa greatly for her to call out his name so desperately, Adam thought. Never in his wildest dreams did he imagine Alexa would form a romantic attachment for Fox. Had he known, he would have made certain things were done differently.

Though Alexa's physical recuperation pleased the doctor, her mental state definitely did not. Her melancholia reached a point where it threatened to destroy her, as the doctor was quick to impress upon Adam. "Is there nothing you can do, Lord Penwell?" he asked worriedly. "Your wife's body has mended nicely but she has lost the desire to live. Was that baby so important to her that her mind refuses to look to the future?"

Adam shrugged helplessly. He had tried to talk to

Alexa but she refused to listen. She blamed him for her baby's death and so far nothing he could do or say consoled her. "I've tried, Lord knows I've tried to get through to her," he told Dr. Lambert.

"Is there no one who can talk to her?" the doctor suggested. "Should there be, I strongly advise you to do it soon."

After that conversation Adam was thoughtful a long time, determined to go to any lengths to bring Alexa out of her despondency. Somehow, someway, he'd find someone or something to save Alexa from retreating from life. Desperate situations called for drastic measures, and considering what he was about to do it was obvious he was driven by desperation.

Alexa sat listlessly in the lounge Adam had thoughtfully pulled up to the window, her hands folded motionless in her lap. She knew she should be out taking exercise in the late winter sunshine but she could not gather the energy to care. Frozen in her own private hell Alexa drew more and more into a shell of her own making.

Hattie was careful to dress her attractively in soft, flowing robes and brush her dark hair until it shone like glass, but it mattered little to Alexa how she appeared to others. She knew both the doctor and Adam were concerned about her but she was content to sit and let the world go by. How could she make them understand she had no intention of dying just yet? When she tried to explain they refused to believe her, especially in light of the way she repeatedly pushed her food away when it was forced upon her. Didn't they realize that she needed little nourishment to sustain her dormant body? What she did need was time. Time to come to grips with her grief and time to evaluate her feelings for Adam.

There were times in the past weeks when she actually felt sorry for her husband. His own grief appeared genuine, but when he attempted to explain about Gwen, she would hear none of it. She couldn't, not yet. Meanwhile she was content to hibernate like an animal whose bodily functions stopped for long periods of time while she existed in a deep, dark void.

As was his custom since her illness, Adam bid Alexa goodnight before he retired to the room he had been using since Alexa's illness. Disappointment etched his features when she barely acknowledged his gesture, as if it was not worth the effort. When Hattie came to ready her for sleep she allowed herself to be handled like a child and tucked into bed. The faithful servant spent a few minutes banking the fire, then left the room, softly closing the door behind her. So deep had Alexa sunk into despair that she was unaware of how close she hovered to total retreat from life.

Sleep. Healing, almost like death but without the same permanence; elusive. As much as Alexa desired it, it would not claim her. Thoughts. Crushing, too complicated to face; painful. They would not stop. And then a noise, barely a breath, yet Alexa sensed it, every fiber of her being attuned to the raspy whisper that sometimes haunted her dreams.

"Alexa, my love."

Adam? No, not Adam. Fox! But how. . . ? Raising on one elbow, Alexa peered into the darkness, imagining a masked face lurking within the shadows. "Who is there? Adam? Is that you?"

"No, Alexa, not Adam." There was no mistaking the husky whisper.

"Fox! Where did you come from? You shouldn't be here, it's too dangerous! The English are determined to have you at the end of a rope."

"Would you care, milady?" he asked, stepping from a darkened corner of the room into the light of the flickering fire. Alexa's breath lodged painfully in her throat at the welcome sight of him, his powerful, well-muscled body moving with the grace of a sleek cat. He looked tough, lean, and sinewy, and Alexa wished he would show her his face.

"You know I would, Fox," came Alexa's low reply. "But why have you come? You know Adam is a royalist. If he found you here he would turn you in. Oh, Fox, please leave now before you are discovered!"

"I'll take my chances, milady," rasped Fox hoarsely. "I came because I heard you were ill. I had to see for myself that you were recovering. I . . . I heard you hold your life in little regard."

A stunned expression marched across Alexa's face. "Where . . . where did you hear that?"

"I have my ways," he said mysteriously. "Is it true? Have you no desire to recover?"

Alexa's dusky lashes swept her pale cheeks, unwilling to show Fox just how close he had come to the truth. "I lost my baby, Fox," she said, as if that explained everything.

"I know," he sympathized. "But you are young, Alexa, there will be others."

"The child could have been yours, you know."

Fox was quiet a long time. "Aye," he acknowledged sadly, quietly.

"There were times when I wished it were."

"Are you so unhappy as Adam's wife? Does he abuse you? Neglect you?"

"N-no, nothing like that. But he doesn't love me. He wants Lady Gwen. What does life hold for me? Why should I live?"

"Life for me, milady," Fox urged huskily as he settled

down beside her on the bed and took her in his arms, noticing as he did the fragile quality of her bones beneath his huge hands.

"For what purpose? I am another man's wife."

"It will make me happy knowing that you are content. A privateer's life is hazardous at best and I would not ask you to share it."

"Will . . . . will I ever see your face?"

"I promise you, Alexa, one day you will know my face."

"You mean it?"

"It's a solemn vow. But you must promise me something in return."

"What?" Alexa asked warily.

"Two things. First you must promise me you will concentrate on getting well." Alexa nodded, then waited expectantly for his second request. When it came it shocked her. "I want you to be happy with Adam." Waving aside the objections on the tip of her tongue, he continued. "Adam is a good man and I believe he loves you."

"You're mistaken," Alexa interjected stubbornly. "He does not love me!"

"What man could know you and not love you?" Fox rasped quietly.

"You would embrace another man's cause?" Alexa's face registered hurt as well as surprise.

"The man is your husband, milady. I would rest easier if I knew you were happy and cared for."

"You want me happy with another man? What kind of man are you?"

"One who loves you and wants only what is best for you. Will you promise me this, Alexa?"

There was a time, before she lost her child, when she fancied herself in love with Adam, Alexa mused thoughtfully. Could she, for Fox's sake, still find an ember of that lost love somewhere in the chambers of her heart? "If I promise to do as you ask will I ever see you again?"

"Didn't I just tell you that one day you would see my face?" he chided gently. "Never doubt it, my sweet lady, we will meet again. It's preordained."

"Then I agree," Alexa gave in grudgingly, "although I truly believe you are wrong to think Adam loves me. Now you must go, Fox. It's too dangerous for you to linger here."

"A boon first, milady. A kiss from your soft lips."

Without waiting for an answer she felt his lips touch hers like a whisper, more of a caress than a kiss. It was as tender and light as a summer breeze and vaguely reminiscent of another's. He attempted no other intimacy as he reluctantly released her lips.

"Fox, I . . ."

"No, Alexa, we've made our pact to one another, there's nothing more to say but good-bye—until we meet again." He was gone before she could form a reply, leaving nothing in his wake but the tender impression of his lips on hers.

10

During the weeks following Fox's stealthy appearance in her bedroom, Alexa amazed Doctor Lambert and Adam by her rapid recovery. "Whatever you did or said," the good doctor remarked to Adam, "worked miracles." Adam flashed an inscrutable smile but said nothing, for he, too, was stunned as well as thrilled by Alexa's complete turnabout. Not only had Fox's words triggered her recovery but her own youthful body reasserted its will, defying her halfhearted wish for eternal rest. Adam was secretly glad he had resorted to drastic measures in order to force Alexa back into the world of the living.

Alexa's appetite returned along with the color in her cheeks and soon she was spending time outdoors and taking meals with Adam in the dining room. Adam knew the time was ripe to tell Alexa that he must leave again soon. First they had much to discuss. That night he accompanied her to their room but did not leave as was his usual custom since her illness.

Alexa, fearing he might want to make love to her and

unsure of what her reaction would be should he try, began nervously pacing the room. "Sit down, Alexa, please," Adam urged, motioning toward the bed.

Reluctantly Alexa obeyed, and Adam followed, settling down beside her. "Did you want something, Adam?" she asked, remembering her promise to Fox. If Adam wished to talk she would listen. She almost giggled aloud at the thought of Adam's resonse should he learn she was willing to listen to him only because another man had requested it. Adam looked at her strangely but did not comment on her mirth.

"Alexa," Adam began hesitantly, "you're completely well now or I would not even consider leaving. But I can delay no longer. I am forced to undertake another mission."

Alexa started to speak, then thought better of it as her jaw clamped shut with a snap.

"I have no choice, my love. Until this war is resolved one way or another I am bound to serve. I want you to understand I do not leave from choice."

"When must you go?"

"Tomorrow."

"Why are you telling me? You never bothered before," Alexa accused hurtfully.

"I deserved that, Alexa. And I'll try to answer you as honestly as I can. When I return I want you here for me."

"I have no place else to go," she reminded him.

"I'm not referring to just your presence in my house," Adam explained with difficulty. "I've come to realize that you mean a great deal to me, Alexa. I admire your courage, your spirit, and yes, damn it, even your temper." Alexa looked at him doubfounded, unable to find her tongue. "What I'm trying to say, my darling, is that I love you."

"Just like that, Adam, and you expect me to believe you?"

"I hope you'll believe me."

"What about Gwen?"

"I've tried before to explain about Gwen. She means nothing to me. She never did."

"Yet you were about to marry her when I came into your life."

"Gwen was part of a plan. I . . . thought I needed her," explained Adam.

"And suddenly you find you no longer need her? Amazing!"

"I have you, my love. When I returned to America I thought I'd never see you again. You were to marry Charles and I knew you hated me for what I did to you. I needed Gwen for . . . for reasons I'm not at liberty to divulge, but certainly not for love."

"That night I lost our child," Alexa accused, her pain still too raw to prevent the tremor from entering her voice, "you were going to bed her."

"I admit it, Alexa, though God only knows I've been punished enough for it. But it wasn't Gwen I wanted, it was you. I had no wish to harm you or my child by forcing my attentions on you. I had planned on visiting a brothel. I was drinking heavily and when Gwen offered herself I recklessly accepted. But I did not do it to deliberately hurt you, never that. Even then I realized I loved you. Gwen was nothing but a poor substitute for the woman I really desired. Don't you think I've cursed my lust over and over since that night?"

Adam's declaration of love stunned Alexa, robbing her of speech. Could it be that Fox was right all along when he said he felt that Adam loved her? How did he know? Should she believe Adam when she knew him to be undeserving of her trust and love? All these thoughts warred within her as she considered life as Adam's beloved wife, not just a woman he was forced to marry.

"Alexa, what are you thinking?" He dared to take her

in his arms and when she did not protest, pressed soft kisses on the top of her head. "Do you hate me still? Has anything I said made any difference to you?"

"I think you're asking too much of me too soon. The baby . . ."

"We'll have other children. Lots of them."

"This one was special."

"What made it so special?" Adam asked sharply.

"It just was, Adam. Why this cross-examination? Suffice it to say that no matter what the circumstances under which he was conceived I wanted it." Even though he might have belonged to Fox, she wanted to add but did not.

"So did I, my love. And I wanted you. I still do, desperately."

"Don't pressure me, Adam. Leave things the way they are until you return."

"Will you promise to wait for me?"

"Aye, I'll be here," she said slowly.

"I can't leave without making love to you, Alexa. I need you. I want the memory of you in my arms to live on in my thoughts during the long nights ahead."

"Do I have a choice?" Alexa asked impishly, suddenly feeling daring. It had been so long since she had been the recipient of Adam's love. Since her wedding night, to be exact. The thought suddenly titillated and excited her.

"No choice at all." Adam grinned rakishly, thrilling to her obvious acceptance of his attentions.

His mouth was dry, his breath a hard knot in his throat as he slowly undressed her, kissing each place he uncovered with agonizing thoroughness. When she was completely nude he undressed himself and gently eased her onto the bed, pausing to worship her with his smoky eyes, whispering his love for each part of her body. The turbulence of his passion swirled around her and drew her inexorably into its vortex, dismayed at the magnitude of her own desire.

His hands moved, gently, touched her breasts, then lowered to the smooth roundness of her buttocks. Gently he touched his lips to hers. His tongue explored the hollow of her slim neck and the crevice between her firm breasts. Then he scooted downward and his lips moved fludly over her thighs, flat stomach, lower, lower . . . She gasped.

She felt herself drifting, vibrating with heat as his hands gently coaxed her thighs apart. And then time stood still as his hands, mouth and tongue explored the very depths of her, thoroughly, with agonizing slowness. And then ecstasy exploded. Only when she stopped trembling and he felt her fingertips touch the softness of his tawny hair did he rise above her, his manhood hard and throbbing against her thigh. He took her hands, encouraging her to explore, and he groaned in pleasure as she took his lead.

Unable to wait another minute, Alexa looked up, gasping in delight as he slowly entered her, his eyes aglitter in the shadows, shimmering misty pools of gray that reflected his need for her. All restraints burned away as they sought the immediate satisfaction of all shared pleasure. In heated, explosive and vibrant need they moved together, slowly at first, then faster as their mutual desire urged them to greater heights.

Alexa breathed in deep soul-wrenching gulps as his expert thrusts sent her to even greater levels of ecstasy than she imagined possible. Higher and higher they soared until the peak of sensual delight was reached and they exploded in a downpour of fiery sensations. Alexa cried out and Adam answered in long surrendering moans.

Adam held her close as contentment and peace flowed between them. "It will always be like this between us, my love," he promised, "if you will allow it." And then they both succumbed to the deep sleep of satisfied lovers.

Sometime during the night Adam awoke her with long, drugging kisses, his hands gentle and coaxing on her flesh. Soon the flames of passion once again burned within them. Their initial urgency gone, they were able now to take the time to explore endlessly, to arouse, to find the tempo that best suited their needs. As he roused her passion, his grew stronger until he rose above her and claimed her, pressing into her until his magnificent length was totally sheathed and she surrendered completely to his masterful stroking. Afterwards, Alexa was astonished at the sense of fulfillment permeating her slender form.

"Perhaps we've begun another family tonight," Adam smiled in the dark. "Would you like that, my love?"

"I . . . don't know, Adam. Not if a child was all that was keeping us together."

"I love you, Alexa. I've hurt you time and again, I know, and all because of a misguided emotion called revenge. I'm asking you now to forgive me."

For some obscure reason Alexa could not give voice to her feelings. It was almost as if she gained some perverse satisfaction by deliberately withholding her love. But after what they just shared together she came to the realization that a kernel of love for Adam remained somewhere in the compartments of her heart. Should she allow it to take root and grow, thereby fulfilling her promise to Fox? she wondered, emotionally drained. Time would tell, and Lord knows she had plenty of that.

Alexa opened her eyes to the graying darkness of predawn light and knew instinctively that Adam was gone. "Oh, Adam," she wailed into the empty room. "I should have told you I loved you before you left!'' The admission was dredged from a place beyond logic and reason. From the very beginning she felt they had something special together but his thirst to avenge his father's death blinded him to her true worth.

Alexa knew that admitting his love had cost Adam dearly; that he had fought against his growing attachment to her and the child she lost. Oddly, she loved him all the more for denying his pride and seeking forgiveness. Come back to me safely, Adam, she silently entreated. Come back to me and let me love you.

Days passed. Alexa had no visitors. None dared come after her fiasco at the General's reception. Though situated but an hour's ride from the city, she might as well live in the middle of nowhere. She heard nothing save what gossip the house slaves repeated. Her one consolation was that she had finally met Mary Forbes, the overseer's young wife. One day she made it a point to ride out to the neat, scrupulously clean cottage Adam allotted to the couple.

Timid, possessing none of the beauty or fire of the slightly younger Alexa, Mary Forbes proved to be a sweet-natured woman who at first was totally awed by Lord Penwell's lovely wife. Her plain but attractive face, surrounded by a wealth of hair the color of ripe wheat, registered shock the first time Alexa appeared at her door. With a babe in her arms and one hanging on her skirts, Mary stuttered an invitation to take tea which Alexa accepted with alacrity.

While Mary Forbes prepared tea, Alexa played with the children, both boys, age one and three. At first Alexa experienced a pang of sadness when she thought of her own dead child. She often pictured him possessing Adam's handsome features and tawny hair. But soon she came to enjoy playing with the two little Forbes boys and took to visiting the small cottage once or twice a week.

Reading also became a favorite pasttime for Alexa. Ensconced in a comfortable chair, she worked her way through Adam's large, well-stocked library. From Adam she heard nothing. She hoped General Prevost appreciated his efforts that kept him away from home for long periods of time.

One month passed and still Adam did not return. Through the slave grapevine Alexa learned that Fox and several other privateers were back harassing the British navy after a short absence of a month or two. By now the English were becoming desperate to capture and hang Fox, and many traps had been laid for him, only to be foiled by the wily Fox who lived up to his name admirably. At times Alexa felt a part of her would die should Fox be caught and executed. Was it possible to love two men? Alexa wondered distractedly.

Mac, too, was constantly in her thoughts and prayers, for though she did not love him as she did Adam . . . or Fox . . . he was a true friend to her and just as dear. How was it possible to love two men? Alexa reflected as her thoughts led her to both Adam and Fox. Adam's love brought her happiness and physical joy while Fox's love bolstered her spirit and fed her courage. Without either of them she would not be a complete woman.

Early in the year 1779, Alexa suddenly became aware that spring was nearly upon her. She could smell it in the fertile earth, see it in the budding trees and foliage turning green before her eyes. Already soft breezes and brilliant sun warmed the days. The slaves were busier than ever readying the soil for planting and Alexa began to miss Adam dreadfully. He had never been gone so long and she began to fear for his safety. She even considered going to General Prevost's headquarters in Savannah and inquring about him. Then something happened that drastically changed her circumstances.

One night, restlessness rode Alexa mercilessly and she remained downstairs later than usual, prowling the darkened rooms. For some unexplained reason tension prickled along her spine and as the night progressed her unease escalated rather than diminished. Given Alexa's pensive mood the frantic scratching at the door was almost anticlimactic.

At first Alexa considered calling Jem, who slept off the kitchen, but quickly discarded the idea. Perhaps it was someone with news of Adam, she thought hopefully as she hurried to open the door. Or maybe Fox had returned to visit her. What she found on the other side of the door curdled her blood. Stretched out on the porch in a widening pool of blood lay the battered body of a man Alexa quickly identified as Mac.

Flinging herself to her knees she cradled his head in her arms, calling out his name. Upon examination Alexa realized that the ugly gash on his head demanded immediate attention and she started to rise to get help when she noticed his blood-soaked shirt. Only then did she realize that all the blood surrounding him could not have come just from the head wound alone which was already beginning to congeal.

Gingerly lifting his shirt away from his body she saw what seemed to be a bullet wound in his side, one that could prove life-threatening. With a desperation born of panic, Alexa pressed her ear to his chest and was rewarded with a steady, albeit weak, heartbeat. She hated to leave Mac lying there but it was impossible for her to move him by herself without adding to his injuries.

Alexa ran for Jem, startling the poor man out of a sound sleep. In one swift glance he took in the situation and went for more help. It took three men to carefully lift Mac's huge body and carry him to one of the spare bedrooms.

"Get Mammy Lou, quickly!" Alexa entreated Jem once they had Mac settled. "Tell her to bring anything she has to heal a serious bullet wound. We can't let Mac die!"

Jem ran for the woman healer while the other two men carefully undressed Mac under Alexa's watchful eye. His side was still bleeding profusely and Alexa knew a moment of intense fear. How could one man lose so much blood and still live? Just then Mac began to moan and thrash about.

"Mac! Lie still, you'll hurt yourself!" pleaded Alexa, tears streaming down her face.

Mac's eyes opened slowly, alarming Alexa by their glazed look. "Alexa," he croaked from between parched lips. "Forgive me for coming here. I wouldn't hurt you for the world."

"You did right, Mac, truly. I'm going to help you. Please, don't talk, save your strength."

"No, let me talk, we both know I might not make it and . . . and I want you to know what happened."

"Shh . . . later, Mac."

"No, Alexa. Please hear me out." Alexa nodded grimly as she clung to Mac's disjointed words. "They laid a trap for us, the British. Always before we escaped, but this time it was different. They wanted Fox badly."

"You were with Fox? What happened to your own ship? What about the *Lady* A?"

"Your namesake is in Nassau undergoing repairs. She was slightly damaged in a skirmish a month ago. I was so anxious to return to the fray Fox asked me to join him aboard *The Gray Ghost* when he put into port two weeks ago." He paused for breath and began coughing, alarming Alexa by his pallor and weakness.

"No more, Mac. The rest will have to wait," Alexa declared firmly. Mac started to protest but just then Mammy Lou bustled in carrying a basket over her arm. Giving Mac a cursory inspection she set to work immediately. Alexa was somewhat eased by her no-nonsense manner.

"It's bad, mistress," Mammy Lou informed Alexa as she set out her instruments and potions. "Powerful bad. He surely will die if that bullet don't come out."

"Can you do it, Mammy Lou?" Alexa asked anxiously.

"Shore can try," the old slave said confidently, turning back to the half-conscious Mac. "Hold him down," she ordered curtly to Jem and the two men who had carried Mac into the house.

Mac screamed as the probing began, but his body soon gave up the struggle as he passed out. "Good," Mammy Lou grunted as she felt Mac relax beneath the hands restraining him.

For the next half-hour Alexa felt her own life draining away from her as she watched the slave probe and prod Mac's torn flesh. Then, uttering a cry of triumph, Mammy Lou drew forth the bullet. In swift order she sewed up the wound, sprinkled it with a white powder and bound it up tightly. Then she devoted herself to the jagged head wound that required nearly a dozen stitches to close. Through it all Mac lay pale and unmoving.

"Will . . . will he live?" Alexa asked fearfully. "He looks terrible."

"If he's lucky." Mammy Lou shrugged noncommittally. "If the fever don't kill him; or the loss of blood; or the shock to his system."

"What can I do?"

"Nothing, mistress, except see that he is comfortable and takes plenty of liquids."

"Thank you, Mammy Lou," said Alexa gratefully. "I don't know what I would have done without you."

"I'll go back to my cabin now, but call me if you need me."

Two hours later Alexa was still sitting beside Mac

when he opened his eyes. "Alexa, are you still here?"

"Aye, Mac, I'm here."

"I must have passed out." His voice was weak but clear.

"Small wonder." Alexa smiled. "But thank God Mammy Lou managed to remove the bullet from your side and stop the bleeding. If she hadn't you wouldn't be here talking to me now."

"Alexa, has anyone—have the English come looking for me yet?"

"No, Mac. No one has come."

"They will! I have to leave here, Alexa! If they find me here you can be charged with aiding and abetting a fugitive. It's a serious charge, one demanding the death penalty." He tried to rise but weakness prevented him from doing more than making a token effort as he collapsed back against the pillow, pain twisting his features.

"Mac, please, don't try to move. You'll only succeed in reopening your wound."

"Don't you understand, Alexa? This is serious. If I'm found . . ."

"No one will find you," soothed Alexa. "Adam is a loyal Tory. Why should they come here looking for you? Do you feel like telling me how you were wounded? And how you came here?"

"Did I tell you I was with Fox aboard *The Gray Ghost*?" Alexa nodded. "The British lured us out into the open by using a decoy. We were patrolling the eastern coastline when we spied what appeared to be a heavily laden ship sailing out of the Savannah River. It looked to be an easy mark so we prepared to attack." Mac paused and wet his parched lips with the tip of his tongue. Sensing his need, Alexa pressed a glass of cool water to his mouth, and he drank greedily before continuing.

"We fired our cannon into the frigate but she did

nothing to defend herself. Almost at the same moment Fox and I realized our mistake, but by then it was too late. From behind one of the small islands at the mouth of the river came six British warships, heavily armed and closing in fast. We piled on the canvas but were unable to shake them despite our superior speed and maneuverability."

"How did you get here?"

"We were somewhere in the vicinity of the secret cove I used when I first brought you to Adam when we took our first hit," Mac continued slowly. "We didn't have a chance. In short order we were surrounded and boarded. I took a bullet in the side and fell overboard."

"And Fox? What happened to Fox?" asked Alexa, beginning to tremble.

"I don't know. He may have been captured, or killed. I shudder to think what will happen to him should they take him alive. But then again, he may have escaped. I know of no man as wily as the Fox."

"Did you swim to shore after you fell overboard?"

"I must have. I don't remember too much after hitting the water. When I realized where I was instinct must have driven me here. But I must leave, Alexa. The British are probably searching for me now. I refuse to put your life in danger. Adam will have my hide."

"We'll talk about it later, Mac," Alexa promised soothingly. "You need to rest. It's nearly dawn and I'm going downstairs to see if cook will prepare a broth for you. I'll be back later."

Refusing to listen to his protests, Alexa left the room, intending to see cook first and then wash and change her clothes. She fully expected Mac to be asleep within minutes of her departure and she was right.

Alexa had just gained the foot of the stairs when there came a loud pounding on the front door. "Open up!" demanded an authoritative voice. "Open in the name of the king!'' Alexa nearly dropped from fright. Had the British found Mac's trail so soon?

"Who is it? And what do you want?'' called back Alexa, gathering her scattered courage. "I am alone. My husband is on a mission for General Prevost,'' she added in an effort to impress the soldiers with her husband's importance. But it appeared to make little impact.

"Open up, or I'll be forced to break down the door! We know the Fox is here. We've been trailing him most the night.''

The Fox! Alexa laughed aloud with relief. He escaped! Of one thing she was certain. Fox was not here. She could safely open the door and know they would not find Fox. The banging began anew and she swiftly moved to open the door before it was torn from the hinges. Hopefully the soldiers would not know who Mac was if they found him.

A half dozen armed men moved into the room and Alexa recognized their leader immediately—that nasty Captain Barrington who was such great friends with Lady Gwen and claimed an acquaintance with Charles.

"Where is he, Lady Foxworth?'' the captain asked as his eyes roamed beyond the entranceway into the darkened room.

"I told you,'' Alexa insisted haughtily, "Fox is not here. And if he did happen to travel in this direction what makes you think I'd give him shelter?''

"Come now, milady,'' sneered Barrington contemptuously. "We are all aware where your sympathies lie. Not too many months ago you as much as declared yourself a traitor before hundreds of people.''

"Surely you know better than to give credence to the words of a pregnant woman,'' scoffed Alexa, feigning disbelief.

"I believe nothing that comes out of the mouth of a traitor. No, milady, move aside and allow my men to pass. I will believe you only after a thorough search fails to turn up the Fox."

"If Adam were here he wouldn't allow this," said Alexa murderously.

"Lord Penwell, much as I dislike the man, would be the first to surrender the Fox to the authorities. He is a loyal subject even if his wife is not."

So saying he bodily removed Alexa from her stance by the door and set her aside while his men fanned out to begin their search. Alexa feared greatly for Mac, for though she knew that he was not the Fox, he nevertheless was a privateer and wanted by the British.

Alexa's heart plummeted to her feet when she heard a triumphant shout echo through the rafters. "I've found him, Captain! He's in one of the bedrooms, sorely wounded!"

"So, the Fox is not here!" sneered Barrington, turning on Alexa. "Then who is the man upstairs? Your lover?"

"That man is not the Fox!" shouted Alexa frantically. "His name is Logan MacHugh and he is Adam's friend!"

Snorting disgustedly, Barrington turned from Alexa and bounded up the stairs. Gathering her skirts in one hand, Alexa followed swiftly, all the while entreating Barrington to believe her. Mac was barely conscious when they reached the room, and burning with fever. One of the soldiers drew the sheet away from Mac's flushed body so the captain could view the wound. He stared fixedly at the bloodsoaked cloth binding Mac's middle and at the gash on his forehead.

"It's the Fox all right," he gloated happily. "We'll be well rewarded for this night's work, men."

"No, no!" persisted Alexa in an effort to save Mac.

"Why won't you believe me? This man is Logan MacHugh. He . . . he's been injured in an accident."

"Likely story," scoffed Barrington derisively. "If this man is not the Fox as you claim, then where is the Fox? And who is he? We trailed him here. Come, Lady Foxworth, if this man is not the Fox take us to him."

Alexa frowned, confusion creasing her smooth brow. "I . . . I . . ." she stammered as she searched for a likely answer.

"The look on your face is answer enough," said Barrington knowingly. "Search the house for evidence," he ordered his men. "Meanwhile, I'll make certain Lady Foxworth does not escape."

"Escape?" squeaked Alexa, panic-stricken. "Wha-what do you mean?"

"You know the penalty for harboring a traitor, milady. I am obliged to take you into custody. You will be jailed in Savannah until your trial."

"Trial! Oh, God!" she moaned, grasping for a chair when her knees turned rubbery and refused to support her meager weight. *Adam, Adam, where are you?* she silently implored. *I need you, desperately.*

Amid much noice and boasting, two of Barrington's men burst into the room brandishing a distinctive black mask emblazoned with the face of a fox. "Here's all the proof you need, Captain!" concluded the man, wagging the damning evidence in his hand. "Found it in a trunk in the attic."

Alexa gasped, her face white in the pale dawn. "I . . . I don't know where that came from!" she denied weakly. Truly, she was more surprised than anyone in the room.

Barrington growled something unintelligible low in his throat before ordering his men to take up Mac and bear him away. "No, you can't! If you take him from bed he'll die!" Alexa cried out frantically.

"It will save us the expense of hanging," shrugged Barrington as two of his soldiers carried Mac from the room, his moans of agony echoing down the hall. "Now, milady, get your cloak, we have a long ride ahead of us." Grasping her elbow in sturdy fingers he hustled her from the room and down the stairs.

"Wait!" cried Alexa, halting when she saw Jem standing in the entranceway wringing his hands. "At least allow me a moment to leave instructions for my people until my husband returns."

Nodding curtly, Barrington released his grip while Alexa hurriedly told Jem what was taking place and asked him to instruct Forbes to instigate a search for Adam on her behalf. Then she had time for nothing more as Barrington, growing impatient, shoved Alexa out the door before him and mounted his horse, unceremoniously pulling her up in front of him.

"I'm perfectly capable of riding one of my own mounts," Alexa complained bitterly as she felt his arms tighten uncomfortably about her middle.

"I'll not give you the opportunity to escape," Barrington replied, leveling an icy glare in her direction. "I intend to see you brought to justice and punished."

It was the most miserable ride Alexa had ever experienced in her life. She had no idea what damage Mac had sustained when he was dragged from his bed and hauled to Savannah. Barrington's men rode ahead and she could see neither them nor Mac. And, to add to her misery, Barrington goaded and taunted her unmercifully the entire way, telling her that he was certain General Prevost was so enraged by the navy's losses to the Fox that he was certain to make an example of her by hanging her forthwith. Alexa could only grit her teeth and pray that Adam would arrive in time to rescue her from her uncertain fate. When they finally arrived in

Savannah she was near collapse, exhausted from her long vigil at Mac's bedside and her terrible fear of what awaited her.

As they passed through the city, Alexa dared to ask, "Where are you taking me?"

"The lower levels beneath the Governor's mansion have been divided into cells to house traitors and like criminals," mocked the captain. "I'm certain you won't find it up to your usual standards, milady, but it will have to do."

"Please, ask the General to send for my husband. I'm certain he will clear up this misunderstanding. What can I do or say to convince you that Mac is not the Fox?"

"Nothing, Lady Foxworth. But rest assured both the General and the Governor will be informed of your treasonous act and will decide if your husband should be sent for. Until then you will be treated no better than you deserve."

Alexa recognized the Governor's mansion as they approached. They did not enter the long, circular driveway but circled the block to a little-used side entrance. Barrington pulled her roughly from his horse after he dismounted and shoved her through the door and down a long flight of stairs. The chill and dampness immediately penetrated her thin dress and cloak, even piercing the soles of her shoes to her feet, and Alexa could not suppress the shiver that shook her slight form.

Soon they came to a large room lit only by two torches set in sconces in the damp wall and lined on both sides with tiny, cell-like cubicles, each sealed off tightly from the world by a heavy oaken door. Cut into each door was a small, grilled opening through which food could be passed and the prisoner viewed. Sheer black fright seized Alexa and she began to shake uncontrollably.

"What is the matter, milady?" The captain grinned maliciously. "Isn't it to your liking?"

"You . . . surely you don't intend on locking me in one of those cells, do you?" she asked tremulously.

Barrington laughed raucously. "Have no fear, milady. You should be housed here no longer than it takes to build a scaffold."

From a smaller room located somewhere off the larger one in which Alexa stood, two guards approached, both registering surprise at the lady of quality to be placed into their dubious care. "Well, look what we have here," sneered the older guard, leering appreciatively at Alexa. "She is a lot better than the usual riffraff we get. Can we take our pleasure with this one like we do the others, Captain?"

"I'll have her first, Bates." The younger man grinned, displaying a row of yellow teeth. "You near killed the last one before I had my turn on her."

"Oh please, no!" wailed Alexa, backing away from the two burly men. Just thinking of what they might do to her shattered what little composure she had left, and she choked back a sob. Somehow she had to keep her wits about her if she was to save herself, and she fought to control her escalating terror. Until Adam arrived to save her she had no one or nothing to rely upon except her own courage and cunning.

Captain Barrington shrugged carelessly. It mattered little to him that a traitor should be ravished by these two sadistic guards and was about to tell them so. In fact, he had half a notion to take her himself. She was even better looking and shapelier than Gwen who had finally allowed him to share her favors. He smiled when he thought about Gwen's reaction when he informed her that Lady Foxworth was incarcerated in a cell below her uncle's home. Just as he was about to tell the guards they could do what they will with Alexa, her words stopped him short, giving him cause for second thoughts.

"What do you suppose my husband will do when he discovers his wife has been—violated by these two brutes?" she asked, thinking fast. "Perhaps he might not agree with my actions but I am still his wife and he will not countenance vile acts against my person. He is an earl and that makes me a countess, and if he so chooses he can ruin you for allowing me to be brutally raped."

Alexa held her breath while Barrington mulled over her words, frowning. At long last he seemed to come to a decision. "I regret, men, that Lady Foxworth appears to be telling the truth. Though she will eventually hang for her crime, she is still the wife of a lord of the realm. Knowing Lord Penwell as I do, I'm convinced he will exact some sort of vengeance should his wife be turned over to the likes of you two to use for your own vile purposes."

Two pair of disappointed eyes viewed Alexa with obvious disgust, having just had their pleasure spoiled. "But that is not to say she should be treated any differently from anyone else incarcerated here for crimes of treason."

Bates nudged his younger companion meaningfully. "Hear that, Grubbs, we can still have a little fun." To Barrington he said, "We understand, Captain. Leave the lady to us."

Nodding curtly, Barrington shoved Alexa toward Bates and the equally odious Grubbs. Though he couldn't be certain either guard would obey his orders in regards to Alexa, at least he had done his duty. Whatever happened to her now was out of his hands.

"Don't leave me!" screamed Alexa, gasping in panic. "I demand to see the Governor!"

"You will, in time," Barrington assured her as he prepared to mount the stairs. "Besides, you are in no position to demand anything."

The moment Barrington disappeared from sight, Bates seized Alexa roughly, passing his large calloused hands over her trembling body. "Damn, Grubbs," he moaned huskily, "this one's got the nicest pair of tits I've felt in a long time."

"Let's have a look," Grubbs suggested, yanking Alexa's cloak from her quaking shoulders. The sight of her breasts straining against the bodice of her low-cut gown proved too much for him and he inserted two beefy fingers in the neckline and ripped downward. Alexa screamed as both her bodice and chemise split, releasing her pale breasts. Both Bates and Grubbs stared appreciatively at the vision of two perfect white mounds crested by rose-colored nubs. Bates reacted first, grasping Alexa's nipple between finger and thumb and squeezing. Alexa screamed, trembling with pain as tears sprang unbidden to her eyes.

Not to be outdone, Grubbs seized the other breast, bringing his mouth to its crest and sucking noisily. Striking out blindly against this forced indignity, Alexa connected with a bulbous nose, eliciting a groan. One knee came up and found a groin and she received tremendous satisfaction when a yelp followed. Her long fingernails imbedded themselves in a pair of eyes and suddenly the sickening pressure was gone from her nipple.

"You heard Captain Barrington!" she gasped, panting from her exertions. "Keep this up and when my husband, Lord Penwell," she stressed for emphasis, "finds out about it he'll make you wish you'd never set eyes on me!"

Both suffering from wounds inflicted upon them by one small woman, Bates and Grubbs wisely decided to heed her words. They had enough problems without an earl coming down upon them like an avenging angel.

Besides, there were other ways and means of obtaining what they wanted from the high and mighty Lady Foxworth. They'd make her wish she had the foresight to share her favors with her keepers who held her well-being in their grubby hands.

Alexa watched with trepidation as Bates unlocked the door to one of the cells and pushed her forward with the flat of his hand placed against the small of her back. It was dark inside but the dim light filtering through the door revealed a square room bare save for a wooden cot covered with a thin straw mat and a dirty gray blanket, a single chair and small table. An odoriferous bucket sat in a far corner.

Reeling into the room, Alexa fell heavily against the cot as the door creaked shut behind her, leaving her in near darkness. Through the grill in the door she saw Bate's grinning face ogling her, and then he was gone. A long wail escaped her parted lips as she gave vent to her despair.

Adam, where are you? she silently entreated. I need you so. And then her misery became too great to bear without the relief of tears as huge sobs wracked her frail body and tears streamed down her pale cheeks.

11

Somehow Alexa managed to sleep for several hours, and miraculously, was not disturbed by her two guards until a meal was passed to her through the grille by one of the men, she knew not which. She was surprised to discover that the food, a rather bland stew of vegetables and unrecognizable meat, was palatable though far from tasty. At least they had no plans to starve her, Alexa thought wryly, for the overcooked, unseasoned mess was nutritious enough to keep her alive. The rest of the meal consisted of a mug of tepid water and a crust of dry bread. As she was soon to learn, the same unvaried meal was passed in to her twice each day. Nothing else was forthcoming.

For two days Alexa saw no human face. There were times she had the distinct impression that someone was watching her, but when she looked toward the grille in the door she saw no one. Because of the dampness and ragged condition of her only dress, she wore her cloak at all times. Most galling of all was having to perform bodily functions in plain view. What was even more difficult to bear was the fact that the reeking bucket she was forced to use had not been emptied for the whole time she had used it.

On the third day of her incarceration Alexa could no longer stand the suspense of not knowing what was to be her fate. Consequently, the next time the grille was shoved aside by one of the guards in order to push through her meal, she cried out, "Wait! Please! Don't go whoever you are!"

Instantly Bates's ugly face appeared at the opening. "What do you want?"

"I want to see Governor Wright, or General Prevost. And I wish to know if Mac is still alive."

"Well, milady," mocked Bates nastily. "From what I hear neither the General nor the Governor wish to see you."

"But I must see them! It's imperative I explain to them about Mac!"

"Tell it at your trial." Having said all he intended to he began to back away.

"Wait! Please!" screamed Alexa.

"What now?" grumbled Bates crankily.

"I'd like some water with which to bathe, and a comb. Perhaps you could send for a change of clothing," she suggested hopefully. Bates slanted her an assessing look.

"Can you pay? Let me see the color of your coin, milady."

"You know I was allowed to bring nothing with me. I possess nothing of value."

"I think you do, milady." Bates leered, his salacious intent clearly evident in his coarse features. "You can trade your favors for all those niceties you crave. Why, me and Grubbs would be only too happy to bring you anything you need, milady, should you show us a little consideration."

"No, no!" resisted Alexa hotly. "How could you ask such a thing of me? I'll never give in to you."

"Never is a long time and from what I hear you haven't much time left. You and Fox are to be brought to trial within a fortnight."

"Then Mac is still alive!" Alexa breathed, expressing a swift surge of joy. "Is he being held here also?"

"You'll get nothing more from me, milady, until you are ready to cooperate and bestow a little of what you've been so jealously guarding. If I forced you, Captain Barrington or your husband might get wind of it and ruin my chances for advancement. But nothing was said about you giving your favors freely."

"Over my dead body!" gasped Alexa, rage mottling her perfect features.

"Perhaps, if you're still warm, I might consider it," Bates hinted lewdly.

"Oh God!" gagged Alexa, sickened. Bates snickered, backing away from the grille. "Wait! At least you could empty the . . . the bucket in the corner. Would you want me to sicken and die of disease before I can be brought to trial?"

Bates gave Alexa an oblique look, carefully weighing the consequences should Alexa die before her day in court. Finally, he shrugged, unlocked the door and carried out the offensive waste container. Thereafter, either Bates or Grubbs provided that service every other day.

Two weeks passed and it seemed to Alexa in her solitary cell that she had been forgotten by the world. Dirty, her hair a rat's nest, Alexa was never so close to giving up in her life. It was no wonder she seriously considered subjecting herself to the base desires of her guards in order to ease her deplorable circumstances. The disgusting odor of her own person became far more offensive than the foul bucket resting in the corner.

What could be keeping Adam? Alexa despaired. What if he failed to arrive in time to save her? Not for one minute did she doubt that Adam would set everything right when he returned. In the meantime she existed beneath the earth in a void as dark and forbidding as the hole she lived in.

Then one day Alexa received a surprise that gave her back her will to survive. Mary Forbes was allowed to visit. The moment the cell door creaked open Alexa was assailed by a terrible fear. Should Grubbs or Bates suddenly decide to renew their assault upon her she was far too weak to resist. But when she spied the slim figure of Mary Forbes outlined in the dim light of the doorway, she nearly fainted with joy. Mary stepped inside and the door closed behind her.

"Ten minutes," warned Bates in a gravely voice.

"Oh, Mary, Mary, how did you get them to let you in to see me?"

Squinting in the murkiness, Mary was shocked to the core by Alexa's bedraggled appearance. It was obvious she had not had an easy time of it these past weeks and Mary's soft heart went out to the younger woman. "Alexa, what have they done to you?" wailed Mary, struggling for composure.

"I'm fine, Mary, really," assured Alexa with a calm that belied her inner turmoil. "But how did you convince the guards to let you in here?" she asked again.

"Tom bribed them," Mary divulged, lowering her voice in a confidential manner. "That pair would do almost anything for money."

"Thank God!" Alexa moaned, her despondency evident in her violet eyes. "I had almost given up."

From under her cloak Mary drew forth a bundle and laid it before Alexa on the table. "I've brought you a change of clothes. I've also included a brush, towel, soap and a few other necessities," Mary confided. "I had much more but they wouldn't let me bring it in."

"Thank you for that much," Alexa said earnestly as she eyed the soap greedily. "But as you can tell by the odor I've not been able to bathe in all the time I've been here. I'm only allowed enough water for drinking purposes."

"Poor Alexa," Mary murmured soothingly. "Tom still has sufficient coins left to secure adequate fresh water for bathing each day. Now sit down while I try to work the tangles out of your hair."

Complying gratefully, Alexa settled on the chair while Mary worked diligently on her long tangled locks. As Mary strained over the snarled mass, Alexa asked the question that burned on the tip of her tongue. "Have you heard from Adam, Mary? Has Tom been able to locate him?"

Mary bit her lip in consternation but knew she owed Alexa an answer. "No one seems to know where he is. He appears to have disappeared into thin air. It's assumed he was captured when General Prevost sent him north on a secret mission."

"Oh, no!" cried Alexa, stifling a sob. "Then I am surely lost! Somehow I expected Adam to return and save me."

"Alexa, don't give up. All is not lost," pleaded Mary, hugging Alexa's slim shoulders. When Mary drew her arms away her hand inadvertently caught in a fold of Alexa's cloak, pulling it away from her body, revealing the gaping edges of her torn bodice and chemise. Mary stared in horror at Alexa's exposed breasts and fading purple bruises marring the pale mounds.

"Oh, God, what have those two brutes done to you?" she groaned. "Oh, my lady, how dare they rape you! You, a countess!"

"They didn't rape me, Mary, honestly," Alexa quickly assured her. "They attempted to but I fought them. They haven't tried since. I'm fine, truly I am."

"Dear God! I can't stand the thought of you in this place at the mercy of those two creatures in charge. If only there was something I could do . . ."

"You've already done more than you realize, Mary. You literally pulled me out of the depths of despair by making my lot more comfortable. I'm eternally grateful to you and Tom for all you've done for me and all you attempted to do."

Casting an anxious glance at the door, Mary said, "My time is almost gone, Alexa, is there anything else I can do for you?"

"Has Tom tried to see the Governor? Or the General?"

"Not a day has gone by without Tom calling on one or the other. But they steadfastly refuse to see him, Alexa. From what Tom has been able to learn, they intend to make an example of you and nothing or no one can sway them. I'm sorry."

"Keep trying, Mary," encouraged Alexa. "If only I were allowed to talk to them I know they'd . . ."

"Your time is up, lady," a gruff voice announced, halting Alexa in mid-sentence. This time it was Grubbs who appeared at the grill. "You were only promised ten minutes."

Grubbs opened the door and Mary reluctantly moved toward it after bestowing one last hug on Alexa, whispering in her ear as she did, "Don't give up, Alexa. I know your husband will arrive in time. Or that the General will relent."

"Out!" ordered Grubbs curtly. Then the door closed and once again Alexa found herself alone, surrounded by a terrible silence.

But miracle of miracles, a short time later Grubbs returned with a basin of water. Bless Mary, Alexa thought as she quickly shed her cloak and dress and stood in her torn chemise. Almost reverently Alexa took up the bar of soap and washcloth, the luxury of soap and water on her skin so sensual she closed her eyes and gasped with joy.

"She'd rather have that water than a man between her legs," goaded Bates from the other side of the grill.

"That's because she's never had a real man," Grubbs gibed crudely.

"Go away!" raged Alexa, holding the towel before her breasts. "Am I to be allowed no privacy? You treat me no better than an animal!"

"Traitor, animal—no difference." Bates shrugged, grinning at his cruel joke. Nevertheless, they moved away, allowing Alexa privacy in which to wash and dress in her clean clothes. She felt like a new person and was amazed at how the feeling of cleanliness lent her courage. It was almost as if fresh blood surged through her veins with the clean clothes. Now she was ready to face anything, or so she thought.

A few days later Alexa had another visitor; one so unexpected and surprising that she was rendered speechless when she recognized the face she knew as well as her own.

"Hello, Alexa."

"My God! Charles! What are you doing here?"

"I could ask the same of you. I never thought to see you again. Certainly not under these circumstances. You've fallen about as low as anyone can go, milady," he mocked cruelly.

"Charles, have you come to taunt me or to help me?" Alexa asked, a spark of hope lighting her eyes.

"Help you, Alexa!" Charles laughed nastily. "You've committed treason against the crown. Surely you don't expect me to lift a hand to save you, do you?"

"We were to be married once, Charles. You said you loved me."

"That's before you showed me your true colors. Your father told me how you became whore to Adam Foxworth who just happens to be Lord Penwell, the man who attacked me in the summerhouse on the night of our engagement. Did you have the whole thing planned in advance, Alexa?"

"Charles! You are despicable! You well know I was taken against my will and . . . and forced. It was all part of a grand scheme by Adam to hurt and embarrass my father."

"You ran off and married the fellow, Alexa," Charles accused childishly.

"And without allowing me the courtesy of an explanation you broke our engagement to marry Lady Diana," Alexa retorted hotly.

"What did you expect?" shrugged Charles haughtily. "You were damaged goods. And as it turned out expecting another man's child." He glared fixedly at her flat stomach.

"I lost the baby," Alexa said softly, surprised at the stab of pain she still felt over the loss. "If you haven't come to help me, Charles, why did you come? To gloat?"

"Perhaps," admitted Charles sheepishly. "Then again, maybe I just wished to see you once more before . . . before . . ."

"Before they hang me," supplied Alexa. "No need to stumble over the words, Charles, I know what they intend for me. But tell me, what are you doing in Savannah?"

"I'm a captain, now," he boasted. "I have a ship of my own, the *Avenger*. My ship took part in the successful attack on Fox. We've been ordered to patrol these waters for several weeks in a concentrated effort to rid the area of privateers. They are creating havoc with our shipping. Now that the Fox has been eliminated our job has been made much easier."

Alexa smiled ruefully. Little did Charles know but the Fox was still at large and no doubt *The Gray Ghost* would rise up from the ashes to harass the British. "Do you find this amusing, Alexa?" Charles asked, his voice laced with sarcasm. "I should think one facing death would show some remorse."

"I have no guilt over what I did, Charles. A man came to me gravely wounded, a friend of my husband. I took him in and cared for his wounds. If that constitutes treason, then I plead guilty."

"The man you conveniently took in was the notorious Fox, a traitor with a price on his head."

"You're wrong, Charles. Mac is not the Fox."

"The authorities think so."

"They are wrong."

Charles shrugged. "What about the careless words you uttered before hundreds of people declaring your sympathy for Fox and the so-called patriots? Barrington told me that General Prevost would have jailed you then and there had you not been pregnant at the time."

Unable to curb her tongue a moment longer, Alexa lashed out heedlessly. "I meant every word I said! These Americans don't deserve the treatment they're getting from the English. They want nothing but freedom from oppression and unjust taxation. They are a hardy and tenacious people and I find I greatly admire their spirit and courage!"

"My God! You are a traitor!" gasped Charles, aghast. "I must admit I seriously had my doubts concerning your guilt, that's one of the reasons I requested permission to see you. But now," he shook his head sadly, "I believe all the charges leveled against you. You've changed, Alexa."

"Of course I have," charged Alexa crankily. "After all I've been through do you expect me to remain the same selfish, spoiled child?"

"When I arrived and learned about you, I felt almost sorry for you. But it's obvious to me you deserve everything that's coming to you. Goodbye, Alexa." Without a backward glance Charles stomped haughtily from the cell, his pride and bearing echoing his disdain for a traitor to her own country, no matter how beautiful and desirable she may be.

"Well, my lady," sneered Bates through the grille, "not even one of your lovers will lift a finger to help you. Now it appears doubtful that your own husband cares enough about you to come to your defense even though he has been back in Savannah for several days."

Stunned, Alexa cried, "You lie! Why should I believe you? If Adam was in Savannah he would surely do his utmost to set me free."

"Why would I lie, milady? Believe what you will but rumor has it he's already courting his next wife."

"Lady Gwen," breathed Alexa as pain shuddered through her.

"Aye, you have the name right, milady," grinned Bates maliciously. "But you need only say the word and old Bates will comfort you in your last hours."

"Go away!" shouted Alexa, covering her ears to drown out his hateful words. When she dared to look again Bates was gone.

Flinging herself on the cot, Alexa gave vent to her pain and misery. Could it be true? she asked herself with fearful clarity. The picture of Adam and Gwen together numbed her brain. What could Adam be thinking? Had he bothered to check the prisoner assumed to be Fox he would surely know that it was Mac being held and not the infamous privateer. Was it fear of losing his Tory friends that caused him to abandon her, the wife he professed to love? Alexa understood none of it. What was Adam up to? Did he intend to sit back and let her hang because of her loyalty to her newly adopted country? Was he so shallow as to allow such a travesty of justice rather than defend his own wife? Or his best friend? Confusion reigned as Alexa's mind reeled beneath the weight of her thoughts.

Somehow, life continued. Nearly a month had elapsed since Alexa had been seized and imprisoned. Each day she begged to be allowed an audience with either Governor Wright or General Prevost—and each day her request was denied. Since the surprise visit by Charles, no one had been allowed near her. For what reason she could not divine.

Then one day the long promised event she had been dreading for weeks came to pass. Grubbs arrived early with her usual basin of water, informing her that she was finally being brought to trial. She was to appear that very afternoon. "The Fox was tried yesterday and promptly sentenced to hang," Grubbs announced glee-fully. "No doubt you'll both hang, side by side."

Alexa rejoiced to learn that Mac still lived but was saddened by the cruel blow fate had dealt them. Abruptly she wondered if Adam would attend her trial, and hoped he would not. She had no wish to see him ever again. At that moment the only emotion she could spare her husband was hatred.

Alexa washed carefully and brushed her long black hair until it glowed like buffed glass as it caressed her slim hips. Looking in the small mirror Mary had thought-fully provided she saw a small pale oval staring back at her. Her smudged violet eyes seemed too large for her face and her skin had a translucent quality bordering on fragility. Her wan appearance startled her for she had never been particularly sickly or fragile. Weeks in a damp, sunless environment had greatly undermined her health and Alexa had never been more aware of it as she searched her mirror for a hint of the beauty that had once been hers.

It was the odious Captain Barrington who came for her a few hours later, looking down his long nose at her bedraggled appearance. Though her body was clean her dress was dirty and stained from weeks of wear. The weather was uncomfortably warm but Alexa threw her badly worn cloak over her shoulders, hoping to conceal her disreputable state of dress.

"Your day of reckoning has finally arrived, Lady Foxworth," Barrington sneered disparagingly. "I must say you look nothing like the beautiful woman who entered this cell a few short weeks ago."

"How can I when I was allowed not one single consideration or amenity?" Alexa replied scathingly. "I was treated worse than an animal."

"Tell the Governor, or General Prevost, when you see them," shrugged Barrington, unconcerned. "Move along," he prodded, hurrying her from the cell in a manner that was anything but gentlemanly.

Alexa blinked rapidly as her eyes adjusted to the light. Immediately she was hustled into a closed carriage which took off with a jolt before she had a chance to settle herself. Beside her Captain Barrington took out a spotless handkerchief and mopped his brow. Never would he become accustomed to the abominable Savannah heat.

During their short ride from the Governor's mansion to the building where Alexa's trial was to be held, Barrington regaled her with news of the war. It seemed that General Henry Hamilton, the British commander at Detroit, had captured Vincennes in Illinois. What Barrington did not know was that Vincennes was even now under attack by George Rogers Clark in a successful bid to recapture the British post. This expedition did much to free the frontier from Indian raids and gave the Americans a hold upon the northwest. All this

Barrington was to learn later in dispatches sent to General Prevost and delayed by the capture of the courier.

All too soon they reached the rather austere building that served as a courthouse and Alexa drew back, stunned to see the crowds of people waiting outside for her appearance, or so she assumed. The moment she stepped from the carriage Alexa knew a moment of sheer fright as her assumption proved correct. At her appearance the crowd turned ugly, hurling insults at her from every direction. If there was anyone who sympathized with her cause, they wisely kept their feelings to themselves lest they face the same fate as Alexa.

"Traitor!" Shouts came from the crowd as bodies closed in upon her. "Hang the traitorous bitch!" It was a nightmare, and Alexa, weak from her long weeks of confinement and inactivity, felt herself drowning in a sea of hostility. She wanted to crawl into a hole, to faint, to disappear, if it were possible. Anything to escape the revilement heaped upon her by the jostling, angry crowd of Tories.

One thing only saved Alexa from making a fool of herself by fainting at the feet of her tormentors. Adam! Across the sea of anonymous faces, one countenance stood out amidst the others. A handsome, arrogant face whose gunmetal eyes pierced her like knives aimed at her heart. Alexa's first thought was that except for the subtle lines of tension etching his features, he looked the same.

Grief tore at her vitals the moment she saw Lady Gwen beside him, clutching possessively at his arm, and hatred rose like bile in her throat, bitter and choking. Alexa felt blackness begin to claim her and summoned all the strength her meager body possessed to subdue it. Never would she give Adam and Gwen the satisfaction of knowing that seeing them together hurt her beyond measure. Her lower lips jutting in angry defiance, jaw set determinedly, Alexa gulped back her nausea as she surmounted the darkness threatening to devour her and moved through the crowd, one step at a time.

In her heart she accepted the inevitable without question. Adam had indeed abandoned her and she was left alone to face an ignominious end.

12

His arrogant features purposely set in harsh lines, Adam nearly dropped his stony facade when he saw Alexa stumble, then right herself the moment she spotted him in the crowd. She looked thin and wan, the tender skin beneath her huge purple eyes bruised with dark shadows. How she must hate me, he thought, nearly rushing to her defense despite his firm resolve to pretend indifference to her plight. But the pressure Lady Gwen applied to his arm brought him back to his senses and he was able to watch with outward calm as Alexa, mustering the courage he knew her capable of, squared her small shoulders and passed through the angry crowd with her dignity intact.

It was bad enough, Adam reflected glumly, watching Mac's trial and subsequent death sentence without batting an eyelash. Especially in view of the fact that he was called upon to testify. Deliberately lying under oath, Adam swore that it was entirely possible for Mac to be the Fox. He further explained that he seldom saw his friend or was privy to his personal life. Through it all

Mac sat apparently unmoved by Adam's testimony. His grave wounds were beginning to heal but Mac was still too weak to walk into the courtroom. It was obvious to Adam that his friend hadn't received the proper care he needed in order to speed his recovery. And judging from the look of Alexa's pale face she had been treated no better.

Once inside the large room the crowd did not diminish as people surged in behind Alexa, jostling for a good seat from which to view the proceedings. Alexa's trial promised to be even more spectacular than Fox's for the simple reason that Alexa was a beautiful woman as well as one accused of treason. Then, too, the previous trial for Fox proved a great disappointment to the Tories. There was nothing romantic or flamboyant about the thin, weak shell of a man carried into the courtroom on a litter. Truth to tell, the entire proceedings proved a gigantic farce.

Therefore, the whole of Savannah looked forward with great relish to Alexa's trial, especially since it was learned that her husband, Lord Penwell, was finally returned from a secret mission and had verbally condemned her actions, refusing to come to her aid or even to see her. As if to verify gossip, Adam immediately began seeing Lady Gwen, whom everyone knew had been very close to being Lady Penwell, until Lady Alexa came out of nowhere to claim that title. When Alexa grew large with child in a disgustingly short time the reason for their hasty marriage became common knowledge. Some went so far as to say the little slut received no more than she deserved.

From one of their own brave men, Captain Charles Whitlaw, came the indisputable information that Lady Alexa had been disowned by her illustrious father, Sir John Ashley; that the lady had done something so despicable that the very sight of her sickened the poor man. And who should know better than Charles who revealed he was engaged to the notorious Lady Alexa at one time. Disgusted by her conduct, he had broken his engagement and married a woman worthy of his good name.

All this Adam heard in a roundabout way from Gwen, refusing to comment, only nodding sagely. He truly wished he could go to Alexa, to offer comfort, but under the circumstances he was forced to cool his heels until the time was ripe, meanwhile feigning indignation at his wife's activities as well as disinterest in her fate.

From Lance Barrington Adam learned where Alexa was being imprisoned and that she was being well-treated and in no immediate need. But seeing Alexa now, Adam realized that Barrington had greatly distorted the truth. God only knows what his lovely wife was forced to endure those weeks she spent in the dungeon-like cell below the Governor's mansion.

It had been less than a week since Adam's return from his prolonged mission for General Prevost and he had not known about Mac or Alexa before then. He returned just in time to attend Mac's trial and was told all the grisly details by General Prevost. Circumstances beyond his control forced Adam to renounce his wife and reaffirm his loyalty to the crown despite his wife's avowed sympathy for the colonists. Governor Wright took Adam at his word and immediately offered him a place to stay until the trials were concluded; an offer Adam gratefully accepted although it placed him conveniently in reach of Gwen's waiting arms.

It was only natural that he should squire Gwen about while he awaited the trials. Certainly he could not be blamed if Gwen made too much of his attentions. He deliberately chose to play at Gwen's game for it suited his purpose. Adam knew that Gwen assumed they had a future together once Alexa was conveniently done away with.

Alexa sat in a chair facing her jury, her spine rigid, her head held high. Only Adam, sensitive to her every mood, noticed the slight trembling of her chin. Her stern-faced judges were before her, seated at a long table. General Prevost held the center position. Ranged on either side of him were Governor Wright, Lance Barrington, Charles Whitlaw and two other officers she did not know. Alexa's heart plummeted. She hadn't one chance in a thousand of escaping with her life and she well knew it. In her mind's eyes she saw herself mounting the scaffold beside Mac.

Suddenly the room quieted as General Prevost cleared his throat and glared down at Alexa. "Lady Foxworth, you are brought to trial today to answer to charges of treason. What say you, guilty or not guilty?"

"Not guilty, General," Alexa proclaimed in a low but clear voice. "I have done nothing that can be construed as treasonous but perhaps speak out of turn."

"You are charged with lending aid and succor to a known criminal with a price on his head. The Fox was apprehended in your home while you stoutly defended him," the General accused.

"Mac is not the Fox. You have tried and condemned the wrong man."

A humorous snicker rippled through the room and grew into a wave of laughter. "So you say," sighed the General dryly. "It would save us all a lot of trouble, milady, if you would confess."

"I confess to nothing," persisted Alexa doggedly. "Mac is not the Fox. Ask my husband. He can attest to the truth of my words."

"We intend to, milady, if you force us to continue, and I can see you are determined to have your name besmirched in court."

"I have faith that all will be explained to your satisfaction and I will be judged innocent," declared Alexa with more conviction than she felt. Everyone, including herself, knew she was being made an example of and likely to hang beside the man wrongly assumed to be the Fox.

"Have it your way, Lady Foxworth," the General signalled wearily. "I will now call upon Captain Barrington to tell how he and his men followed Fox's bloody trail to your house."

Captain Barrington told his story convincingly of how he saw the Fox go overboard after he was wounded in the fierce fighting aboard *The Gray Ghost*. Following in a longboat, the search party spent hours trailing the wounded man to the Foxworth plantation.

"What did you find when you arrived and demanded entrance?" asked the General.

"At first Lady Foxworth refused to let us in, insisting she knew nothing about the Fox."

"Did you believe her?"

"No, sir," smiled Barrington wryly. "Not when I was standing in a pool of blood that proclaimed her guilt more clearly than words."

Barrington went on to describe how he found a wounded man in a bedroom and the mask worn by Fox in a trunk in the attic. When he finished he glanced triumphantly at Alexa and sat down with a flourish. Adam cursed beneath his breath, frowning darkly.

"What is your response, Lady Foxworth?" General Prevost inquired.

"General, you have to believe me," Alexa insisted urgently. "The man Captain Barrington found in my house is not the Fox. His name is Logan MacHugh, a friend to my husband.''

''How do you explain his wound?''

Alexa flushed. He certainly had her there. Mac was still a privateer even though he was not the Fox. ''I . . . I didn't ask,'' she supplied lamely.

''You didn't ask, I see,'' mocked the General, throwing up his arms in disgust. The room buzzed with amused laughter until the General raised his hand for silence.

''And the mask found hidden in the attic? Perhaps next you'll tell me it belongs to Lord Penwell and that he is the Fox.'' Raucous laughter met the General's well-placed jest and Alexa glanced quickly at Adam but he steadfastly refused to meet her eyes.

''I have no idea how that mask found its way into the attic. Perhaps it was meant for a masquerade,'' suggested Alexa amid hoots of amusement. ''And I would be the last person on earth to accuse my husband, Lord Penwell, of being the Fox, for no one knows better than I that he is not.'' Adam exhaled softly, unaware that he had been holding his breath.

''You are correct, Lady Foxworth, we have already tried and convicted the Fox and he certainly isn't Lord Penwell.''

After that Charles was asked to testify as to her character, since he was the person present who had known her the longest. As Alexa had expected, Charles painted a bleak picture indeed of her tarnished reputation. Alexa flinched when Charles launched headlong into the details of how she became Adam's mistress in England, conveniently omitting the important fact that Alexa had not done so willingly. What Charles did stress was that he and Alexa were to be married when she succumbed to Lord Penwell's persuasive charm and was subsequently disowned by her father when Adam tired of her and returned her to her father pregnant.

Shock and disbelief registered on the faces of those present, but surprisingly none of it was directed at Adam. When asked to respond to Charles's charges, Alexa bit her lip and shook her head, declining. What could she say that was not already said? At any moment she expected Adam to jump up to defend her honor but to her acute embarrassment he remained seated, seemingly unmoved. Rage and hate combined to lend her courage when she heard General Prevost call Adam to testify next.

"Lord Penwell," General Prevost asked, "were you aware of your wife's seditious sentiment when you married her?"

Turning to face Alexa, Adam's silver-gray eyes bore relentlessly into her violet ones. To many of the spectators they appeared to reflect his contempt for his wife. But to Alexa they told another story. Was he trying to convey to her that she should take courage? That he had not abandoned her no matter how it might appear? But his cold words and stern visage soon disabused her of that notion.

"Though reluctantly, I must admit, General, that my wife championed the American cause many times in my hearing," Adam said slowly.

Alexa gasped, and whispered softly, "Oh, Adam, how could you?"

Adam turned a deaf ear on her softly spoken words as he continued with cruel deliberation. "As you are well aware, I was necessarily gone from my home for long periods of time and had little or no knowledge of what went on in my absence."

"We heard your testimony, Lord Penwell, as to your relationship to the man you knew as Mac but who in reality is the Fox. Do you believe Lady Foxworth had an . . . er . . . intimate involvement with the Fox?"

Fixing Alexa with an inscrutable look, Adam replied, "I

believe the Fox to be in love with my wife."

Upon hearing Adam's damning words, Alexa's frail shoulders slumped dejectedly. Once again Adam was struck by the fragility of her slim form. He knew her to be near the end of her tether and he dropped his eyes to conceal the extent of the pain he felt at her ordeal. Hang on, Alexa, he silently encouraged. Don't give up now. There's too much to lose.

As if receiving his telepathic message, Alexa straightened her spine, glaring defiantly at the avid spectators and her judges so eager to condemn her. "You may sit down, my lord," the General told Adam. "I know how painful this must be for you but your own loyalty was never suspect."

Governor Wright was the last person called upon to testify and he but repeated the careless words spoken by Alexa months ago at the General's reception. When the Governor sat down, General Prevost asked, "Have you anything to say in your own defense, Lady Foxworth?" Alexa shook her head negatively. What good would it do when there was no one to come to her aid? "If not, I am prepared to pass judgment."

Immediately Alexa came to attention, her breath caught painfully somewhere between her lungs and her windpipe. So soon? How could they come to an agreement so soon? But to the spectators watching with avid anticipation, there was never a doubt as to the final outcome.

"The charge against you is a serious one," the General drawled tonelessly. "You are the daughter of a nobleman, the wife of an earl, and yet you chose to disregard your upbringing and deliberately set out to betray your country.

"Your high station in life does not absolve you of guilt nor should it sway our judgment in any way. There is only one sentence I can render, and that is to find you guilty of treason." Looking to his fellow officers seated beside him, he duly noted and recorded their silent nods of agreement. "As you can see the jury is in complete agreement with my findings."

Alexa let out her breath slowly as pandemonium reigned in the courtroom. Expecting to be found guilty is one thing, hearing it is another. Inexplicably her eyes found Adam's, catching him in the odd moment before he had a chance to disguise his feelings. To her dismay she found pity and compassion lurking in their silvery depths, and a hint of something she could not define. And then her attention turned to the General who signalled for silence.

"There can be but one punishment for treason and that is death. Lady Foxworth, you are to be taken at dawn two days hence and hung by the neck until dead! The traitor you took into your home shall hang beside you. May God have mercy upon your souls."

A great hush fell upon the room as all eyes concentrated on the beautiful, slender woman whose existence was to be terminated in the prime of life. The truth to tell, there were many present who considered it a waste to kill such a lovely creature and Alexa felt grateful for their groans of commiseration. But mostly she was too numb to react. Two days! She had but two days to breathe the air, to dream of the future that would never be, to consider the fickle love of the man who had betrayed her.

Instinctively Alexa knew that had Fox learned what was happening to her things would be different. But she had no way of knowing whether Fox was dead or alive. Imprisoned as she had been these last weeks she had heard nothing of his exploits. Alexa's thoughts were immediately curtailed when she heard her name spoken by the General.

"Have you anything to say, Lady Foxworth?"

Alexa was about to shake her head when she thought better of it. Why should she not speak her mind? What more could they do to her? Certainly not hang her twice. Resolutely she stood to her meager height, turning to face her delighted audience. Her face had gone dead white, and she had to clasp her hands tightly together to keep them from shaking, but her voice was strong and steady, laced with a courage that came from somewhere within her soul.

"What you are doing is wrong," she said in a low but steady tone. "Not only what you are doing to me but to America as a country and her brave people. I freely admit I admire freedom, and courage, and the will to survive against all adversity. But that is the only crime I confess to. Hang me if you will, for I shall become but another martyr to justice and freedom."

Alexa was startled to hear cheers ring throughout the room and wondered if Adam was one of those encouraging her. He was, but only in his mind and heart. Never had he admired or loved Alexa more. If only there were some way to make her aware of his feelings, Adam reflected miserably. But with Gwen suspicious of his every move there was no safe way to approach Alexa. Against his will he was forced to stand by helplessly as Alexa was roughly hustled from the courtroom and into a waiting carriage.

Her supper lay untouched on the table, just where Bates had placed it when he carried it in. Usually he just shoved it through the opening, but this time he chose to enter Alexa's damp cell in order to torment her.

"Didn't I warn you you'd end up swinging from a rope?" he jeered crudely. "You don't have much time left, milady. You have only to say the word and I'd be more than happy to ease your last hours.''

Alexa let him ramble on, too numb to react to his taunts. Eliciting no reaction from Alexa, Bates finally gave up and left her in peace. Somehow, amidst her scattered thoughts of Adam's cruel rejection and Fox's failure to appear at the last minute to save her, Alexa slept. And when she awoke she had but one day left to live.

She thought of many things to do the last day of her life, but did none of them. She wanted to write to Mary Forbes and tell her goodbye; to let Adam know that she had truly loved him once; to explain to Fox that if it were possible to love two men, then he was surely one of them.

Automatically she washed and ate, and the day passed. No one came to bid her farewell; whether by choice or by order, she had no way of knowing. Had she been more aware of what went on around her Alexa would have noted the sly look Bates gave her whenever he passed her cell and glanced through the grille. But Alexa was too miserable to notice the pecularities of her guards.

Somewhere from the depths of her memory she conjured up the image of Fox; Fox making love to her for the first time; Fox coming to her when she was desperately ill; Fox telling her he loved her but advising her to cling to her husband. From there her bleak ruminations settled on Adam, the husband who had proved undeserving of her love.

From the very beginning Alexa knew she meant nothing more to Adam than a means to an end. Oh, it was true enough he was never deliberately cruel to her, though he might have wished to be it was not in his nature to be abusive to a woman, and he soon had her yearning for his lovemaking. He was a consummate lover, considerate, thorough, tender. When she had finally discovered her love for him he sent her back to her father and an ignominious fate while he hastened back to Savannah to marry another woman.

The final blow had come when Adam refused to come to her aid. His cruel rejection proclaimed his complete disinterest in her and her plight. This coming as it did on the heels of his recent confession of love made his refutation all the more painful. But it did not matter now. Nothing did, for at dawn tomorrow her life would end before it had really begun.

When Bates carried in her second meal of the day Alexa knew her time on earth was running out. She grew suspicious when he did not leave immediately, but stood back, silently appraising her. Alexa paid him no heed until abruptly he grasped her by her slim shoulders.

"In hours you will die, milady, and I have yet to see anyone come to your defense or offer you comfort," he said, devouring her with his beady eyes. "And at this late hour it looks as if no one will."

Alexa pulled away but his strength overpowered her. "Take your filthy hands off me."

"You think you're too good for the likes of old Bates, eh? Well, milady, I'm all you've got, like it or not."

"I need no one, and certainly not you!" Alexa flung out insultingly.

"I've been patient for weeks," Bates hinted nastily, "but no longer. I've sent Grubbs out on an errand so I could have you first. If he protests too much I'll share you with him when he returns. Meanwhile, milady, lay down on the cot and spread your legs; you won't be hurt if you do as I say."

"You're mad!" spat Alexa, backing away from the menacing brute whose mind was set on rape.

"Mad with desire, milady." Bates grinned, pursuing her across the room. "And tired of waiting."

Lunging forward, Bates caught Alexa's skirt, ripping it away from the bodice, and Alexa screamed, looking toward the open door as she visibly assessed her chances of escape. "Don't try it, milady. I'm faster and stronger than you are."

The words had no sooner left his mouth than he grasped her by the waist and flung her roughly on the cot where she bounced once on the hard surface before Bates pinned her in place with his considerable bulk. He attempted to kiss her but Alexa's head whipped wildly back and forth, denying him access to her lips. Alexa felt herself weakening but was determined to resist as long as a breath remained in her body.

And then Alexa felt his weight leave her as a growl of outrage rent the still, damp air. "You bastard! What do you think you're doing?" Alexa recognized the voice immediately. Adam had finally come!

"This woman still bears my name," Adam declared with angry indignation, "and I won't have her treated in such a vile manner. Do I make myself clear?"

Picking his bruised body off of the floor, Bates abruptly realized who it was he faced. "I was only having a little fun, Lord Penwell," Bates whined obsequiously. "I didn't mean nothing by it."

"We both know what you were attempting to do," Adam contended harshly. "Or," his gray eyes narrowed dangerously, "has this been going on since Lady Foxworth was placed in your care?"

"No . . . no!" denies Bates quickly. "This is the first time, I swear it!" Fear clutched at his vitals the moment he saw the murderous look in Adam's steely gaze.

Adam glanced at Alexa for verification. "Alexa, is what this man says true?"

Still lying in a daze where Bates had flung her, Alexa

217

nodded, then found her voice. "They—Bates, here, and Grubbs, tried to . . . to . . . but they were unsuccessful."

"Was he 'successful' tonight?" he asked, the menace in his voice apparent.

Alexa shook her head and Adam sighed audibly. "Lady Foxworth has just saved your worthless hide, Bates. Now get the hell out of here. I wish to visit with my wife in private."

"Of course, my lord, of course." Bates bowed, backing toward the door.

"I fully intend to appear before dawn tomorrow and should I learn from Lady Foxworth that you've molested her during her last hours, I'll kill you. Is that understood?"

"Perfectly." Bates nodded, moving with alacrity from the cell in order to escape Adam's threatening glare. He had no wish to tangle with the vengeful lord. In his haste to leave he nearly backed into a small, veiled figure standing in the doorway.

The woman sidled into the cell, stopped beside Adam and slowly raised her veil. Until then Alexa had no idea Adam had not come alone. She gasped in shock and outrage when Gwen revealed her smiling features. Immediately Alexa's violet gaze slid to Adam, searching his face intently, her contempt for him clearly visible.

"Why didn't you let Bates have her, Adam?" Gwen asked innocently. "After all, she's as good as dead. Perhaps she might have enjoyed it."

Adam glared at Gwen, effectively silencing her. "No matter what Alexa has done she doesn't deserve to be treated in a despicable manner. As long as a breath remains in her body she is Lady Foxworth and shall be treated accordingly." He regarded Gwen coldly. "I thought I told you to wait outside."

Adam tried desperately to rid himself of Gwen so he could visit Alexa in private but she had attached herself to him like a leech, refusing to be parted from him for a moment. In the end he was forced to bring her along, hoping she would obey him and wait outside while he talked to Alexa. But it was not to be, and he gritted his teeth in frustration.

"I was lonesome out there," Gwen whined. "Do hurry, Adam, and make your farewells. It's so . . . so . . . dreary in here and I'm anxious to leave."

"I'll leave when I'm good and ready, Gwen," Adam declared icily, turning back to Alexa, "and not before."

"Are you all right, Alexa?"

Alexa nodded her head. "You arrived in time, Adam. Thank you for that much. What I would like to know is why you bothered to come at all?"

Adam flushed. He deserved that, and more. If only he could talk with Alexa alone, explain to her, tell her of his plans. But with Gwen hanging on to his every word there was nothing he could do to ease her tortured mind.

"I couldn't let you go without telling you goodbye. One day we will meet again," he hinted meaningfully.

"In the hereafter, no doubt," laughed Alexa harshly, completely missing his point. "Your farewell is duly noted, Adam, now you may leave, your conscience salved."

"Alexa, if only . . ."

"Oh, for God's sake, Adam, don't get maudlin," Gwen interrupted derisively. "The woman is a traitor, you owe her nothing."

Cursing beneath his breath, Adam tried to convey with his eyes all that he wanted to say but couldn't, bemoaning the fates that refused to cooperate with his plans. First, Gwen had insisted on accompanying him, then he arrived to find Alexa in danger of being raped. And now, there was little chance for him to tell her all she needed to know. He was forced to place his trust in God and pray that everything went according to plan, and that Alexa cooperated without his instructions.

Adam wavered halfway between speaking out before Gwen no matter what the consequences and leaving Alexa thinking he had abandoned her, when Bates, bolstered by Grubbs's considerable bulk, appeared in the doorway.

"Lord or no, I've got my orders," Bates grumbled spitefully. "Ten minutes are all you're allowed. You'll have to leave."

Cursing the fates that created women like Gwen and men like Bates, Adam nodded curtly. But instead of following Gwen from the cell he hesitated a moment and strode swiftly to Alexa's side. Taking her stiffened body into his arms as if to kiss her goodbye, he whispered urgently into her ear, "Have faith, all is not lost." Then he did kiss her, putting into it all the things he could not tell her.

The kiss lasted a long time, demanding, needing one last taste, and Alexa responded without willing it. His tongue curled into her mouth, drawing from it a measure of her unique essence. He wanted never to let her go, to protect her forever. Instead, he must place her into another's keeping. Exerting tremendous will, Adam drew away. As he turned to leave Alexa imagined him to say, "Be brave. I love you." Then he was gone.

Through the stillness surrounding her she heard Gwen complaining bitterly. "Was that necessary, Adam darling?" She did not hear Adam's response for just then the cell door closed with a resounding bang.

Immersed in grief, Alexa failed to comprehend Adam's last words. She remembered only his kiss and the feel of his arms around her. She also recalled his eyes upon her in that brief moment before he turned to leave. It was almost as if his eyes were forming a picture his memory would carry forever. Tears blurred her vision as she realized that she would never see Adam again. Perhaps that was the reason for his probing look and strange words, she thought bleakly.

One thing Alexa could not forget or forgive was that Adam had seen fit to bring Gwen with him tonight. The indignity of his callous disregard for her feelings left her numb and withdrawn. The most she could say for Adam's unexpected visit was that it arrived at a most propitious time, or else Bates would most certainly have raped her. Her stomach heaved in revulsion as she thought of that terrible moment when he nearly had his way with her.

Alexa collapsed heavily on the dingy cot that had served as her bed these past weeks, afraid to sleep, for dawn was but hours away and she wished to savor fully the last moments of her life. Memories both sweet and sad flooded her mind as she relived those moments most dear to her. Somehow, against all odds, Alexa nodded off sometime during the wee hours of morning.

Somewhere in the dark recesses of her mind Alexa noted and recorded the commotion outside her cell, but was too lost in her subconscious reminscing to respond. She lay as one already dead and so did not react immediately to the creaking hinges when the heavy oak door opened. Nor did the sudden appearance of light in her dark cell register upon her befuddled brain. It was the voice that brought her out of her slumberous state. Low, raspy, with a huskiness she would recognize anywhere. Fox!

"Alexa, wake up!"

"Fox! Oh my God! You have come for me!"

"Aye, my love. Hurry now, we haven't much time."

Moving with alacrity, Alexa asked, "Where are the guards? Where are you taking me?"

"The guards are . . . taken care of," Fox rasped as he tenderly wrapped her cloak about her thin shoulders. "As for our destination—the sea, my love. Come along, we must be gone before dawn."

"Wait! What about Mac? We can't leave without him!"

"My men have already seen to him. They await us at the docks."

On their way out Alexa spied her two guards lying in a corner trussed up and gagged. She smiled as Fox, in a parting gesture of contempt, drew a mask from his belt similar to the one he wore and carelessly dropped it beside the two men. Then, taking Alexa's slim hand he led her into the dim light of predawn.

13

Guided by Fox, *The Gray Ghost* cautiously slipped through the English ships lining the harbor as noiselessly as she had entered. Painted entirely gray to blend with the sea and the horizon, sporting gray sails, she quickly left behind Savannah's white-bluffed port. Alexa knew of no other man who would dare such a brazen feat. To sneak into port in the dead of night beneath the very noses of the English took a courage few men possessed. But hadn't Fox always exuded matchless confidence and an undeniable contempt for danger? she reflected as she watched the dark water speed by. A tangible air of brute strength clung to him, making him appear larger than life.

Once they had left the Governor's mansion Fox led her along the dark streets on foot, keeping well to the shadows. Twice they were passed by patrols and Alexa held her breath while she and Fox slipped into a doorway to escape discovery. With Fox's large frame shielding her she felt protected and safe. Never for a minute did she doubt his ability to defend her with his life.

Within a surprisingly short time they approached the dock and Fox unerringly led her to a long pier, the last one in a line of many. He called out softly and the bow of a small boat appeared from beneath the dock where it evidently had been waiting for Fox's signal. Alexa was carefully handed down, followed by Fox, and then a pair of oars cut silently through the murky water as they glided forward with a stealth a cat would envy.

An emotional moment ensued when Alexa discovered Mac to be one of the passengers on the boat. She greeted him with a kiss and tears in her eyes, none of which were lost on a glowering Fox.

It was not until the *Ghost* safely navigated the Savannah River that Alexa sought out Mac in the cabin where he had been taken. Still pale and weak, he nevertheless greeted her exuberantly.

"I thought never to see you again in this world, Mac," Alexa said softly, searching his dear face anxiously. How thin and haggard he looked, she thought worriedly. His face was nearly as pale as her own and it was obvious he had not been fed nearly as well. That he had survived at all was a miracle.

"If only I had been allowed to see you, Alexa, I would have told you all was not lost," revealed Mac with a hint of the old twinkle in his eyes. "Surely you didn't think Fox would let us die, did you?"

Alexa shook her head. "No, but after what you told me Fox could have been seriously injured, or even dead."

"He was injured, Alexa," Mac informed her. "He stayed with a 'safe' family who would not betray him, remaining until he recovered. That's why he was so long in coming. He knew nothing of our plight until a chance visitor mentioned the trial."

"Thank God," breathed Alexa unsteadily. "Fox did what my husband failed to do. Adam would have let us die, Mac, and never raised a hand in our behalf."

"You are wrong, Alexa," Mac shocked her by saying. "Adam arrived in Savannah only days before our trials. When he found out I was to be tried, that the English thought me to be the Fox, he immediately set out to find the real Fox and advise him of our predicament. As it turned out," he smiled mysteriously, "they sort of found each other."

"Are you certain, Mac?" Alexa questioned, openly skeptical. "Not once did Adam visit me or show concern for either of us, until the night before I was to die. And he took up with Gwen again the moment I was out of the picture."

"Believe me, Alexa, Adam had his reasons for the way he behaved. He did not abandon us, as you might think. He was frantic over your plight. Did you truly think he'd stand idly by and let them hang you?"

"Aye," declared Alexa stubbornly.

"By now you should be aware that Adam is the man responsible for our escape. Both he and Fox planned our rescue."

"How do you know all this?" asked Alexa suspiciously.

"When Adam came to visit you last night he passed by my cell and pretended to stop and jeer at me," Mac explained. "What he did was to drop a note to me through the grille while the guards were busy leering at Gwen. So you see she did serve a purpose. The rest I learned from Fox and his men."

"Then you knew Fox was coming."

"Aye, Adam's note explained everything, albeit briefly."

"How can I forgive him for allowing me to think he had abandoned me?" Alexa exclaimed, thoroughly incensed. "In fact, I'm uncertain whether I'll ever talk to him again!"

"You'll see him again, Alexa," predicted Mac cryptically, "and you'll talk to him. Until that day arrives I'll leave it to him to explain everything to you."

It wasn't until the next day that Alexa was given the opportunity to speak privately with Fox. She had slept around the clock when she finally went to bed in the comfortable cabin assigned to her. She awoke to find a tray of food placed next to her bunk. Famished, she gobbled her breakfast, dressed hurriedly, and rushed topside in order to savor the brilliant sunshine, something she had seen precious little of these past weeks. From the bridge Fox watched covertly as Alexa raised her pale face toward the welcome rays. His breath caught painfully in his throat as he drank in her fragile beauty.

She was small and slim, yet her body was rounded and firm. The thick mass of her midnight black hair spread about her shoulders like a rich cloak and framed a face that haunted his dreams. Her skin was a startling white, like fine porcelain, except for the soft pink of her lips. He knew her pallor was due to her imprisonment and he cursed the English for damaging her fragile beauty and undermining her health. He fervently wished he could make up to her all she had suffered on his account.

Her magnetism was so intense that Fox felt himself drawn to her side. Turning the wheel over to Fowler, his first mate, he approached Alexa quietly so as not to startle her. But Alexa, not immune to the mystique surrounding Fox, immediately sensed his presence.

"I haven't properly thanked you for saving my life," Alexa said, turning to face him. She saw he still wore the mask that left his mouth and chin exposed and a black bandana tied about his head pirate style. Alexa experienced a keen disappointment that she was still not to see his face.

"No need, milady," Fox rasped with a flourish. "Had I known sooner I would have saved you those weeks in jail. That couldn't have been too pleasant for you."

"No," admitted Alexa softly, "it wasn't." Anxious to change the subject, she said, "Mac told me *The Gray Ghost* was badly damaged, yet she looks fine to me."

"The original *Ghost* was sunk by the English when they set the trap for us..This ship is a British frigate I took as a prize and outfitted to resemble the old *Ghost*," Fox explained. "She's graceful and nearly as swift, and I have no complaint with her."

"Mac said you were wounded."

"Aye, I took a ball in the shoulder and another in the thigh. I was a long time recovering."

"At a 'safe' house, Mac told me. I take it to mean a patriot aided you."

"Aye. I was lucky. I made it to shore and was found by a colonist who hid me until . . . until your husband found me."

"So it's true. Adam did seek your help." Alexa expressed her disbelief. "Judging from his lack of concern for me I assumed he did not care what happened to me or to Mac. I'm surprised you agreed to help him knowing he is a royalist. Weren't you afraid he would turn you in?"

"No, milady. Adam and I have an . . . understanding which I am not at liberty to reveal at this time. Suffice it to say I know Adam Foxworth well enough to trust him."

"This is all so hard for me to understand," Alexa reflected, shaking her head in defeat.

"One day you'll be told everything, milady, that I promise," vowed Fox in his throaty whisper.

"At this moment I'm of the opinion that nothing Adam

can do or say will placate me. It was despicable of him to deceive me by deliberately allowing me to believe I was about to die. If I never see Adam again it will be too soon."

Through the narrow eyeslits of his mask, Fox searched her face, frowning as he waged a battle within himself. The fight must have been a fierce one for his knuckles turned white where he gripped the rail. Finally his face cleared as his better judgment won out, visibly relaxing as Alexa regarded him curiously. The time for revelations had not yet arrived, he decided abruptly. Declining to respond to Alexa's harsh judgment of her husband, he shrugged and stared out to sea.

"Where are you taking me?" Alexa finally asked, realizing she would learn nothing more about Adam from Fox.

"To Nassau, in the Bahamas," Fox revealed. "You'll be safe enough there. It's in American hands now and I keep a fully staffed house on the island as a sort of home base. I'll see that you're well taken care of."

"Fox, take me with you," begged Alexa suddenly. "Teach me to sail, and to fight, so that I might join your battle."

Astounded, Fox looked into Alexa's glowing face alight with the fires of a personal commitment. It was obvious to him she seriously meant every word she spoke. She was willing to risk all to fight and die for a cause she had readily embraced as her own. Love and pride swelled his heart, but he could not allow her to make that sacrifice.

"No, milady." He shook his head emphatically. "I will not allow you to endanger your life in such a foolhardy venture."

"Why? Because I am a woman?" Her violet eyes defied him, challenged him, but he would not rise to the bait.

"Exactly," he rasped, amused. "I want you safe—I want you—my God!" he croaked hoarsely, unable to continue. He wanted her! Yes, in his life, in his bed, forever. Retreating behind closed lips, Fox clamped his mouth tightly shut, refusing to speak further.

Alexa felt the heavy weight of his disapproval but remained undaunted as she stubbornly continued. "You know I can't return to the colonies, Fox, and I'd be bored sitting out the war in Nassau. I'd be safe with you, and I'd be a part of the fight for freedom. Please, Fox," she begged, her eyes sparkling as she warmed to the subject, "let me stay aboard the *Ghost*."

"It's out of the question, Alexa," he retorted, gritting his teeth in frustration. Though he greatly admired her courage he feared more for her safety. "I'll not hear another word on the subject. You're going to Nassau whether you like it or not. Do you think Adam would thank me should I allow you your way in this?"

"He probably wouldn't care at all," sulked Alexa.

"You're wrong, Alexa. Adam would care a great deal." Almost angrily he turned and walked away, leaving her to brood in silence.

Even Mac refused to listen to her pleas. His own ship, the *Lady* A awaited him in Nassau where it had been undergoing extensive repairs, and Mac intended to enter into the fray again as soon as it was provisioned. He was rapidly regaining his strength and the sun and fresh air worked miracles in restoring him to his former vigor.

To Alexa's chagrin Mac did not take seriously her rantings concerning her desire to fight the English in the same way he and Fox did. If he had known then just how serious she as he would hve listened more closely. As it was he merely shook his head and mumbled something about her safety whenever she broached the subject.

To keep peace Alexa desisted but did not give up. She

continued to plan and scheme, determined to find a way to join the patriots in their fight instead of languishing in Nassau only to worry and fret over the fate of those she cared about.

Two days out of Savannah they encountered an English merchant ship. It was an older vessel, heavy with cargo and no match for the fleeter *Ghost*. Though the British sailors waged a brave battle they were subdued in short order while Alexa was forced to remain below deck out of harm's way, all the while fuming with impotent rage. Why should men be the only ones allowed to defend their country? she bemoaned silently. Why, given the proper training and practice she wagered she could be every bit as good as any one of Fox's men.

Alexa was allowed out of her cabin only after the English crew was set adrift in boats to make their own way to land. She watched in silence, her fertile brain awhirl with ideas as the *Ghost* fired and sank the merchantman. Fox explained that it was too old to be of any value, and Mac concurred.

That night a celebration was held in Fox's cabin attended by Mac and Alexa. They had much to celebrate, it seemed. The hold of the merchantman contained valuable medicines much needed by the patriots as well as guns and ammunition. From the captain's cabin Fox confiscated two trunks packed to the brim with woman's clothing, which he promptly presented to Alexa. Eagerly sorting through them she found them to be elegant and expensively made of the finest materials. Most remarkable was the fact that Alexa had to do very little altering. She wore one of the gowns that night.

Fashioned in violet silk the gown bared her gently sloping shoulders and the upper portion of her breasts, forced upward by the stays of her corset nearly to their pale rose aureoles. The tight waist spanned her nineteen inches and belled out over a deep purple satin petticoat. At intervals the skirt was caught up by violet rosettes to show the intricate embroidery of the underskirt. Alexa felt very elegant in the gown and she was not the only one to think so. Mac appeared entranced and neither he nor Fox seemed able to take their eyes from her shapely form.

Shortly after their meal had concluded, Mac slyly excused himself, his excuse being that he had agreed to take the next watch. Alexa was a little startled by the abruptness of his departure but what truly annoyed her was the manner in which he took his leave. Grinning from ear to ear, his eyes twinkling with amusement, he said, "Enjoy your night, Alexa." Then he was gone, chuckling beneath his breath at Alexa's perplexed frown.

Turning to Fox, she asked, "What on earth did he mean by that?"

Fox shrugged. "It's hard to say. I'm not always privy to Mac's thoughts. But enough of Mac, you look lovely tonight, my love," he whispered softly as his eyes kindled with desire.

Against her will Alexa felt herself respond to the seduction he was weaving about her. "It's the dress," she said slowly. "It was good of you to think of me. My wardrobe left much to be desired."

"I would drape you in silks and satins and adorn you in jewels if you were mine," Fox rasped huskily.

"Fox, please," replied Alexa nervously. Though she had consumed only two glasses of wine she felt her world tilt crazily. From across the table their eyes met and held.

His masculine perfection took her breath away. Below the mask he wore, the sensuous curve of his lips and flash of white teeth gave him a rakish charm she found hard to resist. Fox sensed her intense perusal and rose unsteadily to his feet, passion and need driving him to Alexa's side. Lifting his hands he cupped her bare shoulders as he gently raised her from her chair. Then he slid his palms downward over her upper arms, taking the small sleeves of her dress with him. He extended his thumbs, letting them roam over the tops of her breasts, pushing the tight, constricting fabric down, out of his way. With a small cry Alexa lifted her arms to encircle his neck and her breasts tumbled free.

Fox groaned and swept her into his arms, burying his face in the soft mounds. "Fox, this isn't right!" Alexa cried out. "I'm a married woman!"

"Don't deny me, Alexa, I need you so. To me you are my beloved wife—in spirit if not in name," he quickly amended. "I know you want me as much as I want you."

And then the moist tip of his tongue began its soft sorcery, gently inserting itself between her closed lips and sliding leisurely along them. She was not made of steel, how could she resist the magic the strong appeal he had always held for her? Sighing softly in surrender, she melted into his embrace.

Unable to think beyond the moment, Alexa soon found herself lying in the center of the oversized bunk, trembling with an excitement she was hard-pressed to conceal. She could feel his uneven breathing on her cheek as he settled beside her and held her close. Slowly his hands explored the hollows of her back, her breasts, and against her will she locked herself into his embrace. The sudden magnitude of their passion left them both shaken.

With trembling hands he finished undressing her, savoring every inch of her smooth satiny skin. And then he disrobed himself except for his mask. When his mouth captured one breast and his hands the other, Alexa could not suppress the moan of ecstasy that escaped her throat. Her passion sparking his own, Fox seized her lips, pleasure spiraling through her as his tongue teased hers in a kiss so deep that she was filled with the taste of his magical touch.

His voice a husky purr, Fox whispered, "Touch me, Alexa, touch me with love."

Obeying blindly, Alexa ran her hands experimentally along the broad expanse of his back, down a narrow hip, across a muscular flank and back again where they lost themselves in the curly hair at the nape of his neck below the bandana he wore to cover his hair. Unthinkingly, Alexa tore off the offending cloth in order to allow her hands free access to the thick locks that heretofore had been forbidden her touch. But the wonder of the discovery was lost to her as his tongue flicked across her ribs, setting her afire. Then he found the center of her need and explored it until she was gasping, moaning, calling to him to set her free.

His hands grasping her buttocks to hold her in place, Fox relentlessly plied his mouth and tongue, teasing, exciting, until the pain-pleasure became too much to endure and she exploded with a savage cry of pure delight that spilled out through the porthole to be lost on the crest of rushing water. Rising up he parted her thighs with his knees and entered her slowly, the hard proof of his virility hot and full in her velvet sheath.

"Come with me, my love," he urged, thrusting until she gasped with delight. She started to speak but her words died as he kissed her and were replaced by a shuddering sigh. "Feel my need?" he groaned into her ear. "I'm near bursting with desire. Only for you, my love, only for you."

Once again Alexa felt the tension building within her,

and sensing this, Fox met the fires within her with flames of his own as he grasped her buttocks, pulling her more firmly against his pounding loins. She met his thrusts joyously until the trembling began and waves of rapture convulsed her sweat-drenched body. Shouting his joy, Fox joined her in their spiraling journey beyond the sea and the sky.

Resting side by side as they caught their breath, Alexa reflected upon everything that had just transpired between her and Fox. It was a magical moment. A moment out of time and space where nothing or no one existed but the two of them passionately entwined on the oversized bunk. For a short time Fox had made her world right, inspiring her with all the love and tenderness she had always craved. But it could not continue, she was married to Adam and belonged to him until one of them should die.

Plumbing the depths of her heart Alexa realized that she was in love with two men. Men who were alike in many ways yet vastly different. Alexa found little comfort in the fact that she hadn't meant to betray Adam with Fox, but that knowledge did little to assuage her guilt. Her straying thoughts abruptly evaporated as Fox boldly turned her toward him and slowly began to explore her body in a manner that soon left her gasping with desire.

Alexa closed her eyes and Fox softly kissed the dark lashes that lay like a thick, even scattering of cinders upon her downy cheek. Lovingly he caressed the black hair that streamed over the pillow and atop her breasts like an ebony river. And then he was inside her, claiming her again with all the vigor of a youth about to possess his first woman.

With each movement her body began to pulsate with sweet, tormenting pleasure until she was engulfed in a

maddening rush to attain the summit. When she reached
the crest she waited but a moment for Fox to join her.

Sleep came, deep, satisfying, reviving. But for some
unexplained reason Alexa awoke but a scant hour or
two later. The lamp that ealier had lit their supper had
finally sputtered out and the cabin was cast in darkness
deeper than the depths of hell. But something bothered
Alexa, some little detail that nagged at the corners of
her brain. Abruptly she remembered. Fox's hair! Driven
to mindless passion she remembered that she had torn
off his head covering in order to score his thick locks
with her fingers. Suddenly her fingers twitched with the
need to do so again. To feel those crisp curls against her
palm, so familiar, yet, how could they be?

Then, a rumble of thunder startled Alexa, followed by
a searing blaze of lightening that illuminated the cabin
with its eerie glow. Alexa rose on one elbow to look at
Fox, fearing that the flash had awakened him. But
evidently he was so exhausted from his clash with the
English merchantman earlier that day and from his
vigorous lovemaking that he was oblivious to everything
but the sleep that claimed him.

When the next bolt of lightening scored the heavens,
Alexa found herself plunged into the grip of shock more
profound than the most hideous nightmare. Somehow,
while they were both caught up in passion, Fox's mask
had become dislodged and lay beside him on the pillow.
His face, relaxed in sleep, was as familiar to her as her
own. Her rage—clawing, all consuming—was so intense
it threatened to destroy her. Looking back, Alexa
realized her heart must have known all along what her
mind refused to accept.

There was a certain strength revealed in the hard
planes of his face and the mocking tilt of his brow. His
hair was a thick lion's main of burnished gold and even

in sleep his sensuous lips invited her kisses. Adam and Fox! The same man! If Adam loved her why couldn't he have confided in her? Love is giving yourself, your thoughts, your trust, not just your body.

A feeling akin to hatred rose up like bile to choke her. She thought of her long repressed stirrings of guilt over her belief that she loved two men, that she had allowed Fox to creep unbidden into her heart. She wanted to awaken him, to lash out, to kick, to scream, to curse. But she did none of them, too befuddled to lift a finger in retaliation. She supposed Mac knew, and wondered how many others were aware that the Fox and Adam Foxworth were the same person. His name should have given her a clue but in her mind she could not equate the staunch royalist with the fierce patriot. Evidently, neither had anyone else.

She would pay him back in kind, Alexa silently vowed, for forcing her to unwittingly become a part of his charade. Someday she would find a way to punish him for deceiving her. Alexa wavered between waking him so she might confront him with his deception and allowing him to continue with his ruse, pretending ignorance. Suddenly a thought occurred to her and she smiled deviously. Two can play at the same game, Adam/Fox. She grinned impishly. Was not a vixen more cunning than a fox? Alexa stifled a giggle, more set than ever upon finding a way to tame a fox.

Curving her small body into that of Adam/Fox, Alexa allowed sleep to claim her. When he awoke her near dawn to brand her with his love once again, she did not protest, allowng him to think that she welcomed the embraces of a man other than her husband. As Adam, he no doubt felt a certain jealousy for Fox, knowing that his wife gave of herself so freely, without a thought to her legal husband. And as Fox, he could not help but entertain the thought that the woman he professed to love was not totally his.

On the heels of her astounding discovery came the demise of the woman known as Alexa, and from her ashes rose the Vixen, older, stronger, wiser. Beware!

BOOK TWO

THE VIXEN

14

Booted feet planted firmly on the quarterdeck, that honored elevation on the stern that represented the captain's authority, soft breezes ruffling her long blond tresses, the Vixen's violet eyes skimmed the horizon. She had traveled over many roads during the past six months; progressing from the lady named Alexa, unsuspecting victim of men's whims, to the Vixen, leader of men, captain of her own ship, *My Lady Vixen*, scourge of the English. She laughed softly, a low mirthless chuckle that caused the men working nearby to eye her curiously.

To a man, *My Lady Vixen*'s crew would have laid down their lives for their beautiful captain who led them so fearlessly against the enemy. Foremost among them was her first mate, Drake, who had once been Mac's right-hand man aboard the *Lady* A but who now served her so well.

News of the war was not good as the new year of 1780

began. The British victoriously swept up through North and South Carolina. In September and October of 1779 General Benjamin Lincoln was unsuccessful in ousting General Prevost from Savannah despite the help of French naval and military forces under Admiral d'Estaing, and he fell back to Charleston. In this assault the valiant Count Casimer Pulaski, on the American side, was mortally wounded.

Of some encouragement was word that the Whig population scattered, though without much organization, and formed into groups of riflemen and mounted troops to harass the enemy with little mercy shown by either side. Though casualties on both sides were fearsome, daring and skillful leaders such as Francis Marion and Thomas Sumter kept the spirit of resistance alive by their sudden attacks and surprises on British outposts. And so the war continued, joined by yet another brave patriot, the Vixen.

Mesmerized by the steady rise and fall of the ship beneath her bare legs encased in short, cut-off trousers, Alexa traveled back six months to the day the *Ghost* sailed into Nassau. Two days previously she had inadvertently discovered that her own husband, Adam, was the man known as Fox. Hurt and enraged, she vowed she would one day pay him back in kind. Not even Mac was safe from her plotting, for he too had lent credence to Adam's lie. For the time being it suited Alexa's purposes to keep her secret, allowing Fox his deception.

Guiltless now that she realized she had not allowed a man other than her husband to make love to her, Alexa welcomed Fox to her bed following the first night they had come together so passionately, shocking Fox with her ardor. Alexa chuckled whenever she recalled his puzzled frown at her eagerness to bed him while seeming to forget her husband completely. When, on their last night together, Fox asked, "Do you love me, Alexa?" she was quick to reply without a moment's hesitation, "Aye, I love you, Fox."

"More than Adam? Do you love me more than your husband?" Alexa could feel his breathlessness as he awaited her answer, and she smiled sardonically, wondering what perversity would cause a man like Fox to ask such a question knowing either way he was bound to lose. What devils drove this strong, arrogant man? she wondered.

Her answer stunned him and sent him storming from her cabin in a fit of pique. "It depends on whose bed I'm in when I'm asked," Alexa replied sweetly, her wide violet eyes innocent of guile. The Fox had no way of knowing that out of the mouth of a lady came the words of a vixen.

Fox did not stay angry for long. Their time together was too precious for him to analyze and condemn words spoken in the heat of passion. The next day they arrived in Nassau on New Providence Island, one of the smaller but most important of the islands, islets and reefs that made up the Bahamas. Fox immediately escorted her to his house. Mac did not accompany them. He informed Alexa he would remain aboard his ship while she was being provisioned and expected to sail one week hence. Fox's intention was to stay but one night in Nassau and depart on the morning's tide. Both men expected Alexa to remain dutifully behind, safely ensconced in Fox's small but comfortable house on the island. Both were badly mistaken.

Alexa spoke little during the short ride to Fox's house situated on a bluff a short distance from the harbor. In 1776 Nassau was captured by the young United States navy, but after a few days the place was evacuated, leaving a kind of void as well as a haven for privateers.

Most of the finer dwellings they passed were made of limestone available readily on the island. Huts were constructed of natural vegetation and were more numerous than the better homes. Though it was winter the day was warm with gentle breezes rustling through the trees. Thick woods surrounded the most exquisite beaches Alexa had ever seen, with long unbroken crescents of white sand and sparkling blue sea. Alexa was enchanted and her face must have shown it.

"I knew you'd like it, milady," Fox smiled confidently. "The time should pass quickly for you in this paradise."

"If I don't die of boredom," reposted Alexa wryly. "Fox, won't you please reconsider and take me with you?"

"No, Alexa. It's out of the question."

Alexa bristled but said nothing, her active mind already planning ahead. Before long they stopped before a square, low house built of natural limestone sporting a tile roof and covered veranda forming a wide porch. The house faced the sea and long shuttered windows across the front were opened to garner the breeze.

Alexa found the inside of the house airy and comfortable with furniture fashioned of rattan and bent into shape. Soft cushions provided comfort as well as color. In charge of Fox's home during his long absences were a couple who, Alexa surmised from their features, were descendants of the original Arawak Indians who once resided on these islands, and their lovely young daughter who looked to be about eighteen.

Trini, a handsome woman in her late thirties, served as housekeeper and cook while her husband, Hunter, saw to the upkeep and sometimes served Fox aboard the *Ghost*. Their daughter, Lana, a coffee-hued beauty whose dewy youth and innocence thoroughly charmed Alexa, helped her mother with the chores. Fox's introduction left no doubt in the servants' minds that Alexa was to be considered mistress in his absence. The family proved friendly and respectful and Alexa liked them on sight, especially Lana.

That night Fox made love to her as if he might never see her again, and Alexa responded in a like manner as their lovemaking reached new heights of erotic delight. With hands and lips he brought her time after time to levels of ecstasy never before attained, and she matched his urgency with her own. Never had her pleasure been so pure and explosive. When Fox finally left her at dawn she was filled with an amazing sense of completeness so profound that she barely registered his words when he bid her goodbye and assured her that one day he would return for her.

Fox/Adam was gone, and Alexa's transformation began almost immediately. The first thing she did was to secure Lana's friendship. The young girl reacted favorably to Alexa's initial overtures and within a day or two they were chatting and laughing together like old friends, for there were but two years separating their ages. Alexa was immensely pleased when she learned that Lana was an adventurous sort; being overly protected as she was by her doting parents she longed to taste more fully of life. She confided to Alexa that she greatly admired daring and courage in a woman.

Time was growing short and Alexa, throwing caution to the wind, took a wide-eyed Lana into her confidence. The girl, intrigued and excited by Alexa's daring, eagerly agreed to help. Alexa waited until Mac came to bid her goodbye before setting her plan into motion. Mac, looking fit and healthy after his ordeal, arrived for supper the night before he was to leave New Providence island.

"Alexa, you do understand why Fox left you behind, don't you?" he asked while they were partaking of Trini's excellent meal consisting mainly of conch, a sort of shellfish, cooked in diverse dishes, fresh vegetables and fruits.

"Of course," Alexa replied sweetly.

Though Mac was startled as well as perplexed by Alexa's sudden calm acceptance of her lot, he chose not to delve too deeply into her reason for doing so. He had always found women too complex to figure out. That's why he had remained a bachelor for so long. They talked awhile longer and when it was time to say their goodbyes, Mac tenderly embraced Alexa, placing an almost, but not quite, brotherly kiss on her lips. "We'll meet again, milady," he smiled.

"I'm sure of it," predicted Alexa impishly.

The moment Mac's jaunty step carried him out of sight, Alexa called Lana to her and they began immediately to prepare for Alexa's great adventure from which the Vixen would eventually emerge.

Hurriedly Lana helped Alexa dress in the sailor garb she had collected and helped tailor to fit Alexa's petite figure. Then she departed and returned with a packet of food and a jug of water calculated to provide sustenance for several days, a change of clothes including a bulky sweater and hat to conceal her long, dark hair. Her excitment at a fever pitch, Alexa was finally ready.

Keeping to the shadows, Lana led her long a deserted path to the harbor. Displaying her own mettle and inventiveness, Lana managed to distract the man guarding the *Lady* A long enough for Alexa to sneak up the gangplank undetected. Once aboard Alexa breathed easier, hoping Lana wouldn't be punished too severely for her part in Alexa's wild scheme. She cautioned Lana to display ignorance about her disappearance and hoped the girl would comply.

Thoroughly familiar with the ship, Alexa made directly for a place in the hold that rarely saw any of the crew. The brig used to house crewmen in need of restraint. All of Mac's men, as well as Fox's, were loyal and true and rarely, if ever, required discipline. She would be safe here until she chose to make her presence known, Alexa reckoned. If all went well she expected to remain hidden until Mac was too far from Nassau to turn back.

By frugally rationing her food and water and extinguishing one of the candles thoughtfully provided by Lana whenever she heard someone approaching, Alexa contrived to remain concealed a full week. The hardest part was not seeing or speaking to another soul. But on the eighth day, her food and water all but gone, consumed by loneliness, Alexa timidly ventured forth from the hold. Dressed in her sailor's garb, her hair concealed by a knit cap, she resembled a young lad and was immediately mistaken for such by the first person who saw her as she emerged from her concealment.

A rather stunned seaman noticed her as she crept stealthily from the hold into the light of day, and he immediately challenged her. "You there, lad, what are you doing down there in the hold where you have no business being at this time of day?"

Alexa froze, refusing to face the man. But when he called out again asking who she was and where she came from, she slowly turned in his direction. The dark scowl furrowing his brow alerted her to the fact that he did not recognize her as a crew member. "By Jupiter, a stowaway!" the seaman cried, pouncing upon her. Alexa was too stunned to resist as she was dragged forward by the burly seaman. "Yer lucky it's Captain Mac ye'll be brought before, lad, and not another, for Captain Mac's fair and will let ye work yer passage."

Finally Alexa stood before a frowning Mac, head bowed, eyes downcast. "What have we here, Beggs?" Mac asked, a smile lurking at the corners of his mouth. "No doubt some likely lad who has a yen to fight the British."

"Aye, Captain," nodded Beggs vigorously. "I caught the lad sneaking up from the hold."

"Hmmm," mused Mac thoughtfully, pretending to ponder the dilemma brought about by a stowaway. "Looks skinny, probably starving after a week in the hold. Take him to the galley and tell cook to fill his belly, then put him to work scrubbing the deck. Does that meet with your approval, lad?"

"Aye," murmured Alexa in a voice pitched deliberately low.

"Aye, what?" challenged Mac curtly.

"Aye, sir," responded Alexa.

"What's your name, lad?"

"Al . . . Alex, sir," Alexa answered, thinking quickly.

"Well, Alex," Mac informed her, "it's too late to turn back so it looks as if you'll have your way, though before you're through you may well wish you had remained safely in Nassau." Mac did not notice the triumphant smile lighting Alexa's pert features as he turned away to pursue more important matters.

"Come along, lad," Beggs said gruffly but not unkindly. "But first, seeing as how the Captain has been so generous with ye, the least ye can do is doff yer cap." So saying he yanked the knit cap from Alexa's head. "The Lord preserve us!" he gasped as Alexa's long, ebony locks tumbled freely about her shoulders and down her shapely back in a profusion of tangled curls. "Lady Alexa!"

There was not a man aboard the *Lady* A who did not recognize Alexa from her previous journey with them. During the weeks she had sailed with them across the ocean they had all come to think very highly of her and to a man they would have gladly died for one of her sweet smiles. Beggs, particularly, felt close to her since he was the one who had originally brought her aboard the *Lady* A long ago in England.

Stunned, Mac did not want to believe his ears when Beggs called out Alexa's name. Thinking he was hearing things, he whirled about, only to find he did indeed face a defiant Alexa ridiculously garbed in sailor's clothing yet somehow managing to look feminine and vastly desirable. "My God, Alexa, what are you doing here?" he ranted, imagining Fox's rage once he found out that Alexa had stowed aboard his ship.

"I warned you and Fox I would not tolerate being left behind," replied Alexa smugly. "You both harbor the notion that because I am a woman I am mindless, or too weak to be of any help."

"Do you realize what you've done, Alexa? We're too far from Nassau to turn back. What am I to do with you?"

Alexa smiled winsomely. "Why, you could teach me to sail, to fight, to navigate. You can help me learn all I need to know in order to become a good sailor."

"For what purpose?" Mac asked, disguising his anger. Why couldn't she have stowed aboard the *Ghost* where Fox would be obliged to handle her?

"Who knows?" shrugged Alexa mysteriously. "Someday the knowledge might serve me well."

Suddenly Mac became aware that the entire crew was clustered about them, avidly hanging on to every word spoken, their indulgent smiles making him realize whom they favored in the exchange. Grasping her arm he led her toward his cabin where they were afforded a measure of privacy. Once the heavy oak door shut out prying ears and eyes, Mac began anew to berate Alexa.

"I don't know what to do with you, Alexa," he said, stomping about noisily. "In Nassau I received word that a flotilla of British ships are carrying arms to Savannah to aid in the conquest of the south. If I turn back now I might miss them."

"Then don't turn back," begged Alexa earnestly. "I know I'll be safe with you. And I want to learn, Mac, everything. Please," she pleaded in such a way that poor Mac had no chance at all.

"I can't keep you with me forever, Alexa. Fox is bound to return one day to Nassau and discover you missing. What then?"

"Let's compromise," Alexa hedged, sensing her victory. "Give me three months to learn all I need to know. Just three months, Mac, and then I'll return to Nassau."

She looked so helpless, so appealing, that Mac found himself agreeing to her outrageous demands. "You win, Alexa—three months, then back you go. No pleading, no begging. Agreed?"

"Agreed," Alexa exulted. And so began a period in Alexa's young life that proved a turning point.

The next three months found her working harder and toiling longer than she had in her entire life. Not only from Mac, but from the entire crew who thought it a lark to teach Alexa all their hard-earned skills, Alexa learned to climb the riggings, trim the sails, and wield the rapier with some dgree of proficiency given her limited strength. More difficult was learning to use the sextant to map the course and to read the stars. The latter was taught by Beggs who had been a sailor for more years than any man aboard the *Lady A* save for cook.

All things taken into consideration Alexa proved a quick study and an avid student. There were times when she scampered aloft in the rigging with an agility many of the seasoned sailors admired. Mac held his breath, fearing for her life. And when she came down he scolded her soundly while secretly marveling at her spunk and ability. Among the many things she learned were the rudiments of weaponry, particularly the deadly cannon bolted to the quarterdeck and main deck.

Finally the day arrived when Alexa, strictly against Mac's wishes, participated in a battle. The *Lady* A had taken two ships, both sunk in the fray during Alexa's period of training. When the third was sighted Alexa refused to be relegated to her cabin and showed up on deck during the heat of the battle, acquitting herself admirably with rapier against one or two of the clumsier English sailors. When Mac first spied her it took ten years off of his life and his eyes never left her slim form. She had many protectors that day among her friends aboard the ship. Notably Drake, who considered Alexa his personal charge and under strict orders from Mac became her guardian angel thereafter.

After that first encounter, Alexa crept away and vomited in private, then fell into bed so exhausted she could barely lift her arms or move her legs. The following day Mac ranted and raved at her for her fool-hardy actions, but to no avail. The next ship they attacked, Alexa was where she belonged, in the midst of battle, exhilarated by the skill with which she acquitted herself. The third battle enabled her to prove her merit when she saved the life of Drake who fought at her back and would have sustained a serious injury save for her quick action. Alexa had never felt more confident of her ability as when she was cheered by the crew for her courage and deftness with a sword. Watching in silence,

Mac was eternally grateful the time had arrived to return Alexa to Nassau. He lived in fear that she might be seriously wounded in one of their skirmishes which had become more and more frequent as the weeks went by. Fox would have his hide should he allow anything to happen to Alexa.

Nearly three months to the day Alexa had stowed aboard her namesake, Mac took her aside and told her to plot a course to Nassau. Using her newly acquired skill, Alexa did just that. But as fate would have it they were enjoined in battle one more time before they reached their destination, serving to further hone Alexa's prowess in battle. As a tribute to her bravery Mac awarded her the prize, the ship *Star Chaser*, a sleek English frigate they had just taken. He generously offered the loan of Drake and several of his most trusted men to man the *Star Chaser* for Alexa.

"Drake will make you a good captain, Alexa," Mac told her as he presented his parting gift. "As owner of the ship a share of the profits will come to you and indirectly you will be doing your part in the war." Mac thought it a perfect solution. With the *Star Chaser* to keep her occupied her stay in Nassau should prove less of an ordeal. And with an experienced man like Drake as captain the profits would give her a measure of security no matter which direction her life took. It was not too farfetched to consider the possiblity that neither he nor Fox would survive the war.

If the English proved victorious in the end, Alexa would never be allowed to return to America, and should he or Fox fail to survive, she would be fixed for life. In due course both ships entered the port of Nassau, the *Star Chaser* to be turned into a privateer and the *Lady* A to take on food and supplies.

Alexa was elated with her gift of a ship. Had Mac

known how easily he had fallen in with her plans he would have been astounded. The ship was a plum she hadn't counted on and it literally fell into her hands. When Mac left Nassau a week later to continue his pursuit of the British, he thought he left Alexa in a safe haven for the duration of the war. How little he knew the new Alexa. The moment Mac cleared the harbor Alexa boarded the *Star Chaser* and called together Drake and what crew members from the *Lady A* Mac had left behind. Swallowing her nervousness she faced them squarely and boldly laid out her proposal.

"Men," she said, her voices quivering with excitement. "By now you all know me. For three months we have sailed together and fought side by side. I am confident in saying I have proven myself many times over, in many diverse situations. I do not believe you found me lacking."

Several ayes hailed her words, encouraging her to continue. "What I am about to propose might seem strange at first but I beg you to consider me on my merit alone. Do not allow my femininity to sway your decision."

"What is it you are trying to say, Lady Alexa?" Drake finally asked.

"I intend to sail my own ship and I want all of you loyal men at my side." There, it was out, and Alexa watched closely as shock followed disbelief across the faces of those men she had come to know so well.

Beggs was openly skeptical while Drake's admiration was clearly displayed for all to see. A scattering of disjointed conversation flew about her while the men stared incredulously into the face of their idol. "Lady Alexa, have ye thought of the danger?" asked Beggs in an attempt to dissuade her from her foolish course.

"I've considered everything, Beggs, and my mind is

made up. I fully intend to be at the helm when *Star Chaser* leaves Nasau—with or without the lot of you. Of course," she allowed sweetly, placatingly, "I'd much prefer to have each one of you at my side." She paused dramatically to allow her words time to sink in.

Abruptly, she whirled to confront Drake. "Well, Drake, what say you? Are you with me? Will you be my first mate and right arm? I need you, I need you all."

That's all Drake needed to hear. Already halfway in love with Alexa, he fell completely and irrevocably under her spell. A confirmed bachelor in his late thirites, Drake would have gladly followed Alexa to the ends of the earth and back for one of her special smiles. If he didn't know her to be Fox's lady, a man whom he respected enormously, he would be tempted to win her for himself. Realizing such a thing to be impossible, he would be honored to fight by her side and protect her for as long as fate allowed.

"I'm with you, milady," he shouted to the heavens. "For as long and as far as the winds and the tides and the fates take us."

"Aye, count me in," added Beggs, not to be outdone by Drake.

One by one the others joined in until every man present swore to serve their lady till their death or the end of the war. "Then hear me, men," shouted Alexa, floating on a cloud of euphoria. "Henceforth I shall be known as the Vixen. I will wear a mask at all times so no man may know my identity. I charge you under penalty of death to forget my name, forget my face and address me only as Vixen or Captain. Only you few, my trusted crew, shall know the truth and thereby hold my life in your hands."

A profound silence met Alexa's words as each man mulled over all that Alexa had imparted to them. To be the recipient of such trust filled them with awe. If by chance they hadn't been entirely with her before they were now, body and soul. To a man they would allow their tongues to be torn out before they would betray their lady Vixen.

The cheer that met her ears brought tears to Alexa's eyes. At long last everything she had toiled so tirelessly toward for these past three months was about to be fulfilled. "We sail in a week, men!" Alexa shouted above the din. "As of now the *Star Chaser* no longer exists. Behold, *My Lady Vixen!*" Her slim hands stretched out to encompass the ship beneath her feet.

"*My Lady Vixen!* May God guide her path! English beware! To our captain, the Vixen!" All this and more echoed across the placid water of the bay as the Vixen came into being.

Afterwards Alexa conferred with Drake and Beggs, instructing them as to the refurbishing of the ship, the painting of the new name on the hull and signing on men to fill out the crew. Smiling complacently, Alexa immediately set out to complete her transformation from lady to vixen.

Lana was delighted to have Alexa back safe and unharmed. It took a whole day for Alexa to tell of her exploits during the past three months and Lana sat bug-eyed with excitement during the telling. Lana became truly animated when Alexa confided her newest venture and once again asked the girl's help in creating the Vixen.

Though Lana expressed the desire to accompany Alexa, Alexa felt obligated to deny her request for she would not be so cruel as to deprive Trini and Hunter of their only child. Instead she involved the girl in every phase of her transformation.

The first thing Lana did was seek out a reputable chemist and instruct him as to what she wanted. Slightly startled but willing enough to comply, the chemist soon sent Lana on her way with several bottles tucked in her basket leaving him a good deal richer. Several hours later Alexa's luxuriant black hair had been bleached a silver blond, the color of moonbeans reflecting off the sea. Alexa was startled by the effect and hardly recognized herself in the mirror Lana held up to her. Donning a mask and changing the timbre of her voice, Alexa was convinced no one would recognize her. All in all, she was more than delighted with her appearance.

Her attire was next to come under her scrutiny. Because she wished to present a far more flamboyant picture, someone who would not so easily be forgotten, Alexa abandoned her sailor garb as being unsuitable for her purposes. When she met the English in battle she wanted to be noted and remembered. Lana fashioned skin-tight breeches of shimmering black silk, specially designed to display the long curve of Alexa's shapely legs and thighs. A sheer white silk blouse with billowing sleeves was left partially unbuttoned to provide enticing glimpses of her firm, unconfined breasts. A bright scarf tied about her slim neck provided the finishing touch and lent her a rakish air. She and Lana made several sets of the daring costumes and added two capes of varying thicknesses.

Last but no less important was the mask. Following Fox's example, Alexa fashioned several half masks from black silk, spending several hours painstakingly embroidering the features of a vixen upon the material. The effect was startling, to say the least. By the end of the week *My Lady Vixen* was ready to sail and meet her destiny, and so was her daring captain. What Alexa couldn't know was that in a surprisingly short time the Vixen would become a legend among men, an enigma of unmatched courage. Her beauty and cunning would precede her from port to port. There was not a ship afloat which did not recognize *My Lady Vixen*, but she was feared by no one save the British and occasionally a hapless Spanish galleon which chanced to cross her path.

Surprisingly, the Vixen was not without mercy. Her prisoners were rarely killed outright unless in the heat of battle, but set adrift in boats or sent to port to be ransomed. The legend of the Vixen grew, was embellished upon, and told and retold with great relish until the price set upon her head by the enraged English nearly matched that of her counterpart, the Fox.

When Fox learned of the exploits of the Vixen, he merely smiled mysteriously, but in truth his curiosity was piqued, for she sounded like a woman after his own heart. He knew one day destiny would bring them together; it was inevitable, for wasn't a fox created to tame a vixen?

15

An excited cry quickly aroused the Vixen from her ruminations and she raised her masked face upward to where the lookout posted in the shrouds pointed and gestured wildly. "Ship ahoy!" he called down to those below. "To the starboard, Captain!"

Immediately Alexa brought the glass to her eye to scan the horizon. At first she saw nothing, then slowly a full set of sails came into view above the rise of the sea. From the crow's nest, the sailor, whose vision was more encompassing than that of his mates below, yelled out, "She's English, Vixen! A warship from the looks of her."

Immediately Drake was at her side. "She's probably well-armed, Vixen," he said, following her progress with his own glass. "What are your intentions? Do we engage her in battle or run?"

Alexa eyed him contemptuously. "Have we ever run away from a good fight, Drake? This ship is no different from the other three we've taken in as many months."

Drake grinned. In truth he'd never known Vixen to turn tail and did not expect her to do so now. She seemed to come alive during the heat of battle, and thrived on life at sea. Even now his breath caught in his throat as he watched her, blond hair swirling about her slim form like dancing moonbeams, enticingly displayed in the daring costume that had become her trademark.

"I'll distribute the weapons, Vixen," Drake saluted as he turned on his heel. Alexa nodded distractedly as she continued her tracking of the English warship.

As the ship drew near Alexa saw that she was a ship of the line and appeared to be swift and well-armed, just as Drake predicted. The name on the hull proclaimed her to be the *Avenger* and no doubt out to rid the seas of American privateers. A small frown puckered Alexa's smooth brow. Where had she heard that name before? she wondered as she searched her memory for some hint as to why the name should cause the sudden feeling of unease. Some niggling memory tugged at the outer edges of her brain but failed to materialize. Shrugging her shoulders Alexa concentrated on the approachng ship, quickly discarding any other diversions from her mind.

All about her her brave crew were already springing into action, loading and priming the cannon lining the upper deck and quarterdeck. Each man wore a brace of pistols as well as a cutlass strapped to his waist. It took over two hours before the warship came within range of *My Lady Vixen* and Alexa was gratified to see that her own ship was lighter and possessed of greater maneuverability.

Ordering the crew to strike the colors, Alexa watched proudly as the Stars and Stripes were hoisted, followed by her own personal pennant, the head of a vixen transfixed on the body of a shapely woman. In reply the British ship ran out her own Union Jack, followed by a warning shot that fell short of *My Lady Vixen's* bow. In retaliation *My Lady Vixen* fired a volley of her own.

Employing the expertise gained during the past six months, Alexa ordered the sails brought into the wind, coming up unexpectedly upon the enemy. With a slash of her hand the upper deck guns roared and belched fire. When the smoke cleared away Alexa rejoiced to find at least one of their eighteen pounders had found a home on the deck of the *Avenger*. Almost upon the heels of the eighteen pounders came the thunder of the nine pounders. But the battle was far from over.

The English captain was evidently experienced and cunning for he deftly tacked in a zigzag course at the same time firing his own cannon. But the English captain was not so sly as he thought for he allowed *My Lady Vixen* to come up almost to the prow of the *Avenger*, which could not fire their guns because of the proximity of *My Lady Vixen*. It was a tactic she had learned from Mac and it now served her well. As she came up against the hull of the *Avenger* she ordered the sails lowered and grappling hooks employed. With the ships anchored together and the boarding planks run out, Alexa and her crow bounded onto the deck of the *Avenger*, cutlasses drawn, pistols primed.

In the beginning Alexa was too engaged to take more than a cursory notice of the English captain. When he finally came under her scrutiny her steps faltered and she nearly dropped her guard. A warning shout from Drake who rarely was out of shouting distance from her during battle alerted her just in time to deflect a killing blow. Swiftly dispatching the sailor who was an inferior swordsman, Alexa leaped before the captain who was gaining the upper hand against one of her own men. The sailor, Sykes, quickly stepped aside as his captain moved in to replace him.

"Aha, Captain Whitlaw," Alexa growled throatily, "I

believe I am better suited to your skills than Sykes, good man that he is." The moment Alexa had recognized Charles Whitlaw, her ex-fiancé, she knew why the *Avenger* had plagued her when she first saw the name painted on the hull. It was the ship Charles had been given to command, as well as one of those involved with trapping the Fox several months ago near Savannah.

"You know me?" asked Charles, eyeing Alexa warily as they measured one another over their drawn swords. "I'm certain, Vixen, had I met you I would remember it, mask or no."

Alexa laughed, feinting to the right as Charles neatly sidestepped. "Beware, Englishman," she warned light-heartedly, "for the bite of a vixen can prove fatal!"

Charles gritted his teeth. "I've never been bitten by a lady yet, Vixen. I expect I'll be highly honored for ridding the seas of a menace. The world will never miss you. A woman's place is at home doing her husband's bidding and raising his heirs."

Bright dots of rage exploded behind Alexa's eyes as Charles continued to express his arrogant views. The bastard! she cursed beneath her breath. He's of the same ilk as Fox who expected her to remain meekly at home while he and others like him romped merrily from one adventure to the next. But she'd show them both! she vowed. Charles would soon learn just how dangerous it was to tangle with a vixen. As for Fox, one day he too would feel the Vixen's fangs!

Concentrating on Charles and his flashing sword, Alexa slowly and methodically employed the skill she had honed during the previous three battles and months of training to thoroughly humiliate Charles, who fancied himself quite accomplished in the art of fencing. Alexa proved to him otherwise as she drove her sword through the fleshy part of his arm. Charles yelped, cursing loudly, but somehow he managed to retain his stance and parry her next thrust, which might have proved fatal had it landed.

Then something happened to bring a quick end to the skirmish. One of Charles's chance thrusts flicked across the front of Alexa's silk blouse, accidentally slitting the sheer fabric. The edges parted and Alexa's full breasts tumbled free, so stunning Charles that he momentarily dropped his guard. That moment was all Alexa needed as she brought the sword up and inward as hard and fast as she could, putting all her strength and weight into the blow. The edge of her blade caught his sword just below the hilt, jarring it loose from his hand and sending it slithering across the deck out of reach. His eyes flew up to find a sword pointed at his throat.

His face a mottled red, Charles shouted accusingly, "You take unfair advantage, Vixen!"

Alexa chuckled hoarsely. "A woman uses any means available to gain the upper hand, Captain Whitlaw."

"You're a brazen hussy, Vixen," spat Charles disparagingly, "to bare yourself so shamelessly before all these men."

"Aye, I am," agreed Alexa with equanimity. "But enough of this. It seems my men have won the day and await your presence with your crew on the quarterdeck." She prodded him with the tip of her sword and Charles reluctantly moved forward. Immediately Drake took over and Alexa strode off in the direction of her cabin, only to return a few minutes later with a fresh blouse.

Because they were close to a port controlled by the Americans, Alexa decided to turn the *Avenger* over to the American navy rather than selling or sinking her. She was a good ship and would be used to serve against her own countrymen. She told as much to Charles when she assembled the defeated English crew to inform them of her intentions.

After consulting with Drake, she decided to lock the English crew in the hold of the *Avenger* and let the American government ransom them as they saw fit. Charles loudly voiced his indignation over the arrangements, but to no avail.

"Don't you know your cause has been defeated?" he protested vigorously. "Why don't you give up now and save yourself a lot of grief? One of your own generals, Benedict Arnold, has been tried for treason and subsequently executed. Everyone knows the Americans are all but beaten."

"I have every faith that the Americans will emerge victorious," Alexa retorted sharply. "The fight will continue until the English are driven from American shores."

"I don't suppose you've heard that our dashing Colonel Banastre Tarleton cut to pieces a detachment of your General Lincoln's cavalry followed by the complete destruction of Buford's Virginia regiment near the North Carolina border," Charles bragged. "Why, before the year is out, you, Fox and all the others of your ilk will find yourselves swinging at the end of a rope."

Alexa and Drake exchanged significant looks but refused to rise to Whitlaw's bait. This last piece of news he had so carelessly thrown out came as a surprise to Alexa, but she was not one to discount so easily the Americans' fortitude and stamina in the face of great odds. Charles realized he had imparted staggering information to the Vixen and sought to remain in command of the situation.

"Not even four of your generals combined—Greene, La Fayette, Gates and Washington—succeeded in defeating our General Cornwallis. Gates, the hero of

Saratoga, became overconfident and imcompetent. His rout is the talk of the war. He was immediately replaced by Greene, who is said to be nearly as able as Washington. But then, that is not saying much. By the end of 1780 the Americans will once again be placed firmly under the English yoke."

"You always did talk too much, Charles," Alexa rasped irritably. "I'm afraid your participation in the war has ceased and you are destined to languish in an American prison for the duration. Now, in the hold with you!"

Charles peered at Alexa curiously. Why did the feeling persist that he had met her somewhere? Perhaps it was her own familiarity in addressing him that gave him some basis for his thinking. But surely he would have recognized the flowing silver hair, the hoarse whispery voice, the enticing body, had he seen Vixen before. Still puzzling over the enigma of who had bested him in battle, Charles disappeared into the hold muttering vaguely about vixens and foxes and women who should be home engaged in nothing more taxing than embroidery.

Drake stood beside Alexa as the *Avenger*, now manned with a skeleton crew from *My Lady Vixen*, set a northern course for a port known to be in American possession. Drake felt he knew his captain well enough by now to speak frankly. "Judging from your words, Vixen, I assume you know that English captain."

"I do know him," Alexa shrugged. "Quite well, at one time."

"Do you think he recognized you?"

Alexa grinned impishly. "No more so than you or any of the crewmen who saw me walk aboard *My Lady Vixen* over three months ago."

Drake answered her grin with a smile of his own. "Aye, I remember that day well. Not a man jack aboard thought the silver-haried wench anything more than a gorgeous, lusty woman on the prowl for an easy coin earned on her back. You fooled us all, Vixen, just as I imagine you fooled the Englishman."

A thorough inspection of the ship was made to assess the damage done by the *Avenger's* huge guns. To Alexa's chagrin *My Lady Vixen* had not escaped totally unscathed. A ball went through the hull just above the waterline and another fell into the water doing little harm to the structure of the ship but cracking the rudder. After consultation with Drake it was decided to put into a small uninhabited island off the Florida coast often used by privateers because of its concealed cove and deep water that allowed ships to anchor close to shore. Wood for repairs was readily available as were fresh water and wild fruits and berries. As yet the English hadn't discovered the haven and it was still considered a safe refuge.

Alexa learned from the ship's carpenters that it would take several days to complete the repairs necessary to make *My Lady Vixen* seaworthy, and decided that the crew had earned a short reprieve from their duties aboard ship. As they traveled south Alexa grew anxious to feel land beneath her feet once again and considered sleeping on shore during their stay on the island, just as she knew most of her crew would elect to do. Perhaps she would explore on her own while her men went about their duties. A freshwater bath would feel delicious, and she needed to touch up the roots of her hair with the dwindling supply of bleach Lana sent along.

Two days later *My Lady Vixen* dropped anchor a short distance from the white crescent of sand lining the pristine water of the bay. Almost immediately two boats set out for shore with the landing party. Though they expected to find nothing amiss, precaution was the better part of valor and Alexa was more cautious than most, no doubt due to the fact that she was a woman and must work twice as hard to retain the trust of her men. Two hours later the boats returned, reporting that all was secure.

That evening the entire crew, with the exception of the watch left aboard *My Lady Vixen*, lounged comfortably on the soft sand while the cook prepared their meal over a huge fire built on the beach. A detail of men had scoured the shore for crabs, clams and lobsters and tonight the fare consisted of a luscious mixture of shellfish and rice called jambalaya by their Creole cook. It was delicious and Alexa hungrily gobbled up her share, then curled up in her cape and promptly fell asleep against the romantic backdrop of a full moon, swaying palms and a voice in the background singing a soulful tune.

The next day dawned bright and hot despite the fact that it was late October and 1780 was fast drawing to a close. Alexa had a difficult time equating the heat and humidity of Florida with what she was accustomed to in England.

Shaking the sand out of her clothes, Alexa ate a bite of breakfast, then satisfied herself that the men were getting on nicely with their repairs before gathering up her paraphernalia and informing Drake that she was off for a bath.

"I've been on this island many times, Vixen," Drake told her. "It's riddled with swamps but if you keep to the well-defined path leading inland you'll soon come to a small lake. The lake is shallow and should serve your purposes admirably."

"I'll remember your advice, Drake." Alexa smiled winsomely.

So winsomely, in fact, that Drake was persuaded to add, "Perhaps I should come along and . . . er . . . protect you."

Alexa glanced at him knowingly. Since they first sailed together Drake had never, either by word or action, expressed a desire for her as a woman. Which was fine with Alexa, for the Vixen was a captain first and a woman last. She wanted no relationships to confuse matters or undermine her authority. Not that Drake wasn't handsome enough, for he was. He was also strong, virile, and protective of her. But he was not Fox/Adam—and he was the only man she wanted.

Grinning impishly, Alexa patted her sword and said, "Thank you, but my sword is all the protection I need."

Drake watched her wistfully as she turned and ambled down the path, the provocative sway of her hips sending sharp pangs of desire surging through his veins. He had been at sea too long, Drake thought, shaking his head to clear it of such disturbing ideas. Perhaps he could persuade Vixen to allow the men a much-needed few days of diversion in a friendly port. But Drake was of the opinion that bedding a whore would not solve his particular problem.

Alexa spent the entire morning lolling in the warm water of the small lake Drake pointed out to her. Using a bar of sweet smelling soap she washed her long silver tresses and then touched up the roots with the last of the bleach mixture she brought with her from Nassau. She would have to return soon and purchase more, she thought idly as she soaped her body which had taken on a golden glow from her long hours standing in the sun. Alexa had never looked better and she knew it.

When she finally had enough of the water she lay

down on the sand to soak up the sun while she waited for her clothes, which she had washed, to dry. From force of habit as well as to protect the delicate skin of her face from the drying rays of the sun, Alexa donned her mask and promptly fell asleep.

Within minutes Alexa began to dream. It was the same dream that haunted her nights as well as many of her days. It had been over six months since she had felt a man's touch or experienced a man's love, and Alexa was not made of stone.

In her dream she was truly a vixen, being stalked by a fox, a handsome animal both ferocious and brave. Raw desire raged within the fox, desire to mate with the female of his species. There was no escape for the vixen; she was cunningly cornered by the fox and dragged to his lair. Pouncing upon her, the fox suddenly took on his human form and it was Adam who bent over her own human body, titillating and exciting her until her blood warmed and need sang through her veins.

Had her dream followed its normal course Alexa would wake up at this point bathed in sweat and tense with barely suppressed desire. Then she would clear her mind of those disturbing thoughts and force herself instead to concentrate not on Adam/Fox but on his lies, and the hurt he caused her by failing to trust her enough to take her into his confidence. And as her anger grew, her ardor died. Only then would sleep claim her again.

But today, lying on her back with the sun warming her nude body and her erotic dreams heating her blood, Alexa did not awaken. Her dreams were too real this time and she was too near the thrilling climax to surrender to reality. Instead, she succumbed to the rewarding path where her dreams led, to her erotic fantasies, and finally to ecstasy.

Alexa moaned, a sound immediately answered by a

low chuckle. But caught up as she was in her dream, Alexa did not associate it with reality—until the moment when soft lips lapped at her turgid nipples and rough hands explored the velvet texture of her skin. Her eyes snapped open and a masked face bent over her, a sardonic smile tugging at the corners of his lips.

"We meet at last, Vixen," murmured Fox, his silver-gray eyes roaming the length of her bared flesh with amused insolence.

Automatically Alexa's hands flew to her face and she breathed easier when she felt her mask securely in place. "I've looked forward to this meeting, Fox," Alexa whispered huskily, using the same ploy he did to disguise her voice. "Only somehow I pictured the circumstances different." She started to rise but Fox's large form held her firmly in place beneath him.

"Where do you think you're going, Vixen?" Fox rasped lazily.

"Back to the beach," Alexa insisted. "By now my men must be wondering what is keeping me and will soon come looking for me." That ought to discourage him, she thought smugly.

"No need for that," Fox informed her blandly. "I told your man Drake that I would look after you."

"I can't imagine him agreeing to that!" Alexa replied testily. Then she recalled that Drake was aware of her true identity and no doubt in his capacity as Mac's first mate was privy to Fox's identity also. "What are you doing here on this island?" she asked to cover her confusion.

"Same as you," Fox confided. "We were in need of repairs and sought a safe place to make them."

Squirming beneath him, Alexa declared, "Let me up, Fox. I'm certain my clothes are dry by now."

"No, Vixen," Fox laughed softly. "Not until I make

love to you."

"Like hell!" Alexa roared, almost forgetting to disguise her voice in her anger. "I'm not your plaything! I pick and choose my lovers!"

"I'll not disappoint you, Vixen," Fox assured her with typical male conceit. "By now you should be bored with Drake and the others and welcome someone new to amuse you. You look to be a woman of vast . . . appetites. Give me a try, Vixen, you won't be sorry."

Alexa exploded in a torrent of fury. "You conceited bastard!" she gasped, dismayed by his profound audacity. "I wouldn't bed you if you were the last man on earth!"

"I want you, Vixen," Fox stated, undaunted. "When I came upon you sleeping in the sand I thought you the most beautiful woman I'd ever seen."

"How many women have you said that to?" Alexa demanded mockingly. She could not help but wonder how many women Fox had bedded since he had left her to languish in Nassau.

"Only one other," admitted Fox dryly.

"Where is she now? That other woman, I mean. Do you love her?"

"You ask too many questions," said Fox evasively. "We are wasting precious time when I could be making love to you."

Alexa bristled. "I think not, Fox. You and I have only just met and I'm not even certain I like you."

"Ah, but I like you, Vixen. I've dreamed of meeting you ever since I first heard of your exploits. You're good, Vixen, damn good. My Lady Vixen's record is one to be proud of. There is not an English ship afloat who wouldn't give its eye teeth to bring about your downfall. Your reputation alone made me yearn to meet you, but now that I've seen you I won't be satisfied to settle for mere friendship. I mean to have you, milady Vixen. For what other purpose was a vixen created if not to mate with a fox?"

"Why, to tame a fox, naturally," Alexa taunted coyly. "Now will you kindly let me up?"

"You're wrong, Vixen, it's the other way around." As if to prove his point his lips took hers hungrily, eager to prove his mastery over her.

Alexa fought against the emotions his kiss was provoking in her, excruciatingly aware that the hot blood in her worked to Fox's advantage. He was despicable, she told herself, a charlatan, a liar, arrogant—and worst of all he had deceived her!

His hand rested at the side of her neck, his thumb tracing her jawline in a lulling motion that relaxed her. His kiss was at first light and teasing, then, as his passion flared, deeper and demanding, drawing a response Alexa battled to withhold. Did the arrogant oaf expect every woman to fall in his arms at his slightest whim? Alexa fumed. Well, the Vixen was not just any woman! She had an independent life of her own and would bed no man unless it was her choice. And Fox was acting too self-assured and possessive for her liking.

Marshaling all her strength, Alexa shoved against Fox's massive chest, catching him unawares and sending him sprawling on his backside. Nimbly, Alexa eluded his grasping hands as she leaped to her feet, snatching up her clothes at the same time. Fox roared in protest as his hands clutched at thin air.

"Dammit, Vixen, that was uncalled for! What is wrong with you?"

"The Vixen chooses whom she beds with, and when, Fox," Alexa sniffed haughtily, keeping a safe distance while she slid into her revealing costume.

"Don't I please you?" Fox glared at her. "Is that your

final decision?"

Arching a slim eyebrow, Alexa leveled a pointed look in Fox's direction, promising much but giving nothing. Her soft shoulders rose carelessly. "Who can say?" She grinned mischievously. "It's a woman's prerogative to change her mind. And if I do you'll be the first to know. Unless, of course, someone else catches my fancy."

Alexa's brazen retort did not sit well with Fox. He watched in glowering silence while Alexa dressed, and then, as if to taunt him further, began to brush her long silver tresses which had dried into a tangled mass. Engrossed in her task, Alexa did not note the gleam in Fox's eyes or his devious smile that did not bode well for the Vixen.

When Alexa finished she gathered up her belongings and turned a questioning look on Fox who seemed so struck by her beauty he found it difficult to speak. "Will you walk back with me or come later?"

Fox rose to his feet and sketched a mocking bow. "After you, milady Vixen," he gestured, quickly falling in beside her as she started down the path that led to the beach. To fill the void Fox began to talk of the Vixen's exploits during the past months. "They tell me you are an expert with a sword."

Alexa smiled wickedly. "I'm able to hold my own," she temporized.

"More than just hold your own, I'll wager. Where did you learn such manly skills?"

"From a friend," Alexa hedged.

"I'll bet," Fox commented dryly. Alexa flushed but wisely held her tongue. "Where did you come from, Vixen, and why the mask? Is there some dark secret in your past you wish to hide?"

"I could ask the same of you, Fox. What are you trying to hide?"

"I can't afford to reveal my true identity," Fox shrugged, surprising Alexa with his willingness to talk. More freely than he ever did with his own wife. "I come and go at will in and out of Savannah and am privy to General Prevost's plans. To the world at large I am anything but a privateer and am entrusted with secrets invaluable to the Fox and his crusade against oppression. Even Governor Wright trusts me in my other identity."

And Governor Wright's niece, Alexa wanted to ask but bit her tongue, does she trust you too? Instead she said, "It's strange you do not show your face to your own countrymen."

"It's safer this way," hedged Fox. "But if you are willing to unmask, I will afford you the same courtesy."

"You aren't the only one who has reasons for remaining anonymous," Alexa replied tartly. "So let's call it a draw. We shall both retain our secret identities. Agreed?"

"Agreed," Fox smiled cryptically.

From a distance Alexa heard voices and knew they were near the beach where the crews of both ships were hard at work repairing their damage. But before they came out into the open, Fox grasped Alexa's arm, halting her in mid-step, and swung her around to face him. "We're far from finished, you and I, Vixen. Before either of us leave this island we'll finish what we started back there by the lake."

"No man tells me what to do, Fox," Alexa bristled angrily. "I told you before, only if I wish it."

"I'll make you wish it," Fox rasped softly, "beg for it, even." Then he turned on his heel and preceded her to the beach where he was immediately hailed by his men. Alexa followed more slowly, sorting through her muddled thoughts.

Foremost in her mind was the knowledge that Fox wanted the Vixen. And this despite the fact that he loved Alexa, or so he said. As Adam, he also professed to love his wife. And yet, he felt no qualms about bedding another woman when Alexa supposedly was unavailable. No doubt he had bedded Gwen Wright often enough during the past months when he returned to Savannah as Adam. What a damnable mess, Alexa groaned inwardly. Fox/Adam, Alexa/Vixen. How would it all end? Of one thing she was certain: Should Adam return to Alexa after the war he would never learn from her of her daring exploits as Vixen.

Drake met Alexa at the edge of the clearing. "Did he see through your disguise?" he asked anxiously. "I wanted to go after you myself but Fox wouldn't hear of it."

Alexa blushed hotly, thinking that it might have been Drake who found her nude instead of Fox. "I'm certain I fooled him completely," she assured him confidently. They conferred briefly about the repairs on the ship and then Drake turned to leave, but Alexa put a restraining hand on his arm. "Drake," she said softly, "you know about Fox, don't you? I mean you know who he is."

Drake flushed, embarrassed. "Aye. Besides Captain Mac and Fox's own crew, I am the only other person to know."

"Then you know Fox is my husband." Drake nodded. "For some unexplained reason Adam chose not to confide in his wife so she is not supposed to know he is the Fox."

For a moment Drake looked confused. "Then how . . ."

"Suffice it to say I came upon the truth accidentally, but I kept the knowledge to myself. That's one of the reasons I do not wish Fox to know who I am. The other reasons are too complex to go into at this time. I'm grateful to you for keeping my secret. It means a great deal to me."

"I swore an oath, Vixen, and I intend to uphold it. I know you by no other name but Vixen. And you need have no fear about your crew. To a man they are faithful to you."

Overcome with gratitude as well as profoundly touched by her men's loyalty, Alexa threw her arms about Drake and planted an exuberant kiss on his lips. It was over almost before it began and Alexa turned on her heel, leaving a stunned Drake in her wake. A few yards away, Fox watched through slitted eyes, unable to control the muscles that twitched spasmodically in his tightly clenched jaw.

What kind of game was the little witch playing? Fox asked himself as he watched Vixen swagger down the beach. How dare she put him off while sharing her favors with her men. It took more restraint than he knew he possessed to keep from dragging her back into the woods and making love to her. He'd have his way yet, Fox vowed darkly, his eyes following Vixen's enticing form undulating across the white sane.

The repairs on both ships were progressing well. That night the combined crews held a joint party with food and drink provided equally by Fox and Vixen. Harmonicas and musical instruments were brought out after the meal and Alexa found herself being swung from man to man as the music grew wild and the dancing more frenzied. During those times Fox was her partner they conversed little, for the hectic pace kept them moving. When she finally made her bed beside the fire, guarded by the faithful Drake, she fell into an exhausted sleep, unaware of the wistful glance Fox cast in her direction.

By day the crews toiled diligently, but at night they danced and sang far into the wee hours. It was a time of reprieve from the pressures of war, from the perilous sea, and the men made the most of it.

Gathered around a huge fire one night the talk turned to the skills of their respective captains, and Alexa blushed to hear her men loudly sing her praises. Sitting beside her taking it all in, Fox carelessly flung out a challenge that left Alexa stunned. ''What say you to an exhibition duel, Vixen?'' Immediately sixty-odd voices rose in a roar of approval.

Could she best Fox? Alexa speculated. Seated beside her, Drake voiced his doubts. ''Don't do it, Vixen. You're good but not that good.''

That's all Alexa needed to hear. She would show all these men that she was every bit as good as they were. ''I accept,'' she agreed recklessly. Drake shook his head negatively and looked worried while the crew members of both ships thought only of the entertainment bound to liven up their drab existence. Within minutes bets flew back and forth and before she knew it Alexa found herself caught up in the excitement generated by the prospect of a duel between the two captains. Only Fox appeared unmoved as he sat back, smiling complacently, as if he had just accomplished some great feat.

Almost as an afterthought Fox leaned over and whispered for Alexa's ears only. ''What say you to a wager to make the duel more interesting?''

''What kind of a wager?'' asked Alexa suspiciously.

277

She knew Fox well enough to be wary of anything he might suggest.

"If I win," Fox said smugly, "you share my bed for as long as we're on the island."

"And if you lose?" countered Alexa.

"I won't," replied Fox confidently.

"But if you do," challenged Alexa stubbornly.

Fox thought a moment, then smiled broadly and said, "In the unlikely event you should best me you may unmask me. In private, of course."

Alexa's prudence fled out the window at such an enticing prospect. Not only would Fox face ridicule from his crew should she win but would earn additional embarrassment when he bared his face to her. It was too much for her to resist and, against her better judgment, she nodded her head in agreement.

It was decided that the duel would take place on the beach at ten o'clock the following morning. Alexa retired to her place beside the fire while Drake soundly rebuked her for being goaded into accepting the challenge. Alexa was glad he did not know of the private wager between her and Fox or he would no doubt spend the entire night berating her.

"Of course he'll not hurt you, Vixen," Drake assured her, "but it's bound to be an embarrassment to you."

"What makes you so sure I'll lose?" Alexa flounced angrily. "I've defended myself quite well these past months." Somewhere within the compartments of her heart came the unbidden thought that perhaps she wanted Fox to beat her in order to give her an excuse to share his bed.

"Vixen, I don't mean to belittle your skill, but I doubt there's a man alive who can beat Fox at swordplay."

"Maybe not," she drawled slowly, "but perhaps it takes a woman to accomplish what a man cannot."

They were brave words, Alexa knew, but she would try her damnedest to wipe the smug smile from Fox's handsome face.

16

It was hot. Already the sun was an orange ball high in the sky. Alexa stood in the center of a large circle facing an extremely virile and intimidating Fox. She longed to wipe the amused smirk from his lips and deliberately assumed a confident stance, which, truth to tell, she was far from feeling.

Fox appeared totally awesome dressed entirely in black; from his silk shirt open at the neck to expose a large expanse of curly hairs the color of tawny gold, tight black trousers that displayed bulging thighs and bold manhood, down to his highly polished black boots. A colorful relief was provided by the bright red silk scarf worn at a jaunty angle to conceal his hair. Alexa watched in trepidation as his massive muscles rippled and tensed in anticipation of the match.

Alexa was decked out in her usual costume of skin-tight pants and sheer blouse. With every motion, the filmy white silk shifted, allowing tantalizing glimpses of her full breasts. Like Fox, a colorful scarf held her long silver locks in place. She looked so fetching that Fox deliberately forced his eyes anywhere but at her luscious form in order to concentrate on the duel. Perhaps that's what the cunning little witch had in mind when she dressed so brazenly, Fox reflected, greatly admiring her courage as well as her daring.

Around them gathered eagerly the men of both crews, noisily joking and placing their bets. It was no more than good-natured fun and anticipation for the lively match was high. Members of both crews knew their captains would acquit themselves admirably, yet refrain from inflicting bodily harm on one another. Never before had such a match taken place and it never would again. It was something the men could talk about for years to come when they were old and gray with their grand-children at their knee.

They squared off in a traditional pose, and Alexa's soft, "En garde," sent them both into action. Taking into careful consideration her slighter build and feminine stamina, Alexa allowed Fox to take the offensive, easily parrying his first tentative thrusts. Gradually, the tempo of the attack picked up, and she felt the power behind his blows. Like ballet dancers they circled one another, each wary of the other's abilities and responses, alert for an opening. Alexa concentrated in an effort to keep her guard up and watch for any weakness in Fox's attack. But she could find no flaw in his expertise, marking him a master at the art. But no matter how experienced he was, Alexa intended to put up the fight of her life.

After a number of lighthearted feints and parries, the bout began in earnest. It took all of Alexa's strength and stamina to fend off Fox's swift thrusts and powerful lunges. It seemed she had time for nothing but blocking his strokes. Then slowly she began to turn the tide, assuming the offensive herself. Her resurgence of confidence was evident in her skillful feints and vigorous lunges. Awed by her prowess, Fox could not help but admire her expertise.

They fought steadily for twenty long minutes, neither gaining or losing much ground as the offensive changed sides several times. At times Alexa felt buoyed by her success thus far. At other times her arms ached from the weight of the sword and she was certain her wrists were about to snap each time Fox's thrust was successfully parried. On and on they went, thrusting, lunging, parrying, feinting, sidestepping, leaping, recovering, their eyes never wavering from one another.

Alexa began to tire under Fox's relentless onslaught, but she dared not reveal her weakness. One faltering movement, one false step, would tell him that the contest, as well as herself, was his for the taking.

And then it happened, so quickly that Alexa barely registered the deed. She feinted to one side, bringing her sword up to block his thrust. A low chuckle reached her ears as he effectively counter-parried, forcing her sword aside. So swiftly she barely had time to react, the point of his blade came to rest above her heart. With a slight flick of his wrist, he lightly pricked the skin and one drop of crimson blood appeared on the upper swell of her breast.

A shout of triumph from the crew of The Gray Ghost declared the winner. All around wagers were being paid, backs slapped, and a general air of revelry prevailed. Though the Vixen had lost her crew thought the bout evenly matched and a fair one. They were vastly proud of their captain and showed it by their cries of encouragement and congratulations on a well-fought bout.

But Alexa heard nothing save for Fox's soft— "Touche." Sheathing his sword he bowed low, a mocking gesture, at best, grasped her hand and placed an insolent kiss upon the palm. "To the victor go the spoils," he saluted, grinning sardonically. Then, much to Alexa's chagrin, and amid rousing cheers, Fox swung her off her feet, flung her over his brawny shoulder like a sack of potatoes and headed for the concealment of the trees lining the beach.

"Damn you, Fox, put me down!" raged Alexa, beating ineffectually against his broad back with her fists.

"I will, Vixen, in good time," he declared, thoroughly enjoying her discomfiture as well as his victory over her as he loped off in the direction of the lake.

"Where are you taking me?"

"Where we won't be disturbed."

"I'm perfectly able to walk."

"I know."

"Then put me down."

"I enjoy carrying you."

"You enjoy humiliating me before my men!"

"Now, Vixen," Fox cajoled teasingly, "I won fair and square. Both your men and mine knew some sort of reward was expected by the victor. I'm sure we aren't shocking them."

Unable to persuade him differently, Alexa pursed her lips angrily and suffered the indignity of being toted upended over Fox's shoulder. Only when they approached the spot where Fox had encountered Vixen for the first time did he set her on her feet, grinning wolfishly in anticipation of what was to come.

"I demand payment, Vixen, here and now," he rasped softly, his hands straying to the buttons holding her blouse together.

"And if I refuse?" asked Alexa haughtily.

"It is a debt of honor, Vixen. I doubt you'll refuse."

Alexa stared at him coldly then stooped as if to take off her boots, but instead retrieved the knife she kept hidden there in a special holder. Before he realized her intent the point of the short blade was pressed to his neck.

"I could refuse you, Fox, honor or no," Alexa hissed. "I am perfectly capable of taking care of myself, as you can see. But it is my choice to yield to you, not because you demand it, but because I . . . want it." The knife dropped noiselessly to the soft sand at her feet and Fox's face softened as he pulled her into his arms.

His touch was gentle. He raised a hand to smooth her wild silvery hair from her face, then to stroke the velvety softness of her cheek. She could feel the gentle breeze of his breath on her face and realized she wanted him every bit as much as he wanted her.

He touched her breast, where a drop of blood remained from his sword prick, then lowered his lips to flick it away with the tip of his tongue, leaving a trail of moist kisses from there up her throat to her lips. Abruptly the gentleness was gone, and in its place a splendid savagery as his kiss deepened, became drugging, then demanding.

She raised her hand to his chest, lightly resting on the steely muscles. With one hand about her waist, they sank to the sand. Her back arched so that her taut nipples stabbed into him. His kiss was heady and intoxicating and she drank deeply of its drugging cup. Dwarfed by his size, she reveled in his warm embrace, in his strength, and in return gave freely of her lips.

Then his hand moved to cup one firm breast, kneading it gently, preparing it for his lips as he swiftly removed her blouse and took the extraordinarily sensitive crest in his mouth. His warm, moist tongue tantalized it, teased it, causing her to moan aloud. He took her nipple between his teeth, tugging slightly, the hot torment of his tongue lapping, sucking, rousing a need that demanded assuaging.

Fox drew away for agonizing minutes as he swiftly ripped off Alexa's remaining clothes and then his own. She welcomed him back with a cry of joy as his hand rubbed the flatness of her stomach, then grasped her hips to pull her more firmly against his hard shaft, its steely length making Alexa all too aware of his desire for her. His hand traveled down her thigh and then up along the sensitive inside, all Alexa's thoughts centered on that part of her that ached for him.

And then he touched her there and a soft moan of pleasure rolled from Alexa's parted lips. His strong fingers gently teased the silken web of her delight, parting her to seek a spot that instantly drove her wild as she arched in response, leaving her open and begging for him.

Light fleeting kisses moved against the skin of her rib cage, the sweet curve of her hips, the flat stomach, and paused to nuzzle the tight triangle of ebony ringlets. Alexa gasped, an aching need soaring to life inside her. But the kisses continued against the velvet fur, teasing the sensitive flesh, causing her to cry out in supplication.

Grinning, Fox rose above her, his knees easily spreading hers, his long, hard manhood probing, tormenting, before he finally entered her, drawing out, entering, and withdrawing again until Alexa screamed from the need to feel his full length within her.

He began to move slowly, at the same time kissing her again and again, one hand working magic at her breast. Her hips moved against him in an instinctively arousing way until Fox could no longer restrain himself. Her body encased him perfectly as his thrusts grew more rapid, then frenzied. Sensation exploded within Alexa, every inch of her flesh alive and tense with a pleasure more exquisite than she had ever known existed. Her hands clasped Fox's neck, then slid down his back, finally to clasp the rock-hard muscles of his buttocks, helping him to plunge even deeper as her head drew back, her lips parted and she peaked into shards of glorious ecstasy. Then he began his own climax that was so dramatic Alexa thought for a moment her own might begin again.

They held each other until their bodies began to relax, melting together in perfect pleasure and harmony. Then Fox rolled to his side, pulling Alexa closely into his embrace. "My God, you're incredible!" Fox laughed a bit shakily. "I believe you were right when you said you wanted it. You acted as if it had been some time since you'd tasted the delights of love. Or am I just better than the others?"

"Why you conceited oaf!" Irritation sparked her words. "What makes you think you're better than any other man?"

"Ah, alas," sighed Fox, feigning weariness. "If you do not know, I fear I must try again. Obviously I failed to make a sufficient impression on you just now. But if you bear with me, milady Vixen, I will try to do better."

Alexa's eyes grew wide as he lifted her in his arms and carried her into the tepid water of the shallow lake. Setting her on her feet he slowly began to arouse her again, kissing her masked eyes, her lips, her breasts, until he felt her response ignite and turn into flames too hot to control. Beneath his lips and tongue her nipples grew hard as pebbles as he sucked them deep into his mouth, nipping tenderly. The softly lapping water gave his fingers buoyancy as they parted, probed, entered and withdrew. In a surprisingly short time Alexa found herself panting for breath, her body tense with desire.

Boosting her up by her firm buttocks, Fox wrapped her legs about his waist. Alexa gasped, clinging tightly to his massive shoulders and she rode him to glorious victory. But the victory was not hers alone for Fox quickly became the conqueror as he galloped to his own reward.

Two more days elapsed before repairs were completed on both *The Gray Ghost* and *My Lady Vixen*. They were busy days well spent in activity. But the nights found Alexa and Fox lost in a sensual world of their own making where none but the two of them existed. On each night remaining to them they made love repeatedly, as if they might never again see each other, only to awaken in the light of dawn more obsessed with one another than ever. Often Alexa would catch Fox looking at her oddly, a speculative gleam in his cinder-gray eyes.

Yet they were not prepared to reveal themselves. Had Fox been truthful, then Alexa would have gladly torn off her disguise. But for reasons of their own, they both remained stubborn to the end.

It was decided that the *Ghost* would leave the island first and act as a decoy in the event a stray English ship should be lurking about. *My Lady Vixen* was to follow an hour or two later. When Fox and Vixen stood at the water's edge, each seemed reluctant to take their leave.

"We'll meet again, Vixen," Fox told her, his arm casually draped around her slim waist.

"Aye, I'm sure of it, Fox," Alexa whispered. "Where do you venture now?"

"To Savannah. I've been gone too long already and there's vital information I must deliver to those fighting in the hills."

"What of the special lady you told me about?" goaded Alexa slyly. "Does she bide in Savannah?"

"A lady awaits me in Savannah but she is not the one I

told you about," teased Fox, watching her face closely for her reaction.

She didn't disappoint him as she assumed an affronted look. "I was right, you do keep a stable of women."

"But I love only one, Vixen, and I think you know who she is."

Alexa was stunned. Was he telling her he loved the Vixen? Where did that leave Alexa, his wife? "Are you married, Fox?" she asked abruptly.

Fox laughed raucously. "The Fox is married to the sea."

Perhaps Fox is married to no one but Adam is, thought Alexa ruefully. "What about the man behind the mask?" she asked softly. "Does he have a wife?" Her question was deliberately meant to goad.

Seconds dragged into minutes in which Fox remained mute. Just when the silence became unbearable they were interrupted by one of Fox's men. "We are ready to sail, Captain," he saluted as he acknowledged Alexa with a jaunty bob of his head.

"I'll be there directly," Fox replied, dismissing the man with a wave of his hand. Though he never did contrive to answer Alexa's question he did manage to say, "I fear for your safety, Vixen. It would please me to see you in some safe haven until the war's end."

"But it would not please me," Alexa scoffed. "I fully intend to continue my fight against oppression, Fox. The British have not yet heard the last from the Vixen. Nor have you," she added softly.

Curving her into the warmth of his muscular form, Fox captured her lips in a farewell kiss that promised another time, another place. Alexa responded with all the emotion she was capable of. When it ended, he turned and walked away, fearing to look back lest he fail to leave her at all. Alexa watched until his ship cleared the cove and turned northward.

While her own ship was being made ready, Alexa had much on which to ponder. This past week with Fox/Adam had shown her just how much she truly loved her husband despite his deception. After all, wasn't she playing at the same game? What hurt her most was his refusal to acknowledge a wife and how easily he had fallen under Vixen's spell. Didn't that prove just how fickle and dishonorable he really was? she contended glumly. He made love to the Vixen as if he had never made love to another woman before, as if the Vixen was the only woman in the world for him. She dared not think on their future, if indeed there was a future for them.

From every angle Alexa was assaulted by ugly suspicions concerning Fox's relationship with Lady Gwen while under the guise of Adam Foxworth and living a bachelor's existence in Savannah. Did he care at all for Gwen or was his attention to her only a ploy to allay suspicions concerning his activities against the crown? Would she ever learn the truth?

One hour after Fox and his crew left their island haven, the sails of My Lady Vixen caught the breeze and rode the tide into the Atlantic and into the arms of two British frigates waiting for her like sentinels guarding the entrance to the cove. As luck would have it Fox made it out before the ships arrived from another direction, so was unaware of the trap laid for Vixen. The ships had been sent to patrol the coast from the Carolinas to the Floridas in an effort to rid the seas of American privateers, in particular Fox and Vixen. They now had one of their prey trapped between the bay and open water at the entrance of the cove.

"My God, Vixen, it looks like the bloody English have

set a trap for us!" Drake cursed disgustedly. "Where in the hell is Fox now when we need him?"

"Sound battle stations, Drake," Alexa ordered calmly enough though inwardly she was quailing. "We'll try to slip through. My own ship looks fleeter than those frigates and with any luck we can outrun them."

"Their guns will trap us between them, Vixen, and make mincemeat out of us," warned Drake worriedly.

"It's our only chance. Issue weapons and pile on the sail. I'll take the wheel myself."

There was a mad flurry on deck while Alexa skillfully tacked, making as if to run back into the cove. A brisk breeze aided her cause as she tacked again the moment one of the frigates broke free to follow. Using all the knowledge she had gained in her months at sea, Alexa attempted to bring My Lady Vixen about and scoot past the frigate close on her heels. Her ploy was successful only for the length of time it took the frigate to swing about and give chase.

At that point the twenty-four pounders aboard the second frigate blasted forth, but all the shot fell short. A second volley came closer, as did the first frigate dogging their trail. To Alexa it looked hopeless as her own eighteen pounders answered the English guns. And then both frigates commenced firing as Alexa charted a zigzag course in an effort to escape total destruction. But to no avail. To Alexa's horror she found My Lady Vixen sandwiched between the two British ships.

It almost appeared as if they meant to take My Lady Vixen intact, along with her entire crew, for the guns were stilled as the two ships closed in on either side of the Vixen. But until they were too close to fire, Drake kept their own guns belching forth. One of their volleys brought down the mainmast and sails of the frigate on their starboard, but Alexa's joy was shortlived. Both ships were bumping against her hull, fixing their grappling hooks and running out the boarding planks.

Then Alexa saw a sight that froze her blood and sent her heart plummeting to her feet. Both ships were teeming with British soldiers! And they were swarming aboard the Vixen in ever increasing numbers. As brave as her men were they were no match for the vast number of soldiers who engaged them in hand to hand combat. In swift order Alexa dispatched two of them herself, then wheeled to engage another.

"We meet at last, Vixen," declared her opponent.

Alexa was startled to find she knew the young captain who faced her, his sword raised in mocking salute. Captain Lance Barrington, a nasty sneer twisting his lips, took a stance opposite her. "General Prevost dispatched a dozen ships to search the seas and destroy you. Too bad we couldn't snare the Fox in the same net. But you will do," he declared, thrusting dangerously at Alexa.

Alexa was far too busy concentrating on lunging, feinting, thrusting and sidestepping Barrington's spirited attack to answer. She was certain the final outcome of their bout meant little for she realized by the sounds around her, or rather by the lack of sound, that her men had already been subdued by the scores of British soldiers and sailors. But she fought on bravely, refusing to give over until she won or fell to her death.

"Are you surprised to see soldiers boarding your ship?" Barrington asked, stepping up the tempo. "It's the Governor's idea, really. He convinced the General to place troops on all the ships joining in the search. We've been looking for you and Fox, you know. From the Carolinas to the Floridas. And now we have you. It will be a red-letter day for the English when you're swinging from the gallows."

His words were meant to goad, and Alexa knew it. Still, she could not help but hurl a scathing reply. "It doesn't say much for the English when it takes a platoon of soldiers and the crewmen of two ships to capture one woman."

"Beware, Vixen," Barrington gritted out from between clenched teeth. "It will not go easy on you when I finally take you back to Savannah in irons."

"I can only die once," retorted Alexa brazenly as she skillfully lunged beneath his guard to slice a long shallow cut through his coat along the right side of his chest.

Warm blood soaked Barrington's clothes but his step did not falter. He was good, Alexa thought despairingly, too damn good. Suddenly Alexa was aware of quiet all around her, save for the clanging of her sword and Barrington's. Her arms were like two pieces of lead, responding automatically but feeling nothing except a bone-weary ache. Her legs were so tired they began to tremble, but she fought on, determined to kill or be killed.

At least an hour had passed since the English soldiers had leaped upon the teak decks of My Lady Vixen capturing her crew by their sheer numbers. Now, every eye was focused on the battling captains, Alexa's long, slim legs and bouncing breasts garnering the most attention. She was perfection, from her silvery locks to her leather boots; beauty in motion as she danced and lunged just out of reach.

Until her luck ran out. She never knew what caused her to falter, a turn of the ankle, a misstep, or just plain weariness. Whatever it was nearly cost her her life. She was saved by her quick thinking as she turned aside just as Barrington's sword reached beneath her guard to pierce her heart. Instead the blade sliced through the fleshy part of her left arm. Searing pain engulfed Alexa, nearly paralyzing her. Beads of perspiration broke out on her forehead and her right arm, though uninjured, grew too heavy to wield her sword.

His mouth curled in a derisive sneer, Barrington bleated triumphantly, "I won, Vixen! The day is mine!" The tip of his blade pricked the tender skin of her neck as Alexa's sword clattered from her numb fingers to the deck. Barrington's men began cheering so loudly they failed to hear the shout from the watch stationed high in the crow's nest.

Alexa clutched her left arm with her right hand in an effort to staunch the bleeding. Barrington's blade did not waver from her jugular as defiance blazed from the depths of her violet eyes. "I should kill you here and now, Vixen, but I won't," spat Barrington contemptuously. "I'd much rather see you at the end of a rope. But I will unmask you, my lady pirate."

Alexa stepped backwards as he reached out to remove the silken cloth hiding her perfect features. He laughed harshly and grasped her good shoulder to hold her in place. Quiet descended as every Englishman present realized they were about to see the infamous Vixen unmasked. But at the last moment fate intervened in the form of booming cannon and belching fire.

The thunder of cannon reached them the same instant as the watch who, unable to gain attention from his lofty perch, climbed down from the riggings to warn his mates of the swiftly approaching danger. "A ship, Captain!" the man yelled through the din. "And nearly upon us." His last words were superfluous for at that moment cannon shells exploded into the ship lashed to My Lady Vixen's starboard, setting several small fires.

Alexa's relief was enormous as Barrington relaxed his hold upon her long enough to view the oncoming ship. "My God!" he cried, "The Fox!" All eyes turned to watch the sloop skitter across the water with amazing speed, her big guns firing again into the frigate that had already received the brunt of his initial attack. By now one British ship was already ablaze and it was obvious something had to be done fast. "Cut her loose!" ordered Barrington as his men snapped to obey his command.

"We're a sitting target, sir!" called out one of the seamen. "We'd best get back aboard our own ship before it's too late."

Nodding in agreement, Barrington prodded Alexa forward as he ordered crisply, "Abandon the burning ship! Step lively, men! All hands over the side to our remaining ship!"

"What about Vixen's crew, sir?"

"Leave them. We haven't room to transport them what with two crews and a platoon of soldiers crowded aboard one ship, nor the time to dispatch them. I have the Vixen and that's who we came for. Hurry men, over the side!"

Faint from loss of blood, Alexa was prodded, shoved and dragged onto the English frigate. By now the *Ghost* was close enough so that she could see the magnificent figure of Fox standing on the quarterdeck, arms akimbo, feet wide apart, and Barrington reacted swiftly to the danger, ordering all their sails unfurled in order to escape the range of Fox's cannon. Though Barrington hated to admit it, Fox had caught him off guard and their best defense was retreat. With Vixen aboard perhaps Fox would be reluctant to fire upon them for fear of harming one of his own, allowing them to escape. But Barrington had underestimated Fox's cunning.

Alexa was lashed to the mainmast by Barrington's men, in plain view of the *Ghost*. Though Fox did not fire upon the frigate, he had little difficulty dogging their path. His sloop did not wallow beneath the weight of the combined crew of two ships and numerous soldiers, and could have run rings around the three-masted frigate. He was careful to keep well out of range of the big twenty-four pounders as he stood by helplessly watching the Vixen being lashed to the mast, blood flowing freely from her wound.

Fox considered an all-out attack, tacking in a zigzag pattern in order to avoid the cannon, but suddenly help came from another quarter. The crew of My Lady Vixen, having freed themselves from their bonds, and under the expert direction of Drake, joined in the foray.

The moment Barrington was made aware of My Lady Vixen's pursuit, he roundly cursed himself for neglecting to order the Vixen's crew killed or her ship fired in his haste to return to his own ship to escape Fox. But he still had Vixen and she was his passport to safety, if she lived, he thought wryly as he noticed her waxy pallor and the way she slumped against her bindings.

Immediately his ship came under the guns of both privateers as they fired warning shots across the frigate's bow. The frigate answered with a volley of her own, and when quiet prevailed once more, Barrington cupped his hands to his mouth and shouted across the water.

"If you hit us, Fox, you risk the life of the Vixen!"

"I'll take my chances," bluffed Fox, replying in a like manner. "Between my Gray Ghost and My Lady Vixen, we'll blow you out of the water. We'll trust in luck to rescue Vixen alive."

Fox had no intention of firing on the frigate, and knew Drake would follow his lead, but he did all in his power to convince the English otherwise. "We'll grant no quarter should you force us to fire," taunted Fox, his voice hard and cold. "Every one of you will die unless you give Vixen over to us."

The captain of the frigate, William Crisp, upon hearing Fox's words, approached Barrington. "This is still my ship, Captain, and I'm responsible for it as well as the lives involved. Unless we do as Fox orders and release the Vixen we'll be annihilated."

"I refuse to believe Fox would deliberately take the life of one of his own, Crisp." Barrington shook his head. "I don't believe he'll carry out his threat."

"I believe him," Captain Crisp declared. "The man's utterly ruthless. What's one woman's life to him? He's well aware that she'll face the hangman once she is returned to Savannah. Given her situation death at sea might be preferable. I say we give her over and consider ourselves lucky to escape with our lives."

Barrington was not so easily convinced. He trusted Fox not at all. He knew that the moment Vixen was off his ship the guns of both the *Ghost* and *My Lady Vixen* would not hesitate to blast them out of the water. For the moment Barrington settled on the ploy of wait and see, unwilling to give over his prize and unconvinced Fox would actually fire upon them with Vixen aboard. His answer was not long in coming.

Carefully instructing his gun crew on where to place the shot, Fox ordered a round of cannon aimed at the frigate. It hit well forward, starting several small fires. The frigate immediately retaliated only to find the sly Fox had maneuvered out of range. Next *My Lady Vixen* moved in position to fire which convinced Barrington more than anything that Fox would risk all, even Vixen, to sink an enemy. But Barrington was far from defeated as he slanted a sly glance in Vixen's direction, the beginnings of an idea forming in his mind.

He realized that Fox would not allow the frigate to escape once he had Vixen safely aboard the *Ghost*, so it stood to reason that a ploy must be devised in order to gain them the opportunity to escape the Americans, some sort of diversion. Captain Barrington's devious mind worked furiously as he quickly discarded several ideas, finally settling on one he was certain would work.

"You can have Vixen, Fox," he suddenly called out to the *Ghost* standing off their starboard. "Come and get her, we won't fire."

"If you do, *My Lady Vixen* will put a volley midship," warned Fox ominously.

"You have my word," shouted Barrington. Then he wheeled about to issue orders to Captain Crisp. Next, he went to Alexa, removed the ropes holding her in place and half-carried, half-dragged her to the railing in full view of both American ships.

Alexa was barely conscious, her head lolled from side to side, her mouth slack. Blood still oozed from her wound and she had a large bump on her forehead where she had been struck by one of her captors when she struggled against captivity.

Holding her firmly in place at his side, Barrington waited patiently as the *Ghost* slowly closed the gap between them. When he deemed the time exactly right, with the *Ghost* neither too close nor too distance for his purposes, he lifted Vixen's limp form high in his arms so that she hung partially over the rail. When he was certain he had Fox's full attention, he leaned out over the water, dangling Alexa like bait before him and calmly let her drop, down, down, down . . .

17

From the moment the Fox heard the roar of distant guns and realized it could only be Vixen in some kind of trouble, he was like a man demented. Without a moment's hesitation he ordered the *Ghost* about but it was still over an hour before he came within sight of the British frigates lashed to either side of *My Lady Vixen*. When he was close enough he fired a volley into one of the frigates; one of the balls evidently finding the magazine, setting the ship ablaze. But he had not arrived in time to save Vixen and he watched helplessly as an English officer dragged her aboard the second frigate after setting adrift their sinking mate.

The blood froze in Fox's veins when he saw that Vixen was wounded and bleeding profusely, appearing to be barely conscious. Only when the officer turned did Fox recognize him as Captain Lance Barrington. He nearly jumped into the water to swim to Vixen's aid when he saw one of the Englishmen strike her in the temple with the flat of his sword when she roused herself long enough to resist.

Then help came unexpectedly from the crew of *My Lady Vixen* and Fox hoped to bluff Barrington into releasing Vixen. After conversing with Barrington across the water, Fox took heart when he realized the captain believed he would destroy the frigate with Vixen aboard rather than allow an enemy to escape unscathed.

Relying on his initiative, Fox swiftly closed the distance between the two ships, signaling Drake to stand by with his guns trained on the frigate once he had Barrington's word that he would release Vixen. What happened next would live in Fox's memory forever. Horrorstruck, he watched Barrington, as if in slow motion, raise Vixen in his arms, dangler her over the rail and let her fall. It took a full minute for Fox to gain his wits and react.

Unbuckling his sword, removing his side arms and kicking off his boots, Fox considered nothing but his unwillingness to let Vixen die as he arched gracefully from the quarterdeck into the churning water below. From the deck of *My Lady Vixen* Drake watched as if hypnotied as Vixen's small body disappeared into a watery grave. He reacted in the same manner as Fox, hitting the water at nearly the same instant.

Grinning triumphantly, Barrington gave the signal and his ship, taking advantage of the diversion he had cunningly contrived, raised every sail available to them and turned tail. He was confident neither privateer would move from the spot until Vixen's body was recovered, and not for one minute did he believe Vixen would be pulled from the water alive. In any case, he would not be around to find out.

The shock of hitting the water roused Alexa to the point where she floundered futilely for a few minutes

before sinking helplessly beneath the surface.
Wounded, too weak to swim, she felt herself sinking,
whirling in a dark eddy, deeper—deeper— Her lungs
ached to draw in precious air and Alexa knew the end
was near when a peace descended upon her. Tranquil,
relaxed, mysteriously able to breathe, Alexa floated in a
void very near death until fate intervened.

Suddenly Alexa felt herself rising, being dragged
inexorably upward by her long silver locks. Vaguely she
wondered why the effort was being made for she was
perfectly able to breathe underwater. And then she
knew nothing more.

By the time Fox had located Alexa and dragged her to
the surface, long minutes had passed and she appeared
so lifeless he despaired that she could be fully restored.
With Drake's help Fox carefully handed Alexa into the
longboat that had been lowered the moment Fox hit the
water. Then Fox and Drake were hauled in.

It wasn't until Alexa lay stretched out on the teak deck
of the Ghost that Fox began in earnest to revive the
feeble spark of life left in her frail body. When he
pumped out every drop of water from her lungs and still
she did not breathe, he grew frantic. He couldn't lose
her now! There was too much left unsaid between them,
so much to resolve. He refused to let her die.

In desperation Fox covered Alexa's mouth with his
own, willing her to live by breathing his own life into her.
Again and again he forced air into her lungs, frustrated
when she failed to respond. "Don't die, damn you!" he
cried out, gripping her shoulders to emphasize his
words. "I need you, do you hear? Don't leave me!"

Drake stood beside Fox, tears streaming unashamedly
down his cheeks. "It's no use, Fox," he despaired,
placing a hand consolingly on Fox's straining shoulders.

"I won't give her up, Drake, she has to live! I won't

allow her to die," Fox croaked, shaking off Drake's restraining hand as he bent to continue his breath of life. He knew it was a radical procedure, one that he had heard of but never before tried. But at that point he was willing to try anything.

Suddenly Alexa's chest heaved weakly, once, twice, and then she began to cough and sputter. Jubilant, Fox did not cease his ministrations until he was certain Alexa no longer needed his help and was able to breathe on her own. Only then did he sink back on his heels and raise his eyes to heaven, thanking God for giving him back a woman he could not live without.

Alexa stirred, intensely aware of every bruise and ache in her battered body. A blaze of light pierced her closed lids and she groaned aloud, seeking a more comfortable position. "Alexa, wake up. Please! Speak to me, my love."

That voice! Fox! Fox was speaking to her, imploring her to awaken, calling her his love. Opening her eyes was a painful process but when she did she saw Fox leaning over her, his mouth beneath the mask tense with worry. "Thank God!" he breathed when her violet eyes finally focused on him. "I was afraid you'd never awaken."

"How . . . how long have I been out?" Alexa asked weakly.

"Three days," Fox informed her bleakly. "Three miserable days in which you hovered between life and death."

"You care so much?" Alexa asked, amazed.

"My God, Alexa, how could you even ask such a question?"

Suddenly Alexa tensed, aware for the first time that Fox had called her Alexa and not Vixen. A soft cry of distress rose from her throat as her hand searched her face, knowing even before she touched the soft skin of her cheek that her mask had been removed. "You know!" she accused petulantly.

"Alexa, my darling," Fox told her in a voice tinged with amusement, "I knew who you were the moment I laid eyes on your nude body stretched out so enticingly in the sand."

"You knew then? But . . . how? I . . . I don't understand. I was masked, my hair was bleached and I disguised my voice."

"Did you think I wouldn't recognize a body I know as intimately as my own? I know every inch of your glorious flesh, Alexa. Never would I mistake you for another. Besides," he grinned wolfishly, "there is one spot on your body you did not think to bleach. That special place, my love, was as black as the deepest night."

Alexa blushed furiously, knowing exactly the spot he was talking about. Actually, she hadn't considered bleaching so intimate a place, for she had no intention of allowing anyone a view of her nude body. "Why did you say nothing? Why did you allow me to believe I had fooled you?" accused Alexa hotly.

"At first I was enraged to discover you were the Vixen; that you had deliberately gone against my wishes and placed yourself in a position of danger. When you're feeling better you have much to explain. I'll want to know exactly how the Vixen came into being."

"Yet, in the end you left me to continue my charade, danger or no."

"I could have unmasked you, revealed you for who you were and escorted you back to Nassau. But what good would it have done?" He shrugged philosophically. "You would have found a way to surmount that obstacle and take to the sea again."

Alexa nodded slowly. "Aye, I would have."

"After our duel I knew you to be capable of taking care of yourself. Drake is a good man and so is Beggs. I talked with your men and found them loyal to the point of willing to die for you. Your courage and daring overwhelmed me and against my better judgment I decided it unfair of me to curtail your activities when you felt so strongly about the American cause."

Alexa beamed beneath his praise but was quickly deflated when Fox amended, "But it's over for you, Alexa. You were sorely wounded and I will not allow you to deliberately place yourself in danger again. For all intents and purposes the Vixen died beneath the sea. I'll make certain that the word is spread until it reaches the right ears. Goodbye, Vixen, welcome back, Alexa."

"No, Fox," begged Alexa. "Don't make me sit out the rest of the war in Nassau."

"You've no choice, my love. It will be months before your arm heals to the point where you can use it without causing yourself pain."

"So now I'll wager we're on our way to Nassau," she fumed impotently.

"Aye."

"What happened to the English frigate?"

"She turned tail and ran while we were involved in your rescue."

"Thank you for that," Alexa said softly. "Where is *My Lady Vixen*? Will she put in to Nassau also?"

"No," Fox said smugly. "Drake has taken command of the ship and is giving chase to the frigate hoping to catch up to her."

"What?" Alexa asked indignantly. "I don't believe you! Drake would not act without orders from me."

"I told you it was over for you, Alexa. He saw how gravely injured you were. We all thought you were dead

304

when I pulled you from the water. You scared ten years off my life. That you live at all is a miracle. No, my love, the Vixen has ceased to exist."

Weariness etched deep lines in Alexa's face as she started to protest, but Fox silenced her by placing a finger against her soft lips. "No more, Alexa, you are still far from well. Go back to sleep. In the meantime I'll have something appetizing prepared for you to eat, and when you awaken we'll talk further. There is still much I don't know concerning your transformation from my sweet Alexa to the fierce Vixen."

Alexa nodded tiredly. But before she closed her eyes and drifted off to sleep, she murmured, "Yes, Adam, there is much to tell you and even more for you to tell me." Stunned, Fox could only stare at her, the even movement of her chest telling him she was already fast asleep.

It was dark when Alexa awoke hours later feeling rested as well as ravenous, but still hurting. A short time later Fox came into the cabin bearing a basin of hot water and proceeded to tenderly bathe her face and hands. Only then did Alexa become aware that she wore one of Fox's soft linen shirts as a nightgown and that her left arm was tightly bound and held firmly in place by a sling, making movement awkward at best.

When a tray was brought in Alexa concentrated on the food while Fox sat back and watched, sometimes reaching over to help her cut her meal into bit-sized portions she could manage easily with one hand. His eyes never left her face and Alexa realized that soon there would be no more secrets between them, and inwardly she rejoiced.

Replete, Alexa told Fox she was finished and he set

the tray aside, then settled on the bed beside her. "Do you feel strong enough to talk, Alexa?" he asked in the husky whisper he assumed in his identity as the Fox.

"Aye, Adam, as soon as you remove your mask," Alexa shocked him by saying. "There'll be nothing between us now but the truth."

"How long have you known?" Fox/Adam asked when he finally found his voice.

"I discovered you were the Fox shortly before you left me in Nassau. I must admit it was a shock to learn my own husband did not trust me enough to tell me the truth."

"It was for your own safety, my love," Adam explained as he removed the final barrier that stood between them. "I feared you might let it slip inadvertently had you known who I was. You see, though I was outwardly working for General Prevost, the messages I carried were relayed to Americans. During those frequent missions for the English when my absences wouldn't be questioned, I took to the sea as Fox. Did you ever wonder how Fox was so familiar with the British shipping schedule from England?"

"But damn it, Adam, you knew I was loyal to the American cause!" accused Alexa angrily. "Yet you deliberately deceived me! I let Fox make love to me! All the while feeling terrible guilt because I thought I was betraying my husband!"

"I wondered about that, my love," Adam admitted wryly. "At first it hurt to think you'd allow another man to make love to you so easily. I was bitterly jealous of my other self. But by then you were aware of my identity, weren't you, Alexa?"

Alexa smirked, happy at least that she had confused Adam enough to question her loyalty. "You asked for it, Adam."

"Tell me truthfully, my love, did you mean it when you told Fox you loved him?"

"Aye, I meant it."

"And Adam?"

"I didn't love Adam until . . . until later. You see, Fox took my virginity and I harbored tender feelings for him long before I realized my love for Adam. Besides, in the beginning Adam wasn't deserving of my love. You have to admit Adam was rather despicable."

"You minx," replied Adam, uncertain whether he liked her explanation. Then he made a revelation of his own. "I loved you as Fox long before I allowed Adam to love you." Alexa looked incredulous. "It's true, my love. Fox was free to love who and where he pleased; he had no vendetta against the Ashleys. I think Fox loved you from the moment he saw you. It took Adam longer to admit his feelings."

"Yet you were willing to leave me to face my father and rush back to America to marry Lady Gwen! Why?"

"Gwen was necessary to the cause, or so I thought. While you only complicated my life."

Alexa searched Adam's face, afraid to ask what was burning on the tip of her tongue. But because it was important to her, she overcame her reticence and asked, "Adam, in the months we've been apart, on your trips back to Savannah and Adam, did you . . . make love to Gwen?"

Adam flushed darkly, unwilling to answer until her piercing gaze prompted him to say, "Alexa, I don't want to talk about Gwen. I did what I had to in order to avoid suspicion."

"Tell me, Adam," she repeated softly.

"I did not bed her, Alexa. After Fox rescued you and Mac on the eve of your hanging, Adam disappeared for awhile. It looked very suspicious that I should drop out of sight at the same time you did. When I returned to Savannah from Nassau I told everyone I was out looking for you, that I wanted you hung for your crime as badly as they did. They wouldn't have believed me had I not taken up with Gwen almost immediately. I was forced to keep up the pretense with Gwen or else risk having my identity revealed."

"Thank you for being honest with me, Adam," Alexa said gravely. "How long must your charade with Gwen continue?"

"Until the English are driven from American soil or I am found out and hung."

"I see," was all Alexa said. But try as she might Alexa did not understand how wooing Gwen aided the American cause. "Do you love me, Adam?" she asked abruptly.

"More than life, my love," smiled Adam, his love shining from the depths of his smoky eyes.

"Then I'll try to understand why you must . . . must court Gwen. But I don't have to like it."

"Nor do I," replied Adam so sincerely that Alexa was inclined to believe him.

They talked a while longer of the war. Adam informed her that Cornwallis had marched leisurely into North Carolina but had suffered the loss of two detachments sent at intervals to disperse various partisan corps of Americans. On October 7, 1780, a force of 1100 men under Major Patrick Ferguson was surrounded at King's Mountain, South Carolina, near the North Carolina line, by bands of riflemen under Colonel Isaac Shelby, Colonel James Williams and Colonel William Campbell. After a desperate fight on the wooded and rocky slopes, the British surrendered. Ferguson himself was killed.

Later, in another skirmish, Colonel Tarlton's English troops were practically destroyed by a cavalry attack led by American Colonel William Washington at Cowpens, southwest of King's Mountain. Despite the weakening his army suffered by these losses, Cornwallis marched rapidly through North Carolina, giving General Greene a hard chase. Later still, the two armies met at Guilford courthouse and a virtually drawn battle was waged in which no one came out a clear winner. Tactically, the English were victors given their tenacity and superior numbers, despite the loss of 600 men. A few weeks later, however, Cornwallis abandoned the heart of the Carolinas and Georgia and marched to the coast at Wilmington, North Carolina to recruit and refit his command.

"What about the war at sea?" Alexa asked. "How is it progressing?"

"The French are doing all in their power to aid us," Adam replied. "Admiral De Grasse has orders to cooperate with Washington's armies in a joint operation. It looks like the tide of war is finally turning in our favor."

"Thank God," Alexa fervently prayed. "Is Prevost still in control of Savannah?"

"Aye, unfortunately. But I think I've tired you out enough for one day. Sleep, my love, I won't be far away."

And he wasn't, for some time during the night Alexa awoke to feel Adam's warmth lying beside her, though carefully keeping his distance so as not to hurt her. Sighing contentedly, Alexa cuddled closer and went back to sleep, feeling safe and protected.

Adam awoke at dawn and stared down at his sleeping wife, marveling at the peaceful look on her beautiful face despite her recent ordeal. Over and over he cursed himself for allowing her to continue her charade as Vixen when he realized the infamous privateer was his own wife. It was true, just as he told Alexa, that he had recognized her immediately, especially after he made love to her. If nothing else convinced him, that alone did. He chuckled beneath his breath, imagining how shocked she must have been, knowing that he was Adam Foxworth, to find him so anxious to make love to another woman. It serves her right, the little minx, he thought perversely.

He blamed himself for not insisting she give up the sea and return to Nassau immediately. He should have escorted her there personally. But he knew, determined as she was, Alexa would have found some way to circumvent his orders and bring the Vixen back into being. But this time he meant business. He fully intended to place two guards ashore with her in order to make damn certain she would not slip away once her arm healed.

Alexa opened her eyes, watching the play of emotion on Adam's handsome features in the murky darkness. "What are you thinking?" she asked quietly.

"How much I love you and how I nearly lost you through my own stupidity," confessed Adam unhesitantly. "Have you forgiven me yet for lying to you?"

"I can forgive you almost anything except how badly you treated me while I was imprisoned for treason. I hated you when you showed up at my trial with Gwen."

"I hated myself for hurting you. But as I explained, it was necessary. I had to be free in order to rescue you as Fox. I was shocked when I returned to Savannah to find you were being held prisoner along with Mac. It was everyone's assumption that you would both hang."

"What took you so long in returning?" Alexa asked. "When Mac showed up at the plantation gravely wounded and told me of the trap set for you I feared for your life."

"I was wounded, my love. I took a ball in the shoulder and another in the thigh," explained Adam. "I tried to reach the plantation but passed out in the woods. Evidently the English lost my trail and found Mac instead."

"What happened?"

"As luck would have it I was found the next day by a hunter, one loyal to our cause. He carried me back to his shack in the woods where I recuperated. We were so isolated I knew nothing of what was going on in Savannah until informed by a chance visitor. Then I hastened back to take charge of your rescue."

Alexa trembled. "I shudder to think what would have happened had you not returned when you did."

"Don't even think it, my love," frowned Adam who had often thought the same thing during the past months.

Raising up on one elbow, Adam captured her mouth in a tender kiss, gentle at first but quickly passing the bounds of gentleness as his tongue explored the sensual contours of her lips, then the warm, moist sweetness within. Alexa sighed, wishing she could put both arms around his neck instead of just one.

Adam's mouth left hers, sliding along her cheek, caressing her neck, the soft skin above the shirt she wore. His head raised and his powerful arms lifted her slightly so that he could shove up her nightdress to uncover her breasts. A surge of fiery sparks flew down her stomach to that spot between her thighs with the first hot, wet touch of his mouth full upon that perfect mound, drawing it deeply into his mouth, sucking, then biting gently.

Alexa moaned softly and to Adam it was like a dash of cold water in his face. "My God, Alexa, what am I doing?" he cried. "You're not well enough to make love!" Abruptly he drew back and Alexa experienced a feeling of deprivation, but she knew he was right. She was far too weak to respond as she would wish.

Three days later the Bahamas could be seen in the distance, jewels of verdant green floating in a setting of turquoise-blue and surrounded by crescents of white sand sparkling like diamonds against the sun. Though still weak Alexa was out of bed for the occasion and basking in the warmth of the perfect day. Adam had agreed to let her out of bed but would not allow her to don Vixen's revealing clothes. Instead, she appeared demurely clad in a dress he had taken as booty from an English ship. In fact, there was a whole trunkful of clothing at Alexa's disposal.

As they approached New Providence Island Adam, still under the guise of Fox, climbed the rigging to scan the harbor. What he saw sent his senses reeling. Several English warships lined the beautiful bay and two of them in the process of weighing anchor and heading toward open sea. Thinking swiftly, Fox scampered down the ratlines in record time, hitting the deck on the run. Within minutes the wheel was in his competent hands as he skillfully maneuvered the ship about to scurry before the wind. The English were afforded no more than a glimpse of their stern as the fleet sloop disappeared over the horizon.

Once the British ships were left in their wake and no longer visible, Adam went in search of Alexa whom he sent below fuming at the first sign of danger. "We've outrun them, Alexa," he told her. "For the time being the danger is past. But we can no longer assume Nassau to be a safe place for you."

"What will you do now? Does this mean I can remain aboard the *Ghost*?" she asked hopefully.

"No, my love. I told you I must return to Savannah. It's imperative I find out from General Prevost what the English plan next."

"What about me, Adam? Is there nowhere I will be safe?"

"I know of no place I can leave you and be absolutely certain of your safety," Adam pondered, deeply troubled. "If only I could take you back to Foxworth plantation and keep you with me. We've been parted far too long for my liking."

Suddenly Alexa brightened considerably. "Why not, Adam? Take me to Foxworth plantation, I mean." Excitement colored her words. "Who would think of looking for me there? If anyone comes I'll hide."

"I don't know, my love," Adam hesitated, considering her words. "What if someone should accidentally discover you?"

"I'll remain a blond! It's been months and months since anyone has seen me. If they do by chance catch a glimpse of me they won't recognize me."

"It's risky, Alexa, damn risky. But it could work. If need be I could always hide you away with rebel sympathizers."

"It's settled then!" Alexa rejoiced. "You'll take me back home?"

"I have no choice. It's either that or send you back to sea on the *Ghost*. And I refuse to endanger your life in such a manner again. I told you before the Vixen is dead."

Alexa lamented the death of Vixen as sorrowfully as she would have mourned her best friend. Vixen was a vital part of her and she regretted the loss sorely. But in one thing Adam was right. It would be months before she would be well enough to resume her daring exploits at sea.

Adam waited until dark to bring the *Ghost* into the secret cove. From there he and Alexa were forced to walk to Foxworth Manor. After taking on fresh water the *Ghost* was to take to the sea again under the able direction of the first mate. She was due to rendezvous with Mac in the West Indies and await instructions from Captain John Paul Jones. In six weeks she was to return again for Fox. In the meantime Fox would resume his Adam identity and gather vital information from General Prevost and Governor Wright.

Alexa was so exhausted Adam carried her the last few yards to the house. It was late when he entered and all was dark but for a single lamp left burning in the hallway by Jem who by now was accustomed to his master's comings and goings. Alexa was taken directly to their room where she fell asleep even before Adam tenderly tucked her in.

The next morning before Alexa awoke Adam approached Jem, instructing him to replace all the house servants. Jem was so shocked by the request that Adam took the man into his confidence, explaining why he wanted no one left in the house who might recognize Alexa as his wife. Because Jem had become fond of Alexa he readily agreed to Adam's strange request. But when Adam revealed that the household was to regard Alexa as his mistress, Katy, a name he quickly made up, Jem balked.

"It ain't right, Mastah Adam," Jem remonstrated. "That lady upstairs has been treated badly enough already without the servants considering her a loose woman."

"Would you rather see her dead, Jem?"

314

Once Jem considered the alternative he followed Adam's instructions religiously, so that when Alexa was finally introduced to the new servants they were inclined to look down their noses at a mere mistress, but being slaves, had no recourse but to accept her as their master instructed.

Alexa knew that Jem alone knew her secret, as well as Adam's, and suffered the other servants' contemptuous treatment in silence. What hurt the most was that Adam told her she was not to see her dear friend, Mary Forbes, for fear of discovery. Not only was it best for Alexa's safety but also for Mary's. It had been nearly two years since she last set foot on Foxworth plantation and she was too happy to be back to complain.

A young girl named Missy had been assigned to her as personal maid and Alexa set out immediately to win the girl's friendship. The maid reacted dramatically to Alexa's friendly overtures and from then on Missy would allow no one to speak ill of her beautiful mistress, loose woman or no.

A week later Adam came to Alexa with the news that he must go to Savannah to confer with General Prevost. "I don't want to go, my love, but I must. Something big is brewing and I must learn what it is."

"Adam," Alexa blushed and looked away. "Will . . . will you see Gwen?"

"It's unavoidable, Alexa," he replied, wishing it could be otherwise.

"I won't ask, Adam, if you have to . . . to bed her. You know how I feel about it."

"I will do what I must, my love," Adam said with bitter emphasis.

A wash of tears blurred Alexa's vision and she turned away. Was courting Gwen really the chore he made it out to be? she wondered bleakly. He had not attempted to make love to her since the island even though she was recovering rapidly from her wound. Adam had even left her to sleep alone since their return and she made up her mind not to send him off to Gwen without a reminder of how beautiful it was between them.

Lifting her vibrant violet eyes still shimmering with large drops of pearly tears, Alexa asked huskily, "Do you love me, Adam?"

"My God, Alexa, how can you ask such a thing? You mean everything to me."

"Then make love to me. Now! Take me upstairs and love me!"

A surge of hot desire spiraled up through him at Alexa's impassioned plea. He had deliberately bridled his passion until he was sure she had recovered her full health. "Are you certain, my love?" he asked, his voice harsh with emotion. "Are you well enough? I had hoped . . . but did not want to rush you."

"You aren't rushing me, Adam. Oh, my darling, I want it. I want *you*. Please don't deny me the right to be your wife again when I want that more than anything. If you must take Gwen, I want it to be me you think of me while you're . . . you're making love to her."

"Come then, my love," he gasped, scooping her up in his arms, "I'll make love to you the rest of the day and all night, until you tell me to stop." Racing with her into the hall, up the stairs and past the shocked servants he bore her into her room, setting her on her feet only when the door was firmly shut behind them.

With agonizing slowness he undressed her, murmuring over the perfection of her breasts, the slimness of her waist, the roundness of her hips, her long shapely legs, following his words with soft, feathery kisses on her lips and breasts. When she was completely nude she helped him disrobe, running her hands lovingly through his tawny hair, then twining them into the fur of his brawny chest. Her fingers played shamelessly with his male nipples, surprised when they hardened much like her own. Continuing her sensuous exploration, she skimmed his slim hips, feeling the corded tendons in his bulging thighs. When she grasped that part of him that grew long and hard, he moaned and raised her high in his arms, then slowly lowered her to the bed.

His mouth fell to hers in a bruising kiss, his tongue thrusting into her mouth much as she longed to be pierced from below. One huge hand found her breast, to torment her before it followed a path to her flat stomach, and below, toying with the softly curling hairs there. She yearned for him to touch her, and when he did a moan of intense pleasure escaped her lips. With gently probing fingers he teased and parted her moist flesh while his lips took first one nipple and then the other deep into his mouth until she writhed beneath him, mad with desire.

Alexa cried aloud when his mouth left her breasts for sweeter pastures as his tongue plundered, then retreated, then launched a delicious foray into the moist cavern, piercing the very center of her need. Squirming to escape the exquisite torture, yet fearing he might stop, Alexa moaned in an ever increasing crescendo. But Adam was relentless as he grasped her hips to hold her in place, allowing her no respite from his questing mouth and tongue.

Finally the tension became too great to bear and Alexa screamed as she broke apart into a million blazing pieces, scattering and falling to earth, only to revive again when Adam thrust deep inside her. Alexa felt herself responding to Adam's drugging kisses and words of love as his forceful movements goaded her still higher. Their simultaneous climax eclipsed anything she had ever felt before.

After a short respite Adam took her again, and yet again. All through the day and night, until Alexa begged him to stop. In the morning he was gone.

18

Adam returned from Savannah three days later, and
Alexa welcomed him joyously until he presented her
with several gifts. The moment he handed her a large
box containing a beautiful yellow dress fashioned of the
finest linen she had ever seen, and a smaller box which
revealed a string of matchless pearls nestled in a bed of
velvet, a coldness pervaded her body and refused to be
dislodged. Her first thought was that Adam was
pandering to her for his indiscretions with Gwen. It was
all too obvious that his guilt drove him to extravagance
on her behalf. She made her feelings quite clear when
she contemptuously tossed his gifts aside.

"Don't you like your dress, Alexa?" Adam asked,
puzzled. "Or the pearls? I had hoped to please you."

"They would have pleased me, Adam, were I not
aware of what they represent."

"What do they represent?"

"They were meant to assuage your guilt over Gwen,"

319

Alexa accused sulkily. "I need no such presents, Adam, to remind me that I share my husband with another woman."

"You share me with no one, my love," Adam revealed. "I couldn't make love to Gwen. Not after what we shared before I left."

Alexa stared at Adam incredulously, happiness lighting her flawless features. "Do you mean it, Adam? What . . . what happened?"

"I was careful to avoid Gwen the whole three days." He grinned deviously. "I made a concentrated effort to remain close to General Prevost the entire time I remained in the city."

"Oh, Adam," Alexa cried, throwing herself into his arms. "I do love you!"

"Should I tell you what else I learned or shall I take you to bed immediately?" Adam laughed.

Alexa flushed prettily. Was she so transparent? "Tell me, Adam, please."

"Drake caught up with the British frigate and Captain Barrington. There was a fierce fight and Drake killed Barrington. The surviving crew were set adrift and the ship scuttled. They were picked up by another British ship."

"Good for Drake!" Alexa declared, her eyes gleaming with pride. "What else did you learn?"

"All of Savannah is agog with the news that the Vixen is dead. The survivors of the frigate reported she was mortally wounded by Barrington and subsequently drowned when he threw her overboard. Their belief was reinforced when their frigate was overtaken by *My Lady Vixen* and the lady herself failed to materialize during the fighting. So, my darling, the Vixen is well and truly laid to rest."

Alexa looked so sad that Adam was prompted to ask, "Why so pensive? It's what we've hoped for."

"I feel as if a part of me has been torn out," Alexa ventured. "I liked the Vixen. I liked her independence, her courage, her ability to operate on her own. She was beholden to no man, victim to none. I'll miss her."

"You're wrong, Alexa. The Vixen is dead in name only but she lives on in the heart and soul of Alexa. Nothing or no one can take that from you, nor will defeat claim you. I should know, for once I set out to destroy you only to be conquered in the end by a violet-eyed vixen."

Then Adam carried her upstairs to show by his actions what his words attempted to convey.

Once their passion was temporarily sated, Adam told Alexa that Cornwallis had retired to Yorktown to rest and await developments. Alexa was happy to learn that Adam would remain at Foxworth plantation until the *Ghost's* arrival in about four weeks. It was a time of renewal for them—a month in which Adam rarely ventured to Savannah, devoting his days and nights to his wife. Until one day their bubble unexpectedly burst with disastrous results.

That day in August of 1781 dawned clear and hot like so many other summer days in Georgia. Adam had arisen early as was his custom and, taking advantage of his time on the plantation, was in the fields with Forbes, catching up on the workings of his large holdings. Alexa, finding time heavy on her hands that particular morning, wandered into the study, one of her favorite places because it was quietly located in the rear of the house and accessible not only through the door off the hallway but by French doors opening into the garden. When Adam was in the fields he often came into the house through the garden entrance, since it was closer than going around to the front or entering through the kitchen and disrupting the servants.

Overcome by a strange restlessness Alexa wandered about the familiar room, touching objects Adam had touched, sniffing the pleasant odors of leather and tobacco, wishing he were with her to still the unexplained tension that had gripped her from the moment she lifted her head from the pillow this morning.

Alexa smiled a secret smile, her hand splayed across her flat stomach. She couldn't wait to see Adam's face when she told him of her suspicions. She hoped he would be as pleased as she to learn she was expecting a child. According to her calculations it had happened on the island. She had deliberately waited to tell him until she was certain. There was no longer any need to wait. In seven months she would bear Adam's child.

So engrossed was she in her thoughts of bearing Adam a healthy baby that she failed to hear the altercation taking place at the front of the house. She had no notion of what was transpiring until the door to the study flung wide to admit a fuming Gwen. Jem followed helplessly in her wake, sputtering, "I'm sorry, Mistress Katy. I told Lady Gwen that Mastah Adam was in the fields but she insisted on waiting in here for him."

Alexa felt the color drain from her face. The last person in the world she expected to see this morning was Lady Gwen. Courage, Alexa, she told herself, drawing in a deep, steadying breath. If she passed the test with Gwen it was unlikely she would be recognized by anyone else in Savannah.

"So, it's true!" Gwen ground out from between clenched teeth as she glared contemptuously at Alexa.

"I beg your pardon," replied Alexa, feigning ignorance. "Who are you?"

"I am Lady Gwen Wright, Lord Penwell's fiancée," declared Gwen boldly, "and you don't have to tell me who you are. I heard from my dressmaker that Adam recently purchased a gown for some woman. It wasn't for me so I concluded he must have a mistress tucked away here at Foxworth Manor. How convenient for him."

Alexa flushed but refused to be cowed by Gwen's snide remarks. "Adam's fiancée?" she questioned guilelessly. "I was under the impression that Adam already had a wife."

"He did have a wife but she is dead. She was a traitor and rescued on the eve of her hanging by a pirate. Nothing has been heard of her for years and Adam is convinced she is no longer alive."

"I see," was all Alexa said, turning her face so her long, blond hair partially obscured her features.

"Where did Adam find a lowborn slut like you?" demanded Gwen disparagingly. Alexa refused to rise to the bait, further angering Gwen. "Probably on one of those mysterious trips of his," she sniffed, answering her own question, "that he takes so frequently. Where is your lover?"

"Adam is in the fields, just as Jem told you. No doubt he'll be back shortly. Do you wish to wait?"

While Alexa spoke in a soft, whispery voice she hoped would fool Gwen, a nagging suspicion tugged at the haughty Englishwoman and she peered sharply at the beautiful blond, her eyes narrowed in thought. "Do I know you?" she asked, observing Alexa closely. "For some reason you look familiar."

"No, I've never seen you before," insisted Alexa, stifling the urge to run as far away as she could in order to escape Lady Gwen's sharp eyes. "I've just recently come down from Charleston."

"So, that's where Adam found you," Gwen snarled, in her anger forgetting Alexa's similarity to someone she was certain she knew. "In some brothel, no doubt."

Alexa lowered her head, blushing, which to Gwen was a near admission of guilt. "Ha! I knew it!" crowed Gwen triumphantly. "Surely you must know that a whore like yourself can mean nothing to a man like Lord Penwell no matter how beautiful . . . Adam and I are to be married soon and I suggest you leave of your own accord while you are still able."

Gwen's thinly veiled threat hung in the air like heady autumn smoke. "I will leave when Adam tells me to and not before," Alexa declared, her voice laced with loathing. Try as she might Alexa could not forget that the despicable Englishwoman standing before her had intimate knowledge of Adam's love.

"I don't believe I'll wait for Adam after all," Gwen announced. "It's degrading to me to remain in the same room with his whore. Tell him for me he has much explaining to do and I'll expect him in Savannah within the next twenty-four hours or our engagement is off."

"Somehow I don't think Adam will care," replied Alexa softly. Highly insulted as well and enraged at Adam, Gwen turned and flounced from the room in a snit, unaware that she had dropped her reticule just outside the door in her haste to leave Alexa's daunting presence.

The moment Gwen rushed from the room Alexa's knees began to wobble and she clutched at the back of a chair to keep from collapsing. For one awkward moment during the entire interchange Alexa feared Gwen had seen through her feeble attempt to disguise her true identity. After all, she had done little more than bleach her hair. But thankfully, Gwen's anger had prevented her from delving too deeply into her memory.

Suddenly a loud voice interrupted her ruminations. "Alexa, my love, look who's here!" Alexa whirled as Adam came striding through the French doors followed by Mac and Drake. "I thought I'd find you here," Adam grinned, slipping an arm about her slim waist.

"Adam, please be quiet," Alexa warned, placing a finger to his lips. "Gwen was just here."

"I know," Adam replied, "we saw her carriage drive off as we came through the fields. What did she want? Did she recognize you?"

"I'll tell you later, Adam, after I've properly greeted our friends," smiled Alexa, offering her hands to Mac and Drake. A handshake did not satisfy Mac as he drew Alexa into his arms and planted an exuberant kiss on her soft lips despite Adam's jealous glare.

"Now I can tell you," Alexa said, turning back to Adam. "I don't think Gwen recognized me though she did give me quite a scare. But let's forget her for the time being."

"Alexa, had I known I was creating the Vixen when I taught you to sail and use a weapon I would have refused your request outright instead of letting you wheedle me into doing something that went against my better judgment," Mac declared with a twinkle. "I'm surprised Adam still speaks to me, let alone allows me in his house."

"It's over with, Mac." Alexa smiled almost regretfully, for she did miss the excitement of her former life. "I am no longer the Vixen."

"You don't know how happy that makes me," Drake cut in, greeting Alexa every bit as exuberantly as Mac. "I was hoping when you and Fox clashed on the island he would insist you return to Nassau."

"When did you find out about Fox, Alexa?" Mac asked. "On the island?"

"No," Alexa grinned impishly. "I knew Adam was the Fox long before that."

"I'll bet that's some story," leered Mac wolfishly.

"One that shall remain untold," Adam declared, slanting Alexa a challenging look.

Alexa glared back defiantly. "You kept me in the dark concerning your activities for so long you deserved whatever you got."

"Alexa," warned Adam, tempering his warning with amusement.

"Oh, all right, Adam," Alexa capitulated, feigning defeat. Then she burst into laughter until Adam followed suit, quickly catching Mac and Drake in their hilarity.

Had Alexa and her companions been able to see through the closed door they wouldn't have felt so joyous and carefree. Lady Gwen did indeed leave in her carriage but she hadn't rounded the bend before she missed her reticule and ordered her driver back to the house. Certain that she had dropped her bag in the hallway, Gwen did not bother to knock but slipped through the unlatched door and retraced her steps to the study where she had encountered Alexa a short time earlier. She spotted her reticule almost immediately and bent to retrieve it. It was then she heard loud voices and the names of the infamous pirates, Fox and Vixen, spoken.

Gwen felt no qualms about putting her ear to the door and listening to the conversation. Her eyes grew round as saucers and her mouth trembled in disbelief as she shared secrets no one but the people in the room were privy to. That the woman she had spoken to only moments before was Adam's wife came as no surprise for she had already begun to suspect the blond woman was other than she pretended. But to learn that Alexa was the Vixen was a stroke of luck she hadn't counted upon.

What she heard so stunned her that her legs refused to hold her and she dropped to her knees before the door. Adam Foxworth, Lord Penwell, the man she had hoped to marry was the Fox—that wily privateer who seemed at times to disappear into thin air to stymie his foe! And no wonder! In reality he was a respected member of English nobility. And now, she alone knew their secret.

But not for long. She grinned deviously as she picked herself off the floor and left the house as quietly as she had entered.

Inside the study the four privateers celebrated their reunion oblivious to Gwen's hasty exit as they raised glasses of sparkling brandy in a toast to a United States of America free from English intervention.

"I know the Ghost is on its way here to pick up Adam," Alexa said after their toast had been made, "but what are you two doing here with your ships?"

"Good news, Alexa," Mac revealed, elated. "De Grasse and a large contingent of twenty-eight French vessels and 3300 troops sailed from Haiti for the Chesapeake. We are to rendezvous here with the Ghost, pick up Fox, and depart immediately to join the battle in the north which is bound to be decisive."

"Oh, Mac, you mean the war will be decided by this one battle?" Alexa sparkled.

"It's very likely," Adam forestalled Mac's answer. "We're bound to beat the English with so large a force. From there it's on to New York where Cornwallis is holed up. The end is in sight, my love."

"When must you leave?" Alexa asked shakily, unwilling to part with him so soon. She hadn't even told him yet about the baby.

"In a day or two, as soon as the Ghost arrives."

Alexa nodded solemnly, swallowing the lump forming in her throat. "I understand," she said, blinking her eyes rapidly to dispel the tears gathering there.

Later they shared an excellent supper and then continued their visit over coffee and brandy. It was late when Drake and Mac returned to their ships and Adam and Alexa were allowed to escape to the privacy of their room.

Needing no words to express what they both felt,

Adam undressed her leisurely, her senses fully awakened by his touch. They made love slowly, reverently, almost as if it were their first time, or their last. Words of love flowed freely, unhampered by mistrust or deception. Alexa knew she had no experience for comparison; to her it was an instinctive knowledge that only in Adam's arms could her body, her mind, her love, find such perfect joy.

No other lips had the ability to tease, caress, and titillate as did Adam's. No other hands had the power to elicit so dramatic a response as they explored, parted, probed the secret places of her body. And when he finally pushed his way inside her, she welcomed him with a throaty purr, feeling his desire swelling within her.

Beneath his mouth the rosy tips of her breasts surged and stood erect as his forceful thrusts carried her from darkness into blinding light. When he grasped the rounded mounds of her buttocks to still her mindless writhing as he labored to bring them both to climax, Alexa cried out her joy into the stillness of the night. Only when her tremors ceased did Adam allow his own passion free rein and join her.

They lay closely entwined in the aftermath, basking in contentment and filled with awe at their total surrender to each other. It was a perfect time in which to tell Adam about the baby, Alexa smiled drowsily. But the words she formed in her mind were never uttered.

Both Adam and Alexa were startled from their euphoria by a loud banging on the door and angry voices calling out to them. Alexa froze, recalling that day so long ago when she had been disturbed in the same manner. The day she and Mac had been carted off to prison.

"Open up!" a loud voice demanded. "Open in the name of the king or we'll break the door down!"

"Oh God, Adam! They know!" Alexa wailed, clinging to Adam. "You must get away."

"We know you're in there Fox! You too, Vixen! You won't escape so easily this time!"

"They want us both," Adam said grimly, pulling on his trousers. "I have to get you out of here, my love. Hurry, slip into your robe, I won't allow them to take you again!"

"What are you going to do?"

"I'm going to stall them while you go out through the study doors to the cove where the *Lady A* and *My Lady Vixen* are anchored."

"Adam, no!" protested Alexa. "I won't leave without you!"

The men outside began battering down the door and in desperation Adam grasped Alexa's slim shoulders in an effort to shake some sense into her. "Use your head, Alexa! I'm better prepared to take care of myself than you are! There are ways and means to escape as long as I don't have you to worry about. Go!" he ordered, shoving her roughly. "I want you out of here before they break down the door. Hurry," he called, "tell Mac what happened. And Alexa, I love you!"

Then he was out the door and racing down the steps, sword raised high in a futile effort that did little more than allow Alexa sufficient time to run into the study and out the French doors—into the waiting arms of Charles Whitlaw!

19

Beneath the relentless barrage the door finally splintered and broke apart. Adam was momentarily stunned but not surprised to find nearly twenty men storming through the shattered opening. With sinking heart he realized there was no possible escape this time for the Fox. Maintaining his stance at the foot of the curving staircase, Adam fought bravely but from the onset he knew there could be but one outcome. His one burning desire was for Alexa's escape and that once Mac and Drake learned of his plight they might join forces to rescue him much in the same way he had once spirited Mac and Alexa out from under the noses of the English.

It took a wound in the side and another in the shoulder to subdue Adam, and even then it required four men to pin him down. ''Up the stairs!'' ordered the lieutenant in charge. ''Find the Vixen! I want them both!''

After several long minutes, minutes in which Adam hoped Alexa would make good her escape, the men surged down the stairs to report no one but servants on the upper floors. "Where is she?" asked the lieutenant, prodding Adam with the tip of his boot. "We know the Vixen is here and we know who she is, so don't try to lie."

"I don't know what you're talking about," Adam retorted, feigning ignorance. "There was no one here but my mistress and she returned to Charleston earlier today."

"We know better," snarled the lieutenant. "Lady Gwen told the General everything. By now it is common knowledge that Lord Penwell is the Fox and his wife the Vixen."

"Gwen," spat Adam contemptuously. "I might have known. It's too late, gentlemen, there is no one here but myself."

The entire house was searched thoroughly, and when the study doors were discovered open the grounds were searched as well as the slave quarters. Next the fields, outbuildings and surrounding woods were scoured while Adam lay in a ever widening pool of congealing blood, praying that Alexa would not be found and that the secret cove where the *Lady A* and *My Lady Vixen* lay at anchor would remain undiscovered.

With the advent of dawn the search intensified and the path through the woods leading to the secret cove was indeed discovered. But when the troops stood at the edge of the water not a ship was in sight, and Adam rejoiced when he heard the news, too sorely wounded to realize that had his friends known he was in trouble they would have come to his aid. Only then did he allow weakness and loss of blood to overcome him as he slid gratefully into darkness.

Alexa squirmed and struggled but the arms holding her were too strong. Panic seized her as she realized she was caught as well as Adam and she could do nothing to help him. Now Mac and Drake would have no way of knowing what had happened tonight until they returned to the house and questioned the servants. By then it might be too late.

"Don't struggle so, Alexa, I won't hurt you," said a voice she had thought never to hear again.

"Charles!" Alexa gasped. "How could it be?"

Immediately a large hand was clamped over her mouth. "Quiet, damn you! Do you want that stupid lieutenant to take you back to hang?"

His words confused her. Why would Charles want to save her after what she did to him? Hadn't he heard she was the Vixen? And how had he escaped from a northern prison?

Alexa ceased her struggling as Charles drew her deeper into the woods where he had two horses tethered and waiting. "Up you go," he boosted her. Then he surprised her further by tying her hands to the pommel with his scarf. His eyes raked her thinly clad body insolently one long moment before he sprang on his own horse and grasped the reins of Alexa's mount, urging them both through the dark woods. They were miles down the road by the time the English soldiers took their search outside the house and into the surrounding area.

Alexa jogged behind Charles for over an hour until finally they came to a small house located on a deserted street on the outskirts of Savannah. He halted before the gate, untied Alexa's hands, helped her dismount and pulled her inside the darkened interior. He left her for a moment or two while he lit a lamp, then turned back to study her features.

"So it is true," he muttered, eyeing her blond hair with barely concealed lust. "I could hardly credit it when

Lady Gwen announced to one and all that the Vixen was alive and none other than Lady Alexa Foxworth."

"Why is it so difficult to believe?" asked Alexa curiously.

"It seemed impossible that the bewitching lady who bested me in a duel could be the same woman I was once engaged to. I had no idea your body was so lovely until I saw you aboard your ship in that revealing costume. Even as I cursed you I wanted you. You were magnificent standing proud and defiant on the quarter-deck."

"The last I saw of you you were on your way north to prison," Alexa said. "What happened to bring you back here? Did you escape?"

Charles snorted. "I spent six miserable months incarcerated in New York before I was exchanged and returned to Savannah. During those bleak months I was unable to cast the Vixen from my mind. I vowed one day we would meet again and when we did I'd have her—in my bed, writhing beneath me."

Have her? Alexa asked herself fuming. My God, what did he intend? "I thought you hated me, Charles. You said as much when you visited me in my prison cell."

"That was before I knew you were the Vixen. I was devastated to learn Vixen was dead, but when Lady Gwen informed us otherwise I knew I could not let you hang. When I knew you as Alexa you were nothing to me but a contemptible traitor, unworthy of my pity. But then I met the Vixen, and though she defeated me I could not rest until I had conquered her just as she did me."

"If you have any feeling at all for me, Charles, let me go so I can help Adam. They'll hang him for sure and I can't let that happen. I love him."

"Of course they'll hang him," allowed Charles dryly. "I'm counting on it."

"What do you intend for me?"

"My ship is being sent back to English waters and you'll be on it. By the time we reach our destination the Fox, or Adam Foxworth, if you will, will already be dead. We'll marry as we were meant to years ago."

"You're crazy, Charles, I'll never agree to marry you! Besides, you already have a wife."

"My wife died in childbirth recently," Charles announced without remorse. "I am free to marry again."

"I won't do it!"

"Would you rather die beside your husband?"

"Aye! There's no shame in dying for something you believe in." But then Alexa thought of the child she carried, Adam's child. Could she condemn an innocent baby to death? Perplexed, she bit her lip, struggling for an answer.

Charles must have gleaned something of her thoughts, for he asked, "What is it, Alexa? What is bothering you? Are you afraid to face death?"

"N-no, it's not that," hesitated Alexa.

"Then what? What is worrying you?"

"Charles, I'm pregnant. I'm expecting Adam's baby. I don't mind dying for myself but to condemn an innocent baby . . ."

Charles's eyes gleamed as he silently appraised Alexa's slim form barely concealed beneath the folds of the thin nightgown and robe. "Then it's settled, we'll marry after you've given birth. We'll farm it out and one day have children of our own."

"No Charles," Alexa resisted firmly. "I'll not give my child up nor will I marry you, even if it costs me my life."

"And the life of your baby as well?"

"Not even then. The Vixen has taught me a lot of things, one of which is to fight for the right to live as I see fit. Never again will I become a victim. If I must die for my convictions then so be it."

"Those are rather lofty words, Alexa," Charles declared.

"I mean them, Charles, so you may as well turn me in now if you intend to force me to marry you and give up my child."

Alexa has indeed changed, Charles mused silently when the stubborn tilt of her chin told him she was fully prepared to thwart his desires by going to the gallows. But there were more ways than one to change her way of thinking, he thought deviously. "What would you do to save Adam from the hangman? How far would you go?" he asked slyly.

"Charles! My God, can you do that?"

"For you I would do it, Alexa. The thought of possessing the Vixen excites me beyond bearing. My dreams are filled with the sight of long blond hair and a body more enticing than any I have ever known."

Alexa was stunned by the depth of Charles's desire for the Vixen. In fact, it went beyond desire, into the realm of enchantment. But there was no doubt in Alexa's mind. She would risk anything, sacrifice all for Adam. Even her own happiness meant nothing in comparison to the life of the man she loved beyond all reason. "How do I know you're telling the truth, Charles?"

"To prove my words I'd bring your husband aboard my ship so you might see him before we sail. With your own eyes you can watch him leave so you'd know and be satisfied that he is free to go where he will."

"It's a big risk, Charles," Alexa said doubtfully. "What makes you think you could free Adam so easily?"

"I have my ways," Charles hinted mysteriously, but did not elaborate.

"If you could truly free Adam, Charles, I would go with you, willingly. But first you must agree to two stipulations."

Charles' shaggy brows lifted suspiciously. "What stipulations, Alexa?"

"First, I absolutely refuse to give up my baby, and . . . and second, you must agree not to touch me in . . . in that way until after my child is born."

"You're in no position to dicker, my dear," Charles hissed angrily.

"It's the only way I'll agree," declared Alexa belligerently. "If you want me badly enough you'll wait." To Alexa's way of thinking, once she got Charles to agree to her demands any number of things could happen between now and the actual time she must capitulate. Besides, there was no way they could marry as long as she had a living husband. She told him as much.

"I'll admit that having your husband alive does complicate matters, but nothing is insurmountable when my uncle is a member of parliament and can easily obtain your divorce from a man who is a known traitor."

How easily he made things sound, Alexa thought, still unwilling to trust him. "Then you agree to my terms?"

"With one exception, my dear. As long as you are demanding, I shall make two demands of my own. One, you must keep your hair blond, it excites me." Alexa nodded warily. "And when you see your husband you must promise not to tell him about our agreement. You are to tell him that you are going with me of your own free will and that you intend to divorce him and marry me."

"My God, Charles, he'll never believe me!" exclaimed Alexa, anguish creasing her lovely features.

"Then you must do all in your power to make him believe it."

"I can't, he'd know I was lying!"

"Do you want him to die?"

"No, of course not."

"Then what is your answer?"

"You agree to my terms?"

"Aye, I give my word, you can keep your child and I'll wait to take you to my bed. I'd not enjoy it anyway knowing you had another man's brat in your belly."

A long, painful silence ensued. A silence in which Alexa carefully considered all her options. Even if she agreed to all Charles's terms, it did not mean she intended to live by them. Anything was possible once Adam was free. She'd make him believe she no longer loved him but she knew in her heart that once he was free he would come looking for her, and when he did everything would be explained. In the meantime she would hold Charles off indefinitely. Once she was back in England maybe she could enlist her father's help. He owed her. Her own happiness meant nothing as long as Adam and her baby were safe.

"You win, Charles, I'll go with you. After I've seen Adam and know he's safe."

Alexa spent a long miserable week in the house Charles had rented for his foul purposes. He was making arrangements, he told her, for Adam's release. She was aghast when he informed her how much it was costing him for bribes, but she knew money was no obstacle for him. She was giving up more than money to see Adam free. He would probably end up hating her without ever knowing just how much she was giving up for him and the suffering she would endure because of it.

It seemed that Charles was full of surprises. A trunkful of her own clothes appeared at the house the day after she arrived. Charles told her all Adam's property had been confiscated in the name of the crown, and that he had gone to the house himself, which was locked and deserted, and packed her clothes without anyone the wiser. She was grateful to him for he had thoughtfully included those gowns that were designed for her during her last pregnancy, but she was not gulled by his attempts to please her.

Though Alexa was technically not Charles's prisoner, she was not allowed to leave the house. When Charles told her why she agreed with him totally. "All of Savannah is looking for you. There are patrols out searching the entire area and environs. For your own safety you must remain hidden."

"Charles, what about Adam? Are you seeing to his release?"

"These things take time, my dear, but the arrangements are nearly complete. The bribe has been settled and both Bates and Grubbs agreed to bring him out to my ship. After you've spoken with him the rest will depend on his own ability to leave the city undetected and make his own way."

"Bates and Grubbs! My God!" Alexa cried, distraught. "How can you possibly trust them? Bates tried to rape me while I was a helpless prisoner, and would have succeeded had Adam not intervened."

"Don't worry, Alexa," Charles assured her, "there is too much involved here for them to betray me. I am making rich men out of them." Charles fidgeted nervously as he talked, shifting his eyes often from Alexa's searching looks, but somehow he managed to convince her everything would take place as planned. It's too bad she wasn't present to overhear the conversation between Charles and the two disreputable guards later that night.

"Is everything all set, men?" Charles asked as they sat at a table littered with empty bottles in a shabby dockside inn.

"Tomorrow night," Bates answered in a low voice. "Are you sure we won't get in trouble for this? The Governor is set on hanging the man."

"What does it matter how he dies as long as he no longer lives to harass us?" Charles scoffed.

"I don't understand why we're to bring the Fox aboard your ship," Grubbs grumbled, scratching his thatch of shaggy hair.

"You don't need to understand," shot back Charles sharply. "I'm paying you enough to do as you're bid and ask no questions. You are to row Fox to my ship and leave, but remain hidden near the docks where you can watch and wait for him to return."

"Then we're to follow him and kill him," grinned Bates evilly.

"After he's out of sight of the ship," added Charles, exasperated by the low mentality of the men he had chosen to do his bidding. "That's very important. Wait until he turns the corner before you attack him. Are you certain the two of you can handle him?"

Grubbs snorted gleefully. "Are you kidding? The man is weak as a kitten. He's still recovering from the wounds he received when he was taken and he's been beaten daily besides. The man can barely walk."

"Ease up on him, men," Charles advised thoughtfully. "I want him on his feet and fairly lucid when you bring him to me."

"I can't see . . ." complained Bates bitterly.

"Don't question me, Bates," Charles warned icily. "You're not being paid to understand. In keeping with our agreement you'll receive half of your money now and the rest after the job is done. You are to collect it from my lawyer whose name you already know. There will be no problems or questions from him for he knows the money is to go to you."

Bates grumbled crossly and Grubbs complained about the arrangements, but Charles was adamant. "What if neither the Governor nor the General believe Fox was killed trying to escape?" Bates was emboldened to ask.

"You're being paid to make them believe it," Charles snapped disgustedly. "Must I do your thinking for you? Tell them anything, but that bastard better be dead or I won't sail until the both of you are made to pay for bungling the job."

"Don't worry." Grubbs flushed angrily. "The man is as good as dead. The moment the deed is done we will signal the ship with the lantern just like we agreed."

Charles smiled slyly. He was going to a lot of trouble just to possess a woman he lusted after, but in truth all he was doing was cheating the hangman out of his due by hastening the Fox's death a mere day or two. He dared not risk leaving Fox alive for fear he might by some miracle escape the gallows and find his way to England where Charles expected to be living with Alexa.

"You won't forget the words you're to say to Fox before you kill him, will you?" he asked anxiously.

"We remember them, word for word," promised Bates, "you can depend on us. We won't fail you."

A few minutes later Charles handed over a heavy bag to Bates, shook hands all around and went back to his rented house where Alexa anxiously awaited word of Adam's release. That night he told her all the arrangements except for the cruel ending he had planned for Adam. Charles sounded so sincere that Alexa did not doubt him, accepting everything he told her as the truth. Had she bothered to examine her conscience, Alexa would have realized that she did not want to suspect that Charles might betray her, or that he might wish Adam dead. She effectively blocked out all but the thought that Adam would live as long as she did as

Charles wished.

"I'll take you aboard my ship late tomorrow night, Alexa," Charles confided. "In a closed carriage. You'll be heavily veiled. I don't want anyone to see your face, not even my own men."

"When will I see Adam?"

"Around midnight. Are you certain you can convince your husband you no longer love him?"

"I'll do what I must," Alexa gritted out from between clenched teeth.

"I'll make it up to you, Alexa, I swear it." Charles promised. "I'll make you happy, you'll see. You were prepared to marry me once."

"So I was, Charles, but you wouldn't have me."

"I must have been crazy. You're the loveliest, most exciting woman I know. I want you, Alexa, any way I can get you."

Charles had deliberately kept his distance from Alexa these past days for he did not trust himself around her. He had given his word he would not touch her until after her baby was born and the only way he could honor it was by remaining apart from her. He did not wish to destroy the fragile beginning they had made by forcing her, but she looked so appealing standing before him, so soft and feminine, he could not resist her.

"Alexa," Charles groaned hoarsely, pulling her clumsily into his embrace, "I want you now. I can't wait." His lips were soft and fleshy and Alexa nearly gagged when he kissed her, wondering how she could have ever considered marrying him and how terribly young and inexperienced she must have been at the time.

Alexa struggled, pushing against his chest with all her strength. "You promised, Charles! Surely you can't want me now that I'm carrying another man's child!" she temporized, playing for time.

At the mention of the child, Charles's ardor cooled perceptibly. His pride would not allow him to take a woman with another man's seed growing in her belly. And since the man was the contemptible traitor, Fox, the act was even more reprehensible to him.

"You are right, Alexa," Charles uttered disdainfully, shoving her aside rudely. "I wouldn't have you now. I can wait, but once you're free of that bastard you carry you won't find me so easily appeased. And don't think you'll escape me once we get to England," he added nastily, "for I can still turn you in to the authorities. Then what will become of your precious brat?"

"My baby is no bastard!" Alexa defended hotly. "He has a father. My marriage to Adam is legal and binding."

"Until death do you part, eh, my dear?" He laughed with malicious humor. "Or divorce. Whichever comes first." His laugh chilled Alexa to the bone.

"So help me, Charles, if you fail to keep your word, you'll live to regret it. I was the Vixen far too long to be taken advantage of by the likes of someone like you. I'm doing what I must for Adam, and for no other reason. I'm giving you fair warning, don't even think of betraying me."

Charles experienced a shiver of apprehension. They fury that filled her violet eyes was not one he cared to see directed at him should she find out what he really intended for her traitor husband. Composing himself, Charles lied smoothly. "I'll keep my part of the bargain as long as you keep yours. It's up to you. You must convince Fox you no longer care for him and never want to see him again." Alexa nodded grimly, her eyes bright with unshed tears.

The night was moonless, as dark as the deepest Hell. A storm was brewing offshore, perhaps one of those damned destructive hurricanes so prevalent this time of year. It was nearly midnight, the watch had just disappeared around the corner of the Governor's mansion and the lights in the barracks housing the guards had just winked out. All was quiet.

Dressed all in black, their faces and hands darkened with charcoal, hats pulled low, Mac, Drake, and six of their strongest and most trustworthy men hugged the shadows. Mac had found out only today that Fox was being held in the same dungeon-like cell that he had occupied months ago. For nearly a week Mac's men, those he knew wouldn't be readily recognized as privateers, prowled Savannah for some word of Fox. Nothing had been heard about him since he was taken from his home by soldiers. Nor of Alexa. Mac began to fear that they were both dead, executed immediately by the vindictive English in fear that they might escape the hangman once again.

But a few nights ago, through a stroke of good luck, one of Mac's men overheard two privates talking in an inn near the docks. Both were well into their cups and appeared to have more money than they should have given their occupation and rank. Each man had his arms around a doxy and was haggling over the price of their favors. The man called Grubbs left immediately fondling the posteriors of both whores as they climbed the stairs together. The other man, Bates, remained behind long enough to buy an extra bottle to take above stairs. Mac's man, Drew, sidled up to Bates.

"Could I buy you a drink, mate?" asked Drew, flashing a toothless grin. "It gets a mite lonesome drinking alone."

"Not tonight." Bates smiled foolishly. "I've more important things on my mind." He leered wolfishly toward the stairs and at his departing comrades. Then, much to Drew's chagrin, he took his bottle and turned to follow his friends. Almost as an afterthought he whirled about to face the disappointed seaman. "You look like a good sort, mate. Meet me back here tomorrow night, late, and you can share a bottle with me and Grubbs."

The next night Drew arrived early at the inn in time to see both Bates and Grubbs seated at a table with an English officer. Drew sat in a far corner, hat pulled low over his forehead, until the officer left, then he approached the pair. Both men appeared extraordinarily pleased as Bates weighed a hefty bag in his large hands.

"How about that pint now, mate?" Drew asked innocently.

Bates peered at him a few minutes as if searching his memory, then broke into a wide grin. "Aye," he agreed amicably, nodding toward the chair Charles had only recently vacated. "Seat yourself."

Drew let out his name, then ordered ale all around, carefully counting out the coin. Both guards responded by revealing their own names plus the information that they were important men charged with guarding a desperate criminal. Drew became immediately alert but wisely exhibited nothing but mild curiosity and a measure of awe. But as the drinking became more serious, the men loosened up, boasting of their importance in order to impress the insignificant seaman.

"What's your ship, mate?" Bates asked, swiping at the line of foam gathered on his lower lip.

"Sea Lion," said Drew, replying as he had been instructed. "A merchantman out of Liverpool."

Bates nodded, evidently satisfied. What he did not know was that both the *Lady A* and *My Lady Vixen*, along with Fox's *Ghost*, rode at anchor in the harbor, all three flying the Union Jack and with new names painted across their hulls. There were so many English ships cluttering the harbor that three more raised little interest.

After a while Grubbs left the inn to return to duty but Bates still had a few free hours so he remained with Drew, finding his company pleasant. Finally, Drew inhaled sharply and asked, "Are you really guarding an important prisoner?"

Bates cast a blurry eye about him, then whispered wetly in Drew's ear, "Aye. Did you ever hear of a traitor they call the Fox?" Duly impressed, Drew nodded. "He's in the dungeon beneath the Governor's mansion. But not for long," Bates hinted slyly.

"I've heard of the man," said Drew in a conspiratorial voice. "I hope they hang the bastard."

"That's exactly what will happen to him day after tomorrow, but someone wants him done in before that." Bates laughed raucously, unable to focus his eyes on a shocked Drew.

"You?" asked Drew.

"Naw, I couldn't care less how he dies. But some toff wants him out of the way badly enough to pay me and Grubbs to do it sooner. Tomorrow night, in fact. It's all arranged."

"You're going to do him in? What will the Governor say to that?"

"The Governor will probably thank us for saving him the expense of a hanging. He'll be taken from his cell and . . ." Suddenly Bates realized what dangerous information he was about to divulge and clamped his mouth tightly shut. "Never mind, it's not for the likes of you to know the where and why. When Fox returns from the ship we're to take him to, he's a dead man and me and Grubbs are rich beyond our wildest dreams.

"Ship? What ship?" But Bates refused to utter another word on the subject. Soon afterwards Drew left to report everything he had just learned to Mac and Drake.

After much deliberation the two privateers came to

the conclusion that Fox was to be taken from his cell, to some ship, and then killed when he left. Of Alexa they heard nothing and it worried the two men who both had a certain fondness for the lady. It was decided that Mac, Drake and six men would go ashore after dark and watch the dungeon entrance of the Governor's mansion for any sign of activity. If nothing happened by midnight they would storm the prison and forcibly remove Fox.

"It's nearly midnight," whispered Mac to the men crouched beside him. "We'll give it another half-hour and if nothing seems amiss, be prepared to . . ."

Abruptly a crack of light showed around the door they were watching, serving to effectively cut off Mac's words. The crack widened and into the abyss stepped two men, half carrying, half dragging a third. "Fox," breathed Mac, clenching his hands into tight fists. It was obvious his friend had been handled none too gently by his captors.

Making certain there was no one about, Bates and Grubbs dragged the Fox through the deserted streets the short distance to the docks. Mac, Drake and the others fell in behind, following at a discreet distance. Beforehand they had agreed to do nothing until they learned where Alexa was being held. They would not leave her behind to fend for herself. They decided to allow Fox to be taken aboard the ship, for according to his guards he wasn't to be killed until he returned to shore. As much as they wanted to remove Fox from immediate danger, it was more important to rescue both the Fox and his Vixen. The anxious men watched apprehensively as Fox was placed into a longboat and rowed out to a ship anchored amid the many others in the harbor.

That week spent in the dungeon-like cell was the most miserable one in Adam's life. His wounds had been crudely treated and slow in mending. The pain he lived with both day and night was not nearly so bad as his suffering over Alexa's fate. He had heard nothing of her. He had seen no one but his sadistic guards who took great pleasure in beating him daily despite his wounds and weakness. Just yesterday an officer had appeared and told him curtly that he had already been tried and found guilty months ago and that his hanging, long overdue, was to take place day after tomorrow.

When he questioned the officer about Alexa he was gratified to learn she was still at large. The only conclusion he could draw was that Alexa had made it to safety and told Mac what had happened, just as he hoped. But could he expect an eleventh-hour reprieve? he wondered bleakly. He would give his soul to be able to live out his remaining days with his love, but as long as she was safe he would ask for nothing more.

On the night before he was due to hang, Adam lay on his cot staring desolately into the darkness. Sleep eluded him, but he did not mind. He had too many memories to relive, too many beautiful thoughts of Alexa filling his mind and heart to give in to sleep. Amid his waking dreams of those sweet moments he had first taken her in the guise of Fox, he was rudely interrupted when both Bates and Grubbs entered his cell.

Bates sneered at him, his mouth twisted with hate. He had not forgotten that day when Fox/Adam had prevented him from having his way with Lady Alexa, who as it turned out was the Vixen. During the past week he had vented his anger often enough on the wounded man by administering severe beatings. But now, being given the opportunity to do the man in was the ultimate pleasure.

"Get up, Fox!" Bates ordered, prodding him ungently.

Adam grunted, struggling to sit up. "Can't you wait till morning to beat me?" he asked, wincing in pain from his previous beating. "Or are you afraid the hangman will deprive you of your sadistic pleasure?"

"Get moving," Grubbs commanded, shoving Adam toward the door. "Someone wants to see you."

"Now? It must be nearly midnight."

"Aye," agreed Bates. "It's time." Between them they prodded Adam from the cell and out the door.

Limping and struggling to keep up, a myriad of thoughts went through Adam's brain. Where were they taking him? Surely they didn't intend to hang him in the middle of the night, unless, of course, they feared some kind of rescue by Fox's friends. But when they hurried him past the newly erected gallows standing like sentinels of death in the deserted square, Adam was truly perplexed.

A glimmer of hope beat in his breast when he was shoved into a boat and rowed to a ship anchored in the harbor. Perhaps these men had been bribed by Mac to let him go, Adam wrongly surmised. But as they drew close to the ship, Adam's heart sank when he realized he was being rowed to an English warship. Obviously his fellow privateers would not send him to the enemy.

It was then Adam considered jumping from the boat into the water, making a break for freedom. But weakness soon changed his mind. That and the overwhelming desire to see this to the end in the unlikely event he might yet encounter Alexa. With a toughness born of determination, Adam gathered what little strength remained in his battered body in order to meet his fate with courage, unaware that eight of his comrades waited on shore for his return.

20

The rowboat nudged the hull of the ship, the hooks attached, and winched up to the deck. When prodded, Adam stepped out and watched dispassionately as the boat was immediately lowered to begin its return journey. Adam was not loathe to see the last of Bates and Grubbs.

The total darkness was such that at first Adam did not recognize the man who greeted him. "Come along, Fox," Charles nodded curtly, "there is someone who wishes to see you."

His leg stiff and unwieldy from the wound to his thigh, Adam stumbled awkwardly after Charles until the captain was forced to lend him a helping hand. It was obvious that the guards hadn't eased up on the beatings as he had suggested. Charles only hoped Alexa would not back down when she saw Fox's sorry condition.

Alexa paced the cabin, nearly sick with worry. What if Adam refused to believe that she no longer loved him? she asked herself grimly. Charles had brought her aboard his shp over an hour ago and she had been unable to relax since. Now that the time for her meeting with Adam was at hand she wasn't convinced she could go through with this charade. But when she thought of her child and what would happen to Adam if she failed, she knew she must.

Charles opened the door to the cabin and Adam was momentarily blinded so that he did not immediately see Alexa, or the look of outrage descending upon her pinched face. "Adam, oh my God, what have they done to you?"

"Alexa!" cried Adam, joy and incredulity coloring his words. "Oh my love, you're safe!" Only then did he recognize Charles who had moved into the light provided by the lantern swinging from the bulkhead, and sheer black panic seized him. "Charles Whitlaw! What is this all about, Alexa?"

"Tell him, my dear," urged Charles delightedly.

"What is it, my love? Why have I been brought here?" Though Adam wanted to ask more, he wisely refrained.

"You've been brought here to bid your wife goodbye," Charles goaded relentlessly. "That much I'll tell you. The rest is up to Alexa." He looked toward her expectantly.

"Adam, are . . . are you all right?" Alexa began hesitantly. "You look terrible."

"I'm well enough," replied Adam, his eyes like ashy cinders never leaving her face. "What is it you have to tell me?"

"I'm going away with Charles," she blurted out, knowing of no easier way to tell him. "To England. I've . . . already become his mistress," she lied, lowering her sooty eyelashes until they were dark smudges against her pale cheeks. "I intend to obtain a divorce once I arrive in England."

"I can hardly blame you for wanting to save your life,

Alexa," Adam said slowly, waiting for her to explain more fully.

"You're mistaken, Adam," Alexa replied, her voice deliberately cold. "I've chosen Charles of my own free will. He would have let me go but I wished to return to England with him. I'm tired of running, of war, and . . . and of you. I want a better life and Charles can give it to me." Forgive me Adam, she silently implored.

"Surely you don't expect me to believe that, do you, my love?" Adam scoffed wanly. "What of our love for one another? Although I am soon to die I did not expect you to forget me so easily."

"You won't die," interjected Charles grandly. "As a gesture of good faith as well as a token of my love for Alexa, I have arranged, at great expense, I might add, for your release. When you leave this ship you will be allowed to go where you will."

Openly skeptical, Adam spat, "I don't believe you, Captain Whitlaw!"

"For Alexa I would risk anything," Charles shrugged. "If I allow you to die your death will always stand between us. I'm doing this for myself as much as for my future wife."

"Is that true, Alexa?" Though Adam's face was devoid of all expression, Alexa sensed the bleakness and despair behind his words.

"Aye," she lied, watching his gaunt face take on a hardness she hadn't seen in years as Charles moved beside her and curved an arm possessively around her slim waist.

"Come with me, Alexa! I love you," Adam implored desperately.

"It's too late, Adam. Don't you understand? I'm Charles's mistress!" She was almost shouting. Cleverly, Charles picked that moment to move his hand upward to cup Alexa's breast, his thumb rubbing back and forth across her nipple which seemed to surge and harden beneath his tender ministrations. Charles smiled salaciously but Adam turned away, momentarily defeated.

"I believe this interview is at an end," Charles said, nuzzling Alexa's neck, all the while edging her toward the bunk, leaving Adam no doubt as to his intentions. "My mistress and I wish to be alone. You'll be taken ashore in a boat and left on the dock. After that you are no longer my responsibiilty."

Haunted by the knowledge that Alexa no longer loved him, Adam ignored Charles, addressing Alexa instead. "Have you nothing more to say, Alexa? Do I mean nothing to you after all we've been through together?" He waited, challenging her to reply.

Alexa swallowed hard, lifted her chin, and boldly met his gaze. "Goodbye, Adam. It is over between us. Don't come after me for I. . . ," she faltered, choking on the words, ". . . I never want to see you again."

"Your wish is granted, Alexa. If I live through this you'll not be bothered by me, ever. Get your damn divorce. I wish you both well."

Blurry-eyed, Alexa watched as Adam limped from the cabin, bent beneath the weight of his wounds and the terrible blow she had just dealt him. "You bastard!" she lashed out at Charles. "You didn't have to touch me like that! What are you trying to do, destroy him completely?"

Charles grinned nastily. "I had to do something, my dear. It was obvious he didn't believe you."

"He does now! He'll go through life hating me!"

Charles nearly laughed aloud, knowing that Fox had little time left on earth to hate anyone. "You did very well, Alexa. I'm proud of you."

"To hell with you, Charles! One day you'll be sorry, I swear it!"

"Come along now, Alexa," Charles cajoled. "You'll get over it soon enough. You have me and your child to console you. Don't you want to see how well I kept my word?" He led her out of the cabin and to the rail where they could just see the dim outline of the longboat scraping against the dock.

The sky was beginning to lighten and Alexa watched with trepidation as Adam pulled himself painfully from the longboat and limped off down the quay, not once looking back. She had done her job well, Alexa thought ruefully. He had rounded the corner, already out of sight, but Alexa could not force her feet to move. Beside her, Charles's attention was concentrated on the shoreline. To Alexa it appeared as if he were waiting for something or someone.

Skulking in the deep shadows of the quay, Mac, Drake and their men kept anxious eyes trained on the English ship to which Fox had been taken. They saw the two prison guards return and disappear around the corner but did not follow. If Fox did not return soon one of the men was prepared to summon the crew of all three ships into a formidable force and attack under the cover of darkness. The time was growing short when Mac saw a boat being winched down into the water. As the boat came close to shore, he could barely distinguish the figures of three men, hopefully one of them Fox/Adam.

Their patience was rewarded when the boat bumped into the quay and Adam emerged with all the speed his lame leg afforded him. The boat departed almost immediately, leaving Fox a lone figure outlined against the midnight sky. Adam paused for one last look at the ship, his eyes bleak. Then his face hardened as a coldness settled over his features and he limped off rapidly in the same direction taken by the two guards, Bates and Grubbs.

"Shall we call out to him?" Drake asked as Adam prepared to round the corner out of their view.

"Not yet," cautioned Mac. "We know that Fox isn't supposed to leave the area alive. Let him get out of sight of the ship and see what happens. We'll be close behind to offer protection."

Drake led the way, each man following single file, Mac last, their dark clothing making them all but invisible. They turned the bend and discovered Fox to be a few yards ahead of them when the very thing they had been anticipating occurred. Two men jumped from the shadows into Fox's path, both brandishing knives in a threatening manner. Fear for Fox's life released Mac's feet as he charged forward, Drake and the others close on his heels.

Adam lapsed into a state of shock, his meeting with Alexa hurtling him into a deep abyss as her cruel words came back to haunt him. The undeniable and dreadful facts were that Alexa did not love him. He should have foreseen such an event, should have known the nature of an Ashley to be anything but trustworthy. How could he have expected anything different from a woman with a devil for a father and a whore for a mother? he asked himself disgustedly. It was true when he told her he did not blame her for wanting to live, but did she have to fall into Whitlaw's bed so soon? Or admit it so brazenly?

Adam almost wished he had the gumption to tell Charles to go to hell, that he wanted nothing from the man, not even his own freedom. But he could not. He would live yet another day to see his country drive the British back across the sea. When Alexa became the

Vixen, she had changed irrevocably, Adam thought grimly, and not for the better.

When the boat scraped against the pilings of the quay, Adam scrambled out, his muscles flexed despite his weakness, half expecting the two sailors rowing the boat to jump out and attack him. He would put nothing past Charles Whitlaw. But the men merely pushed off to return to their ship. After a moment's hesitation Adam took off down the quay, hoping to find a way to return to the secret cove to see if *The Gray Ghost* was waiting for him.

Anticipating some sort of trickery, Adam was therefore not the least bit surprised when two men leaped from the shadows, knives drawn and menacing. "You didn't really think you would go free, did you, traitor" asked Bates whom Fox had recognized along with Grubbs.

"Not really," Adam admitted dryly, helpless to defend himself against such overwhelming odds.

"Before we kill you, Fox, we have a message for you," Bates sneered.

"Aye, from a lady," echoed Grubbs. "We're to tell you that she wants no reminders of her past left alive to haunt her."

"And she commends your soul to hell," added Bates, repeating the words Charles had drilled into him.

So saying, Bates lunged forward, but Adam deftly sidestepped, determined to resist as long as breath remained in his body. Just as Grubbs prepared to join in the fray to put a quick end to any ideas Adam might harbor about resisting, Mac reached them, followed in swift order by Drake and six burly seamen. A short-lived but bloody battle ensued in which Bates was killed and Grubbs wounded.

"Don't kill him!" Adam shouted as Drake was tempted

to put a quick end to Grubbs's miserable life. "I want to question him." Then he turned to Mac. "I'll never forget this, Mac," he said softly, unable to express in words what he felt in his heart.

"Just returning the favor." Mac grinned cockily. Then he sobered quickly as he saw at close hand Adam's deplorable condition. "My God, man, you look dead on your feet! What have they done to you?"

"Later, Mac," Adam replied grimly. "Let's see if Grubbs here can give us some answers. Who paid you and Bates to kill me?" he asked, grasping Grubbs by his blood-soaked shirt.

At first Grubbs refused to answer but Drake's knife pressing into the tender skin of his neck soon changed his mind. "The captain—Whitlaw, I think his name is. We were to wait here for you and kill you."

"What about the lady?" Adam queried relentlessly.

"I don't know anything about a lady!"

"You gave me a message from her."

"But I never saw her. Honest."

It was obvious Grubbs knew little of Charles's affairs, or of Alexa, and Adam turned away, disgusted, but then he suddenly thought of something and whirled to confront the cringing Grubbs. "How was Whitlaw to know if you succeeded in killing me? Knowing Charles he would leave no loose ends."

Grubbs licked his dry lips, tasting blood. Nothing mattered now but preserving his own life. "We were to wave a lantern from the quay as a signal that all went as planned."

"Where is the lantern?" Mac demanded harshly.

"In . . . in the corner behind those bales of cotton," Grubbs pointed out, his eyes glazed with fear.

Mac turned and grunted out instructions to one of his men who moved with alacrity to follow his captain's orders. While the sailor was preparing the lantern so that he might give the prearranged signal Charles was anxiously awaiting, Drake made short work of Grubbs, tossing his body and that of Bates into the dark water of the harbor.

Adam did not watch for Mac had drawn him aside and asked worriedly, "Adam, where is Alexa? We can't leave without her."

Adam laughed harshly, a sound raw with emotion. "She's aboard that ship out in the harbor," he revealed curtly. "I've just seen her."

"My God, why didn't you say so! But don't worry, we have enough men at our disposal to storm the ship and take her."

"I'm not worried, Mac, and there is no need to storm the ship on Alexa's behalf," Adam replied bitterly. "She's there by choice. She made it perfectly clear that she wants nothing more to do with me. In fact," he snorted derisively, "she has already become Charles Whitlaw's mistress."

"Adam, you're wrong!" protested Mac, aghast. "You have to be. Alexa's not like that. She loves you. She's always loved you."

"You wouldn't think so had you heard her, Mac. She wanted me dead so I couldn't interfere with her new life with Charles. It's over. I never want to hear her name spoken in my presence again."

"Think, man!" Mac advised. "Use your brain! Alexa is sacrificing herself for you."

"You didn't see her, Mac, or Whitlaw fondling her before my eyes. They were consumed with lust for one another. I'm certain they are in bed together right now. I can't fault her for wanting to live, but did she have to fall in bed with her ex-fiance at the first opportunity?"

"Alexa couldn't have changed so drastically in a week!"

"She's an Ashley!" Adam grated out illogically, as if

that explained everything.

Their conversation halted when Drake approached to inform them the ship had answered their signal and was preparing to weigh anchor.

"Damn you, Adam! Are you going to stand by and allow Alexa to walk out of your life forever?" Mac challenged, enraged.

No answer was forthcoming as Adam turned his back on his friend and limped off. Shaking his head sadly, Mac followed.

"A patrol is coming!" hissed one of the men posted as a lookout.

"This way," whispered Mac, propelling Adam toward a deserted quay where they had hidden their boat beneath the pilings. The last man barely managed to scramble from sight as the patrol drew abreast of the quay, and sensing nothing amiss, moved on. When they passed out of sight the boat left its concealment as the oars noiselessly cut through the murky waves.

Once they were a safe distance away, Adam asked, "How did you come to be here tonight, Mac?"

"Some of my crew were in Savannah the night the squad of English soldiers set out in the direction of Foxworth," Mac explained. "My men had no idea where they were going, or why, but they raced back to the cove to warn me and Drake. Thinking they might suspect we were anchored in the cove and send foot soldiers in conjunction with a sea attack, I thought it prudent to leave and anchor down the coast a ways in open water. Not in my wildest imaginings did I dream they were after Fox or Vixen."

"When did you learn what actually took place?"

Once we were certain no ships were forthcoming. But it was the following morning before we returned to the cove where we found Jem waiting for us on shore. He explained everything."

"When I heard Alexa had made good her escape I assumed she had found you and was safely aboard *My Lady Vixen*."

"If she came to the cove," Mac revealed, "she would have found it deserted." A long pause ensued. "Adam, I just can't believe . . ."

"Forget it, Mac. I know what you are going to say and I don't want to hear it. Alexa never reached the cove. She went straight to Charles. Tell me how you learned I was to be taken from my cell tonight."

"For nearly a week we heard nothing," Mac said, "and we feared you were already dead. Then Drew, one of my crewmen, hit it lucky." Mac went on to explain what Drew had learned from Bates. "It wasn't much to go on, but by putting two and two together we managed to be at the right place at the right time."

"Thank God for that!" breathed Adam, nearly at the end of his endurance. "I see the *Ghost* out there. When did she arrive?"

"She arrived in the cove for our rendezvous three days ago. We spent the time since then painting out the names from the hulls and turning ourselves into English merchantmen."

"What are your plans?" Adam asked wearily.

"We sail immediately for Chesapeake Bay to join up with de Grasse's fleet."

"Good! The *Ghost* will be there beside you."

"Are you sure you're fit enough, Adam?" protested Mac. "It's obvious your wounds are far from healed. And Lord knows what else they did to you."

"Well enough, Mac," Adam insisted, "once I feel the deck beneath my feet and fill my lungs with good salt air."

Reluctantly, Mac had Adam rowed to where the *Ghost* lay at anchor, then boarded his own *Lady A* nearby while Drake continued on to *My Lady Vixen*. Within the hour all three ships sailed from Savannah harbor, plotting a northerly course.

A week later *The Gray Ghost*, *Lady A* and *My Lady Vixen* joined the forest of masts of the great fleet of de Grasse from the West Indies anchored just inside Fort Henry. The date was September 5, 1781. There they met the combined forces of Admiral Hood and Admiral Graves. A poorly executed British attack prevented the British from winning the day. Later the French and the Americans were joined by Admiral DeBarras and his eight ships of the line, and the British were decisively outnumbered. Graves sailed for New York after the battle which proved to be the decisive battle of the war.

Meanwhile, Cornwallis, in Yorktown, Virginia, his supplies and men badly depleted, awaited relief from Clinton in New York. Clinton's promise that a fleet of twenty-six ships and 5000 men would arrive for his relief, buoyed his hopes, and Cornwallis continued his resistance. On October 13, 1781, with the promised reinforcements still missing, Cornwallis tried to retreat across the York River, hoping to reach a position favorable to a relieving fleet for supplying him. Failing in the attempted retreat and in urgent need of supplies, Cornwallis's troops fell under the combined forces of General Washington and the Comte de Rochambeau, de Grasse's French fleet and additional French infantry led by Lafayette. After an unsuccessful bid for escape, Cornwallis surrendered on October 17, 1781, bringing to an end, for all practical purposes, the war in America.

From small beginnings developed one of the greatest naval wars in history. The fleet operations which in a few weeks decided the fate of Yorktown and of the American cause, were merely incidental to the vast naval campaign carried on over a period of five years in Carribbean, European and Indian waters. Taking part in these great navy operations were not only famous names such as John Paul Jones, but hundreds of privateers. Brave, freedom-loving people like Fox, Vixen, Mac, Drake and countless others who formed the nucleus of the American navy.

With the articles of peace yet to be worked out, hundreds of royalists fled to Bermuda and other British-owned islands, while loyal Americans were free to move back to their lands without fear of British reprisal for their activities against the crown.

It was the spring of 1782 before Adam was free to return to Foxworth plantation. He was accompanied by Mac. Drake was amply rewarded for his loyalty by the gift of My Lady Vixen which he intended to use to found a lucrative shipping trade. But no matter what Adam said, Drake would not change the name of his ship. My Lady Vixen was a legend, a proud name Drake refused to alter.

But Adam was not allowed to remain long at his plantation. Because of his record as a fearless and relentless defender of freedom, he was called before the Continental Congress and sent on a mission he at first refused, but later, persuaded by Mac who was to accompany him, accepted. In April of 1782, Adam and Mac boarded The Gray Ghost and sailed for England. It had been seven months since Adam had last seen Alexa.

But the adage "out of sight, out of mind" did not apply to Adam. He thought constantly of Alexa, but not always with fond memories. The love he once bore her turned to ashes in his mouth. A thousand times over he relived their all too brief times together in the past and wondered how she could have changed so drastically. Perhaps it was only Charles who wanted him dead, Adam thought hopefully. But in the end it mattered little who actually ordered his death, Adam reflected glumly, for his wife was the one to benefit most from his demise.

Although his thoughts of Alexa were often harsh and unyielding, he couldn't help but remember her as the Vixen. God, she was magnificent! Like no other woman he had ever known. All woman—beautiful. Yet proud and courageous too. There was no possible way to forget her, nor forgive her. Her adventurous life as the Vixen meant more to her than her role as his wife, Adam reflected bitterly.

But despite, or because of, those memories, hate began to fester in him like a cancer. Such was his state of mind that he feared should he ever see Alexa again he would be tempted to kill her.

21

London 1782

The journey across the water to England was a night-mare Alexa hoped never to experience again. She was seasick the entire time at sea, no doubt due to her pregnancy. The only good to come out of it was that Charles did not approach her sexually. In fact, she rarely saw him, consumed as he was with his duties as captain.

Unbeknownst to Alexa, Charles and much of the world save for America, by the time they reached English soil Cornwallis had already surrendered and the war was all but over. But the news would not reach them yet for many weeks. In the meantime, still weak and far too thin, Alexa was virtually Charles Whitlaw's prisoner.

Charles whisked her from his ship to his London town-house without allowing her to see or speak to anyone. Truth to tell she was in no condition to face family or friends and was grateful for the seclusion of Charles's house where she might rest and recuperate.

By this time Alexa's pregnancy was clearly noticeable

and Charles ordered her confined to the house. But after a mere two weeks of rest and wholesome food Alexa's condition improved greatly and the inactivity was galling, especially after her activities as the Vixen. Though Charles provided excellent care, and his servants were informed that she was soon to become Charles's wife and they should treat her accordingly, Alexa longed to visit her father to learn for herself if he still harbored strong feelings against her. Mainly she wanted to enlist his help.

Then there was her old retainer Maddy, who was more of a mother to her than servant. Two weeks was long enough to remain in bed and Alexa was determined to go to Ashley House despite Charles's warning to the contrary.

Though Charles still wanted Alexa, her state of pregnancy definitely turned him off sexually, and he was content to visit his clubs and cavort with actresses until she was rid of her unwelcome burden. It was not Charles's nature to remain faithful to one woman for any length of time, and since he could not possess the woman he wanted at the moment, he felt no compunction about taking his comfort elsewhere. Nevertheless, he demanded Alexa's presence in his house, threatening to turn her over to the authorities should she leave him for any reason. The name Vixen was well-known in England and he was careful to point out that she would most certainly hang the moment her child was born should she be revealed. Unreasonable as it might sound, as long as Alexa's hair remained the color of pale gold, she lived in Charles's eyes as the Vixen. A woman he wanted above all others. A woman around whom dreams were spun.

Alexa was gratified that she was not called upon to satisfy Charles's sexual needs and that he left her much on her own. It presented her with the oppportunity to seek her own diversion. One beautiful spring day she deliberately disobeyed Charles's orders and set out for Ashley House in a hired conveyance. A wide cape concealed her rounded shape and she tugged nervously at her blond hair, wondering if her father would recognize her and allow her entrance.

Hesitantly, Alexa lifted the brass knocker and let it drop with a resounding bang, then stood back to wait. Nothing. Twice more she used the knocker with no results and was about to give up when a small, white-haired woman peeped out through a crack in the door.

"Can I help you, miss?" asked the woman in a kindly manner.

"Maddy?" Alexa gaped, shocked at how much the housekeeper had aged. "Is that you Maddy?"

"Do I know you, miss?" Maddy asked, peering owlishly at Alexa over rimless glasses.

"Oh, Maddy, it's me, Alexa!"

"Oh, no, miss!" Maddy protested vigorously. "Lady Alexa had hair as black as night, and I heard she is in America. For all I know she could be dead."

"Not dead, Maddy. Very much alive. And I've come back." She stepped closer to the nearsighted woman. "Take a good look then tell me you don't know me."

Wordlessly Maddy obeyed, staring at Alexa an inordinately long time before abruptly bursting into tears. "Oh, Lord, oh dear God, it is you, my lady. You've come back!"

The door opened wide and Alexa stepped inside. The hall was cool, the house, from what she could see, clean and orderly. But somehow Alexa sensed it had been unoccupied for a long time. The feeling persisted as she followed Maddy into the drawing room, becoming an eerie premonition when she saw dust covers shrouding all the lovely furniture she remembered so well.

"Maddy, why is everything covered up?" Alexa asked, alarmed. "Where is my father? Surely he can't still be in the country. Is he sick?"

Maddy's tears grew more copious as she regarded Alexa pityingly. "Sit down, Lady Alexa," she urged, whisking a cover from one of Alexa's favorite chairs. Certain she was not going to like what Maddy was about to tell her, Alexa obeyed.

"What is wrong, Maddy? It's all right, you can tell me."

Knowing of no way to soften the shock, Maddy said, "Your father is dead, my lady. He lived but one year after you left. The doctor said it was his heart. It came on so sudden I never expected . . ."

"Dead! And I never knew!" Alexa lamented, recalling not those terrible moments when she had been forced to leave home, but the good times when she was growing up the adored daughter of Sir John Ashley. Without a moment's hesitation she forgave him for any wrong he might have done her, for in his own way he had been terribly hurt by her mother. Now it all seemed so long ago and insignificant.

"We tried to find you, Alexa," Maddy continued sadly. "Your father's solicitor traced you to America and learned you had married that Lord Penwell. Is it true?"

"Aye, I married Adam. It's a long story and one day I'll tell you. But why were the lawyers trying to find me?"

"Why, to settle the estate, of course," Maddy said, surprised that she should even ask. "It's all yours now, this house, the country estate, the land, all the money; your father left everything to you."

Alexa's eyes popped open and she gaped at Maddy in disbelief. "My father did not disinherit me? After all he said and did?"

"You didn't see him after you left, my lady. A sorrier

man you've never seen. Once you were gone I think he began to realize just how much you meant to him. He wasn't the same after that."

"But to leave everything to me," Alexa whispered, still shaken.

"It was his way of making amends," Maddy told her. "And believe me, Alexa, your cousin Billy Ashley was enraged to learn everything had gone to you. I expect he was counting heavily on your father's wealth."

Alexa frowned, remembering Billy as a distant cousin, a brash young man who would go through her father's fortune like water through a sieve.

"Now that you're home you have but to sign the papers and move into your home," Maddy expounded happily. "Is . . . er . . . your husband with you?"

Immediately Alexa looked so distraught that Maddy was sorry she had asked. "N-no, Maddy, Adam is still in America," Alexa finally answered.

"No matter," Maddy replied briskly. "I'll have your room prepared immediately. Most of the old servants are still employed to keep the place in order. The same is true for the country estate."

"Maddy, wait! I can't stay here. Not yet, anyway."

"Can't stay here?" Maddy blinked. "Why ever not? Where will you go?"

"I told you it was a long story, Maddy, but I'm staying with Charles Whitlaw for the time being."

"Charles! Your ex-fiancé? The man who deserted you? Surely you jest!"

"I wish it were a joke, Maddy, but it's the truth. And . . . and I'm not at liberty to leave his protection."

Maddy bristled indignantly. "What's that scoundrel up to, my lady? Have you left your husband for Charles? I think you'd best tell me everything."

"Oh, Maddy, I don't know where to begin or how to

tell you all I've been or done."

"At the begining, Alexa," Maddy said softly, settling her ample frame more deeply into the chair. "Start from the day you left here carrying Lord Penwell's child. Where is the child, by the way? Did you leave it at Charles's house?"

"I lost the baby," Alexa sighed heavily, recalling vividly that painful time in her life. Then she went on to relate all that had happened to her during the intervening years, leaving out nothing but her present pregnancy. When she began the story involving the Vixen, Maddy grew round-eyed with shock.

"Oh, no, my lady! There's not a person in England who hasn't heard of the Vixen or the Fox. Are you truly her?"

"Truly," smiled Alexa impishly. "Blond hair and all. And Adam is the Fox. Only I didn't know it for a long time."

"I've always known you were incorrigible, Alexa, but I never realized to what extent. You must love your adopted country greatly to defend it so vigorously. It's obvious that you love your husband also. I'm happy you've found true love after all you've gone through."

"Oh, Maddy, I haven't told you everything yet," wailed Alexa, clearly distraught. "Adam thinks I've left him, to be with Charles. He thinks I no longer love him. I was forced by Charles to say terrible things to Adam and he probably hates me."

Comprehension dawned and Maddy drew in a deep breath. "Charles knows you are the Vixen and is holding it over your head! He released Adam only after he had your promise to accompany him back to England."

"Aye," Alexa flushed darkly. "I had no choice in the matter. They were going to hang Adam. What else could I do? Evidently Charles wanted me enough to agree to my conditions. We have a . . . pact."

"And what of your husband, Alexa?"

"He's alive, Maddy, that's all that matters. One day I'll go to him and explain. After the war is over and Charles no longer is a threat to either of us."

"I wish there was something I could do to help you, my lady." Maddy shook her head sadly. "The thought that you are forced to . . . to . . . bed that cur against your will is reprehensible. If only your father still lived this wouldn't be happening. This time he would protect you."

"I had hoped for as much, Maddy. That's why I came today. But . . . I haven't become Charles's mistress, not yet, anyway. You see," she confided, flinging aside her concealing cape, "I'm pregnant. With Adam's child. I've been able so far to hold Charles at bay because of it, but once my baby is born, I don't know."

"You've still a few months, Alexa. We'll think of something before then," Maddy promised, measuring Alexa's girth with an experienced eye.

"Perhaps," Alexa sighed uncertainly as she started to rise. So much time had elapsed as she related all the events since she left England that Alexa had not realized the lateness of the hour. "I really must go, Maddy. Charles will be furious should he come home and find me gone."

"That coward hasn't harmed you in any way, has he?" Maddy asked anxiously as she scanned Alexa's features for telltale bruises.

"No, nothing like that," Alexa said, stifling a giggle. "I think he's half-afraid of me. Of the Vixen, anyway. He's seen her in action and knowns what she is capable of. But should he choose he can still turn me over to the authorities, and for now that gives him the advantage. That and the fact that I'd do almost anything to protect my child."

Soon afterwards Alexa took her leave, but not before

Maddy reminded her to pay a visit to her father's solicitors as soon as possible.

Alexa did not arrive back before Charles. Fearful that it might prove too difficult to leave the house again, she decided to call on her father's lawyer immediately. Mr. Carter, a partner in the firm of Carter and Bigelow, was extremely happy to see her, for his firm had spent considerable time and money looking for the lost daughter of Sir John Ashley.

"I'm relieved you've finally showed up, my dear young lady," enthused Carter vigorously. "We had just about given up hope. To make matters worse we've had that damn, ahem, excuse the language," he apologized, ". . . rake, Billy Ashley riding us. He is determined to have himself declared heir. If you hadn't shown up soon . . . well, you're here now, and that's all that counts."

"Thank you for not giving up on me, Mr. Carter," Alexa smiled winningly.

"It's what your father wanted," confided Carter. "I was with him when he died, you know. He charged me with telling you he was sorry for everything and hoped you'd forgive him. He said you'd understand what he was talking about."

"Aye," nodded Alexa, choking back the tears. "All has been forgiven."

"Then let's get to the papers, Lady Alexa. I've had them prepared and waiting for just this moment. You'll find everything is in order."

"I'm certain they are, Mr. Carter," Alexa smiled as she began the process of affixing her name to the legal documents.

Then suddenly Carter noticed she was signing as Alexa Ashley Foxworth, Countess of Penwell. "You've married, my lady!" he exclaimed.

"Aye, is there a problem with that, Mr. Carter?"

"Well, no, not really. It's just that under the law all your property passes into the hands of your husband."

Alexa had in fact forgotten those archaic laws but in this instance it made little difference to her. Should Adam ever come back to her and forgive her, she would gladly hand over to him everything she owned. Aloud she said, "When Lord Penwell returns to England I'm certain he will be happy to administer my estate."

Carter sighed audibly, relieved that the sticky situation had resolved itself so effortlessly. "Then I hope everything has been handled to your satisfaction. Will you move in immediately?"

"No," Alexa hedged, rising slowly to accommodate her bulk. "Perhaps later. For the time being I've made . . . other arrangements. But I wish the staff retained and paid from the estate funds until either my husband or myself can see to things ourselves."

"Of course, Lady Alexa," Carter assured her competently. "My firm will continue to handle your affairs just as we've done since your father's death. I can see you are in no condition," he tried not to ogle her bulging abdomen, "to take care of these matters yourself. Rest assured your interests are in good hands."

"Thank you, Mr. Carter," Alexa said graciously.

"If you are in need of funds," Carter reminded her as she prepared to depart, "you have only to draw them from your bank account. I'll apprise them immediately of your return and instruct them accordingly."

Charles was waiting for Alexa when she returned, anger turning his handsome features almost ugly as his mouth twisted in a menacing snarl. Alexa had hoped he hadn't returned yet from his duties, or his club, or wherever he disappeared to during the day. It had been a long, eventful day and she had not eaten since breakfast. Hunger gnawed at her and the beginnings of a headache threatened.

"Where in the hell have you been?" Charles demanded to know. "I distinctly remember forbidding you to leave the house. I arrived home early today so I might have dinner with you, we spend so little time together. But I arrived to find you gone and the servants not even aware of it. Where have you been sneaking off to?"

"You don't own me, Charles!" Alexa challenged hotly.

"I damn well do, my lady Vixen," contended Charles, sneering complacently. "Have you forgotten you owe me your life? And the life of your child? Not to mention your husband."

"I've forgotten nothing, Charles," Alexa retorted. "And I've kept my part of the bargain. I went to see my father, that's all. Why didn't you tell me he was dead?" Alexa asked, her violet eyes so filled with accusation Charles was forced to turn away.

"I've just found out myself," Charles defended weakly, shuffling his feet uncomfortably. "I would have told you when the time was right." Deliberately, Alexa turned her back on the enraged Charles. "Don't play the haughty aristocrat with me, Alexa," he warned, grasping her arm to swing her about. "Everyone knew your father disowned you and left his entire estate to Billy Ashley, a distant cousin."

Alexa's eyes gleamed but she wisely refrained from informing him of her father's change of heart. Instead, she shouted, "Take your hands off me, Charles! I'm tired and hungry and in no condition to deal with your childish tantrums!"

"Childish tantrums!" Charles stormed, his face mottled with rage. "How dare you call me names! You're a slut, my fine lady Vixen! Everyone knows you gave yourself to that impostor, Lord Penwell, on the eve of our wedding. I have a good notion to take you right here on the floor, big belly or no. You deserve no better from me."

As if to reinforce his vile intentions, Charles flung her to the floor and calmly proceeded to unbutton his trousers. "You lay one finger on me, Charles, and I'll kill you!" gritted out Alexa from between clenched teeth. "No man has the right to make a victim of me. I learned many things in my role as the Vixen, and one of them was how to defend myself. If you harm me or my child I swear you'll find a knife in your back when you least expect it."

Charles froze, his fingers, already on the fly of his pants, stilled as a shudder passed through his body. He was certain he never wanted the look in Alexa's eyes directed at him more than once. "What about our bargain? You're still a traitor and it's not too late to bring you before the authorities. From what I understand King George would feel little remorse over your death."

"I will keep my word, Charles, as long as you hold to yours. You are not to touch me, either in anger or . . . or otherwise, until after my child is born."

"And afterwards? You'll share my bed willingly?" Alexa nodded, hiding her crossed fingers behind her back. Flushing darkly, Charles turned and stomped from the room.

After that scene, Charles moved swiftly to curtail Alexa's outside activities. She found herself guarded both day and night by a burly thug whom she was certain Charles had hired off the streets. She was not allowed to leave the house except to walk in the gardens, and then only in the company of her guard whose name she did not bother to learn for she had neither the occasion nor the inclination to speak to him.

Unbeknownst to Alexa, Charles had gone so far as to

engage a midwife of unsavory reputation who was quite willing, for a price, to fall in with his devious plans. It was arranged between them that when Alexa's baby was born she would be told it had died. The small coffin Charles intended to bury would be empty and the baby given to a couple who would raise it in the country away from London. Charles wanted no whining brat around to remind Alexa of her dead husband.

Alexa had seen no one since she had called on Maddy and her father's solicitor weeks before. Though not ill-treated by Charles she nevertheless remained wary of him, uncertain whether or not to trust him or the midwife he had engaged for her. She had even gone so far as to suggest that Maddy come and attend her, but Charles quickly disabused her of that idea. In the end Alexa realized she had no one but herself to rely upon.

Soon afterwards something happened to irrevocably alter the fabric of Alexa's life. Insulated as she was from the world outside Charles's home, Alexa heard little news but for servants gossip. So you can imagine her shock when she heard the butler and footman discussing the news that was on the tip of everyone's tongue. The war in America was over! A ship just recently arrived from America bearing word that Cornwallis had surrendered and Clinton was sailing back home to England. For all intents and purposes the war was all but ended. Later a delegation of Americans would arrive to work out the terms of the peace treaty.

Alexa was jubilant. Along with peace came the end of her subjugation to Charles. Her word was no longer a valid reason for remaining under his domination. Nor was the fear of being unmasked as the Vixen, for one of the terms of the treaty was bound to be amnesty for all persons convicted of war crimes. At long last she was rid of Charles, Alexa rejoiced, and once her baby was born she was free to return to America to find Adam. She prayed fervently that he had come through the war unscathed. He looked so wretched the last time she saw him.

Alexa began to pack immediately, determined that she would not remain with Charles a moment longer than necessary. When he returned home late that night after cavorting passionately for long hours with an actress talented in more than one of the arts, Alexa was waiting.

"Why aren't you in bed, Alexa?" He frowned when he found her seated in the drawing room with several lamps lit and her arms folded stubbornly. "Is it the baby? If so you should have had one of the servants summon the midwife."

"It's not the baby, Charles. The war in America is ended. The English are beaten and have sued for peace."

"Oh." Charles replied blandly. "I had heard talk of some such today."

"Is that all you can say? My God, it's over! Don't you understand? You no longer have any say over me! I'm free to go and do as I please!"

"And what is that, my dear?" Charles asked snidely. "Where will you go and what will you do?"

"I have a home, Charles. I didn't tell you before but my father left everything to me, the houses, the land, all incomes. I am wealthy and shall want for nothing. I am more than capable of providing for myself and my child."

"When did you learn all this?" Charles asked curiously. "I suppose that housekeeper of your father's imparted that information to you the day you went to Ashley House."

"Aye." Alexa admitted defiantly. "I visited my father's solicitors that day, too. I signed the papers and everything is now mine."

"And you saw fit to keep that information from me," contended Charles, glowering.

"It had nothing to do with you."

"What about your word, Alexa? Does the word of an Ashley mean so little that you break it so easily?"

"I consider the promise I made to you under coercion now null and void. It was given under duress. I never intended to keep it. Once my child was born I would have found a way to keep from honoring my promise to . . . to become your mistress, or wife, if that's what you intended."

"I had thought to marry you, Alexa," Charles admitted crossly. "Had I known you were wealthy I would have already done so."

"Have you forgotten something, Charles? I already have a husband. I would not commit bigamy and you have made no move so far to obtain a divorce, not that I would have agreed to it."

Suddenly Charles burst out laughing, shocking Alexa. He laughed until tears slid down his cheeks, until Alexa thought he was mad. "What's the matter with you? Have you gone crazy?"

"Oh, Alexa, how naive you are," Charles gasped, wiping away his tears of mirth. "Did you really believe I would allow Fox to live so that he might come after you one day? Give me more credit than that!"

"What . . . what are you talking about?" Alexa paled, her body tense with dread as she stared fixedly at Charles. "I saw Adam leave the ship with my own eyes. I watched him disappear into the night."

"What you failed to see were the two men I hired to kill him the moment he walked out of your sight," Charles informed her, grinning maliciously. "That man had nine lives and I dared not trust the hangman to claim him. A rescue was always possible no matter how well-guarded he was."

"You despicable bastard!" spat Alexa, quivering with impotent rage. Then abruptly something occurred to her. "How do you know for sure he is dead? We sailed almost immediately and he could have escaped your trap. Didn't you just say he had more lives than a cat?"

"No danger of that," Charles smiled complacently. "You saw for yourself just how weak Fox was. He had been beaten daily by his guards and his wounds were still festering."

Hope stirred in Alexa's breast as she replied, "He still could have escaped. Any number of things could have happened without your knowing it."

"Not likely," Charles said slyly. "I know for a certainty that Fox is dead. Remember the light we saw on shore before we sailed? If you recall you even remarked on it." Alexa nodded, dreading the words she knew were coming. "That was the prearranged signal telling me that Fox, or Adam, if you prefer, was dead. Not until I was certain he no longer lived did I take my ship from Savannah. Now, I'm not convinced it was worth the effort," Charles confided sourly.

Exerting gargantuan effort, Alexa hauled herself from the chair and rushed at Charles, nails bared, opening deep tracks down his cheeks. "You vile beast!" she screamed, grief driving her beyond sanity. "If I had a sword I'd run you through! You killed a better man than you can ever hope to be! I hate you! One day, Charles, when I'm not burdened with child, we'll meet on even terms and then I'll take great pleasure in killing you. So help me God!"

Charles experienced a shiver of fear. Never had he seen a woman so grief-stricken as to be bordering on insanity. Wrenching her clawed hands from his blood-streaked face he managed to free himself with great effort. He knew enough about Alexa and the Vixen to realize she had not spoken idly. One day, when he least expected it, he would find himself facing the sharp edge of a sword, and more than likely sudden death at the hands of a vengeful woman.

"Calm yourself, Alexa," Charles hissed, "remember your child."

"I am remembering my child. I'm thinking that he or she will never know a father's love."

"I think it's best that I leave, Alexa. You're becoming distraught and I fear for your sanity," Charles said, backing away.

"You fear for your life, coward, as well as you should! Get out of my sight! If I ever see you again be prepared to die!"

Charles needed no further urging as he turned and fled from the house, muttering darkly about women who thought themselves equal to men and refused to be subjugated by them. Never again would he attempt to tame such a woman. Give him a timid, demure woman whose existence depended upon her husband's good will.

Alexa hauled herself up the stairs step by painful step, her fragile, swollen body wracked with sobs. Dead! Adam was dead! A dull ache gnawed at her vitals and sapped her rapidly diminishing strength. She had no reason to doubt Charles, for she distinctly recalled standing at the rail of Charles's ship and wondering about the lantern winking at them from shore. For some unexplained reason she chose not to question Charles at the time despite the fact that he seemed extraordinarily anxious until he spied the twinkling light that she since learned was a signal proclaiming Adam's death.

It seemed impossible that she would never experience his lovemaking again, or hear his low, sensuous voice whispering to her of his love. What really hurt was the knowledge that he had died without ever knowing about the child he fathered. Safe in her room, Alexa locked the door and sank gratefully into bed, her grief too difficult to bear without the relief of tears.

Early the next day Alexa arrived complete with luggage at Ashley House where she collapsed weeping into Maddy's comforting arms. "I hoped you'd come home, my lady," Maddy soothed, "the moment I heard the news about the war. You're safe now, lovey. Charles can no longer harm you."

"Oh, Maddy, Charles has already done me more harm than you'll ever know. He killed Adam! He ordered my husband's death!"

Leading her to a chair, Maddy did her best to console Alexa once she was told the full extent of Charles's deceit. "Perhaps it didn't happen as Charles said," suggested Maddy hopefully. "Try not to carry on so, lovey. You're doing your child no good."

"You didn't see Adam that night. He was sick, and so weak he could barely stand," wailed Alexa, bitterly defeated. "He's dead, I just know it!"

Attempting to change the subject, Maddy asked, "Did you see Charles this morning before you left? Did he try to stop you?"

Alexa laughed harshly through a wash of tears. "That coward? He knew better than to try to stop me. He was nowhere in sight when I left. The servants told me he failed to return home last night. I think I frightened him, Maddy. I promised to kill him and he knew I meant it."

Maddy's eyes nearly bugged out of her gray head and she clucked her tongue as she viewed the instant transformation of her beloved, sweet Alexa into the cold-blooded Vixen. There was no doubt in her mind that Charles had best look to his own safety.

With Maddy's help Alexa settled into the familiarity of
her childhood home. Though she had spent a great deal
of time at her father's country estate, Ashley House in
London was equally dear to her, and she made tentative
plans to spend the summer in the country with her
newborn baby. Perhaps there, in the peaceful
atmosphere, she would at last come to terms with her
grief and learn to live without Adam.

In her heart Alexa knew there would be no other man
for her. Thanks to her father she had no financial
worries. Though life no longer held any meaning for she
she would make the best of it for Adam's child. Thank
God she still had that small part of him, Alexa sighed
gratefully as she cradled the bulk of her stomach in her
arms. For the next two weeks a calmness settled over
her—a calmness that often preceded childbirth.

On May 12, 1782, Alexa felt the first pangs of labor.
For many hours she hid her distress from Maddy who
fussed far too much over her as it was. But by early
evening it was all too apparent to the housekeeper that
Alexa was deep in labor and she hastily summoned the
midwife. Earlier, Alexa informed Maddy that she did not
want the same woman Charles had engaged so the
housekeeper made inquiries and found a competent
woman noted for her cleanliness and compassion.

At ten o'clock that same evening Alexa gave birth to a
son she promptly named David Ashley Foxworth. Davie,
for short. As births go it was relatively uncomplicated,
and afterwards Alexa was able to lie back with her son in
her arms and marvel at the miracle of his birth. Each tiny
finger and toe was perfect in every way, as were his
beautifully formed head, small ears, and miniature
features like his father's. How dearly she loved him!

Alexa was sorely disappointed when her milk failed to
come in, forcing her to engage a wet nurse. She

supposed the failure was due to the shock of learning about Adam's death shortly before she gave birth. But whatever the cause, Alexa was devastated the first time she saw Davie suckling contentedly at the breast of a woman other than herself.

Alexa's recovery was swift and without incident. Motherhood agreed with her; she was radiant, lovelier than she had ever been. By this time her hair had returned to its former lustrous black and her figure had regained its perfect proportions. Nevertheless Alexa continued to shun society. She could not force herself to go out in public or seek the company of others. Not yet. Maddy scolded her repeatedly for living the life of a recluse.

"You can't hibernate, my lady," Maddy chided gently. "You're young. You have your whole life ahead of you. One day you'll find someone else you can love."

"No, Maddy," Alexa denied hotly. "There is no other man for me. If I can't have Adam I don't want anyone." Maddy began arguing against Alexa's reasoning until Alexa added, "Why don't you pack our things, Maddy. I think it's time we returned to the country. It's been years since I've been there and I am so looking forward to it."

As it turned out, Maddy, Davie and the wet nurse departed for the country a few days later. At the last minute Alexa was prevented from joining them. Just as she was about to depart with the others she received word that Lawyer Carter wished to see her about an urgent matter. Rather than detain the others she sent them ahead without her, promising to follow as soon as possible.

Carter's summons proved to be a matter of concern to Alexa as she soon learned when she faced him across his desk. "Lady Alexa, I find myself the bearer of grave tidings." Her features set in determined line, Alexa nodded for him to continue. "Your only male relative, distant though he may be, has challenged the legality of your father's will."

"Billy Ashley? But . . . what could he do?"

"First you must answer me truthfully, Lady Alexa. Is it true your husband is dead?" Gulping back the lump in her throat, Alexa nodded again. "Somehow Billy learned of it and now considers himself your legal guardian until you reach the age of twenty-five. he wants to be made trustee of your estate."

"My God!" Alexa gasped, horrified. "I just turned twenty-two. In three years he'll beggar me!"

"I'm in complete agreement, Lady Alexa," sympathized Carter.

"Can he do that to me?"

"He's gone so far as to petition the king. You are to appear before the court in ten days to show just cause why you should be allowed to manage your own estate."

Alexa groaned. What else could go wrong in her life? she wondered dismally. Why should a wastrel like Billy Ashley be allowed to govern her life? Must a woman be deemed incompetent solely on the accident of being born female? She'd go to America and claim Adam's estate before she'd buckle under to the likes of Billy Ashley! Alexa vowed in a surge of unbridled rage.

"Does Billy know I have a child?" Alexa asked suddenly.

"Why, no," Carter admitted slowly. "You kept yourself in strict seclusion. I doubt anyone knows."

"Good," Alexa sighed. "I don't want Davie dragged into this. He's on his way to the country and I'll keep him there for as long as it takes to resolve this mess. I know your firm will do its best for me, Mr. Carter," Alexa said in parting.

Back at Ashley House Alexa considered enlarging her

staff while she remained in residence, the bulk having left with Maddy, then decided against it. There was only herself to care for and the pair of old retainers left here to care for the house in her absence was sufficient for her needs. Owen could serve as butler and general care-taker while Bertha, his wife, could take care of what little cooking was needed to satisfy her as well as do the house-work. Though the couple lived in a small apartment above the carrige house, which meant Alexa would be alone in the house at night, she decided she had little to fear there. As soon as Brown, the coachman, returned from the country she'd send him back with a note to Maddy explaining everything. Alexa hated to part with her baby for ten days but there was no help for it. She thanked God for Maddy, knowing she could be trusted to care for Davie properly in her absence.

22

His long legs stretched out before him, Adam stared morosely into his glass of ale. Despite the fact that each one of his arms encircled the bare shoulders of an attractive woman seated on either side of him, his mind was anywhere but on his companions. Since his arrival in London three days ago he had tried everything from drinking to whoring in order to keep his mind from the only woman he had ever loved. Alexa! So close yet out of his reach. Had he tried he could not have counted all the times during these past months he had dreamed of confronting her, of laughing in her face at her failure to do away with him, and of the punishment he would mete out to her should she be unfortunate enough to come under his scrutiny.

Dear God! The thought of her nearly drove him insane. The scent of her, the taste; the way her violet eyes sparkled when he made love to her, and how she callously turned her back on him when he needed her most. Had he not heard her say the words Adam would never have believed her capable of, hating him to the point of wanting him dead? What had happened to change her? Had she only pretended love, Adam pondered, until the right moment arrived in which to exact vengeance for the way he had taken her from her home in order to destroy her father? Aye, Adam decided dejectedly. That had to be the answer. It was not love for him she harbored in her heart, but hate.

"What's wrong, luv?" asked the woman on his right, a pert brunette with bowed lips painted a bright red and green cat eyes. Her name was Lucy, an actress of dubious renown whose greater success lay in pleasing the male patrons of the theater.

"What makes you think something is wrong?" scowled Adam darkly.

"Do you scowl like that all the time?" pouted Lucy prettily.

"Perhaps he needs some cheering up," piped up the blond occupying Adam's left arm. Fannie, somewhat older than Lucy but no less enticing with her overblown figure and bewitching smile, was not averse to sharing any man who took her fancy. And Adam had definitely taken her fancy. His brooding good looks attracted her the moment she spied him in the audience, his bored expression a challenge she couldn't resist.

Adam, in his rush to self-destruction, boldly invited both women to share supper with him, hinting of better things to come. Both Lucy and Fannie accepted with alacrity. They were waiting now for Mac who had been invited by Adam to share the favors of one of his lively companions.

Due to Adam's unstable state of mind and his frequent bouts of depression these past months, Mac rarely left Adam's side. Their meetings had been postponed for a few weeks and Mac cursed the inactivity that left Adam at loose ends. As he walked into the inn now and saw

Adam carelessly fondling the two women, both obviously actresses or whores, he cursed roundly. How he wished he could bring Adam and Alexa back together. But he was not even allowed to mention her name in Adam's presence. Adam also forbade him to call on Alexa, but Mac decided he would do as he pleased in that respect. He felt obligated to speak to Alexa at least one time in order to learn the truth of what had happened to cause her to leave Adam. He found Adam's story about Alexa wanting him dead hard to digest. To Mac it just didn't make sense.

"Mac," Adam gestured, waving Mac toward his table the moment he saw him enter the crowded room. "You're in luck tonight. These two lovely ladies are willing to share their . . . er . . . time with us. Sit down, our food is ready."

Mac seated himself and immediately the brunette sidled over and placed a slim hand high up on his leg. "I'm Lucy," she batted her lashes invitingly as she bent over to give him an unhampered glimpse of white breasts bared nearly to the nipples.

Mac smiled his appreciation to Adam who promptly raised his glass in a silent salute. Somehow Adam muddled through the meal, suddenly hot to bed Fannie with those tempting red lips that promised to dull his memory of violet eyes surrounded by thick dusty lashes. As soon as it was decently possible he took Fannie by the hand, excused himself and propelled her up the stairs to his room. He hadn't had a woman since Alexa, in fact, hadn't desired one.

"God, you are eager," Fannie laughed, licking her red lips expectantly. No sooner had the door closed behind them than Adam grasped Fannie by the waist and flung her on the bed, falling heavily atop her. "Wait, can't you?" she gasped. "At least let me take off my clothes."

"No," grunted Adam, raising her skirts to hover about her waist. "Later. I want you now!" He tore into her unprepared flesh and she groaned. But it wasn't long before she began moaning not from pain but from desire as Adam dug his fingers into her buttocks to press even closer in order to sheath himself more fully between her quivering thighs.

"Oh, yes, yes," Fannie gasped, oblivious to all but Adam's pounding haunches. Adam exploded first, but being the considerate lover he continued until Fannie followed him only seconds later.

Afterwards, guilt-ridden over the way he had shamelessly used Fannie as a means to exorcise the woman he really wanted in his bed, Adam undressed her and made love to her more leisurely. Completely beguiled by the first man considerate of her own pleasure, Fannie would have killed to have Adam exclusively hers. Late that night she left considerably richer and with a promise that Adam would see her two nights hence for a repeat of what they had just shared.

Though physically sated, Adam remained wakeful, unable to corral his wayward thoughts. For him there was no peace. Pulling on his clothes he wandered below stairs to find that everyone had settled down for the night; Mac was nowhere in sight and rather than awaken him for conversation Adam bought a bottle and returned to his room to drink himself into a stupor.

The next morning found Adam in a foul mood as well as badly hungover. He consumed a gallon of tea before the liquor was sufficiently diluted to allow him to function with minimal pain to his head that seemed to have grown to monstrous proportions.

Sometime during the interminable night Adam had come to the inevitable conclusion that he must face Alexa, if for no other reason than to prove to her he still lived. Perversely he wondered if she had already committed bigamy by marrying Charles Whitlaw. What a joke on her when she discovered her new marriage to be illegal. Perhaps she already carried Charles's child, Adam thought, grimacing with pain. The possibility was too terrible to contemplate.

Unable to eat breakfast, Adam left before Mac awoke to question his destination or his motives. Boldly he approached Charles's house and rapped on the door. An elderly butler answered the knock. "I'd like to see your mistress," Adam said in a voice brooking no argument.

"The mistress, my lord, has been long dead and buried," replied the old retainer, undaunted by Adam's threatening tone. "And the master is on his way to India." He started to close the door but something in Adam's face stopped him.

"Dead!" gasped Adam, staggering backwards. "No, it can't be! Alexa can't be dead!"

Upon hearing Alexa's name spoken in such grieving tones, the butler's face immediately cleared. "I'm speaking, sir, of Lady Diana, Sir Charles' wife who died giving birth. The Lady Alexa left here some months ago."

So relieved was Adam to hear that Alexa was alive that he drew in deep gulps of air, unaware that he had been holding his breath. "Do you know where I might find Lady Alexa?"

"No, my lord," replied the butler. In truth he knew exactly where Alexa had gone but he had grown so fond of the lady that he wished no harm visited on her. Hence, he lied, for he cared little for Adam's dark, brooding looks. Let him locate her himself if he was so intent upon finding her, that good man decided as he closed the door in Adam's face.

Still shaken, Adam returned to the inn for lunch—
having missed breakfast he felt the first stirrings of
hunger. Well into his meal Adam could not help but
overhear the conversation between two men seated at
the next table, making him grateful that he had returned.
From what he had heard so far the men were obviously
a lawyer and his client.

"What kind of a chance do I have, Wayne?" the
younger man asked. He looked to be over thirty with
thinning blond hair and sharp features. The pronounced
bags under his eyes led Adam to believe he was well
along the path to dissipation.

"It's difficult to judge which way the court will decide
in a case such as this, Billy, but I truly believe your
chances of controlling the Ashley fortune, at least until
your cousin, Lady Alexa, turns twenty-five, to be
excellent. Unless, of course, she remarries."

"I'll make certain that doesn't happen," smirked Billy
knowingly, "unless she's willing to settle for me."

"Are you absolutely certain the lady's husband is
dead, Billy? If not all this is a waste of time."

"I heard it directly from Charles Whitlaw before he left
for India, Wayne," Billy assured him smugly. "He's the
one who brought Lady Alexa from America after the
death of her husband. He was in his cups one night and
hinted to some deep secret in her past but refused to
divulge just what it was. Believe it or not he appeared
frightened of my esteemed cousin."

Adam nearly choked as he smothered a laugh. The
Vixen's anger could be formidable, as Charles well
knew. He wondered why Charles and Alexa had split,
especially since this Billy Ashley appeared on the verge
of wresting Alexa's holdings from her. Until that
moment he hadn't realized John Ashley was dead. As
often as Adam had wished for Ashley's demise, it no

longer seemed important to him. But at least he now knew where Alexa was living. She obviously was staying at Ashley House. But rather than face her at a time when he was far from feeling his best, Adam put the meeting off until the following day when he deemed himself better able to cope with his emotions.

Before Adam presented himself at Ashley House the following evening he had accomplished many things. One of which was to pay a visit to Lawyer Wayne. He smiled to himself as he recalled the encounter as well as the stunned look on Billy's face, who just happened to pay a visit while Adam was speaking with the solicitor.

Claude Wayne nearly fell off his well-padded posterior when Adam was shown into his office and introduced himself. "You . . . are the husband of Lady Alexa Ashley Foxworth?" he gasped in disbelief. "That's impossible, sir! Adam Foxworth, Lord Penwell, is dead."

"You have proof of that?" Adam asked coolly, flicking an invisible speck from his impeccably clad arm.

"Well . . . er . . . that is, proof enough," Wayne hemmed and hawed. "Do you have proof of your identity, sir?"

"Actually, I do," announced Adam, enjoying himself immensely. Then he proceeded to extract several documents from his pocket including a letter of credit and a large bank draft bearing his name. Wayne studied everything very carefully before handing them back, his face mottled, clearly distraught by the turn of events. He and Billy Ashley had grand plans to bilk Lady Alexa out of the bulk of her estate before that young lady reached her majority. The unfortunate appearance of the lady's husband had effectively put a damper on their well-laid plans.

At that point Billy Ashley sauntered into the office, not

bothering to knock or be announced. "Wayne, what do you hear from the courts?" blustered Billy before he saw Adam sitting in a chair. "Are our bribes sufficient to assure me the Ashley estates?"

Wayne paled, motioning frantically at Adam who rose to his full height as he faced Billy. "Who is this man, Wayne?" Billy asked, an unexplained frisson of fear stiffening his spine.

Wayne cleared his throat, shifting uncomfortably in his chair. "I'm afraid you're in for a shock, dear boy," he replied in a voice much too high. "This is Lord Penwell, Alexa Ashley's husband, who has been miraculously resurrected."

Billy started violently, his face twisted with rage. "Impossible! Charles would not lie! This man is an impostor!"

"There are too many people in England who could verify my identity," Adam said lazily. The dangerous gleam in his icy gaze was not lost on Billy Ashley. "I believe lawyer Wayne is quite satisfied with my credentials. As for Charles Whitlaw, I fear his information was false. As you can see I certainly am no ghost."

With an exaggerated bow Adam left, the loud curses of Billy following him out the door. He laughed heartily, something he hadn't done in months, experiencing a surge of elation that held until he stood resolutely before the elegant door of Ashley House. It was very late, for Adam had first attended the theater and postponed his date with a furious Fannie until the following evening.

Though Mac had begged to be allowed to accompany Adam when he called upon Alexa, he was denied his request. Mac's all-consuming fear was that Adam might do his wife bodily harm when he finally faced her, but Adam promised he would not hurt her. "I wouldn't dirty my hands on her!" Adam spat derisively.

"You've gone to a lot of trouble in her behalf, Adam," Mac reminded him. "You could have stood by and done nothing while she lost everything to Billy Ashley."

"No I couldn't, Mac. Sooner or later my name will be made known as one of the Americans here to negotiate a peace treaty with England. I should never have allowed you to talk me into coming here in the first place. Besides," he calculated slyly, "Alexa's possessions are mine by law. I couldn't allow so valuable an estate to pass into the hands of a man like Billy Ashley."

"I wouldn't tell Alexa your views." Mac grinned implishly. "I imagine she fancies the estate hers."

"The law is the law, Mac." Adam smirked as he imagined Alexa's face when he told her he was taking over her properties. "I'm on my way there now to inform her that her husband is very much alive despite her efforts to the contrary."

The house looked deserted. Only one dim light was visible, and that coming from a window near the rear of the house. But Adam was not deterred. He knew Alexa had to be there. With a determination born of long months thinking of just such an encounter, he grasped the knocker firmly in strong fingers and set up a furious pounding. For several painful minutes there was no answer. Then, when he was on the verge of giving up in disgust to return in the morning, the door slowly opened.

Alexa had fallen asleep curled up in a chair in her father's den, an opened book lying in her lap. Owen and Bertha had already retired to their own quarters and Alexa, unable to sleep for thinking about her appearance at court in a few days, had wandered into the study and fallen asleep. The racket at the front door startled her awake, but only after several minutes was she able to gather her wits sufficiently to move. In a daze she walked to the door, halfway between waking and sleeping. It never occurred to her to wonder who might be visiting at so late an hour, or that to open the door might invite danger. What she did think of was Davie, and that something might have happened to him. With lamp held aloft to light her way, Alexa slowly opened the door.

Adam's first glimpse of Alexa, her lovely features flushed from sleep, her ebony hair falling in disarray about her slim shoulders, caused his body to swell with desire and his heart to beat erratically in his breast. Reining in his stampeding emotions, Adam felt himself drawn into the fathomless deep violet depths as Alexa's eyes grew wide with shock the moment recognition dawned.

"You!" Her voice was a throaty rasp reminiscent of the Vixen. "It can't be! You're dead!"

"Not dead, Alexa," Adam replied coldly. "But very much alive, no thanks to you."

Alexa's slim hand fluttered upward to clutch convulsively at her throat. "Adam! Thank God!" Then she did something she only did once before in her life. She fainted.

With the grace of a panther, Adam swooped her up before she hit the floor, at the same time stomping out the fire from the smashed lamp she had dropped when she fell into her swoon. Glancing about, he saw no servants lurking in the shadows, having no doubt been dismissed for the night. Closing the front door with his foot, Adam scowled at Alexa's limp body resting peacefully in his arms, then came to a swift decision. He felt a thrill of excitement pounding through his blood as he bounded up the stairs, picked the first bedroom he came to and deposited her unceremoniously on the bed. As fate would have it, it was Alexa's own room.

He moved about lighting a lamp and wetting a cloth to place on her forehead, stopping to stare at her as he feasted his eyes on her beauty so long denied him. When he had looked his fill he placed the cloth on her brow and loosened the buttons of her bodice. After a few minutes Alexa began to stir, moaning softly and thrashing about. When her eyes finally focused she discovered Adam sitting calmly beside her on the bed, a sardonic smile curving his sensuous lips.

"Oh, Adam, Adam, my love. It's true, you are alive! I wasn't just dreaming."

"Why, Alexa," Adam said mockingly, "how can you doubt it?" Struggling, she sat up, noticing for the first time Adam's stern countenance, his cold eyes, the cynical twist to his lips. Oh, God, she groaned inwardly, he hates me! He'll never forgive me!

"You left me in little doubt of your feelings the last time we met," Adam accused, giving her a look of intense animosity. "Why did you wish me dead, Alexa? I can understand everything but that."

"No, Adam. It's not true. It was Charles! He's the one who wanted you dead! He arranged everything without my knowledge. I just recently found out that he paid to have you set upon after you left his ship. What happened?"

"Somehow Mac got wind of what was planned and arrived in time to save my neck. So you see, my love," he stated with bitter emphasis, "I foiled your attempt to end my life. Your lover should have left me for the hangman had he wanted me dead."

"Adam, you must listen to me," Alexa begged desperately. "I acted as I did to save your life. Charles promised to set you free if I returned to England with him."

"As his mistress?"

"Aye, but . . ." Suddenly Alexa was aware that Adam was no longer listening to her. His eyes were drawn to that enticing portion of her upper breasts and neck that showed through the opening in her bodice where the buttons gaped apart.

With a will of their own his hands thrust forward, his long fingers caressing her throat and the tops of her breasts. "How was Charles, Alexa?" Adam asked softly, accusing. "Did he make you moan as I did? Did he do all the things you love? All the things I taught you?"

Alexa gasped, unable to speak as his strong hands suddenly tightened about the slender column of her neck, his face a contorted mask of pain. "Adam," she gagged, "please. You're hurting me."

"No more than you hurt me, I'll wager." His fingers tightened, Alexa's face grew white, then red, and she knew that death was imminent.

"I . . . love . . . you . . ." she managed to gasp out only seconds before the pressure to her throat eased.

"Oh, Jesus, Alexa!" Adam shuddered convulsively. "Do you realize I nearly killed you; how near death you were?" He flung himself away, unable to control his emotions. For months he had dreamed of facing Alexa, of punishing her in some way too horrible to contemplate. And he nearly succeeded! Oh God, what had he become? What had she done to him? Breathing deeply in an effort to gain control of his rampaging emotions, Adam whirled about to glare murderously at Alexa. "What happened between you and your lover? Has he tired of you already? Or have you tired of him?"

Alexa tried to speak but couldn't; her mouth was dry, her throat sore and raspy. Sighing disgustedly, Adam poured her a glass of water from a pitcher sitting nearby and waited impatiently until she could form the words she wished to say. "I . . . I left Charles the moment word was received in England confirming the war's end. I knew then that he no longer presented a threat to me."

"A threat? Do you think me stupid enough to believe that Charles forced you into his bed?"

"Yes . . . no . . . I mean, you're not stupid, but Charles did not force me. Not into his bed, I mean. I never shared his bed."

Adam sighed wearily. "You lived with Charles for months and you expect me to believe you never shared his bed?"

"Aye. Oh, Adam, I was . . ." She paused dramatically, then clamped her mouth tightly shut. No, she would not tell Adam about Davie. Not yet. Not until she knew what he intended for her. Once he learned he had a son he might be tempted to take him away from her and she couldn't allow that. Davie was her whole life and she would kill to keep him with her.

". . . was what, Alexa?" Adam asked, eyeing her curiously.

"Nothing . . . I meant to say I was unwilling."

Sarcastic laughter met her ears and Alexa felt herself tremble. From the first moment she met Adam she had never really feared him until now. "Your flimsy explanation does not do you justice, my love. Somehow I expected better from you." His smoky eyes blazed with an unholy light as he boldly raked her figure from head to toe.

Realizing Adam wasn't going to believe her no matter what, Alexa wanted him gone. Far away where he wasn't likely to learn about Davie and lay claim to him. "What are you doing in England, Adam?" she asked, sullenly. "Did you come all this way just to tell me you hated me?"

"I had no intention of seeing you at all. I came to

England as part of a delegation sent to negotiate a peace treaty. A relative of yours, Billy Ashley, is what brought me to Ashley House."

"Billy! What has he to do with us?"

"I accidentally learned your father died leaving you a wealthy woman," Adam casually explained. "I also heard Billy Ashley was attempting to wrest your holdings from you by having himself declared your guardian. I quickly disabused him of that notion. You can forget about Billy Ashley and any plot he may have hatched."

Alexa was dumbfounded. "You did that for me? But . . . I don't understand. If you hate me so much why . . ."

"Don't flatter yourself, my love," Adam said contemptuously. "I did it for myself. I am your lawful husband and your holdings now belong to me. Did you really think I'd allow your wealth to slip through my fingers so easily?"

Red dots of rage exploded behind Alexa's eyes. "You bastard!" she cried, nearly knocking him off his feet as she sprang at him. "Get out of here, I don't need you!"

"I hear Charles is on his way to India. With whom have you replaced him? A woman of your passions cannot live long without one man or another." His words were spoken with deadly calm as he captured Alexa's flailing arms, pinning them to her side and pulling her plaint form hard against his maleness. Through the thickness of her skirt she felt him grow large and prod between her legs.

"Damn you, Adam, leave me alone. I won't give in to you. If it's a woman you want, go find a whore!"

"I have one," he laughed crudely, flinging her on the bed and settling his considerable bulk on her frail form, making it impossible for her to escape him. "You're also my wife, Alexa, or have you forgotten?"

"I've forgotten nothing, and I don't deserve your contempt, Adam. I saved your life, damn you! I should have let you hang!"

"Maybe you should have, Alexa," Adam agreed softly. Before she could offer a tart reply, Adam's hard mouth claimed hers, slanting first one way, then the other in a kiss meant to punish as well as show his contempt.

Struggling beneath him, Alexa felt her breath leave her soul as his kiss deepened and his tongue ravaged the soft inside of her mouth, stabbing, probing, insulting in its boldness. His fingers dug hurtfully into the tender flesh of her upper arms and Alexa whimpered, wishing she had the comfort of a sword in her hand.

At the first touch of her mouth against his, Adam was driven beyond reason, beyond time and space as his blood took fire and blazed white-hot through his veins. Lifting himself slightly he began ripping and tugging at her clothes until he finally bared her beautiful breasts to his hot gaze.

Abandoning her lips, his eager mouth fell to a nipple, dusty rose and pouting prettily beneath his gaze. "This is rape, Adam!" Alexa managed to gasp out.

Ignoring her taunts, Adam continued to nuzzle and suck at her breasts, vaguely thinking that she had somehow changed since he had last had her; her breasts seemed fuller, more firm. His mouth continued its brazen assault as he tugged off the rest of her clothes and tossed them on the floor. Then he worked furiously to free himself of his own constricting clothing before renewing his salacious attack.

"You've changed, Alexa," he murmured, his hands skimming sensuously over her body, discovering once again all the secret places he had forbidden himself to think about these many months. Passion, as well as anger, caused his hands to grasp roughly, almost hurt-fully, at her tender flesh.

"If you're trying to hurt me, Adam, you're succeeding," Alexa complained, flinching beneath the onslaught of his ardor.

"I should hurt you, my love. You deserve to be hurt, damn it!" cursed Adam. "But for some unexplained reason the need to possess you, to lose myself in your warm flesh, is far greater. If I can't punish you with one weapon I shall use another; one you are accustomed to."

"Adam, I won't . . ." began Alexa stubbornly.

"You will," Adam interrupted harshly.

Before she could reply Adam's lips were once again claiming hers, forcibly at first, then softening, swallowing her cries of protest deep in his throat while his hands played at her breasts. With the heel of his palm he molded the mounds, caressing the taut nubs with a thumb. Alexa whimpered, drawn against her will into the vortex of his passion.

Then his lips replaced his hands at her breasts and Alexa stiffened and arched as he drew first one and then the other into his mouth, his tongue working wetly in ever widening circles. Moving downward he nipped at her rib cage, lapped at her navel and the smooth surface of her stomach. Lower still, to the crisp nest of ebony curls which he parted with his tongue, searching for and finding the tiny bud of her femininity.

Alexa gasped, tugging at his hair. "Oh, God, Adam, don't do this to me!" No answer was forthcoming as Adam's fingers found her moistness, as his mouth continued to plunder.

Alexa was panting now, crying out, begging. "I can't stand it, Adam! Stop! Please! You're torturing me!"

But Adam was relentless, enjoying her helplessness,

reveling in the knowledge that he was driving her wild with desire. Unable to control her response, Alexa exploded in a million pieces, writhing, shuddering, crying out mindlessly. And then she felt herself stretching as Adam reared up and shoved himself inside her.

"I've forgotten how good you feel," he groaned, feeling her tighten around him. And then words were forgotten as his own passion took over and he thrust, withdrew, thrust again, moving smoothly into her welcoming flesh.

Alexa moaned as she felt herself responding again in a way she never thought possible. It had been so long since she had been made love to, since she had been touched with love, if Adam's angry passion could be construed as love, that she felt herself grow tense and finally disintegrate once more, melting inside as he stroked her to another climax. A few moments later Adam allowed his own passion full reign and he cried out harshly, joining her in her ecstatic journey.

Alexa was allowed little sleep that night. Adam seemed unable to get enough of her, using her repeatedly, forcing a response from her by employing his hands and mouth in ways that drove her to the very brink of insanity. With ridiculous ease he had her writhing and moaning beneath him time and again, despite her resolve to remain unmoved. Morning found her exhausted, her violet eyes smudged with dark circles, her body stiff and sore.

The sun was already high when Alexa awakened to find Adam sleeping peacefully beside her. With his brow smooth and relaxed he looked so young Alexa almost forgave him for treating her so shabbily. Almost, but not quite. If only he would listen to her and believe her, Alexa thought miserably. If only there was some way to persuade him that she loved him. Though he professed to hate her, Alexa had to admit he hadn't hurt her, at times making love to her most tenderly. But then, she remembered the Adam from old whose very nature cried out against physically abusing a woman. He had no need for violence for he was an expert at finding other, more subtle means of punishment, and would not hesitate to use them.

Alexa's ruminations were halted unexpectedly when the door to her room opened and Bertha entered bearing a breakfast tray. "You overslept this morning, my lady," the elderly woman said cheerfully, "so I thought you'd like your breakfast in bed for a change."

Alexa sat up so suddenly the sheet fell away, baring her breasts to the astonished woman, vivid purple bruises clearly visible on her otherwise flawless flesh. When Bertha's eyes fell upon Adam still sleeping peacefully beside her mistress, the tray clattered noisily to the floor from her nerveless fingers, scattering food in all directions. Startled by his rude awakening, Adam reared up, exposing a nude, well-muscled body to the thoroughly confused woman.

"Oh, my lady!" she gasped, eyes bulging dangerously. "I'm so sorry! I did not know!" Embarrassed beyond bearing for disturbing her mistress and her lover, the poor woman threw her apron over her head and wrung her hands helplessly.

"It's all right, Bertha," Alexa soothed as she quickly donned a robe and Adam fell back into bed covering himself with a sheet. "This is Lord Penwell, my . . . my husband."

Slowly the apron descended. "But . . . but . . . I thought . . . we all thought . . ."

"I know, Bertha, everyone thought Adam was dead but as you can see he is very much alive. Go back to the kitchen and I'll come down later and explain everything to you."

Slanting a furtive glance at Adam's amused face, Bertha retreated after quickly retrieving the tray and removing most of the spoiled food from the floor. The rest would have to wait until later.

Alexa fumed beneath Adam's sardonic grin, challenging him with hands resting on her slim hips. "You nearly shocked that poor woman to death, Adam Foxworth!"

"She'd better get used to it," he drawled lazily, "for I intend to move in. This is much more comfortable than my present quarters." And if that wasn't enough, he added, "And this place is so large I think I'll invite Mac to join us."

"Mac is in London?" asked Alexa, evidently overjoyed by the news.

"Aye," said Adam sourly as his cold eyes narrowed in speculation. "You appear inordinately happy to learn Mac is in London."

Alexa flushed. "Mac is my friend."

"I wouldn't be too sure of that. Not after what you did." He bounded out of bed and began gathering his clothes, walking about nude and totaly unconcerned. Alexa lowered her eyes, thinking no man had a right to be so beautiful despite the scattering of scars over his muscular form.

"I'll have Bertha prepare a room for you," Alexa said, her eyes straying to his masculinity so boldly displayed.

"This one will do fine," Adam smiled obliquely. As if sensing her eyes upon that certain part of his body he began to grow hard before her eyes. Alexa gasped and raised her eyes to his grinning features. "Are you still hungry for me, Alexa?" he asked. "Charles must have been gone a long time to make you so greedy."

Alexa gasped. "N-no, Adam, I was just . . ." Just what? she chided herself, turning crimson.

"Don't play shy with me, my love," he warned, eyeing her dangerously. "Either get back in bed or stop looking at me like that."

"Go to hell!" Alexa shouted angrily. "You're a conceited bastard, Adam Foxworth!"

"And you're an insatiable vixen!" He laughed, grabbing her about the waist and falling with her into the rumpled bed.

Another hour passed before Adam finally dressed and left the house, telling Alexa he'd be back later that evening with three dinner guests, Mac and two others he failed to name. Alexa's vile curses followed him out the door.

Alexa spent half the day explaining to Bertha and Owen why they couldn't tell Adam about Davie, and the other half hiring a crew of servants to staff the house and prepare for guests. She wasted little time wondering who besides Mac Adam was bringing to dinner. She was much too busy for that. She sent off a hasty message to Maddy explaining the situation at Ashley House and begged her to care for Davie until she knew what Adam intended for her.

If she had to, Alexa was prepared to take Davie and go someplace where Adam could not find them. Especially if he continued to humiliate and debase her. Still, she was his wife and from all appearances it looked as if Adam intended to exert his husbandly rights. Evidently her wealth meant a great deal to him and he had no intention of letting it slip through his fingers no matter what it took to keep it.

Oh, why did she love him so? Alexa wondered miserably. One day, she hoped, he'd listen to her, really listen, and understand that she acted as she did to save his life. If only Charles hadn't taken himself off to India she might have persuaded him to speak in her behalf and tell the truth. The coward! Her threats must have frightened him to make him go away so suddenly.

Sometime during the day Adam's trunks, along with Mac's, arrive, and Alexa had them carried upstairs. She smiled impishly as she directed Adam's to be placed in a room at the far end of the hall, knowing full well he would not like it. The thought gave her a small amount of pleasure as she went serenely about her duties. At least, she sighed gratefully, she no longer had to worry about Billy Ashley and his nefarious scheme to bilk her out of her inheritance.

23

Mac arrived late in the afternoon, and Alexa, happy to see his merry face, threw herself into his arms. "Mac, it's so good to see you!" she cried warmly. "I'm glad you'll be staying with us."

If Alexa noticed that Mac's greeting was less than exuberant she said nothing. After all, she surmised, Mac was still under the impression that she had left Adam to die an ignominious death. "This wasn't my idea, Alexa," Mac said, shrugging. "I had no idea you and Adam had . . . er . . . resolved your differences. When I returned to my room at the inn this afternoon I learned my trunks had been sent here and I was expected to present myself at supper. What's this all about, Alexa?"

"You've not seen Adam today?"

"No, he didn't return to the inn last night and I left on business before he returned today." He paused, searching her face intently. "Was he with you last night, Alexa? What did you say to change his mind about you? For months he could not tolerate the sound of your name."

Alexa felt her face grow hot. "He hasn't changed his mind, Mac," she said with bitter emphasis. "Adam still hates me. What he did was to realize that I am suddenly extremely wealthy. That alone persuaded him back to me."

"Can you blame him, Alexa?" Mac accused sourly. "Not once did he hold you responsible for wishing to save yourself, but it was cruel of you to let him know you had already become Whitlaw's mistress."

"I know it sounds damning, Mac, but it's not all what it seems."

Mac looked doubtful. "You didn't order Adam's death?"

"How could you even think such a thing?" cried Alexa, angry as well as terribly hurt. "You of all people know how much I loved Adam!"

Mac watched the play of emotion upon Alexa's lovely features, thinking it was time to discover the truth for himself. "I think you'd better tell me about it, Alexa," he said gently, leading her to a chair. "I want to believe you but the facts speak for themselves."

"I tried to explain to Adam, but he refused to believe me. Why are you any different?"

"It didn't happen to me, I can afford to be more objective. Now start with that night the soldiers came for you and Adam."

Though still somewhat reluctant to bare her soul, Alexa told Mac everything up to the moment Adam knocked on her door the night before. The one thing she was careful to omit was the fact of Davie's birth. But Mac knew her better than she knew herself. For several poignant minutes he stared at her, digesting all she said. To his way of thinking her story lacked some essential part. It was as if Alexa had deliberately omitted an important piece of the puzzle.

He startled her when he finally asked, "What aren't you telling me, Alexa? What have you left out? I know you. The Vixen would never allow a man like Charles to bend her to his will. She would have run him through and taken her chances on escaping with the man she loved."

Alexa sighed wearily. "Perhaps you don't know me as well as you thought, Mac."

"So Adam would have me believe," Mac replied dryly. "Will you please tell me, Alexa, how Charles managed to keep you under his thumb for so long?"

"You win, Mac," Alexa conceded. "I would never have fallen in so easily with Charles's plans if I . . . I hadn't a good reason."

"The reason, Alexa. . . ?"

"I . . . was pregnant."

"You were carrying Adam's child!"

"Aye! And I had to protect it, no matter what. I thought Charles would hold to his bargain and allow Adam to go free as he promised, otherwise I would never have agreed to his terms."

"He threatened to turn you in if you didn't submit, the bastard!" Mac said, comprehension dawning.

"Aye, I would do anything to protect Adam's babe. But I never became Charles' mistress! Never!"

"You told all this to Adam?" asked Mac, astounded. "I can't believe Adam would continue to feel as he does after he learned about his child. Is it a girl or boy?"

"A boy," Alexa smiled fondly. "I named him Davie. And . . . and I never told Adam about his son."

"Not told him! My God, Alexa, are you crazy? You can't keep something like that from Adam!"

Alexa's chin rose belligerently. "I can and I will!"

"But why? It doesn't make sense."

"It does to me. What if Adam decides to take his son

away from me? He has the right, you know. I told you he hates me."

"Did he spend the night with you, Alexa?"

"Aye," she admitted grudgingly.

"Then he can't hate you that much, can he?" Alexa stared at him dumbly. "He did make love to you, didn't he?"

"Aye, but he's a man," Alexa replied tartly, as if that explained everything.

"Tell him about his son, Alexa," Mac urged gently.

"No, Mac, not yet. I will, but not until I can make him love and trust me again. I won't take the chance of losing my son. He can have all I own, but not my child. Davie is all I have."

Mac shook his head, thoroughly disgusted. "Do you want me to tell him?"

"No, Mac, please, you must promise me! Let me do it in my own way!" Alexa pleaded, her sudden pallor alarming Mac. "I'd die if Adam took Davie from me! I'll tell him, truly. Just give me time to convince Adam I love him and never meant him any harm."

Alexa became so distraught that Mac was forced to agree, albeit reluctantly. "All right, Alexa, but if this gets out of hand I swear I'll tell Adam myself."

Shortly afterwards both Mac and Alexa retired to their respective rooms to dress for dinner. Adam had not yet returned and Alexa suddenly recalled that she had forgotten to inform Mac about the other dinner guests Adam had invited. She wished that she had remembered so she could ask him who they might be.

Alexa appeared in the dining room to find Mac already there though Adam was still curiously absent. "You look enchanting, Alexa," Mac complimented, his eyes dancing appreciatively over her trim figure clad in apricot silk. The gown, which bared her neck, throat and shoulders, was caught up at intervals around the skirt with maroon rosettes to reveal a maroon petticoat deeply flounced with apricot. Loose puffed sleeves displayed dimpled elbows and slender arms.

Alexa hoped that Adam would concur for she had gone to great lengths to look her best tonight for him and his friends. Thinking about those mysterious guests, Alexa was about to ask Mac if he knew who they might be when she heard voices in the hallway.

"Ah, it seems your errant husband has finally arrived," Mac said, turning expectantly toward the doorway.

Adam chose that moment to grace them with his presence and Alexa knew immediately he was not completely sober. He still wore the same clothes he had on last night and he looked thoroughly rumpled. He slanted an oblique look at Alexa, a look that told her nothing. Ignoring her, he addressed Mac. "You received my message, I see," he drawled lazily, careful not to slur his words. "I'm glad you decided to come."

"You left me no choice," Mac intoned dryly. "I returned to my lodging to find you had all my trunks sent here."

"I trust my wife made you comfortable?" His icy eyes slid to Alexa, widened slightly when he noticed for the first time how fetching she looked, then turned toward the door where two women poised uncertainly on the threshold. "Come in, ladies." He smiled charmingly.

Mac groaned aloud, "Oh, no, Adam, how could you?" He shifted his gaze to Alexa who stood rooted to the spot, a statue made of cold marble, and just as beautiful.

Gallantly escorting the women into the room, Adam announced rather smugly, "Alexa, I'd like to present Lucy and Fannie, both well-known to theatergoers about London. Ladies, you already are acquainted with my good friend, Mac. And this," he gestured expansively, "is my wife, Lady Alexa."

"Your wife!" squealed Fannie, dismayed. "But you never told me you had a wife!"

"Does it matter?" Adam shrugged carelessly. "Has it ever mattered to you?"

Fannie's China blue eyes grew wide as she looked from Adam to Alexa. What she saw in Alexa's steady gaze must have soothed her ruffled feathers for she immediately snuggled close to Adam, smiling up at him in a flirtatious manner. After all, half the men she took to her bed were forced into loveless marriages they didn't want. She made their life more bearable by providing what their wives could not or would not. "No," she cooed silkily, "It matters not at all, luv, else why would you have brought me to your home?"

Alexa finally found her voice. "This is my home and I strongly suggest, Adam, that you take your . . . er . . . friends elsewhere to dine. I refuse to entertain your doxies." With a flip of her hair and a tilt to her chin she prepared to leave the room, but Adam's steely grip upon her arm prevented her.

"This is my home, Alexa, and these are my friends. Now sit down so we can enjoy our meal."

Mac thought to intervene but found no need to when Alexa drew herself up to her meager height and said with all the contempt she could muster, "Go to hell, Adam!" In a froth of swirling silk she was gone, leaving only the tantalizing scent of her perfume.

The moment Alexa exited the life seemed to have gone out of Adam, leaving him totally deflated. After that he became surly to the point of rudeness, relying on Mac to carry the conversation despite his friend's rage at Adam for playing the fool.

Adam barely touched his food, but it did not stop him from imbibing freely. He was angry. Angry at Alexa for refusing to remain and be humiliated by him, and angrier still at himself for bringing the whole mess down on his own head. In the beginning it seemed such a good idea. He meant only to hurt Alexa as she had hurt him. He never really wanted Fannie. During the interminable meal he could not help but contrast her coarse beauty and overblown figure with Alexa's refined loveliness and petite form, and the actress fared poorly.

He had thought it would amuse him to watch Fannie and Alexa eating at the same table, knowing that they shared the same man. But it hadn't worked the way he planned. A wry grin lurked at the corners of his mouth when he remembered the way Alexa's eyes had spit violet fire at him. So like his Vixen. His Vixen! Bah! His and Charles's, and how many others? he asked himself, his thoughts turning sour.

Across the table from Adam, Mac seethed inwardly with silent rage. How could Adam act such a perfect bastard with Alexa? If only he hadn't promised Alexa he'd keep her secret, Mac chided himself, for if Adam continued to act in such a despicable manner Mac was uncertain how long he could hold his tongue. He itched to get Adam alone and give him a thorough tongue-lashing.

As things turned out Mac did not see Adam alone that night. After their prolonged dinner, Mac was pressed into escorting Lucy back to her lodging and once there the pert brunette had little difficulty persuading him to her bed. Mac was after all a virile man.

As for Fannie, she was more than happy to place herself in Adam's care. Her body trembled with anticipation, and when they reached her rooms, Adam suddenly found himself reluctant to partake of what the lady so freely offered.

It was very late when Adam let himself into Ashley House. Grumbling loudly, he stumbled through the darkened house, found the stairs with great difficulty and climbed them cautiously. He paused before Alexa's room, rattled the doorknob and cursed roundly when he found it locked. "Damn it, Alexa, let me in!"

Startled out of a deep sleep, it took Alexa several minutes to gain her wits. In the meantime the pounding continued. "Did you hear me, Alexa, open the door!"

"Go away, Adam," Alexa shouted back. "Your room is at the end of the hall!"

"This is my room!"

"No it isn't! What's the matter, Adam, did you tire of your whore so soon?"

"Fannie has nothing to do with this. Let me in!"

"Go to hell!"

Fury nearly choked him as curses fell from his lips. "There's no door strong enough to keep me out!"

Alexa froze, chillingly aware of his formidable strength when roused to anger. Still, she could not help calling out once more, "Go to hell!"

The angry retort hardened his features with determination as he began slamming his shoulder into the thick panel. Alexa heard rather than saw the lock begin to weaken. She leaned over and lit the lamp just as the door crashed open, and suddenly he loomed above her, his expression thunderous, his breath ragged with impotent rage.

Alexa paled, clutching the sheet about her throat, her own temper rising in response as she flashed him a look of defiance. Her accusing tone stabbed the air. "What are you trying to do, Adam? Humiliate me? Punish me? Well, you succeeded nicely by bringing your doxy into my home. But that doesn't mean I am obliged to cringe before you and pretend to be the dutiful wife!"

God, she was magnificent, Adam conceded grudgingly. How could he ever think another woman could satisfy him? Alexa was his wife no matter what she did and he wanted her. Now!

Alexa watched, stunned, as his anger turned to lust before her eyes. "No!" she warned. "Stay away from me!"

He cupped her chin in his palm, forcing her face upward to meet his gaze. Then he halted her frantic words with his mouth as he fell heavily atop her reclining form. The feel of her sweet flesh against him released all the fury, all the anger that had gnawed at him for months. He held her head steady, forcing her to accept the punishment of his kiss. He pried her lips apart and thrust his tongue into her mouth, knowing he was bruising her soft lips, yet unwilling to stop.

She felt his manhood huge and hot against her belly through her thin nightgown, and she closed her eyes tightly. "I will hate you for this, Adam," she whispered, gritting her teeth.

She heard his hissing breath. "The feeling is mutual!" he snarled, hating himself for his words as well as his complete loss of control. Unable to halt his course of retribution, he quickly tore off his clothes, reared up, pulling apart her thighs, and plunged into her unwilling body. He did not touch her with love as he wished to do, ignoring completely her pounding fists and cries of rage and pain. He grasped her hips and drew her upwards to impale her completely. He knew he was hurting her and wanted to fling himself away and beg her forgiveness. She screamed when he thrust brutally, spilling his seed into her. Then he jerked out of her and rolled off to the side, his breath heaving.

Alexa refused to cry; she was beyond tears. She felt degraded and used. Not even in their earliest times together did Adam treat her so shabbily, taking her in a hurtful manner with neither love nor compassion. In her heart she knew it was over between them. His actions just now proved he really did hate her.

Adam spoke, so low Alexa had to strain to hear him. When she understood what he was saying she could do little more than stare at him, mouth agape. "I'm sorry, my love. God, I didn't mean to hurt you! I drank too much and when I returned to find you had locked me out I became like a wild man. I never meant to force you. Rape isn't my way."

"Why did you come back at all, Adam?" Alexa asked softly. "Your actions tonight made it perfectly clear that you preferred Fannie. Well, you're welcome to her. She's nothing but a cheap little tart who doesn't know enough to keep her legs together. Was she unable to satisfy you, Adam? I know how demanding you can be," she added sweetly.

"Damn it, Alexa, I didn't bed Fannie tonight if that's what you're thinking."

"No? You reek of her cheap perfume!"

"Who are you to talk, my love? You were Whitlaw's mistress."

"Never! I was never Charles's mistress!"

Adam felt his anger build again. One minute he was ready to kill her and the next he wanted . . . Suddenly his anger dissolved as his need for her consumed him. He rolled toward her, taking her lips gently, seducing her with his tongue. He kissed her mouth, her wet eyelids, the tip of her nose. He slipped his hand between their bodies and let his fingers find her belly, pressing lower, teasing her, probing her gently.

"No," Alexa moaned softly, but her body was straining against him as her resistance ebbed.

"You are moving against me, Alexa," he breathed into

her mouth. "You are growing moist and warm beneath my fingers and I feel you quivering with passion."

"No! I won't listen!"

"Feel how much I want you again," he said, pressing her belly against his hard manhood, molding her soft hips against him. "I want to feel myself deep inside you."

He kissed her breasts and she felt ripples of pleasure course through her. She writhed against him for relief, an ache beginning at the center of her femininity. Sensing her need, he slipped his knee between her thighs and pressed upward. Crying out, she moved against him wildly, by now far beyond herself.

He continued to kiss and suck at her nipples while his hands moved torturously between her legs and into her moist flesh. He removed his knee and knelt over her, savoring every part of her beautiful body. He lowered his head and began to nibble at her belly; her soft cries made him tremble with desire. He lifted her buttocks and her legs opened of their own accord, offering herself to him. He nuzzled and teased her with his tongue, wanting only to give her the greatest pleasure possible to make up for hurting her earlier. When he felt her stiffen on the verge of climax, he raised up, parted her and thrust his full length into her warm, moist body. Just as he was thrusting inside her, he captured her mouth, his tongue thrusting in the same manner.

Beside herself, Alexa wrapped her legs about him, bringing him deeper still, and Adam felt his control dissolve. He rode her boldly, and she met his every thrust until her body began to convulse with the painful pleasure and she was falling, swirling, merging with him into an abyss, possessing, being possessed. He heard her final cry, felt the tremendous shudder, and released the tenuous hold he had on reality.

* * *

Adam was gone when Alexa awoke and she experienced the same disappointment that she did all those other times when she had awakened to an empty bed, never certain if her husband would return to her. She was surprised, therefore, to find him not gone at all! but in the dining room eating breakfast.

"Good morning," he said cheerily. "Did you sleep well?" Alexa quirked a slim brow, trying to decide if he was being nasty or merely pleasant. "Have you nothing to say, my love?"

"Adam, I fail to understand you," Alexa finally said. "One minute you hate me and force yourself on me; the next you are making love to me as if . . . as if you meant it."

"I always mean it when I make love to a desirable woman," he replied blandly.

"You're a fool Adam," Alexa said softly. "I've never loved anyone but you."

"I'd be the happiest man in the world if I could believe you, my love," Adam replied, just as softly. Then he arose abruptly, afraid he had admitted too much, excused himself and left the house.

Alexa smiled mischievously at his departing back. Already she felt a softening in his attitude toward her. If they continued like this it wouldn't be long before she could tell him about Davie. She missed her baby desperately and even considered spending a day in the country with him. In fact, the idea appealed to her so much Alexa did just that a few days later.

Adam seemed to be caught up during the next several days with his duties as a delegate on the peace treaty commission. He and Mac left early in the morning and returned at dinnertime. He treated her politely during the day and made love to her furiously during the night. He did not try to force her again. There was no need. To

Alexa's joy she felt him teetering on the brink of total capitulation and lived for the day she would have his love, completely.

It was during one of these busy days in Adam's life that Alexa took herself off the country to see Davie. She spent so long playing with her baby, who had grown inches since she had last seen him, and filling in Maddy on all that had happened, that she was late getting home. At first Adam thought nothing of it, but Alexa's flushed face and nervous manner soon aroused his curiosity and he began questioning her.

"Where have you been, my love?"

"Shopping," she shrugged carelessly.

"Where are your packages?"

"Nothing took my fancy."

"Are you certain you went shopping?"

"For God's sake," interjected Mac, nearly certain he knew where Alexa had gone. "Why the inquisition? Surely Alexa is free to come and go as she pleases." Adam did not miss the grateful smile Alexa bestowed on Mac.

Adam eyed them both narrowly, his lips turned down sourly. "Are you trying to protect her, Mac? Is there something I should know?"

Mac flushed guiltily, loudly protesting Adam's insane accusations. Giving Alexa a knowing look, he replied, "I don't know what you are talking about."

Glaring hostilely at Alexa, Adam asked pointedly, "Have you taken a lover?"

Alexa relaxed, laughter bubbling up from her throat. "I'm afraid you leave me little energy for a lover, Adam." Her answer seemed to satisfy him—for the time being.

Two more times during the following weeks Adam returned home early to find Alexa gone, and once again he suspected her of taking a lover. In fact, he was so convinced she had that he perversely decided to punish her in a like manner.

Adam had not seen Fannie since he returned her to her lodgings that night he made the mistake of bringing her home to dinner. With Alexa now sharing his bed willingly he had grown far too satisfied and complacent, forgetting how she had left him to die. Once again allowing his hot head to rule his heart, Adam unwisely decided to teach Alexa a lesson by using Fannie as an instrument of his retaliation.

Meanwhile, Alexa knew that Adam was growing suspicious of her frequent absences but she couldn't bear not seeing Davie for long periods of time. She realized that she would soon be forced to tell Adam about his son, and for some reason she no longer found that thought too painful. They had come a long way in the last few weeks and she felt he was beginning to trust her again, perhaps even to love her. And then something happened to change her whole way of thinking.

Alexa inadvertently learned that Adam was being unfaithful to her. That he was seeing Fannie again. Perhaps he never stopped seeing her all these weeks he made love to her as if she were the only woman in his life. She saw him by chance one afternoon as he was entering the theater where Fannie was performing. She was riding in her carriage and asked her coachman to pull off to the side of the road where she might wait and watch. About a half-hour later Adam reappeared with a beaming Fannie hanging on his arm. Alexa was devastated, but nevertheless made her presence known to the pair when she stepped out of the carriage to confront them.

"Alexa!" Adam said, secretly pleased to be found out so soon. He had thought only to squire Fannie around for awhile until Alexa got wind of it. Gossip traveled swiftly in London and he had no doubt that she would hear of his latest peccadillo from either Mac or one of the servants. "What are you doing here?"

"I could ask the same of you," Alexa replied with a calmness she struggled to uphold.

"As you can see I'm calling on a . . . friend."

"How nice for her," Alexa replied sweetly.

"Jealous, my love?"

"No more than you," she replied blithely.

With an enticing swish of her hips Alexa regained her carriage and without a backward glance directed the coachman forward.

"Damn!" cursed Adam, his face mottled.

"Don't mind her, luv," Fannie soothed. "Let's go to my place. I'll make you forget all about that insipid witch."

"Insipid!" shouted Adam angrily. "Why that lady is more of a woman than you'll ever hope to be. She's proud, courageous, foolishly brave, and . . . and . . . magnificent!"

Suddenly Adam became aware that Fannie was staring at him, her mouth wide open. "My god," he groaned, "what am I saying?" But it was too late to take it back even if he wanted to, which he didn't. He meant every blessed word he said and he'd be damned if he'd let another man have her. Despite everything she was his alone and would remain his.

Grasping Fannie's arm painfully he began pulling her along the street. "Where are you taking me?" she demanded to know.

"To your lodgings, unless there is some other place you'd rather go."

"You're going back to her." Disgust colored her words. "I thought you couldn't stand her!"

"That's correct, Fannie, I am going back to my wife, and aye, there were times when I couldn't bear to have her name spoken in my presence. But I never stopped loving her."

"You were using me," Fannie accused sulkily.

"I'm sorry. I never meant to hurt you."

Fannie laughed mirthlessly. "Hurt? Don't be an ass. I knew where I stood from the beginning. Women like me take their pleasure where and when they can and expect little in return. I enjoyed you, Adam, while it lasted, but the moment I saw your beautiful lady I knew there was little chance for me."

"You're a good sort, Fannie, and I admire your spirit. I sincerely apologize for using you," Adam repeated. Then he reached in his pocket and handed her a sheath of bills. When Fannie made to refuse, Adam persisted. "You deserve it, my dear. If not for me you'd be free to pursue . . . er . . . other interests. I wish you well."

Then he was gone. He and Alexa had much to make up for. He'd be ten kinds of a fool to stand idly by while another man stole the affections of the woman he loved more than his own life.

They had shared too much, traveled too far together to throw it all away.

24

Trembling with barely suppressed rage, Alexa returned home only minutes before an urgent message from Maddy was put into her hands by Ferdie, the coachman from her country estate. Davie was ill and she must come immediately. It took her less than half an hour to throw her clothes into a bag and tear out of Ashley House as if the devil himself was after her. She paused only long enough to tell Owen where she was going and why, cautioning him to tell no one, not even Adam whom the old man had come to admire. Then she was hurtling down the street with Ferdie whipping up the horses to a brisk trot.

Sometime later Adam entered Ashley House expecting to find Alexa there and was somewhat irritated to learn the house was empty save for the servants. He sat down to wait, and as time passed and Alexa failed to return he began to worry, rising to pace anxiously back and forth, imagining all sorts of things. She might have been upset enough after seeing him with Fannie to leave him. God he was a fool!

Somehow the idea of Alexa leaving him took root in his brain and grew until he pictured her in the arms of another man, some faceless lover who made her cry out and beg to be loved. With those depressing thoughts riding him Adam rushed upstairs to their bedroom, cursing himself for not thinking to check there first. Flinging open the wardrobe, Adam groaned aloud when he noticed several of Alexa's dresses were missing, just as he suspected. The drawers were equally bare of more intimate articles of clothing. He needed no other proof to concluded that Alexa had left him and he had no one to blame but himself!

Returning downstairs Adam sought to question Owen but learned next to nothing from the servant who had loyally served the Ashleys for many years. "Are you certain you have no idea where my wife could have gone?" Adam questioned, thoroughly disheartened.

Owen lowered his gray head, unwilling to look Adam in the eye as he told the lie Alexa demanded. His first loyalty lay with the Ashleys no matter how much he admired Lord Penwell. "No, my lord, she told me nothing save that she was leaving and would return in a few days."

"Are you certain she said she'd return?" Adam asked sharply.

"Aye, my lord, I believe she intends to return." Owen nodded sagely.

"That's all, Owen," said Adam, dropping dejectedly into a chair. "Wait, bring me a bottle."

That's where Mac found Adam when he returned to the house hours later. Only the bottle was empty and Adam was roaring drunk. "Adam, what in the hell happened?" Mac asked, shaking his head disgustedly. "Owen told me you've been sitting here for hours. He also hinted that you were 'well into your cups,' his exact words, I believe. Where is Alexa?"

"Gone," mumbled Adam, reeling out of the chair. "To her lover, no doubt. Can't blame her, though. I drove her to it."

"Adam, you're not making sense." Mac sighed exasperated. "Alexa doesn't have a lover. There's only one man she wants and that's you."

"That might have been true once, Mac, but no longer."

"Tell me what happened." Adam's slurred words were not always clear but somehow Mac pieced together all that had taken place that afternoon. "You're a bigger fool than I thought." He shook his head when Adam's disjointed explanation came to an abrupt halt.

Adam nodded in complete agreement. "I love her, Mac."

"It's about time you admitted it." Mac grinned. "Come on, I'll help you up to bed. Things will look brighter in the morning."

But in the morning Adam and Mac received word that the treaty committee was about to reconvene and they were expected at court immediately. The next few days found Adam too busy to do little more than rage inwardly over Alexa's continued absence. He left the house early and did not return until late, usually too late even for supper.

One night after a particularly exhausting day, Adam was too keyed up to sleep. He longed to feel Alexa's responsive body beside him, curled up warmly in his arms. If only these damned meetings he was obliged to attend would end, he fervently wished. Almost everything had been agreed upon and the king's ministers had only to affix their signatures to the document to make it legal, thus freeing him to pursue his own business.

After pacing the floor for an hour Adam suddenly decided he was hungry and made his way through the silent house to the kitchen. A crack of light rimmed the door left slightly ajar and soft voices reached Adam's ear. Owen and Bertha were seated around the kitchen table drinking a cup of tea before retiring to their own quarters. Adam was about to barge in when he heard Alexa's name spoken and paused just outside the door to listen.

"The poor man." Bertha shook her gray head. "It just ain't right what Lady Alexa is doing to her poor husband."

"It's not for us to condemn or condone," rebuked Owen gently. "Lady Alexa must have good cause to continue with this charade."

Bertha clucked her tongue, evidently sympathizing with Adam. "She should tell Lord Penwell. He has a right to know about David."

Adam froze, his imagination running wild. David! Was that the name of Alexa's lover?

"Mind your tongue, Bertha," Owen chided. "What my lady does in the country is her business. She'll be back soon and she can explain to her husband why she took off so suddenly for the Ashley country estate."

Adam did not wait around to hear the rest of the conversation as he rushed upstairs, needing privacy to ponder the servants' words and their meaning. At least he now knew where Alex had gone and with whom. He trembled to think that even now she could be making love with some man named David. How long has the affair been going on? he wondered bleakly, suddenly recalling all those occasions he returned home to find Alexa gone. It was galling to think that all the time she was making tender love with him, she was giving herself to another. What a fool he was to trust her again!

The next morning Adam left as usual with Mac, but instead of attending the sessions, he asked to be pardoned for several days, citing a family crisis that called for his immediate attention. After some consultation, he was reluctantly excused and he hurried away, leaving a bewildered Mac in his wake. Adam deliberately refrained from telling Mac what he intended for he knew his friend would attempt to restrain him from doing what he must, what his pride demanded. There was little doubt in Adam's mind that he was on his way to kill the man he found with Alexa, though he had not yet decided what punishment he would mete out to his unfaithful wife.

Mounted on one of the finest horses from the stables at Ashley House, Adam set out for the country. His sword rode comfortably on his lean hips and as an extra precaution he jammed a pistol in his belt. His face was grim, his eyes flinty; a muscle twitched along the stern line of his jaw. Before too many hours had passed, Adam wagered, one man would lie dead, either Adam Foxworth or David.

On the day that she was summoned, Alexia reached the country house in record time to find the doctor from the village already attending her baby.

"Oh, my lady, I'm so glad you've come," Maddy wailed the moment Alexa sped into the house. "The doctor is with Davie now."

"What is it, Maddy? How sick is Davie?"

"He's been feeding too little the past few days but we thought nothing of it until he broke out this morning."

"Broke out! Oh, my God, Maddy, is it smallpox?" Alexa asked, immediately thinking the worst.

"I . . . I don't know, my lady, the doctor hasn't come out of his room yet to tell us."

Wasting no further words, Alexa rushed past the sobbing Maddy and into the baby's room where the doctor was still bending over his tiny form. Alexa cried out in alarm when she saw the angry red pustules covering his tiny body. The doctor turned at the sound of her voice. "My lady, I didn't hear you come in."

"Is he going to die, doctor?" Alexa asked, her eyes awash with tears. "Is Davie going to die?"

The doctor smiled indulgently and Alexa couldn't help but wonder why he was smiling in the face of tragedy. If she lost Davie she felt her life would end on the spot. "Your child has chicken pox, my lady," the doctor told her. "A common childhood disease."

"Not smallpox? You're certain?"

"Aye, my lady, not smallpox; although chicken pox can become quite serious I'm certain your son will have no lasting effects other than a small scar or two. He's healthy and well-nourished and within a few days should begin to heal nicely."

Alexa nearly collapsed with relief as she cuddled her son who began whimpering the moment he spied his mother. She had never been so frightened in her life, not even when she faced the hangman. Davie's close call made her stop to think how very precious life was, and how short. It also made her realize how wrong she was not to tell Adam about Davie. Her son needed a father and Adam had a right to claim and love his son. As soon as Davie was well again, Alexa resolved, she would bring Davie back to London for the long overdue meeting with his father.

Just as the doctor predicted, Davie's illness soon ran its course. The only visible scars were a tiny one just above his right eyebrow and another below his left ear. During those long days when she selflessly nursed her son back to health, all tension seemed to have drained out of Alexa, due, she supposed, to her decision to unite father and son. What she stood to lose in all this, Alexa did not know, for during her absence Fannie could have become deeply entrenched in Adam's affections. He was more than likely to be enraged with her for disappearing so mysteriously without a word to anyone.

But now that she had reached her decision Alexa hoped Adam would come to understand what had driven her to leave with Charles. At least the motive behind her actions would finally be revealed and hopefully Adam would believe and forgive.

Once the doctor pronounced Davie well enough to travel Alexa informed Maddy of her plans. "Praise the Lord!" Maddy sighed, raising her eyes in thanks. "It's about time Davie met his father. If you weren't so stubborn Lord Penwell could be enjoying his son right now."

"I had my reasons," Alexa replied sourly. "But somehow they no longer seem important. Pack Davie's clothes. We'll leave tomorrow."

Adam arrived that same afternoon to send the entire household into a tizzy.

Each mile Adam traveled seemed like ten, every minute like hours. He pictured Alexa's lover in so many guises that the end he threw up his hands in disgust. He knew Alexa to be a sensuous and responsive woman, but somehow he liked to think she was that way only for him. When he had finally come to forgive her for Charles, this David came along and set them right back where they started. Did Alexa somehow find him lacking that she felt the need to seek out another man? His anger escalated until his fingers itched to feel his sword pressed against the throat of a faceless man named David.

Adam left his horse at the stables after apprising the astonished stableboy of his identity. Then he walked to the huge front door and calmly made his presence known. A few minutes later an elderly woman looked up at him inquiringly, her bright eyes shining at the sight of the powerfully built man who exuded strength and self-confidence.

"Can I help you?" Maddy asked, realizing immediately the identity of the handsome man despite the fact that she had never set eyes on Alexa's husband.

"Who are you?" Adam asked curtly.

"Lady Alexa's housekeeper," Maddy replied proudly. "My name is Maddy."

Adam pushed his way inside, past the surprised Maddy who was unaccustomed to such rudeness. "I'm Lord Penwell, Lady Alexa's husband," Adam announced, glancing furtively in all directions but seeing nothing amiss.

"I thought you might be." Maddy smiled warmly. "My lady has spoken often of you. I . . . had not expected you to look so fierce."

Adam's features immediately softened. No sense in frightening the servants, he decided, realizing that Maddy was the woman who had been like a mother to Alexa. Often in the past Alexa had spoken of her warm regard for the kindly housekeeper. "Where is my wife?" Adam asked, a harshness creeping into his voice despite his resolve to tread lightly before the woman.

"She's in the bedroom with David," Maddy beamed.

Her words brought a ferocious scowl to Adam's face and Maddy wondered what she had said to cause it until Adam bellowed, "My God! Has the woman no shame? Has she now descended to cavorting openly before the servants?"

Before Maddy could explain he bounded up the stairs

two a time, determined to break down every door if
need be until he found Alexa and her lover. "Third door
on the left," called out Maddy, sensing Adam's intent.
"But you've got it all wrong, David is not . . ." Poor
Maddy got no further as she heard a loud crash and
Alexa's startled scream.

Sagely, Maddy decided to retreat and allow Alexa
time alone with her husband so that they might come to
terms with their feelings. Besides, Alexa had much
explaining to do. She realized, and rightly so, that
finding out about Davie would present quite a shock to
Adam and Maddy wanted no part of what was bound to
follow. She advised the rest of the servants accordingly
and they quickly vacated the front part of the house,
leaving Alexa and Adam quite alone.

Alexa lay full-length upon the bed, cooing love words
to her son. She loved to watch him smile and gurgle
nonsense in return. "My darling David," she murmured,
tickling his chubby stomach, "I love you more than my
life. I'd do anything to keep you safe and happy."

Adam paused before the door long enough to hear
Alexa's startling words before outrage turned him into
an avenging angel. His sword flew out of its scabbard as
he raised one booted foot and kicked the door open,
chagrined to find it had not even been locked and he
could have pushed it open with a lot less bravado. His
icy gaze settled on Alexa reclining on her side in bed,
her lover shielded by her shapely form.

The moment the door crashed inward Alexa's first
thought was for Davie as she bent over him protectively,
craning her head sideways in an effort to identify the
source of the danger. What she saw made her gasp in
shock.

Sword drawn, thunderclouds gathered in his gray
eyes, his thatch of tawny hair falling across his forehead,

Adam stood poised in the shattered doorway. "I've caught you red-handed, Alexa! Let loose of your lover so that he can defend himself. Or is he a coward who prefers to hide behind a woman's skirts."

"Adam!" Alexa gasped, startled. "We were coming back to London tomorrow."

"We! Were you bringing your lover with you? Move aside, Alexa, and let him up. I want to see the man's face before I kill him. No one takes my wife from me!"

Alexa began to giggle, unable to control her mirth as laughter bubbled up from her throat. "Adam . . .I . . . I . . ."

"What's so damn funny, Alexa?" stormed Adam angrily. "Who is the bastard? You belong to me, Alexa. I love you!"

"What? What did you say?"

"I said I wanted to kill the bastard who thinks himself man enough to steal the woman I love!"

"Do you mean it? Do you truly love me?"

Still wielding the sword aloft in a ridiculous pose, Adam paused thoughtfully. "So what if I do?" he asked evasively. "Don't think you can use my love for you to protect your lover."

Slowly Alexa pushed herself into a sitting position, suddenly drained of all laughter. "I've always loved you, Adam. But we can talk about that later. There is someone I'd like you to meet."

"Ah, the elusive David, I presume," Adam gritted out, clutching his sword tightly. "Let me at the bastard!"

Alexa reached around and scooped up Davie, thrusting him forward for Adam to see. "Meet your son, Adam. His name is David but I call him Davie. And he's no bastard. His father is the ferocious Fox, his mother, the Vixen, Fox's mate."

Adam's sword slipped through numb fingers,

clattering noisily to the floor where it lay unheeded at his feet. His mouth gaped open and his eyes glittered dangerously. A baby! David was only a baby, and if Alexa could be believed, his own son! Walking on legs suddenly gone rubbery, Adam gingerly approached the bed to gaze longingly at the babe. A pair of gray eyes to match his own stared soberly up at him. Adam poked a tentative finger at him and Davie immediately clutched at it, attempting to bring to his pink mouth. He laughed merrily at his father, who, enchanted by his son's antics, immediately fell in love.

But Alexa did not fare so well in Adam's regard. "Why, Alexa? Why didn't you tell me about Davie? Do you hate me so much to punish me so heartlessly?"

Alexa felt herself grow crimson beneath Adam's furious scowl. "It was the other way around, Adam. You hated me. I intended to tell you about Davie once you came to realize that you loved me and believed that I had never become Charles's mistress."

"Damn it, Alexa, that is no excuse!"

"I was afraid, feeling as you did, that you'd take Davie away from me!" Her obvious anguish tore at Adam's heart. Had he really been so inflexible in his attitude toward her?

"My God, Alexa, for a man to be denied knowledge of his own son . . . His own flesh and blood!" The statement hung in the air like dense fog between them.

Adam reached out for Davie and Alexa gladly placed him in her husband's arms, watching the play of naked emotion on his face. She knew now how wrong she had been to deliberately separate father and son but at the time it seemed the right thing to do. While Adam held and cuddled his son, Alexa began speaking softly, telling him why she had acted as she did to protect Davie when she learned she was pregnant. She also thought she was saving Adam's life.

"I was going to tell you that I was carrying your child but the British arrived at Foxworth that night before I had the opportunity. I ran out the study doors and right into the arms of Charles Whitlaw who had come out to Foxworth to warn me when he heard that troops were on the way to arrest us.

"Once he learned I was the Vixen it fired his imagination and he decided he wanted me for himself. He took me to Savannah and insisted I return to England with him."

"You went with him because of the baby," Adam said, comprehension finally dawning.

"For myself, I would have gladly died at your side, but I couldn't condemn your child to the same death. He deserved to live. In order to gain my compliance Charles hatched this elaborate plot in which you would be allowed to go free. I . . . I readily agreed to become his mistress, even marry him, to save your life."

"Only Charles never intended for me to live," Adam said bitterly. He sat on the edge of the bed, carefully placing the baby between them. "And he gained himself a mistress."

"No!" cried Alexa. "I was never Charles's mistress! He did not fancy taking a woman already swelling with another man's child. He agreed to wait until after the baby was born. Then the war ended and I was free of him. I no longer had anything to fear from him."

"I was told he went to India."

Alexa laughed uproariously. "The coward! When he told me you were dead I promised him I would come back to kill him once my child was born, and he must have believed me. He had one clash with the Vixen and evidently that was enough."

"Would you? Have killed him, I mean?"

"Without a qualm," Alexa assured him, her chilling tone reminiscent of the Vixen who had killed often in the name of freedom. "He told me you were dead, that he paid to have you killed, and my hate for him knew no bounds. I think, my love, if I hadn't been carrying Davie, I might have taken my own life, such was my grief."

"Thank God for Davie," Adam murmured gratefully. "And thank God for Mac or I wouldn't be here now."

"Amen," agreed Alexa solemnly.

"Have you two managed to make up without doing each other bodily harm?" Maddy stood in the doorway calmly surveying the shattered door that still hung loosely on its hinges. Other than that nothing else appeared damaged.

"Maddy, how did you ever manage to control this hellion?" Adam asked, his harsh voice edged with humor.

"Now you know what to expect from Master Davie," chuckled Maddy. "And speaking of the young man, it's time for his nap."

Reluctantly Adam passed the child into the housekeeper's waiting arms. But not before he fixed her with a stern look and said, "It's only because I'm in an expansive mood, having just discovered I am a father, that I am inclined to forgive you for aiding Alexa in her harebrained scheme to keep me and my son apart. But if you or anyone else should conspire against me again I won't be so lenient."

Properly chastised, Maddy could only nod in agreement. "Aye, my lord." Then she carried her small charge out of the room, carefully closing the ruined door behind her.

"That goes for you, too, my love," Adam admonished sternly, winding a hand through her luxurious hair and tugging gently until she was forced to lean into him.

"Don't you ever try to keep anything from me again."

"What about Fannie?" retorted Alexa tartly. "I haven't forgiven you yet for bedding that slut."

"I haven't bedded Fannie since I moved into Ashley House," Adam admitted grudgingly. "I wished only to make you jealous, my love, when I thought you had taken a lover. How could I bed Fannie after making love to you?"

Alexa's eyes grew wide. "If you're lying to me, Fox, I'll run you through," she warned with a twinkle. "I may have birthed a child but I haven't forgotten how to duel."

"I bested you once, or have you forgotten?"

Her chin tilted stubbornly, Alexa retorted pertly, "A lucky thrust."

"The only lucky thrust I've ever managed was the one that claimed your maidenhead." Adam grinned diabolically.

"Adam!" exclaimed Alexa, blushing furiously.

His lips were so close his name was lost, mingled with his own breath. Then his mouth claimed hers in a kiss that seemed to go on forever. Her lips parted and she savored the taste of him, his tongue moist and hot as he searched her sweetness. Slipping his hands beneath her robe he cupped her breasts, freeing them from the loose garment, bringing his head down to flick lightly at the nipples with his tongue, then taking them into his mouth to suck gently at first, then more vigorously.

Alexa moaned low in her throat as he quickly stripped off her robe to press feathery kisses on her stomach, tracing her navel with his probing tongue, then burying his face against the crisp curls between her thighs. She trembled beneath him as he drank deeply of her honeyed essence, tasting, savoring, prodding her until she cried out in supplication.

A sweet fire between her legs caused her to moan and move her hips as he continued to probe her with his tongue, flames kindling within her with every movement he made. Cupping her tightly his tongue moved faster as she writhed in his grasp. He pushed relentlessly against her until she surrendered helplessly to the ecstasy he brought her.

Watching her lovely face contort with passion was more than Adam could bear as he swiftly shrugged out of his clothes. "I can wait no longer, my love," he panted as he crouched above her, his hands moving to part her thighs. "I want to feel you close around me, to caress me as I stroke. God, you're marvelous!"

"Quickly, my darling," urged Alexa breathlessly.

Groaning loudly he thrust wildly into her, wanting to claim her once and for all, to proclaim his ownership in the most primitive way. As if in complete agreement she thrust up her hips to meet him and heard her own moans of pleasure over his raspy breathing, the impetus of his thrusts increasing with the sound of his deep, ragged gasps. He was piercing the very core of her. Then Adam felt the wild shuddering of her body as the power of her climax triggered his own. He cried out, burying himself deep within her.

After a few minutes Adam rolled to the side, bringing Alexa into his arms. "I never dreamed anything could feel so good." He sighed contentedly. "How could I ever want another woman with you in my arms? We're a family now, my love—nothing and no one will ever part us."

"I've waited so long to hear those words, Adam. I prayed you'd love me again."

"I do, my Vixen, and I will. All night long if you'll let me."

"As long and as often as you want, my darling."

"Then we'd better make the most of the time we have left," he teased, his hands and lips beginning the slow art of arousal once more.

Only this time he was rudely interrupted by a commotion coming from below stairs. Alexa jumped up but Adam was faster, pulling on his pants and shirt and rushing out the door in record time. It took Alexa a little longer to dress as she listened to the voices wafting up the staircase. She was at the top of the stairs when she recognized Mac's voice.

"I came as soon as I could when I learned where you had gone, Adam," Mac said grimly. "What have you done to Alexa?"

"Nothing I haven't done many times before," replied Adam, amusement tugging at the corners of his mouth.

"You haven't harmed her?"

"Should I have?"

"Damn it, Adam, don't play games with me! Have you seen your son?"

"You know about David?" Adam asked sharply, scowling darkly.

Mac flushed guiltily. "Aye."

"How long? How long have you known?"

"From the beginning."

"And you didn't tell me? What kind of friend are you?"

"I promised Alexa that I would give her time."

"Time for what?"

"Time to make you fall in love with her again."

"Good God, man, I never stopped loving her!"

"You certainly went to great lengths to make her believe otherwise," Mac challenged. "That little subterfuge you carried on with Fannie was reprehensible. I fully intended to tell you about David until you flaunted that whore before Alexa. That and your refusal to believe Alexa made me change my mind. I decided you deserved to suffer a little. Besides, I had Alexa's promise she would tell you about Davie when the time was right."

"Between the two of you I didn't have a chance, did I?" Adam laughed, his mood suddenly lifting. "I'm surprised you didn't try to take Alexa for yourself."

"I would if I thought I had half a chance."

"What are you two arguing about?" Alexa intervened saucily. "Adam, don't be angry with Mac. He's the best friend we'll ever have."

"Aye, Alexa," Adam agreed soberly. "I'll give you no argument on that score."

Mac looked from Adam to Alexa, leering slyly when he suddenly noticed that Adam was barefoot, his shirt buttoned crookedly and hanging loose outside his pants. Alexa did not look any less disheveled; her face was flushed, her lips passion-swollen. "Did I interrupt anything?" he asked innocently.

"Damn right you did!" Adam thundered, feigning anger.

"Adam!" protested Alexa, flushing becomingly.

"It's all right, my love." Adam laughed. "By now Mac knows we've settled our differences in bed."

"Good news indeed," Mac concurred heartily. "But I have a bit of welcome news myself. The peace treaty we've been working on has been ratified. The ministers signed it this morning. It needs only the royal seal. We're free to leave, Adam, anytime we please."

Adam turned to Alexa, waiting for her reaction. "It's up to Alexa, Mac. We can stay in England if she wishes, or return to America."

"Adam, how could you even ask?" Alexa scolded. "I fought for my adopted country. I was ready to die if need be. Our new country has great need of men like you, darling. Men to mold and guide her as she glides into a new century."

"God, I love you, Alexa," Adam said, eyes glistening suspiciously. "I hoped you'd say that. But what about all your holdings here in England—Ashley House, the country estate, all your lands?"

"Hold them in trust for Davie and his brothers and sisters. Lawyer Carter can see to everything for us. I trust him implicitly."

"Are you planning on a big family, my love?" Adam asked, vastly amused.

She looked at him coyly. "Your virility was never in doubt, darling."

"I think I'd better get myself back to London." Mac smiled indulgently. "But not until I've seen Davie. He must be quite a young man by now."

"You'll have dinner with us and spend the night," Alexa insisted, poking Adam until he echoed her invitation.

"Of course, it's senseless for you to return to London tonight. We'll all go back tomorrow and prepare for our trip home. I'll have Maddy show you to your room. Alexa and I have some . . . er . . . unfinished business to attend to."

Then to Alexa's chagrin and Mac's amusement, Adam scooped his wife up in his strong arms and carried her up the stairs to the bedroom. He set her on her feet and immediately began pulling frantically at the fastenings of her dress. "Just what is this . . . unfinished business, Adam, that is so important to cause you to forget your manners? It was rude to leave Mac like that."

"My business, my love, as well as my mission in life, is to take a Vixen," replied Adam huskily, pushing her backwards onto the rumpled bed, "and to make love to her endlessly."

"And mine is to keep a sly Fox happy and content, but

never bored," purred Alexa in a breathless whisper, wrapping her arms about his neck as their lips met in a long, delicious, lingering kiss that was as sweet as honey, warm as springtime, and full of promise.

EPILOGUE

Preliminary articcles of peace, signed on November 30, 1782, were followed by a definitive treaty concluded September 3, 1783. The south, Savannah and Charleston were evacuated in late 1782; New York on November 25, 1783.

There were many reasons for Great Britain's misfortunes and failures. Among them were misconceptions by the home government on the temper and reserve strength of her colonists, a population of mainly good English blood and instincts; disbelief in the probability of a protracted struggle covering the immense territory in America; consequent failure to dispatch sufficient forces to the field; the generalship of Washington; and finally, most decisive of all, the French alliance and European combination by which at the close of the conflict Britain was without a friend or ally on the continent.

Make the Most of Your Leisure Time
with
LEISURE BOOKS

Please send me the following titles:

Quantity	Book Number	Price
_____	_____	_____
_____	_____	_____
_____	_____	_____
_____	_____	_____
_____	_____	_____

If out of stock on any of the above titles, please send me the alternate title(s) listed below:

_____	_____	_____
_____	_____	_____
_____	_____	_____
_____	_____	_____

Postage & Handling _____

Total Enclosed $_____

☐ Please send me a free catalog.

NAME _____
(please print)

ADDRESS _____

CITY _____ STATE _____ ZIP _____

Please include $1.00 shipping and handling for the first book ordered and 25¢ for each book thereafter in the same order. All orders are shipped within approximately 4 weeks via postal service book rate. PAYMENT MUST ACCOMPANY ALL ORDERS.*

*Canadian orders must be paid in US dollars payable through a New York banking facility.

Mail coupon to: **Dorchester Publishing Co., Inc.**
6 East 39 Street, Suite 900
New York, NY 10016
Att: ORDER DEPT.